DATE DUE		

STORMY WEATHER

STORMY WEATHER

A CHARLOTTE
JUSTICE NOVEL

PAULA L. WOODS

W. W. NORTON & COMPANY

NEW YORK • LONDON

"Stormy Weather (Keeps Rainin' All The Time)." Lyric by Ted Koehler, music by
Harold Arlen. Copyright © 1993 Mills Music, Inc., Copyright renewed 1961 Arko
Music Corp. All rights for the extended term administered by Fred Ahlert Music
Corporation on behalf of Ted Koehler Music. All rights administered by S.A. Music on
behalf of Harold Arlen Music. International copyright secured. All rights reserved.

"Stormy Weather (Keeps Rainin' All The Time)." Lyric by Ted Koehler. Music by
Harold Arlen. © 1933 (Renewed 1961) Ted Koehler Music and S.A. Music and S.A.
Music Co. All rights for Ted Koehler Music administered by Fred Ahlert Music
Corporation. All rights reserved.

"When You Are Old" by W. B. Yeats reprinted with permission of Scribner, a Division
of Simon & Schuster from *The Collected Poems of W. B. Yeats,* Revised Second Edition
edited by Richard J. Finneran (New York: Scribner, 1996).

While some historical events depicted in this novel are factual, as are geography and
certain locales, and certain persons and organizations in the public view, this is a work
of fiction whose characters and their actions are a product of the author's imagina-
tinon. Any resemblance to actual persons, living or dead, organizations, or events is
entirely coincidental and not intended by the author, nor does the author pretend to
private information about such individuals.

For information about permission to reproduce selections from this book, write to
Permissions, W. W. Norton & Company, Inc.,500 Fifth Avenue, New York, NY 10110.

The text of this book is composed in Bembo with the display set in Copperplate Gothic.
Composition by Adrian Kitzinger
Manufacturing by Quebecor Fairfield

Library of Congress Cataloging-in-Publication Data

Woods, Paula L.
    Stormy weather : a Charlotte Justice novel / Paula L. Woods.
       p. cm.
    ISBN 0-393-02021-5
    1. Police—California—Los Angeles—Fiction. 2. African American motion
picture producers and directors—Fiction. 3. African American police—Fiction.
4. African American women—Fiction. 5. Los Angeles (Calif.)—Fiction.
6. Policewomen—Fiction. I. Title.
PS3573.06414 S76 2001
813'.54—dc21   2001024004

W. W. Norton & Company, Inc., 500 Fifth Avenue, New York, N.Y. 10110
www.wwnorton.com

W. W. Norton & Company Ltd., Castle House, 75/76 Wells Street, London W1T 3QT

1 2 3 4 5 6 7 8 9 0

FOR GUY AND PRISCILLA,
WHO'VE GOTTEN IT RIGHT

Skim milk masquerades as cream,

Things ain't always what they seem.

—Sylvester "Uncle Syl" Curry (1920–   )

STORMY WEATHER

CHAPTER 1

TRUESDALE, JUSTICE, AND THE AMERICAN WAY

When we Justice kids were little and we'd finish watching a movie with my parents, my mother would always ask, "And what was the moral? What have we learned?" And while we would squirm and make faces over how that question intruded on our fantasies, I think I've finally figured out what Joymarie meant.

It's like death. I've probably worked hundreds of homicide cases over the years and they've all meant something different to me, just like my favorite movies. Some homicides pull at your heartstrings—the murder of an innocent child or a battered woman—and haunt you long after the case is closed. Others—gangbangers, a homeless person—make you wonder how our society could stoop so low. Point is, you never know how death will slap you upside the head, or what a homicide investigation will uncover about the victim, the suspects, or yourself.

The Wednesday before Thanksgiving found me downtown at my desk at the PAB, aka Parker Administrative Building, reading the newspaper and trying to get motivated to eat the tuna sandwich I'd bought off the local roach coach. It was unusually quiet in the third-floor bull pen that housed the ten men and two women in the Homicide Special unit of the department's Robbery-

Homicide Division. Almost everyone was out in the field; the rest had cut out early to get a head start on an extended holiday weekend. Among the absentees was my partner, Gena Cortez, who had decided at the last minute to take a few days off.

We should all be so lucky, I grumbled to myself as I began unwrapping the stale sandwich before me. I was saved from my mean cuisine by Ma Bell in the form of a call from Billie Truesdale. Billie and I had worked a couple of homicides during the Rodney King riots and had ridden out the ensuing publicity storm together. Our trial by fire had forged a sisterly bond between us, despite the difference in our sexual orientation. That and the fact Billie worked South Bureau Homicide, location of some of the city's most brutal murders, while I was firmly, but increasingly unhappily, entrenched as the only black woman in the celebrated and celebrity-driven RHD.

"Hail to the conquering heroine," I teased Billie by way of a greeting. "I was just reading about the verdict in the Little Angel of Mercy case in the *Times.*"

A year ago, Billie and her partner had hooked up a registered nurse for the murders of several terminally ill hospital and nursing home patients. An employee of HealthMates, a South Bay home health agency, Angelo Clemenza had just been convicted of moving through a dozen healthcare facilities and private homes, leaving a trail of dead bodies in his wake. His "mission" had gotten the diminutive, soft-spoken man tagged by the right-to-die fanatics and the media as the Little Angel of Mercy, a loose translation of his name in Italian.

The fact that over half of Clemenza's victims were elderly black men had raised the specter of the Atlanta child murders back in the eighties as well as the more recent Jeffrey Dahmer case, and had stirred up the CTs, or conspiracy theorists, from here to Chicago. Billie Truesdale and her partner had done a heroic job during the investigation, even appearing with the LAPD Public Relations commander at town hall meetings and on black radio programs while following Clemenza's devious trail through the

South Bureau's jurisdiction as well as several neighboring suburbs. Clearing the Clemenza case was what my acronym-spouting father would call a CEA—career-enhancing achievement—and I was as happy for Billie as I would have been for myself, conspiracy theorists be damned.

"At least now you can get the CT contingent off your back," I joked.

Taking note that Billie didn't laugh along with me, I was even more curious when she asked, her voice uneasy and low, "Are you tied up on something, Charlotte?"

I looked at the forms on my desk. Steve Firestone, my team leader, was heading up a task force composed of me and Cortez, a couple of detectives from Robbery, and some uniforms loaned out from Central Bureau and assigned to solving a series of home-invasion robberies and murders that were occurring in L.A.'s most exclusive neighborhoods.

But despite the nature of the case and my years on the job, I had been relegated to maintaining the murder books and all of the related paper for the Home Invasion Task Force. My sixth sense kept telling me that my string of back-room assignments was part of Firestone's ongoing campaign to get me into his bed or break my spirit and either get me to quit the department or transfer out of RHD.

Not that those thoughts hadn't occurred to me, especially after the trail of blue slime I'd seen left in the wake of the Rodney King fiasco. For over thirteen years now, my career had been the center of my life, part of my personal mission of restoring the balance in our communities disrupted by crime. But what I had seen and experienced in the past few years had been so disillusioning, sometimes I wasn't sure what good I could really do.

But if I left the LAPD it would be for my own reasons and under my own steam, not because a jerk like Firestone railroaded me out of the department. Shoving the paperwork to a corner of my desk, I replied: "Nothing that couldn't wait. What's up?"

"Meet me at Teddy's."

———

She was already at the diner when I arrived, ruining her lungs with a cigarette under an awning in the drizzling rain. Although I hadn't seen her in a couple of months, Billie Truesdale looked great. Her pixie haircut had grown out a little, soft black tendrils framing her heart-shaped face and the three moles that rode under her right eye. She was wearing a red, short-jacketed pantsuit that contrasted nicely with her sepia-toned skin and fit her smallish frame perfectly. But her hug was perfunctory and her right eye, always a bit lazy, was way off kilter, a sure sign she was stressing about something.

Helga Roosevelt, a grandmotherly German immigrant who'd lived in Los Angeles longer than I've been alive, gave us both a Brunhildean hug and showed us to my regular booth, a sun-cracked relic near the back. While Helga was getting our drinks, Teddy, her husband and co-owner, saluted us from his post at the grill. "Well, if it ain't Truesdale and Justice," he shouted over the sound of frying food. "All y'all need is the American Way!"

Groaning at Teddy's pitiful Superman pun, I shot back: "For a man whose mother actually *named* him Theodore Roosevelt, you sure got your nerve, old man." Teddy's was one of my favorite hangs, as much for the good-natured dozens the elderly black man played with his customers as for his double chili cheeseburgers, which in my mind were the eighth wonder of the world.

Teddy came out from behind the grill to take our orders himself, a bantam rooster in a chef's toque. "Saw you on the news, Detective," he said, beaming at Billie. "Glad it was you who caught that Angel of Mercy lowlife. Doubly glad it wasn't one of *us* what did the deed, if you take my point."

Billie ducked her head and scooted around in her seat.

"Always happy to see cullud folks gittin' ahead," he went on, oblivious to her discomfort, " 'specially in a plantation like the LAPD. They gon' make you gals overseers soon!"

Teddy was old enough and crotchety enough that he could call grown women "gals" or black people "cullud" and not give offense. And I could call him an old man and get only a mock-insulted wave of his dish towel in my direction and a chuckle and nod of agreement from his long-suffering wife.

Billie, however, seemed unable to join in our good-natured banter, unable to look even me in the eye.

"I've got a potential problem," she began as soon as our drinks arrived and Teddy was out of earshot.

"Is it the Little Angel of Mercy case?"

Her good eye fixed on mine. "How did you know?"

"You didn't seem too enthused when I mentioned it on the phone, and with Teddy just now . . ."

"Guess that's what I get for talking to a detective." She laughed, but her fingers were locked tight around her glass, another sign of trouble.

"So?"

"I'm beginning to wonder if we hooked up the wrong man."

"Is this a legitimate concern, or is this just you second-guessing yourself in some sort of 'I don't deserve all this attention' crisis of confidence? Because if it's the latter, you're just going to have to get used to it, girlfriend."

She gestured quickly with one hand, said, "It's nothing like that," and knocked over her iced tea in the process. She jumped to wipe up the mess with napkins while Helga ran for a dish towel.

"Well, be careful," I cautioned, moving my glass out of the way. "You can see where that kind of notoriety has gotten me—ostracized and targeted by my D-III as if I had a bull's-eye on my back."

"Steve Firestone is a skirt-chasing wannabe!" she said heatedly as she passed Helga the wet napkins. "Did you ever tell your lieutenant about him coming on to you?"

My jaw and neck muscles tightened, but I forced a smile and shook my head. "Nice try, my sister-in-blue, but we're not here to talk about my troubles. Tell me why you think you hooked up the wrong man."

Billie slid forward in the booth, her voice low. "What have you heard about Maynard Duncan?"

"Just what was on the news this morning." I sipped my drink and remembered: "Seventy-six-year-old black filmmaker and community activist died last night of cancer, right?"

"That's what the paramedics first thought," Billie replied. "Duncan had suffered from lung cancer for a year and a half, so they were prepared to chalk it up to respiratory failure. But when they were examining the body last night, one of the paramedics noticed something funny and called out a black-and-white from the Wilshire division."

"And they called you?"

"No, actually it was Mikki Alexander. When she arrived on the scene behind the detectives, she discovered the vic had been a patient at Green Pastures Nursing Home last summer. Four of Clemenza's victims were patients there, and she'd investigated those cases for the coroner's office."

"But hasn't Clemenza been in custody for the last year?"

She leaned in a little closer, the aged Naugahyde-covered seat beneath her squeaking in protest. "That's what's been gnawing at me since Mikki called this morning," she whispered.

Although California voters had recently defeated an assisted suicide proposition, it had stirred an intense debate between a vociferous few who supported the concept of euthanasia and those in the medical ethics and religious communities who felt passage of the bill would lead down a dark path Americans were not equipped to travel. In the current climate, and with the Clemenza case so fresh in her mind, I had a pretty good idea where Billie was headed. "So you're thinking what . . . that this old man's death was an assisted suicide made to look like Clemenza's work?"

"Or maybe," she whispered, her errant eye wandering from her clenched hands to my face, "a second Little Angel of Mercy working in tandem with him."

Billie proceeded to tell me how, during a search of Clemenza's apartment, she and her partner had discovered a detailed scrapbook, complete with pictures of his victims, obituaries from the newspapers, and lengthy letters and diary entries addressed to someone Clemenza called "the Twin." Clemenza seemed to think this twin's and his destinies were intertwined, a fact he wrote of in more than one hundred items taken into evidence. "We initially thought he meant a literal twin—until we found out he was an only child," Billie explained. "So the DA's investigators started checking out his friends and coworkers, but no one seems to have been that close to him. They finally concluded the letters and the rest were a bunch of delusional nonsense."

She shifted uneasily in her seat. "But with this new victim sounding like the others, I'm wondering—what if we were wrong and the defense was right? What if Clemenza was being framed with those vics? Or maybe there were two of them doing these old men together."

Los Angeles had endured its share of infamous serial killers, some of whom were suspected of working in tandem. The idea of another deadly duo caused the hairs on my arms to tingle. "Who's the primary over at Wilshire?" I demanded, digging into my purse for my notebook.

"Ron Neidisch." A look of frustration crossed Billie's face. "But he just 'bout bit my head off me when I called over there to give him a heads-up."

Her response brought me up short, forcing me back in my seat. I remembered Ron Neidisch from the Academy. Why would he be uncooperative with a detective from another shop, especially as closely as the neighboring South Bureau and Wilshire had to work together?

"Neidisch's response just seemed weird to me," she continued, echoing my thoughts. "That's why I'm pulling your coat on this one. The original Little Angel of Mercy case stretched across so many jurisdictions, you guys should have handled it from the get-go, but you know our CO wasn't about to let RHD get its foot in the door after what happened when you came in on one of our cases the last time. But now . . ."

Her voice trailed off as Helga put the chili cheeseburgers before us, two masterpieces of grease and goo. Billie studied her burger, but made no move to pick it up. "My CO would have me shot at dawn if I even *hinted* that RHD should be called in on this thing," she confided. "But with Neidisch getting all hincty, I was thinking . . . you know Mikki Alexander pretty well . . . maybe you could chat her up, get something concrete you could take to Armstrong . . ."

Captain MacIverson Armstrong was the pony-playing commanding officer of Robbery-Homicide Division. I knew for a fact he was pissed that Billie's CO had managed to keep the Little Angel of Mercy case in South Bureau, but I wasn't sure if he'd want to disrupt his social calendar to get caught between two hard-charging homicide units.

"He and the chief coroner are pretty tight. I can always put a bug in his ear and see if he ferrets out the details."

"Anything you could do would help," she replied, her hands relaxing for the first time since we sat down. "I just don't want somebody from Wilshire futzing around with the Clemenza case and undoing what I know in my bones was a solid collar. After all the good press South Bureau's gotten on this case, having it blow up in our faces would be a disaster all the way around."

For the bureau as well as the detectives on the case—my friend and colleague chief among them.

"You know I'd love to help you out, Billie. But RHD's taking over the case doesn't mean our team would be the ones working it. There're a whole bunch of detectives senior to Firestone, Cortez, and me who line up for the celebrity cases. And twinning serial killers . . . they'll be tripping over their tongues to get put on that one. I bet we'd be the last team who'd get an assignment like that."

Billie sighed as if the weight of the world was on her shoulders and said, "I'm sure you're busy anyway," pushing her plate aside.

Taking another healthy bite of my burger, I studied the lines furrowing my friend and colleague's brow and knew I'd find the time to help her out somehow. "Let me see what I can do."

"Thanks, Charlotte. I owe you one."

"You sure do." I slid the check in her direction with a smile. "And don't think I won't collect either."

When I got back to the office at two, I left heads-up messages about the Duncan case for my lieutenant and captain and reluctantly went back to my paperwork. I'd been at it for a couple of hours when Manny Rudolph walked up to my desk, a mess of files under one arm. A D-II like me, Rudolph had been assigned to the Home Invasion Task Force from the Robbery side of the shop, but was already managing clues and chasing down leads while I stayed virtually chained to my desk. But that didn't stop me from liking Rudolph, who was always quick with a joke that was never off-color, never insulting to women or minorities like some of my so-called colleagues on the job.

A lanky man with skin the color of cooked lobster, Rudolph scratched at the corner of his gray-blond mustache. "Hey, Justice," he drawled, his voice betraying a bit of Tulsa, Oklahoma, that thirty years in California and even four in Paris at the Sorbonne studying art history had yet to dispel. "Firestone wants these filed into the murder book before you go home tonight."

I cut my eyes across the bull pen to Firestone's empty desk. "Why didn't he tell me himself?" But that was just like Steve Firestone, putting someone else up to doing his dirty work. Always ready to throw a rock and hide his hand.

Seeing my reaction, Rudolph ducked his head and blushed a deeper red. "He had to leave early to pick up his kids from his ex for the holidays."

I could feel my cheeks getting hot, too. "Is that ex number one or ex number two?" Eyeing the stack of files under his arm, I figured I'd be in the office until eight trying to catch up. Why had I promised my mother I'd help her peel apples for pie this evening? "What is that stuff? More tips on the home invasions?"

"Yeah," he replied, almost sheepishly. "Since one of the victim's families offered a reward, we've been busier than a bunch of one-armed paper hangers." He laughed quickly and released the files onto my desk with a thud. "We been runnin' these down over the last week, and they're all dead ends. But . . ."

"I know." I tried for a smile but felt my face settle into a grimace. "They've got to be logged and filed in case we need to come back to them later."

Rudolph sat at Cortez's vacant desk across from mine and toyed with his mustache some more. "You're a real good sport to be doing this, Charlotte."

I avoided his hazel eyes. "It's my job, Rudolph, that's all."

"But I woulda thought Firestone coulda had one of the uniforms assigned to the case doin' this kind of stuff. You and I should be makin' headway out in the field. I've heard you've got excellent interviewing skills."

"Woulda, coulda, shoulda," I muttered to myself.

Rudolph frowned. "Huh?"

"I'm sure we could," I said a little louder, "but as the D-III on the case, that's Firestone's call, not mine." *Or yours, Rudolph, quiet as it's kept.*

He blushed again. "If you keep doing that, Manny, I'm going to have to start calling you Rudolph the Red." I smiled at him, trying to lighten the mood.

The perplexed look on his face didn't go away. "I don't usually work with you Homicide folks, Charlotte, so excuse my ignorance, but is there some reason you're always behind a desk?"

Dropping my head, I busied myself by examining the files to hide the color I could feel betraying my face. "None that I know of, Rudolph," I mumbled. *Except that you won't sleep with your D-III,* a little voice in my head reminded me.

Eventually Rudolph slapped his knees and rose to his feet. "Well, I'm gonna talk to ol' Steve about it when we get back from the holidays."

I kept my head down to hide the mounting anger I felt radiating down my neck to the pit of my stomach. "Suit yourself, Rudolph, but I'd stay out of it if I were you."

I could feel Manny Rudolph's eyes on me, hear him sigh and move away as if he finally got the picture. I guess all that time at the Sorbonne was good for something. "Whatever you say, Detective Justice. Have a nice Thanksgiving," he drawled.

Surveying the mountain of papers, thinking of the grand diva fit my mother would have when I called to tell her I wasn't going to be able to help her tonight, I mumbled: "I wouldn't take any bets on that if I were you."

CHAPTER 2

THIRD
NATIVE FROM
THE LEFT

That was because Thanksgiving dinner at the Nut House, my parents' home in View Park, an upper-middle-class black neighborhood of Los Angeles, was an extravaganza that my mother spent weeks planning. Between her obsessive preparation and the combustible potential involved in getting our eccentric, nut-colored brood together, Thanksgiving dinner could be heaven or hell, in living color, with all the trimmings.

My contributions to the festivities were cranberry sauce and a couple of videos for us to choose from after dinner. And to my mother's delight, this year's culinary contribution wasn't going to be my usual can of Ocean Spray, but homemade cranberry pear relish made by Aubrey Scott, a childhood friend of my brother's who I'd been seeing since he treated me for a dislocated shoulder in a hospital ER during the riots.

Even though I'd dated a few men since I'd lost my husband and daughter some years ago, I was always hesitant to bring them around my family, fearing somehow I was being a traitor to Keith's memory. Or the poor guy would find our family's wild ways and cut-'em-low film criticism too abrasive. Or, in Aubrey's case, even worse—that my mother would start campaigning to make me the

next Mrs. Dr. Scott. So I'd eased him in with a few family barbe-
cues in the spring and summer, thinking that by the time we started up our monthly Justice Family Film Night in the fall, either he
and I would have parted company or he would be accustomed to
the Nut House crew.

Thinking back on it now, I don't know why I was tripping in
the first place; Aubrey had his own history with my family, dating
back to when he shot hoops in our driveway with Perris and
worked part-time in my father's cosmetics lab during summers
home from college. In his adult incarnation he'd even managed to
endear himself to my mother, swapping recipes and taking great
pains to admire her perfectly presented meals.

It was Joymarie's suggestion that Aubrey make the cranberry
relish. "Given the fact your job hardly allows you to open the
refrigerator, much less a cookbook," she'd complained when she
called to review the menu and my assignment the beginning of the
month, "I think letting Aubrey do it would be the best bet."

Which, while I knew she was right, made me a little uneasy.
Although Aubrey Scott had been seducing me with food—and a
few other things—for six months, I wasn't sure whether putting
him in my mother's domestic crosshairs was a particularly wise
thing to do.

It was twelve-thirty Thanksgiving afternoon and I was reviewing a couple of the home invasion files when Aubrey arrived. He
was dressed in brown corduroy slacks and a tan flannel shirt that
accentuated the golden tone of his skin and his broad shoulders.
He stepped through the door, his hands finding their way around
my waist as he bent over to give me a long, sensual kiss. "You
weren't supposed to be here until one-thirty," I noted.

"You're wearing this to dinner?" he asked, fingering the silk
of an old kimono I'd thrown on.

I was about to answer when Beast, my Boxer, trotted into the
living room, a rubber ring in his mouth. "Don't let him sucker you
into that," I warned. "You'll be here all day."

Aubrey bent down and started scratching the dog's ears. "It's
okay. Besides, what's the rush? We don't have to be there until

three." He gave me a suggestive look. "You aren't even dressed yet."

Moving to the files on the dining-room table, I said, "I thought I had an extra hour," trying not to make my voice chiding. "And we don't have as much time as you think. *Dinner's* at three, and if we don't get there at least an hour ahead of time to receive General Joymarie's last-minute orders, there'll be hell to pay. I'm already in the doghouse for having to work late last night and not being able to help her make the pies."

"She didn't mean that crack about the doghouse, fella," Aubrey whispered in Beast's ear, then stood up to face me with an encouraging smile. "Charlotte, relax. Your mother's the most capable woman I know—next to you. And with your sister Rhodesia and Louise and Grandmama Cile to help her, I'm sure everything is totally under control."

He walked to where I was standing in the dining room, tugged at the sash on my kimono, let the silk tie flutter to the floor. "We've both been so busy with work, we haven't seen each other for a week," he murmured, his honey-colored eyes lighting up when he saw what I wasn't wearing underneath. "Why don't we just slow down and have a little pre-Thanksgiving feast of our own before we go over there?" He moved closer, caressing, then kissing the side of my neck. "I *am* a little hungry," he admitted.

I felt my body stiffen, tried to brush away the realization that in the six months we'd been together, Aubrey and I had seldom made love in my house, the house I'd bought with Keith. Besides, the files on the table were calling me, the clock on the breakfast-room wall reminding me we had to hurry. But soon my guilt gave way to an insistent tingling that spread over my whole body. "Me, too," I admitted reluctantly and let myself be led to the leather sofa.

It was two-thirty by the time we got to the Nut House—guilty but satisfied—our holiday assignments firmly in hand. My worst fears were confirmed when my mother answered the door, one hand propped firmly on her slim hips and hopping mad. "You *know* dinner's at three," she scolded. "And you know how I hate tardiness." She eyed me suspiciously. "Was that godforsaken job of yours making you late again?"

"Hey there, Mrs. Justice," Aubrey interrupted, kissing my mother on the cheek and handing her a plastic container of cranberry relish. "I figured you had a special dish you'd want to put this in."

She returned his kiss with a peck on the cheek. "I do, Aubrey," she replied, cutting her eyes at me, "but it needs to be rinsed out."

Aubrey heard the tone in her voice, looked around for an escape route. "Where's Mr. Justice?"

"In the den watching football with the twins, Perris, and Uncle Syl. You can join them, if you want. Charlotte can help us in the kitchen."

Taking the videotapes from me, Aubrey gave me an encouraging "You can handle this" look and hightailed it toward the back of the house while I dutifully followed my mother into the kitchen, aka Thanksgiving Command Central. The battle stations were fully manned: Perris's wife, Louise, a chef's apron over her clothes, was stirring gravy at the cooktop; my youngest sister, Rhodesia, her dreads pulled into a topknot, was putting monkey bread into one of the wall ovens; and I could see Grandmama Cile through the doorway, lining up the pies in the butler's pantry. I also noticed Macon, my middle sister, was not in attendance. I wondered what excuse she'd used not to come down from Oakland this time.

"Hey, girl," Louise greeted me. "Where's that gorgeous man of yours?"

"Who, Aubrey?"

"Like there's anybody else," Rhodesia noted with a snicker.

"Watching the game," I replied, embarrassed by my baby sister's teasing. I edged my way to the door. "Which I'm going to do, too. You've got plenty of help here, Mother."

Joymarie blocked my exit, her gray eyes flashing like lightning. "Not before you tell me why you couldn't make it over last night to help your grandmother and me."

I tried to get around her, knowing now why my younger sister Macon would not subject herself to this mama drama for the holidays. "You know I'm useless in the kitchen, Mother. Besides, I called and left you a message saying I had to work late."

"The night before *Thanksgiving?*"

"Look, I wasn't too keen about it, either. But my D-III left me with a lot of paperwork that had to be filed on the Home Invasion Task Force—"

"Is that the half-white fool who's been tryin' to get in your pants?" Grandmama Cile called out from the pantry.

I hissed a warning to my grandmother through clenched teeth, but it was too late.

"He *what?*" my mother practically shrieked.

"I never told Grandmama that," I swore to my incredulous mother. "She must have me confused with someone else."

My grandmother had come back into the kitchen by this time, a stricken look on her face. "I'm sorry, Baby Girl, but I can't lie—I *did* overhear you talkin' to Matt about it at our last Film Night."

"I'm going to watch the game," I muttered, and tried again to get away.

"No you're not, young lady." My mother's eyes were accusing and her pale-as-an-almond-shell skin had turned a mottled red. "You mean to tell me you told your father about some white man on your job harassing you and you didn't tell your *mother?*" She was practically sputtering with rage.

"Half-white," I mumbled. "And can you blame me for not saying anything? Just look at how you're behaving!"

My mother was trembling now, and there were tears in her eyes. She grabbed me by the arm. "Did he put his hands on you? Did he hurt you?"

I twisted away from her grip. "Quit overreacting, Mother. I can handle myself. It's not that big a deal."

"Not that big a deal!" Joymarie threw up her hands, looking to the others for confirmation of my lunacy. "I bet Henry Youngblood wouldn't think so!"

"Leave Uncle Henry out of this! The last thing I need is the deputy chief of police getting in the middle of my business, even if he is my godfather!"

Joymarie had screwed up her mouth to say something else when, dreadlocks flying, Rhodesia stepped between us, put a hand on my arm, and asked my mother: "Is four seventy-five the right temperature to warm up the bread, Mom?"

"Good heavens, child, you'll burn it up!" Joymarie exclaimed, pushing past us both to the oven. Rhodesia gave me a wink and sauntered over to the stove to listen to my mother lecture her about proper reheating techniques for bread. I could see that doctorate in psychology my baby sister was getting was actually coming in handy.

It only took Joymarie a few seconds to turn down the oven and check the bread. "I'm not finished with you yet, young lady," she warned me, finger pointing.

I was about to reply when Louise broke in. "Let's just everybody calm down so we can have a peaceful meal. We have a lot to be thankful for this year."

"Not the least of which is the love and *concern* we all feel for each other," Rhodesia added.

"Amen to that," Grandmama Cile agreed, looking anxiously between my mother and me.

While the tension from my run-in with my mother had subsided by the time we sat down to dinner, I was left feeling edgy, as if my body was waiting for the next storm to roll in. But everything seemed to have blown over, Joymarie beaming contentedly as she watched us devour the five-course, five-star meal she'd so painstakingly prepared.

Two hours later, we were scattered about the den like beached whales, listlessly watching my niece Ebony and nephew Ivory playing tag near the pool outside. Behind them a thick layer of dark clouds was gathering in the twilight, a portent of wet things to come. Among the dinner's other casualties was my mother's brother, Sylvester Curry, who'd been roused from the sadness of spending his first Thanksgiving without his beloved Jackie by an old family album.

"There I am!" Uncle Syl exclaimed, pointing at a yellowed photograph. "Second native from the left."

I peered over his shoulder at a publicity still from a thirties Tarzan movie, of a bright-skinned, impossibly young man with rings in his lip and ear. "I thought you were supposed to be helping out on the costumes," I teased, rubbing his shoulder playfully, "not trying to get an Oscar nomination on the sly."

Uncle Syl chuckled briefly, falling back on the sofa and wagging his silver-gray head. " Helping out? Shoot, Baby Girl, I practically saved that white woman's job! See, she was a wardrobe mistress who didn't want to get close enough to the extras to fit the costumes on them." His big hands fluttered like flapping birds as he pursed his lips in imitation: " 'I'm not touching those *Negroes,*' she tells Mama. So she convinces her good friend, the noted 'French' fashion designer Madame Violette—that was the alias your Grandmother Vi used when she opened that dress shop up on Wilshire—to let her borrow one of her colored 'helpers' to do the dirty work. My reward for playing the Sambo role was getting a loincloth of my own."

He smiled in sad triumph as he ran his finger along the row of grimacing extras. "Your grandmother was mortified, but what could she do, tell that white woman I was her son? So I went out to the studio with her and did the fittings, then put on my own costume and snuck onto the set."

Despite the offensive denial of her race—and her son—in my late grandmother's little charade, you could tell that it was clearly one of the best days of Uncle Syl's life. "That's Maynard Duncan, right next to me." He pointed out a soulful-eyed, dark-skinned young man, taller and more handsome than Johnny Weissmuller, his arm entwined in a thick jungle vine.

I took a look, then joined Aubrey on the love seat. "This is the director who died yesterday?" I asked, trying not to appear too eager to pick my uncle's brain.

"Yup. Third native from the left. You'da never known he had all that talent, playing those sorry African bushman parts, would you, Cile?"

Grandmama had just entered the den with a tray, bearing slices of her special pecan pumpkin pie. She paused, squinted through her trifocals at the photo, and sighed. "I'da climbed that man's tree any day," she declared as she started passing the dessert around. "Even if I had to knock that wife of his out of the way."

Uncle Syl glanced away, his shaggy eyebrows drawn together and his mustache puckered with some unspoken emotion, probably relief that my mother was still in the kitchen. My father's mother had a way with words that got under her daughter-in-law's skin worse than a tick in summer. And Grandmama's unabashed admiration for "show people" was something Joymarie Justice, a third-generation Angeleno and sometimes too much her mother's daughter, just could not tolerate—despite her own husband's and brother's lifelong, albeit behind-the-scenes, involvement in the industry.

Grandmama Cile sighed and shook her head sadly. "But Maynard Duncan, God rest his soul, wasn't any different from any other Negro in this country. He and Ivy had to wear a bunch of hats just to survive. Especially in Hollywood."

"You know you're telling it now, Cile," my uncle chimed in. "We did whatever it took to make it back in those days—took bit parts in bad movies, fitted wardrobe, swept up behind the elephants—and in between started costume companies or talent agencies or directed, like Maynard."

"And it *ain't* changed," Grandmama Cile added. She sat down next to my uncle on the sofa and handed me a slice of pie. "It's like them young girls, after you to make a movie about what happened to you durin' the Uprisin'."

"I don't blame these young actors." My father's voice boomed from over by the entertainment center, where he stood looking through some videotapes. "You gotta make some noise if you wanna get some attention. It's the only way to make it in this man's town. Take me, for example. If I hadn't've spoken up about

Miss Horne, I'd still be a starvin' artist moonlightin' as a janitor somewhere." He held up a tape. "How 'bout *Panama Hattie?* It was Miss Horne's first big studio film."

Lena Horne was my father's favorite, ever since he worked at Max Factor's Studios as a teenager during "Dub-yu Dub-yu Two" and convinced the chemists there that a broom-pushing colored boy knew enough about "war paint" to formulate makeup for her MGM film debut. My father's formulas would eventually provide the company with a whole new market for makeup, but his so-called impertinence got him fired.

Lucky for us it did. Matthew Justice went on to change his major at UCLA from art to chemistry, and to formulate makeup for everyday black women and, quiet as it was kept, for the best-known black stars for more than forty years. But he always had a soft spot for Miss Horne, his first inspiration. Consequently there was always a debate when we got together at my parents' home about which black classic film we should watch.

"Now, Mr. Justice," Aubrey began, with a nudge and a wink of a honey-colored eye in my direction, "I love me some Lena, too, but how about a little something different tonight?"

"I brought *Carmen Jones* with Dorothy Dandridge and Harry Belafonte," Rhodesia offered.

"And we brought a couple of Charles Burnett films," I added.

Louise suggested, "How about Ruby Dee and Sidney in *A Raisin in the Sun?*"—dodging the daggers in my brother Perris's don't-go-there look. Was my sister-in-love's suggestion of the six-ties film—the story of a black family's conflict over moving from their rented ghetto apartment to an integrated suburb—coinciden-tal, or a not-so-subtle salvo in her ongoing battle with Perris to buy a house away from the golden ghetto of View Park? Ever since the riots she'd been on a campaign for my brother to move her and the twins to a home in one of the city's gated communities—or at least to put up a wall around their house in the old neighborhood.

Or, I thought, maybe there was something else going on between them. I heard Perris say, "Let's watch *Amos 'n' Andy*," a look on his face of pure devilment—that, and the effects of the

Chardonnay he'd been sneaking sips of all day. Ignoring his teeto-taling wife's warning look and the ensuing uproar, he contended loudly, "I don't care what you say about the stereotypes, it's just as funny as that show they got now with that fool comedian and his friends!"

Bearing cups of coffee and tea on a rattan tray, Joymarie Curry Justice swept into the room on the tail end of the outcry, but she had heard enough to have made up her mind. "A Sidney Poitier movie is fine, but I will *not* allow my grandchildren to be exposed to those ridiculous stereotypes in our home," she declared, sounding for all the world just like her late mother.

"But Duncan was the uncredited director on a whole tapeful of *Amos 'n' Andy* episodes I've got here!" my father complained.

"What else do you have of his?" I asked.

"I've got every movie he ever made," my father said proudly. "Maynard Duncan was one of a kind."

"Can I borrow them? Sounds like Maynard Duncan was one of those unsung heroes."

"No different from me, your father, or a dozen other success-ful Negroes Hollywood would just as soon forget," my uncle asserted with a forcefulness that was unusual for him.

"And he was only seventy-six," my grandmother added, blowing thoughtfully over the top of her coffee cup and wiping an eye. "We *should* watch somethin' of his tonight, just to commemo-rate the man's passin'. Maynard Duncan worked on more than them jigaboo films, you know."

My grandmother was particularly shaken by the news; I knew from the papers that in addition to being more than ten years younger than she, Duncan was chairman of Still We Rise, a grass-roots rebuilding effort backed by a coalition of black churches, hers included.

"You got *Murder in Mudtown* over there, Matt?" Uncle Syl asked. "It was Maynard's directorial debut."

" 'Mudtown'?" Louise asked suspiciously. "Is that some kind of racial slur?"

Grandmama Cile let loose with a half-chuckle. "They *claimed* they called Watts Mudtown 'cause of the floods it used to get, but it was also the section of the city where they stuck all the colored folks. But Negroes was glad to be there, 'cause it was one of the few places in Los Angeles you could buy property. So lots of *our* VIPs lived there, from Arna Bontemps to Charlie Mingus."

I pulled away from Aubrey, who was whispering something lascivious in my ear, to ask, "And Maynard Duncan set his first movie in Watts?"

"Sure did," Grandmother Cile replied. "Nineteen forty-one. It was the first movie ever filmed in Watts, and I want to say it was the first mystery movie directed by a black man."

"Uh-uh," my uncle broke in. "That woulda been Oscar Micheaux, back in the twenties. Now mind you, Duncan's and Micheaux's mysteries were long before those blaxploitation films you kids were so wild about in the seventies. And talk about creative! *Murder in Mudtown* had songs and dancing, like a Fred Astaire and Ginger Rogers film. And I'll swear and be damned that rolling-dolly shot Spike Lee and a bunch of other directors use today—with the actors looking like they're being pulled on a little wagon—they got from Maynard Duncan's work in *Murder in Mudtown*."

Mention of Spike Lee's name set off a spirited sidebar discussion between Perris, an ex-cop turned lawyer, and my grandmother, the family rabble-rouser, about the merits of his latest film and its chances of getting any Oscar nominations. "I think Denzel deserves a nomination for *Malcolm X*," Perris argued.

"You know they only give Oscars to Negroes for certain kinds of roles," Grandmama Cile noted sarcastically. "Malcolm X was too dangerous for white people to recognize in real life, never mind in a movie. Negroes winning Oscars for acting are typically playing buffoons or 'noble' Negroes, not someone as in-your-face as Malcolm."

"You tell him, Grandmama," Rhodesia chimed in with a nod of her dreadlocked head.

"And as for poor Spike," my grandmother continued, "outspoken as that child is, you know they gonna pimp him. When has a black man ever won an Academy Award for best director? Never! And Best Picture? In your *dreams,* grandson. It's like Langston Hughes once said—as far as Negroes are concerned, Hollywood might just as well be controlled by Hitler!"

Uncle Syl hugged my grandmother into silence. "Now, Cile, we'll get to Spike and Langston later." He asked the rest of us, "Are we going to watch *Murder in Mudtown* or not?"

There was general agreement around the room, my mother the only holdout. "Don't we have enough murder and mayhem in our midst without seeing it on the screen, too?" she complained, cutting her eyes in my direction.

Aubrey reached for my hand, gave it a secret squeeze. "Thanks for the vote of confidence, Mother," I muttered.

"Come on, Mom," Rhodesia pleaded. "What did we agree to in the kitchen?"

"Can't a mother be concerned for her daughter's safety?"

"I don't want to hear this tonight," my father warned. "This is a film, not a referendum on Charlotte's career!"

My father cued up *Murder in Mudtown* in silence and then plopped down in his easy chair. "Maybe we could watch Lena in *The Duke Is Tops* afterward," he said finally, a dejected tone in his voice. "I named my Bronze Nightingale line of face powders after her role in that film. Biggest-selling products I ever developed."

As the credits rolled, my uncle leaned over to the love seat and whispered behind the back of his hand, "Why are you so interested in Maynard Duncan?"

"No particular reason," I lied, collecting pie crumbs on my plate with the back of my fork. "It's just when I heard about his death, and how he was a contemporary of yours and Daddy's, I got curious. Occupational hazard, I guess."

My uncle ratcheted up a bushy eyebrow, trying unsuccessfully to stare me down. Finally he gave up, saying, "Well, whether he ever gets the recognition or not, Maynard Duncan was a great man and a trailblazer among those of us in show business."

"It sounds as if Mr. Duncan led an honorable and meaningful

life." And may be the victim, I told myself, of a suspicious death that deserved all the attention I could give it.

"Unfortunately, it was a life that was only meaningful to us, Baby Girl," my uncle replied, a faraway look in his eyes. "Only to us."

CHAPTER 3

A BUNCH OF HAS-BEENS AND NEVER-WERES

Not surprisingly, I discovered the next Monday that my CO didn't even know who Maynard Duncan was. MacIverson Armstrong's lack of knowledge about anything outside of department politics and the thoroughbred horses he so religiously followed had prompted me to give him a nickname, one that corresponded to his initials—Captain MIA.

Captain MIA's ignorance about Hollywood's black VIPs worked both for and against me. On the plus side, my tip on Duncan's death, plus a concerned call from the mayor's office, got the case pulled from Wilshire Division and assigned to our unit. While I knew it was probably due to Clemenza, I couldn't help but hope that maybe the mayor felt the same way I did about doing the right thing in investigating the director's death.

But there was a significant downside, too. "You're going to have to work the Duncan case solo for the time being," Lieutenant Kenneth Stobaugh informed me in a meeting that morning.

"But, sir, six days have already passed since they found this guy. You know as well as I do that cases that go beyond forty-eight hours are just that much harder to—"

Stobaugh cut off my protest. "Big Mac wants us to hook up a

suspect on these home invasion robberies ASAP, so Firestone's working clue management directly with Rudolph and a couple of uniforms out of Central Bureau." He consulted his notes, peering over the tops of his gold-rimmed reading glasses, a recent concession to middle age. "Ron Neidisch at Wilshire Division is prepared to turn over the Duncan case to us, and you can liaise with Truesdale over at South Bureau if you need any background on the Clemenza connection."

"How about Cortez working it with me when she gets back?"

Stobaugh looked up from his notes and out the window to the rain-heavy clouds. "What do you think, Steve? Can you spare both Justice and Cortez from the task force for a few days?"

Steve Firestone sat in the other chair before Stobaugh's desk, jiggling his feet. In addition to being Cortez's and my direct supervisor, Firestone was responsible for the work of all of the detectives on the Home Invasion Task Force, which in our shop was a real coup for anyone under the age of fifty.

Firestone interrupted his chairbound cha-cha long enough to ask why the case couldn't be kicked back to South Bureau. "If they half-assed on Clemenza, let them clean it up. They're the ones who were so gung ho to hook up that grandpa whacker in the first place." He raked his fingers through his hair, which made him look like an exasperated Airedale. "I can't afford to have two of our detectives pulled to cover South Bureau's asses while the trail gets cold on the home invasions. All they'll do is get caught up schmoozing with a bunch of Hollywood has-beens and never-weres anyway. These home invasion murders are high-profile."

As if the suspicious death of a pioneering film director potentially connected to the Clemenza case wasn't. But the Home Invasion Task Force was Firestone's big opportunity to shine, and he naturally wanted all the help he could get in burnishing his rising star, not mine or South Bureau's. I suspected, though, that there was another reason he was downplaying the Duncan case. Call it my own twisted version of the Lucy Van Pelt School of Five-Cent Psychiatry, but I had noticed over the years that black victims rarely stirred Steve Firestone's sympathies. Which was sad, especially because he was half black himself, something he desperately tried to hide despite the hint of melanin in his skin and the persistent kink in his hair.

"Believe me, I don't really give two whoops in Hades about the Hollywood connection." I looked each man square in the eyes just to reinforce my position, glad neither of them knew I'd spent the weekend watching and being entranced by Maynard Duncan's films. "If I ever hear from another movie or television person again, it'll be too soon."

Firestone rolled his eyes, but Stobaugh chuckled softly and bobbed his graying blond head. Son of a fabled detective and a real go-getter himself, Stobaugh knew about Hollywood's interest in my life story, had even helped me out by intercepting some insistent phone calls from film producers for me. I decided to make my plea to him. "Lieutenant, we all know this case should've been RHD's from jump street, but South Bureau pulled the okeydoke behind our backs. And if we don't get control of it now, the whole thing could blow up in the department's lap and all over the press, especially in the black community. And I know I don't need to remind you that several of Clemenza's victims were African American. But"—I glanced at Firestone with an elaborate rolling of my shoulders and eyes that would have done Stepin Fetchit proud—"if you want to deal with the conspiracy theory crowd, you go right ahead."

Firestone started backpedaling in his chair; the radical black press was the last thing he had time or inclination to be bothered with, and we both knew it. Meanwhile, our lieutenant's fingers were steepled in front of his mouth, his index fingers lightly tapping his nose as his eyes shifted from me to Firestone and back again. When he finally told Firestone, "There's no way Big Mac is going to relinquish this case to South Bureau," I realized I'd been holding my breath, realized solving the case meant more to me than I dared admit. "Besides, Steve, with you chasing down leads in the home invasion cases and our other teams tied up, Justice is our best bet to do the groundwork on this one. And she's more than capable of balancing this case with her other workload."

Firestone was grinding his teeth so hard I thought he might crack a molar. I directed a brief smile of gratitude in my lieutenant's direction. "I'm sure I can work this in. I'm pretty much on top of paperwork for the task force."

My lieutenant gave Firestone an unreadable look before saying to me, "But you're going to have to handle it solo for now. And I want a rundown on where you are in the investigation tomorrow afternoon, and a full report by Friday. If a second Little Angel of Mercy is out there, we need to get a team on it right away."

After we were dismissed, Firestone followed me back to my desk in the corner of the bull pen that was home to RHD's homicide units, his jaw still working furiously. "Don't you ever pull a stunt like that in front of Stobaugh again!"

A few inquisitive heads popped up like groundhogs testing the winter air, then ducked down as the other detectives shuffled already neat papers, answered silent telephones, and otherwise pretended not to be eavesdropping.

I met Firestone's hot glare. "And what stunt might that be?"

He took a step toward me. "Trying to make it look like I'm shuffling you off to Buffalo on the task force."

I stepped back a little and put on an innocent face. "Excuse me, but I guess I'm confused. There have been seventeen home invasion robberies since July and now this latest rash of robberies and homicides on the Westside. What would you say if you were consistently left with just the paperwork on a case of this magnitude while every other detective assigned to the task force was being given substantive investigative duties in the field?"

"I'd say I was being a good team player," he snapped, jabbing a finger in my face for emphasis. "Which obviously you aren't."

Sensing the anger migrating from the back of my neck to my cheeks, I gathered up my purse and hurried into my jacket. Firestone trailed me out into the hallway, still pointing. "You're becoming the worst kind of detective we could have in RHD— ready to step over your colleagues, your own partner, even your superiors, to grab a headline. You'll never be a leader that way!"

I could feel my stomach knot and my breath grow shallow as I made my way to the elevator. This was worse than the sexual innuendos and come-ons Firestone had subjected me to in the past; now he was hitting me where I lived by attacking my professionalism. Had he said the same thing to Stobaugh when he was writing my evaluation for promotion to D-III? I looked around to be sure there was no one else in the elevator lobby before saying, "That's a crock of shit, Firestone, and you know it!"

I tried to calm myself as Manny Rudolph headed our way. I managed a tense smile, which he briefly acknowledged while giving Firestone a high five. So much for his talking to "ol' Steve" on my behalf.

As I stood waiting for the elevator, I tried to set aside my fears. And tried even harder to ignore Steve Firestone. But like my dog with a chew toy, he wouldn't let go. "Oh, I get it," he said, all up in my face. "Maybe you've found another way of getting that promotion to supervising detective." He stood back and leered. "I didn't know the lieutenant was a breast man."

So angry I felt light-headed, I buttoned my jacket over my gun holster and squared my shoulders. "Is that the only way you think a woman can get ahead in the department—on her back? Hard as this may be for you to believe, Firestone, most of us are more than qualified for the jobs we hold, even though assholes like you discriminate against us and harass us half to death!"

Firestone's mouth twisted into a mean little smile. "So if you're so qualified, why *do* you sleep with the lieutenant? And for the record, Justice, those affirmative-action catchphrases won't work on me. Don't forget, I'm black, too."

"Only when it suits you," I shot back, glad the elevator door closed between us.

As disturbed as I was about my run-in with Firestone, my problems seemed insignificant compared to those of the people of Pico-Union, a partially barricaded, crime-infested neighborhood I cut through on my way to the Wilshire station. While everyone talked about South Central and the damage it suffered in the riots, the impact on this neighborhood just west of downtown was like a nuclear bomb, leveling dozens of businesses and throwing thousands of minimum-wage-to-slave-wage-earning Latino immigrants out of what little work there was. Traveling west on Pico Boulevard, I saw dispirited clusters of men huddled under an assortment of mostly broken umbrellas. They were stationed on the corners of what was once a bustling business district, hoping for someone to pick them up for day labor jobs that wouldn't pay enough to buy their children some Payless imitation leather shoes, not to mention Christmas presents.

But help was on the way. A plethora of public and private redevelopment efforts, with upbeat names like Rebuild L.A. and Still We Rise, had blanketed the city like smog, had been touted by the mayor and the media as if they were the best thing since the fax machine, and had attracted a wealth of talent. Or was that talent attracted to getting wealthy? The opportunists who flocked to the ravaged South after the Civil War were called carpetbaggers. My father called the dashiki-wearing fly-by-nighters who got rich off of the post-Watts chaos in the sixties and seventies poverty pimps. With the exception of the attire and hairstyles, I was hard pressed to see how the current crop of cell-phone-toting vultures I'd seen in the newspapers and on television had done any better by the innocent people ravaged by this latest wave of destruction.

I eased my car into a space in the Wilshire Division's parking structure and hurried inside to find the primary detective who had caught the Duncan case. Tilted back in his chair with his feet propped up on his desk, the receiver cradled under his jutting jaw, Ron Neidisch still possessed the hawklike good looks and buttoned-down style I remembered from our time together at the Academy.

But I could tell this was to be no happy reunion by the way his lip curled a little when he saw me. He abruptly hung up the phone and, skipping the pleasantries, got straight to the point: "You know, every time a minor celebrity goes tits up, it's no reason for you Red Hot Dogs to come big-footing onto the case." The green flecks in his brown eyes sparked as he slung a three-ring binder in my direction and put his feet back up on his desk. From where I was sitting, I could see the beginning of a hole in his sole. At least there was *someone* in Wilshire Division who recognized Duncan as a VIP, albeit an insignificant one. "Us taking over this case has nothing to do with not trusting Wilshire's ability to handle it," I assured Neidisch as I opened the blue murder book and got out my notebook. *Or anyone trying to cut you and your partner out of your fifteen minutes of fame,* I said to myself. To him I explained, "With the heat from the mayor's office and all, the honchos in the PAB just want to be sure this one's not connected to Clemenza."

Neidisch's aquiline nose wrinkled up in a sneer. "Honchos in the Parker Administrative Building? You must mean the Pinstriped Doughboy."

Neidisch was referring to our new police chief, who had earned that nickname among a host of less flattering ones for his girth and seeming affinity for business suits, a sartorial preference in direct opposition to the former chief's command-and-control, uniform-wearing style. I made a noncommittal noise and turned my attention to Section Four of the murder book, which contained the Death Investigation Report.

According to the report, the Wilshire Division watch commander received a call at 1900 hours on Tuesday from one of the city fire department's paramedic units. Ivy Duncan, the vic's wife, had called them at 1830 hours to come to the couple's home in the exclusive Fremont Place section of Hancock Park after she found her husband, Maynard, dead in his bedroom on the second floor.

Although the paramedics had pronounced him at the scene, the signs of an apparent drug overdose had prompted them to call for a couple of Wilshire Division uniforms, who in turn contacted the night watch detective and proceeded to set up a crime scene. The night watch detective got to the residence at 2000 hours and, after her own assessment, called Neidisch and his partner, Joe O'Donoughue, who arrived at 2115 hours and started investigating the scene.

"The paramedics swore they hadn't moved him or disturbed his IV," Neidisch offered when I got to his partner's diagram of the crime scene. It showed in the crudest of detail the position of the body in the bed, his head pointing in what appeared to be a northerly direction. My four-year-old niece and nephew could have done better. When I questioned its accuracy, Neidisch waved away my concern as if I was a gnat on a fruit bowl. "Joe figured he'd fill in the blanks when we got the photos from SID."

"It's not up to the flash hounds from the Scientific Investigation Division to cover for our lack of thoroughness," I said, wondering why couldn't Kate Delafield or some of the other competent Wilshire Division Homicide detectives I knew have caught the case instead of these two sluggards. Neidisch knew as I did that one of the first rules of an investigation was never to rely on memory, especially with the kind of defense attorneys we encountered these days—attorneys who could confuse a jury so thoroughly by twisting the facts they could make them mistake day for night. Therefore, a detective's written notes, observations, and diagrams keyed to each item of evidentiary value were critical. Without them, an attorney could have a field day speculating why another detective would complete a crime scene sketch several days after the murder, and what he, or someone else, could have planted there in the meantime.

I read on. "What's this in the medical history about a continuous fusion pump?"

"That's a little box hooked up to his IV that the vic used to give himself a hit of morphine when he was in pain. But there were other narcotics on the premises, too—pill bottles were all over the bedside table and overflowing the medicine cabinet, too. We stashed the lot of it in an evidence locker."

Although it wasn't indicated in the medical history, the list of drugs was scribbled in the evidence inventory along with their dates of prescription, strength, and quantity remaining. I recognized the name Ampicillin as an antibiotic I'd once taken myself, but the names Oramorph, Demerol, and Vicodin also stood out among the list of a dozen or so bottles found in the cabinet.

Among those found on the bedstand were a bottle of Tylenol with codeine and a bunch of herbs and vitamins.

"His wife stated before he went on the pump, he used to take a half-dozen of those painkillers a day." He snorted and shook his head. "Any one of those could knock me on my ass in ten minutes flat."

Which might improve your disposition, I wanted to say.

"And can you imagine he was still smoking despite all that?" Neidisch was saying.

"What do you mean?"

"We found a gold lighter under his desk and cigarette ashes in the carpet by the bed."

I checked the inventory list. Sure enough, beneath the list of drugs was written: *lighter, antique, gold, ornate inscription, "To My Pilgrim Soul."* "You sure this was his?" I asked, making a note in my book.

"His wife identified it."

"But there are no cigar or cigarette butts listed in the inventory. No ashtray either. Anybody figure out what he was smoking?"

"That bothered me, too," Neidisch agreed. "So we looked around when we were going through the trash cans both inside and out, but we couldn't find anything. We concluded the vic must've sneaked a smoke and then flushed it down the toilet."

"Maybe it was marijuana. There are doctors who'll prescribe it for cancer patients."

"I thought about that, but an old guy like Duncan didn't seem the type."

Although Neidisch's voice carried a cocky assurance that was common to cops, I sensed an uncertainty that made me think maybe he hadn't considered the possibility. "So his widow consented to the search of the premises?"

Neidisch's feet came off the desk. "Hell, yeah." His jaw stood out boldly and his eyes flashed again. "You tryin' t'say I don't know my job?"

"I wasn't inferring that, Ron. I just wanted to know if she was cooperative." I let the silence stretch a little, hoping Neidisch's anger would drain through that hole in his sole. "You interview his home health nurse?"

"She left for vacation the day our—your—boy bought the farm."

"You have any idea where she went?"

"No, and neither does her supervisor at the agency where she works, or her neighbors. O'Donoughue was about to call her job again, see if she's back yet, when we got the word RHD was taking over."

I couldn't help but think if I conducted an investigation of a case this way, Firestone would be on me like a case of head lice. But as my father, Matt, would say, there's no use COSM—crying over spilt milk. I swallowed the bile I could feel rising at the back of my throat and noted aloud that the nurse's name and the agency where she worked weren't in the book.

"Isn't it in there?" Neidisch scanned the report, frowned, then made a show of looking through the papers on his desk. "Here it is," he said at length, and unearthed a card from his desk drawer. "Alice Thomas. She worked for HealthMates, a—"

"Home health agency in the South Bay," I finished. Neidisch didn't say another mumbling word, and the mock-innocent look he was giving me made me want to put my size nines square in his behind. After another beat, I prompted, "It was the agency that employed Angelo Clemenza."

"Who he?" he asked, and shrugged.

Without divulging my conversation with Billie, I responded as calmly as possible, "Come on, Ron. Don't tell me you haven't heard of the Little Angel of Mercy case out of South Bureau. It's been in all the papers." *Not to mention every "in custody" bulletin coming out of South Bureau for almost a year, you jackass.*

"Sorry, Justice, but I've been too busy closing cases to have time to read the papers."

I knew no detective worth his salt wants to be made to feel he can't handle a case, so that wasn't the intent of my line of questioning. Neidisch knew as well as I did that this was what RHD was created to do—take the burden of a time-consuming or inordinately complex case off the shoulders of field detectives so they could concentrate on the day-to-day murders in their jurisdictions. And while there could always be some interdepartmental feathers ruffled when we take over a case, Neidisch's churlishness seemed a little much. And even if he was pissed at RHD, for the life of me I couldn't figure out why he felt the need to diss Billie Truesdale and South Bureau in the process.

Whatever the reason, my former classmate's attitude was pissing me off to the nth degree. But, like so many things on this job, I decided to let it go, give an old friend the benefit of the doubt. Until I realized there was no attempt to contact the victim's physician mentioned in the death report either, and practically lost my mind.

"Don't get your pantyhose in a knot, Detective," Neidisch reassured me, consulting his notebook. "She's on vacation until this Wednesday—at one of those hippie Zen retreats—and the office manager wouldn't discuss Mr. Duncan's condition without the doctor's express permission."

"So why hasn't anybody gotten hold of her? It's been six days since you found this guy already!"

"Place has got no phones, no fax, and it's a three-hour drive from San Francisco to get there."

I started to remind him that the local sheriff's department could have helped or he could have gotten a search warrant for the victim's medical records, but I sucked my teeth and held my tongue. In my mind, it was pure laziness that was making Ron Neidisch drag his feet on the case. Didn't he know that kind of sloppiness could not only undo a case but come back to bite him personally in the ass?

Or maybe that only happened to me.

At least there were notes from interviews conducted at the scene with the wife and sister. Ivy Duncan described her husband as being physically weakened from his last illness, having lost about sixty pounds over the course of surgery and chemotherapy. She also acknowledged he was in a lot of pain, disoriented at times, but with intermittent periods of extreme lucidity. She informed

Neidisch she had found the body on Tuesday evening at 1800 hours. After informing the victim's sister, Mrs. Duncan had called the paramedics at 1830.

The two women were the only ones in the house when the body was found, although a number of servants, workers, and visitors, in addition to the home health nurse, had been there earlier in the day. Under the heading "Persons at the Scene" were the names of the home's inhabitants and visitors that day, which were provided by the women and checked by O'Donoughue against the log-in sheets, obtained through a search warrant from the guard stationed at the development's gatehouse:

> Ivy Duncan, wife. Calif. Driver's Lic. #XD 1483992, DOB 5/19/20. Address: same as victim's. Occupation: co-owner, Soulful Celebrations Catering. Found and identified vic as Maynard Duncan.

> Delphine Giles, sister of victim. Calif. ID# R4504432, DOB 8/15/09. Address: same as victim's. Occupation: co-owner, Soulful Celebrations Catering. Visited victim in his room around 1030 hours. Was working in backyard greenhouse when body discovered.

> Others in house on 11/26 (per Ivy Duncan and Delphine Giles statements):

> Dolores Amargosa, housekeeper. Address: 4122 1/2 West 62nd Street. Arrived before 0700 hours, took FedEx delivery to vic's room at 0945 hours. Went up again at 1230 hours to serve lunch to vic and Pastor Henley (see below). Left at 1430 hours with Otto Randall (see below).

> Otto Randall, catering manager, Soulful Celebrations Catering. Address: 6510 Romaine Avenue #14, Hollywood. Arrived at 0900 hours to prepare food for a Thanksgiving dinner being catered by Soulful Celebrations. Took Dolores Amargosa to Hollywood to catch bus for LAX at 1430 hours.

Senior Pastor Clayton Henley, Peaceful Shepherd Missionary Baptist Church. Address: 3896 Crenshaw Boulevard, Los Angeles. Arrived at 1200 hours, had lunch with vic at 1230 hours, left shortly after 1300 hours.

Alice Thomas, home health nurse, HealthMates. Work address: 4491 West 118th Street, Hawthorne. Home address: Hollywood Tower, 6200 Franklin Avenue, Hollywood. Current whereabouts unknown. Arrived at 1300 hours, reloaded pump with morphine, left at 1330 hours.

Victor "Skip" Sheffield, Jr., CEO, UCN (Urban Contemporary Network). Address: 3845 Hollywood Way, Burbank. Arrived at 1345 hours, met briefly with victim, left at 1400 hours.

Deliveries by FedEx driver (approximately 0945 hours), Soulful Celebrations staff (approximately 1115 hours), but neither entered the residence.

"You talk to all these people yet?"

"Other than the wife, sister, and that preacher, we haven't had time."

In six days? "Where are the field interviews with the neighbors? They hear any arguments coming from the house, see any unusual comings or goings?"

"O'Donoughue has the FI cards in his desk somewhere. Most of the neighbors were out with their housekeepers doing last-minute grocery shopping for Thanksgiving dinner or already gone for the holidays. The few the uniforms could catch at home didn't notice anything, but we handed out business cards and put them in the mailboxes of the ones out of town, in case they saw or heard anything."

I flipped to the end of the death report, and noted the conclusions section was blank, which was to be expected so early in the case. "You've been working homicide a long time, Ron. What's your take on how he died?"

My acknowledgment of his expertise improved Neidisch's disposition a little. Up went the wingtips on the desk, his hands behind his head. "The house was ordinary in every way. Nothing inconsistent with what you'd expect for an old man dying at home, which is why we didn't isolate and search the whole place as a crime scene. The wife and the sister were upset at his death, but not inordinately so, nor did they seem rattled when we questioned them about the quantity of narcotics in the house. Way I see it, this old guy's at death's door anyway, crazy out of his mind with pain. He probably got his pills mixed up and took too many of the wrong ones."

"But it says here most of the painkillers were found in the medicine cabinet. If he was as weak and disoriented as his wife described him, how'd he have the presence of mind to get up and find them among all the other pills in the bathroom?"

Neidisch nodded, knowing where I was headed. "I hadn't ruled out the possibility that he got an assist from someone in the house that day. But I figured I'd hold off making the final call until after the autopsy is done and the fingerprint results come back."

"Who lifted the prints?"

"Herman Wozniak."

I exhaled, relieved that someone competent from the Latent Prints section of SID was assigned to the case. "You get print cards on everyone at the house that day?"

"O'Donoughue's got them for the women at the house and the minister. As for the rest . . ."

"You don't have to tell me," I said, making a note to get those taken care of as soon as possible. "When is the ME making the cut?"

"I was just about to call over there," he admitted. "Then word came down that you were taking over. So I figured I'd—"

"I know . . . let me deal with it."

"You catch on quick, Justice," he marveled, the faint hole in his sole staring at me. "No wonder you and your dykey buddy over at South Bureau are the media darlings."

So *that* was it: Neidisch had a case of what my father called

DJS—delayed jealousy syndrome—with a dose of homophobia and sexism thrown in for good measure. But if I let on that it bothered me, I knew there'd only be more where that came from. I closed the murder book. "You got time to come over to the Duncan house with me, introduce me to the family?"

"Too much to do around here." He and his shoe winked at me. "But a smart cookie like you—I know you can handle it on your own."

I gave my former classmate a megawatt smile in return and made a point of thanking him for his "cooperation" before going to the Property Room to retrieve the evidence collected at the crime scene.

"No problem, Detective," he called after me. "Anything we can to do help, you be sure and let us know."

CHAPTER 4

WORSE THAN MAGGOTS IN A HEAD WOUND

My next stop was to see Mikki Alexander, the investigator who had caught the case from the coroner's department and called Billie. I found her in between runs, having a rare lunch at her desk with Dr. Cassie Reynolds, a medical examiner I'd worked with before. Reynolds, whose blond curls and childlike appearance obscured the steely personality beneath, looked even smaller and younger than usual sitting down, while Alexander's usual heavy veil of Halston was a little lighter, clues to me that she'd not been called out on very many—or very pungent—cases that day.

"Hey, Justice," Alexander mumbled around her sandwich as I pulled up a chair. "Hear they've put you on Duncan. Good to see someone other than the gray-hairs catch a celebrity case."

"As if the dead aren't all the same," Reynolds muttered.

"It's not the dead they're concerned about," I reminded them. "They're hoping there's some producer out there waiting in the wings to make a movie-of-the-week about their lives."

Alexander tossed her head and batted her blue eyes. " 'Mr. Spelling, I'm ready for my close-up.' " While I knew she was trying for Norma Desmond in *Sunset Boulevard,* her short skirt and mane of streaked hair made Alexander look more like one of those hair-tossers on *Melrose Place* than Gloria Swanson.

"Medical examiners haven't gotten that kind of attention since *Quincy*," Reynolds joked. "Not that I'm looking for it," she hurried to explain. "I hate these faking-and-shaking show business people worse than maggots in a head wound."

"Better maggots than those Hollywood leeches," Alexander added with a snort. "At least maggots can help you estimate a vic's time of death."

"What's the story on my vic?"

"From just the preliminary physical examination and checking out the meds at the scene, it's a pretty clear-cut case of a drug overdose," Alexander said.

"So you'll do a full tox screen?"

Reynolds bit into a pear. "Yeah, but I still intend to open him up, take a look at those stomach and bowel contents just in case."

"How soon can you make the cut?"

"Could have done it today," Reynolds answered, "but we don't have the patient's medical record. When we called over to the doctor's office for it, we learned the deceased's attorney has filed a motion to quash."

I felt the hairs on my neck rise up. That made the second time we'd been stopped from getting details on Duncan's illness. "On what grounds?" I demanded.

"I haven't seen the paperwork," Reynolds replied. "The doctor's office clammed up, and neither the family nor their attorney would talk to me."

"What about the home health agency, HealthMates?"

"I called them, too, but got the grand runaround. As you can imagine, with their connection to the Little Angel of Mercy case, no one over there was too anxious to cooperate."

"Well, we can certainly get a search warrant for the records, but I'd rather call on the widow first, see if I can find out what this is all about."

"I wish you luck," Reynolds replied. "She sounded like a real piece of work on the phone."

I made a mental note, grateful for the warning. "Where's this continuous infusion pump he was hooked up to?"

"I'll go get it." Alexander rose from her chair and returned a few minutes later with a large padded bag. Inside was a rectangular box made of metal and plastic, about the size of a hardcover book. Attached to it were coiled plastic tubing and two partially used bags of IV solution.

"How does this thing work?"

"It's really quite simple," Alexander said. "The pump is attached to the bags of IV solution. Inside is a cartridge of the narcotic—which in this case is MS, morphine sulfate—which is programmed to be mixed into the IV solution at a rate set by the patient's physician and administered by the home health nurse."

I had gotten out my notebook and started writing. "What's a normal dosage?"

Alexander deferred to Reynolds, who explained, "Depends on a patient's body weight. But if the patient's been on the drip for severe pain for a while, like your guy, he could be getting several times the normal amount. I've seen them brought in here during the last stages of their disease taking as much as five hundred milligrams per hour. That's enough to kill all of us and have some left over."

"So it'd be hard to figure out how to give someone in Duncan's condition an OD?"

"It would be for the average Joe Blow," Reynolds replied. "But as a rule of thumb, if you dramatically increase the drip rate, or the concentration of narcotic being mixed with the IV solution—say four times the regular dosage—that would probably do it. So would a bolus, an injection, directly into his IV."

While I was writing, I noticed that dust from what was probably Herman Wozniak's, the print technician's, effort had stained the plastic attachments and dulled a shiny lock next to the manufacturer's name on the top of the pump itself. "Who has the key to this thing?"

"The home health agency for starters," Reynolds said as she crunched a potato chip.

"Not to mention any nurse caring for chronic pain patients who worked with this model," Alexander added. "The keys are interchangeable."

"So anyone might have access to a key?"

"Before you jump to conclusions," Reynolds warned, blond curls bouncing, "just being able to open the pump wouldn't do a killer much good. They've got to punch in the right code to activate the machine and then be able to program the dosage."

"Could the vic have done it himself?"

Alexander chewed and swallowed another bite of her sandwich. "For him to give himself enough MS to overdose, he'd have to go to some extraordinary lengths."

"But if he *could* get his hands on a key and the code, would watching his nurse program the machine on enough occasions help him figure it out?"

"It's possible," Alexander acknowledged reluctantly, "but I'd be surprised if this guy had the strength or the concentration, Charlotte. Between the cancer and the chemotherapy, his wife said he was down to under a hundred and thirty pounds. For his height, that's all of a person's fat and most of their muscle. He woulda been pretty weak."

"How much time do you think he had left?"

"Cancer can be pretty tricky," Reynolds said. "Given the amount and variety of painkillers he was taking, it's safe to assume his cancer wasn't localized—had maybe spread to his peritoneum or his ribs, or even his spine or liver, for that matter. The medical record will give us those details, but in any of those scenarios—although the pain would be dreadful—he could still hang on for six months to a year, maybe even longer."

The thought made me shudder. "But what kind of life would that be?" I wondered aloud.

The room grew quiet—we were all so used to dealing with death, the end of life was a little bit out of our league. Mikki Alexander, her head down, ventured a softly voiced opinion. "For some people it's pure agony—for them and their families—while others find redemption of a sort in suffering. My mother died of breast cancer, and it just about tore our family apart. My sisters and I still don't speak to each other behind some of the shit that went on."

"Mikki, I'm so sorry," Reynolds and I chimed in unison.

Alexander looked up and squared her shoulders as if startled that she'd said anything at all. "All I'm saying is that the degree of suffering people can tolerate depends on the individual's makeup and the family dynamic."

Which was something I would have to learn about Maynard Duncan and his family if I was going to determine how, and at whose hands, he died. I gestured toward the pump. "Do either of you know how to program this thing?"

They shook their heads. Reynolds suggested I call the manufacturer to send out a rep. "They can do it," she assured me.

There was a little metal tag on the bottom of the pump, listing the manufacturer's name and a location and phone number down in Irvine. I used the phone on Alexander's desk while she and Reynolds finished their lunch, and left a message with the company's general manager to call me at the PAB. When I was done I said, "I'll need to take this with me."

Alexander nodded. "You can take the pump, but we'll need to keep everything else for testing, see if there are any traces of narcotics injected into the IV tubing."

While Alexander detached the pump from the bag and tubing, I asked Reynolds how long it would take for an overdose to kill a man in Duncan's condition. "The time could vary based on whether he got it though the IV, in a bolus, or by ingestion. Layer on top of that his weakened physical condition, and I'd say ten to thirty minutes as a ballpark."

Alexander added, "Given all of the possibilities, plus what we gleaned from the body temp and signs of rigor at the scene, we're calling it between noon and three P.M."

I made a few calculations in my notebook, arriving at a time of between roughly eleven-thirty and two-thirty for administration of the fatal dose. A time frame which, unfortunately, encompassed the visits of all seven of the people logged in by the gatehouse guard that day.

I closed my notebook, signed out for the pump, put it back in its padded envelope, and exited through the morgue lobby. Two techs were decorating the fish tank in the corner with gold-foil garlands and fake holly berries. It was hard to believe it was almost December, only a couple of dozen shopping days until Christmas.

I took the items from the Wilshire detectives and the coroner's office back to the PAB, where I examined them and checked them into an evidence locker.

After grabbing a burger at Teddy's, I headed west on Third Street, all the while pushing buttons on the radio of my department-issued Chevy, hoping for a sign. Everyone has one—the day the tree goes up in Rockefeller Center, receiving the Needless Markup catalog in the mail, or hearing a favorite song that unequivocally signals "'Tis the season." In my family it was Nat King Cole's recording of "The Christmas Song." As I cruised through Hancock Park, which boasted one of L.A.'s more extensive collections of mansions, I remembered the stories my parents told me about how the Cole family had moved there in the late forties only to have a cross burned into their lawn, allegedly by the local "protective association," in a perverted version of the neighborhood Welcome Wagon. And although the incident was before my time, the legacy of the outrage bubbled to the surface every Christmas when Nat's version of the classic Mel Tormé song was played at the Nut House, sort of a Justice family Yuletide–cum–civil rights anthem.

I stopped at a corner to watch an immaculately attired Korean man emerge from his gated property to walk his Labrador retrievers across the intersection. I wondered how Nat's white-collared, red-necked "neighbors" felt when more undesirables—like this man or even the city's black mayor—followed in the Cole family's footsteps. By then they'd probably pulled up stakes and moved somewhere else, San Marino or behind Orange County's invisible curtain, circling their wagons against the encroaching yellow, black, and brown hordes.

I doubted if their last stand would have been inside the guarded gates of Fremont Place, a Hancock Park enclave right off Wilshire Boulevard and not more than a mile from Nat Cole's former residence. Even though the development's perimeter was protected by a rent-a-cop in a gatehouse, thorny bougainvillea-covered walls, and filigreed wrought-iron work, they couldn't hold back the tide of integration. Lou Rawls and Muhammad Ali had crashed those gates, as did black, Latino, and Asian bankers, lawyers, and corporate chiefs. Yet, much to the chagrin of my Grandmother Vi, it was not one of her blue-veined, socially connected friends who got to break that residential barrier but actor/filmmaker Maynard Duncan and his beautiful wife, Ivy, who were the first black folks to integrate the exclusive development more than thirty years ago. I was guessing at the date, guided by the style and rusted condition of the aluminum awnings that shielded the windows of Duncan's dirt-streaked Greek Revival–style mansion. That and the dim recollection of seeing those same awnings in brand-new condition in a fifties pictorial on black stars' homes in *Ebony* magazine, which set my Grandmother Vi off on one of her memorable "show people aren't *our* people" tirades.

After dropping off my card at the neighboring houses, I went to the trunk of my car to get my briefcase and run through my three objectives for visiting the Duncan residence. One, to reconfirm the information supplied to Neidisch by the dead man's wife and sister on their movements and those of visitors to the house on the day of his death. Two, to get a better feel for the crime scene than I had from O'Donoughue's piss-poor sketch. And three, to figure out those family dynamics Mikki Alexander mentioned, especially why Mrs. Duncan was so insistent on blocking the coroner's access to her husband's medical record.

Passing the weathered concrete lions and making my way up the worn mosaic-tiled front steps, I entertained myself with the thought that if this were an old mystery movie and a detective called at a house like this, the faithful retainer—typically English, white, and male—would be there to intone, "I'll inform Mrs. Nitwittingham that you're here." But if that retainer was American, female, and black, there would be much clutching at bosoms and drawling, "Oh, Lordy, I'll get the missus right away!" So I was a little discombobulated when an elderly woman—closer to Aunt Jemima in color but Jeeves in her carriage—answered the door, took my card, and introduced herself as Maynard Duncan's sister.

Despite amazingly upright posture for a woman Neidisch's murder book indicated was eighty-three, on closer inspection Mrs. Delphine Giles seemed like a woman teetering on the edge of hysteria. "We've lost our housekeeper, too," she stammered as she let me in, excusing the sudden appearance of tears that slipped from behind her oversized gold-framed glasses. "Dolores and Maynard in the same week." A sob caught at the back of her throat. "They say the good Lord doesn't give us any more than we can bear, but when things like this happen, they truly test one's faith."

"May I come in, Mrs. Giles? I have a few questions to ask you."

She pursed her lips, revealing a web of fine lines around her mouth. "Yes, of course." She nervously fingered the cross at her neck and opened the door wider to admit me. I trailed her slowly retreating form and the scent of mothballs across an enormous wood-paneled foyer and turned left down four slightly worn carpeted steps to the living room. Two Louis XIV sofas with matching chairs and chaise longues were carefully arranged in the room, all covered in what appeared to be a seafoam-green brocade pattern underneath a layer of protective plastic slipcovers straight out of my childhood.

We were soon joined by another woman, whose refined appearance placed her squarely in the rarefied social stratum my mother so cherished and my late husband, Keith, disdainfully called "the L.A. niggerati." This one was tall and slender in a way that suggested a lifetime of careful eating and regular visits to one of those chi-chi resorts favored by my mother and her Saks-shopping girlfriends. Her otherwise pale skin had that honeyed, spa-induced glow and her eyes were deeply set atop high cheekbones that had yet to see a plastic surgeon's knife. And even though I knew from the murder book Neidisch had started that she was seventy-two, this woman could probably still walk outside the grounds of

Fremont Place and down Wilshire Boulevard and stop traffic in either direction. A living example of Grandmama Cile's adage "Black don't crack."

She, too, was somberly but exquisitely dressed, her vintage suit—designer-made, I guessed from the detailing—and graying French roll echoing the older woman's. "This is Ivy Duncan." Mrs. Giles's eyes blinked back tears behind her outdated glasses. "My dearest friend, business partner . . . and my brother Maynard's wife. This is Detective . . ." She consulted my card. "Justice, Ivy, from the police department. She has some more questions for us."

Mrs. Duncan approached me briskly, bringing with her the sweet scent of one of those fifties perfumes my mother used to wear, My Sin or something. She offered a slightly mottled, bejeweled hand and gave me and my briefcase a cool, appraising smile. "What happened to Detective Neidisch and Detective O'Donoughue?"

"The case has been turned over to RHD, Robbery-Homicide Division. We're a unit at headquarters that investigates special cases."

Ivy Duncan frowned. "I see." She turned to her sister-in-law. "They won't budge." To me she explained, "We wanted to have the memorial services on Wednesday, but our attorney informs me the coroner's office won't release my husband's body until they do the autopsy. Did you and your RHD have something to do with that?"

"No, ma'am. The holdup is because of your motion to quash . . ."

Ivy Duncan's mouth compressed into a thin line, and she shook her head in warning, hand slightly raised as she watched her sister-in-law wander over to the piano by the picture window.

"We're having my brother laid to rest at the same memorial park where Hattie McDaniel is buried, you know." Mrs. Giles ran a gnarled finger lovingly around a silver-framed picture of the smiling actress, dressed not in her familiar *Gone with the Wind* mammy's outfit or black taffeta maid's drag, but in a beautifully tailored suit. The photo was inscribed "To Maynard, with admiration and respect," and was nestled among more than a score of photos of early black Hollywood stars, some alone, others in animated poses on movie sets or stages or in nightclubs. Maynard Duncan and his sister were in many of them, showing up in the right places and being seen with the right people, everyone from Eddie "Rochester" Anderson to Lena Horne and Billy Strayhorn. One picture in particular caught my eye, of a group riding in a convertible in front of Central Avenue's Club Alabam. It featured the towering, darkly handsome Duncan, Ivy, his sister Delphine, and another man whom I'd seen dancing in *Murder in Mudtown.*

"Remember Hattie's funeral, Ivy?" Mrs. Giles blurted out suddenly.

Duncan's widow nodded, her eyes never leaving mine. "It was one of the biggest turnouts for a Negro actor this town has ever seen."

"*The* biggest for its time." Mrs. Giles returned to one of the sofas, gestured vaguely for me to be seated on the one opposite. "Over a thousand cars in the procession to the cemetery," she said wistfully, eyes locked behind her oversized glasses on some distant point in the past. "Maynard was one of the honorary pallbearers. And remember the repast at her mansion over by First A.M.E? It seems like yesterday, but it has to have been forty years ago!"

Ivy Duncan positioned herself next to her sister-in-law on the plastic-covered sofa. She reached up to smooth a loose strand of the older woman's hair back into place. She then took her hand, rubbed it vigorously, and shifted to face me. "I'm afraid there's really not much we can add to what we told the other detectives. Perhaps I should put you in touch with our attorney. He's handling this matter."

"I want to hear what Detective Justice has to say," Mrs. Giles broke in, motioning me to remain seated.

"First of all, please let me express my sorrow at your loss. Mr. Duncan was a fine filmmaker." Duncan's widow accepted my condolences warily, but his sister looked forlorn as a seashell washed to shore. Mrs. Duncan rubbed Mrs. Giles's hand a little harder, lending courage. "But the circumstances of his death necessitate—"

"The *Times* obituary wasn't even ten lines, you know," Mrs.

Giles interrupted petulantly. "Over fifty years in show business and just ten lines!" Her voice grew shrill, her eyes wild. "And here they'll give these godless white directors accolades right and left for half the work my brother accomplished!"

While I understood how she might feel, I was struck by how unchristian Delphine Giles's rambling had become. And now the older woman had started to weep, causing her sister-in-law to pull a tailored linen handkerchief out of her pocket and wrap an arm around her. "That's just not true, dear," Mrs. Duncan soothed. "Maynard's contributions to the film industry will not be forgotten. The Black Filmmaker Foundation called just this morning about mounting a retrospective of his work next fall."

Ivy Duncan's words did little to comfort the overly distraught Mrs. Giles. The faint shrill of a teakettle echoed from somewhere deep in the house. "Del, dear, do you want me to make you a cup of tea?" Mrs. Duncan gently asked the crying woman.

I could see it was going to be some time before Delphine Giles would be composed enough to talk to me. I picked up my briefcase. "Before you do that, perhaps you could show me where you found your husband."

I watched her body stiffen. "Certainly, Detective."

I followed Ivy Duncan as she made a detour to the kitchen to turn off the kettle, then led me up a wide mahogany staircase. The glossy wood of the risers soared up to the landing and was echoed in the hand-carved banister, which formed a dark border up the stairs and all the way around the open hallway of the second floor. I grasped the smoothly polished wood under my hand and leaned over to gaze at the marble checkerboard floor of the foyer below.

The southeast bedroom, closest to the stairs, overlooked the backyard, where I could see a four-car garage with an apartment above, and a barren rose garden and a dilapidated greenhouse beyond. The room itself held a massive king-size bed with a carved headboard, eyelet-trimmed white linens, and several carefully placed orchids on the night tables. In the northeast corner was another master suite, dominated by another large bed, this one covered in an old-fashioned burgundy-and-black-striped satin spread.

A closed and LAPD-sealed door separated this bedroom from another room in the northwest corner of the house. The small LAPD seal positioned across its doorjamb told me it was where Maynard Duncan's body had been discovered, the door next to it probably to the bathroom where the drugs were found.

"We set my husband up in this front room when he came back from the nursing home," his wife explained. "I don't know why the other detectives felt they had to seal it up. We weren't going to bother it."

"That's to protect the integrity of the scene. Who found Mr. Duncan's body?"

"I did," she admitted in a hushed voice. "I came up here at six, to see if Maynard felt up to eating some dinner. He hadn't eaten all day, and he'd lost so much weight in the past few months, his doctor recommended we try and get him to eat whenever we could. Anyway, when I came up, he was so . . . I don't know, peaceful, I assumed he was sleeping. I remember thinking what a blessing it was he was finally getting some rest. It was when I went to touch him that I knew."

I saw the quiet sadness in her eyes and thought so far her statement was consistent with that she gave to Neidisch. "What did you do next?"

"I went to tell Delphine what had happened."

"Where was she?"

"In the greenhouse, repotting some orchids. I didn't want her walking in on Maynard and being frightened to death. Then I called the paramedics."

I examined the LAPD seal, verified its integrity, and opened the door. Ivy Duncan hung back a little, her hand covering her nose and mouth as I entered the room, and I immediately understood why. Although the ceiling fan was turning and the hospital bed had been stripped by the crew from the department's Scientific Investigation Division, Maynard Duncan's sickroom still harbored the smell of death, that unmistakable combination of urine and fear. The bedside tables looked as if they had been denuded of human presence, too, except for the telltale black residue on the wood surfaces and portable phone that indicated Wozniak and the lab rats from SID's Latent Prints section had been there.

"Oh, dear!" Mrs. Duncan exclaimed, peering in. "What a mess." She then launched into a stream of nervous prattling about how the fingerprint powder had ruined all of their housekeeper's work.

"Excuse me, Mrs. Duncan," I interrupted, feeling a headache coming on, "but can you wait for me outside? I'm going to need a few minutes up here alone."

She inhaled quickly, as if she'd been slapped. "Of course, Detective," she stammered, smoothing back her hair. "I'll just be downstairs."

CHAPTER 5

AN UGLY
WAY TO DIE

Once she was gone, I got out my notebook and tape measure to make my own detailed sketch of the crime scene. It annoyed me that I had missed seeing Duncan's body as it had lain here, that I had to rely on the sketch Neidisch's partner had thrown together and the photos from the crime scene team. As morbid as that might seem to others, being there from the beginning—seeing the body with one's own eyes, letting it tell its sad secrets—was an essential step for me in the successful resolution of a crime.

The room, which measured sixteen feet long by fourteen wide, appeared to be less of a bedroom than an office converted to a makeshift sickroom. On the right wall, beyond the columns of bookcases, was a sealed door, which I opened to reveal a pink-and-black-tiled bathroom, whose outer door I'd passed earlier. The bathroom was covered in colored dust from Wozniak's work, including the toilet, the medicine cabinet, and the underside of the sink. After drawing a diagram of the room, I turned and measured twelve feet from the medicine cabinet to the narrow hospital bed, which was parallel to a large bank of windows overlooking the street. On the side of the bed closest to the bathroom was a night table that held a portable phone and a multicolored orchid that gave off a sickly-sweet smell. On the floor below was a hap-hazard pile of newspapers, including last week's issues of *Variety* and *The Hollywood Reporter*.

Fifteen feet of bookcases on that side of the room held a grouping of unfamiliar statuettes and awards on the top shelf. Below them, a dozen well-thumbed books on herbal medicines, natural healing, and creative visualization shared space with black film books and assorted entertainment biographies. The remaining shelves contained row after row of alphabetized videotapes, including films by Julie Dash and Marlon Riggs, Oscar Micheaux and Gordon Parks, as well as the Tarzan movies I'd seen pictured in my uncle's album over the holiday and Duncan's own work, including *Murder in Mudtown*. I jotted down a few of the unfamiliar titles, possible suggestions for Justice Family Film Night.

In front of the bed loomed one of those three-foot-wide televisions atop a metal table, which also held some computer diskettes, a lot of technical-looking video equipment, and a dozen or more unlabeled tapes. Among the clutter was a five-by-seven note pad imprinted with a logo of Maynard Duncan's name on a director's chair. I lightly shaded a pencil over the pad, brought up some unintelligible writing and Maynard Duncan's signature—the last things written there. I slipped the pad into a plastic evidence bag and marked it to take back to the office.

I searched the drawers of the desk facing the window, came up with nothing remarkable. On top of the desk was a document called *Stormy Weather*, composed of blue, yellow, goldenrod, and green three-hole pages and held together with brass brads. A few yellow pages had fallen to the floor, where they lay amid little bits of pink confettilike paper. Also on the desk were a computer, some carefully labeled diskettes, and a stack of FedEx mailing materials.

I picked up the pages, which seemed to be about the death of Dorothy Dandridge, and tried to see where they fit within the rest of the script lying on the desk. There were still ten pages missing. I riffled through the diskettes, but none of them seemed to have the script file on them, either. Something made me package up the whole thing for examination back at the office.

I resealed the bedroom door and returned to the living room to find that Ivy Duncan had rejoined her sister-in-law on the sofa. She rose when I entered, an apprehensive look marring her otherwise striking face. "Is everything all right, Detective?"

"Why don't I give you a hand with the tea, Mrs. Duncan?"

Her eyes searched my face, uncomprehending for a moment. "Oh, I almost forgot!" she exclaimed, hand to forehead. She led me up a few steps and through the dining room—dominated by a huge table covered with a slew of silver coffee urns and chafing dishes—and into the kitchen. She saw me checking out the silver serving equipment, the industrial-grade range, and the stainless-steel refrigerator in the kitchen. "That stuff's for our catering business," she explained as she prepared a bitter-smelling tea. "Soulful Celebrations. Perhaps you've heard of us."

"How long were you and Mr. Duncan married?"

"Fifty years this past September. We met in 'forty-one, when he came into this after-hours club where I was singing in an amateur night contest." Her face softened and her lips twitched into a sad smile. "I'll never forget it. He was wearing a white cashmere overcoat and a black fedora." She allowed herself another smile, but this one stuck around. "He was so good-looking, genteel almost, but detached at the same time. I knew right then and there I was going to marry him, but it took a year of home cooking and his sister working behind the scenes before he saw the light."

Ivy Duncan blinked back to the present and shook herself. "But you didn't come in the kitchen just to hear an old woman reminiscing. There's a problem, isn't there, Detective?"

"Yes, ma'am, there is. In order for the medical examiner to conduct an autopsy, they need to compare their findings with your husband's medical record."

"I told our attorney I don't want Maynard cut on!" she exclaimed "He's suffered enough indignities over the past year and a half without putting him through that, too."

"I hate to be the one to tell you this, ma'am," I said softly, "but if you intend to have your husband's memorial service the day after tomorrow, the coroner's office needs to get those records so they can do their work and release his body to the mortuary. Dropping that motion will help move things along."

"Why can't you people just leave us alone, let us bury Maynard in peace?" she complained, still swirling the bitter tea in the pot, still not looking at me.

"I know this is a difficult time, Mrs. Duncan, but your cooperation would allay a lot of unnecessary suspicions."

Ivy Duncan searched my face, anger lurking behind her deep-set, glittering eyes. "What's this all about, Detective Justice? First one group of detectives barges in here, turns Maynard's room and this house upside down like we're common criminals, then won't tell us anything. Now here you come talking about allaying suspicions. Why can't you let us grieve in peace?"

"Because," I replied, watching her face carefully, "the coroner's office suspects Mr. Duncan might have died from a drug overdose."

I saw it first in her eyes, which grew dull and lifeless. Then her mouth crumpled and soon every inch of her body seemed weighed down by the gravity of my words. She groped her way blindly to a stool at the breakfast bar, sat down heavily. "I don't understand," she confessed to a spot on the counter, her voice thick. "The drugs seemed to be working, and he was working like crazy to finish *Stormy Weather.*"

"What's it about?"

"It's a documentary. A five-part history of blacks in film and television, from *Birth of a Nation* to *Malcolm X.* He was almost finished with it, I think."

"Think?"

"My husband was very secretive about that film, didn't want us to see it until it was finished. Said we could jinx it if we saw it prematurely."

"Was it scheduled to be released soon?"

She shook her head. "He'd sent demo tapes to some people at BET and Turner Entertainment, but nothing came of it. So he'd started making the rounds to other studios and cable stations."

"That must have been exhausting, given—"

"You'd have to have known my husband to understand his

illness didn't matter. He had worked ten years on that film and he was going to finish it, even if he had to fight his own body to do it. That's why he was willing to experiment with different drugs. Up until he was diagnosed, Maynard was the type who never took anything stronger than an aspirin, but he was willing to do anything to get *Stormy Weather* completed."

Thinking back to the unaccounted-for ashes in the carpet, I started to ask her if "anything" included smoking marijuana, but decided to let the toxicology screens give me that answer.

Ivy Duncan picked up and cradled the sugar bowl in one hand, the fingers of the other tracing circles over its floral pattern. "But it still was an ugly way to die," she whispered, more to the sugar bowl than me. "He tried to continue working in between the chemotherapy treatments, but he got so sick we had to put him in a nursing home. And he actually rallied, started talking about wanting to get back to work. So we arranged for him to come back home in August and have a nurse come and give him his daily pain medicine as part of an in-home hospice service. They thought Maynard would last maybe a month, but he surprised us all."

"It must have been very difficult for you," I murmured, thinking of Mikki Alexander and her mother, and what my Uncle Syl went through in caring for his partner in his final days.

"It was a struggle," she admitted, getting up and putting the sugar bowl on the tray. "Although Medicare paid for his hospitalization and part of the hospice care, it didn't cover his medication or the nursing home, which were thousands every month. We were constantly dipping into our nest egg, but what with Maynard having tapped into it and other resources so many times over the years to finance his research and interviews for *Stormy Weather,* there wasn't anything left. We ended up having to take out a substantial private loan on our house just to keep things going."

I was struck by the way Duncan's widow interpreted the word "difficult" from a financial, not an emotional, perspective. I reexamined the kitchen more closely and noticed this time that the appliances, while highly polished, were probably a good fifteen years old. I replayed other details of the house in my mind—the shabby appearance of the exterior, the plastic-sheathed furniture, and the women's vintage clothes. While a far sight better off than most people, the Duncans were probably hanging on to the good life by the skin of their teeth—if not living exactly from hand to mouth, then certainly at the very edge of what were apparently not limitless resources. I wondered how the sacrifices affected Mrs. Duncan's outlook on life.

"Del even threw in her little bit of savings from her work in films," Mrs. Duncan was saying, and added under her breath, "Not that she ever made any real money at it."

There was an awkward second or two before she hurried to add, "I'm not saying that to be cruel. We all acted, but my sister-in-law was primarily a dancer. You're probably too young to remember Mo and Del."

The picture of Delphine and the other man on the piano suddenly made sense. "Actually my family just watched them dance in *Murder in Mudtown*. Your sister-in-law seems to be taking the news of her brother's death pretty hard."

Mrs. Duncan sighed and nodded. "Her doctor's had her on tranquilizers since last week to keep her somewhat stabilized." Her eyes grew soft. "You see, Delphine and Maynard were inseparable. She adored her little brother, protected him like a mother lion protects her cubs. And he was equally devoted to her, especially when her career was on the skids."

"How so?"

She rummaged around through several cupboards until she found a Tupperware container, which she opened to reveal little lemon-scented cookies. "By the mid-forties, the studios's infatuation with those all-Negro musical and dance films was just about over, so there weren't a lot of calls for specialty acts like Mo and Del's. Of course, they still performed at Club Alabam and theaters like the Lincoln and the Orpheum and such, but the money wasn't nearly as good as working in films. Mo ended up opening a little dance studio on his own, and although Del helped out, her heart wasn't in it.

"I fared a little better, having a bit of a reputation from working in the soundies—the equivalent to what the young people call music videos nowadays—but since Lena, Nat, and a few other Negroes already had the singing game sewed up as far as the television shows and the white-owned nightclubs like the Cocoanut Grove and Ciro's were concerned, there wasn't as much work for me, either."

She arranged the cookies in a sunburst pattern on a gold-rimmed plate. "Maynard was the only one of us who successfully made the transition, began to catch some breaks directing small films and television. First ten years of our marriage, he was in New York and on location more than he was home. But it was his idea for Del and me to start Soulful Celebrations, keep us occupied and capitalize on our contacts in show business. 'They can move all the Negro acts up to Hollywood they want to, but they aren't about to start frying chicken in Ciro's,' he'd say. 'What're the white folks gonna do when they get a hankering for some down-home cooking?'

"He was right, of course. We catered for everybody—from birthday parties at Louis B. Mayer's to pool parties at George Cukor's. We did press parties at Universal and the wrap party for *Carmen Jones* at RKO. Old Jack Warner might have told Chester Himes he didn't want any niggers writing films for his studio, but he sure didn't mind us cooking in his kitchen! And when they got bored with Southern-fried chicken and collard greens, we switched to canapés and caviar. Made enough money to put a big down payment on this house. Del and I proved black women can succeed in a white man's world."

Her voice held that odd mixture of harshness and triumph that I'd heard in my uncle on Thanksgiving day, a peculiar sound I'd heard more than once from blacks who'd outsmarted whites at their own game. As I laughed with her, I glanced at my watch. We'd been talking for almost fifteen minutes, enough time for me to gain some insight into the family's dynamics and her to get comfortable with me as the new lead detective on the case. "I feel that same pressure to succeed in my job, Mrs. Duncan," I confided. "So it would really help me with my bosses if you would talk to your attorney. Withdrawing that motion will save everyone a lot of aggravation, and allow you to bury your husband with the respect he deserves."

She gave me a laser-eyed warning. "Just don't mention any of this to Del. I don't want to upset her any more than she already is."

"I *will* need to speak with Mrs. Giles privately."

She looked skeptical. "Her mind tends to wander a bit on those tranquilizers."

"I promise I'll make it brief. One more thing, though." I slipped my note pad and pen out of my other pocket. "Who referred you to HealthMates?"

"I don't remember exactly, but it was someone on the staff at the nursing home."

I found that interesting, given that the scandal over Angelo Clemenza was well known by that time. "What about Mr. Duncan's nurse, Alice Thomas? Did she ever make any unusual comments about your husband's condition? Or seem particularly upset at his suffering?"

"Not that I recall," she replied rather stiffly. "But Alice generally was very shy around Del and me; it was Maynard who seemed to draw her out. She always took a few minutes out of her visit to chat with him, watch a bit of one of his old films or the *Stormy Weather* project. I think she saw more of it than Del or I did." She half-turned from me, gestured awkwardly toward the tray. "Would you mind carrying that for me, my dear, while I turn up the thermostat? It's gotten very chilly in here."

I hoisted the tray, noting the change in her demeanor, and followed her out of the kitchen. "What time did Ms. Thomas arrive last Tuesday, Mrs. Duncan?"

"One o'clock, her usual time. She gave Maynard his pain medication, they visited for a while, then she came downstairs about one-thirty to tell us she was going on vacation and who'd be her replacement from the agency. Which was strange, when I think of it in retrospect."

"Why 'strange'?"

"Alice's vacation came as a total surprise to Del and me. She swore she'd mentioned it to Maynard, but he must have forgotten to tell me."

"**D**id Ms. Thomas say where she was going on vacation?" I asked the women as I set down the tea service on the coffee table and sat on the sofa opposite Mrs. Giles.

"She sent Maynard a postcard," Mrs. Giles replied vaguely. "I don't know where I put it, though. Maybe in my address book."

Duncan's widow excused herself, returned with a battered leather binder, and began to look through its bulging pages. It took her a moment to find it, but it was well worth the wait. On the reverse side of a photo postcard of Maui's Road to Hana, Alice Thomas had written that she was staying at the Hyatt Hotel.

"We started to call and tell her about Maynard, but we didn't want to ruin her vacation," Delphine Giles explained hesitantly, a slight quaver in her voice.

"You did the right thing, Mrs. Giles." I pocketed the postcard. "When is Ms. Thomas due back?"

"Thursday. I assume her office will tell her about my husband when she gets back. I'd hate to have her come all the way over here for nothing."

"Who else besides Ms. Thomas was in the house the day Mr. Duncan died?"

The women looked at each other, then seemed to silently agree that Duncan's widow would be the one to take the lead. "We were here most of the day with Otto Randall, our catering manager, experimenting with appetizers for a large dinner party we were working in Bel-Air on Thanksgiving Day."

Randall had arrived at nine that morning, Mrs. Duncan recalled, and worked with the two women until two-thirty. "Would he have gone upstairs to visit with your husband?" I asked.

Mrs. Duncan nodded. "Although Maynard was in a lot of pain, he insisted on seeing people, no matter how bad he was feeling. He was very fond of Otto, so I'm sure he did. I just couldn't say exactly when."

"I think he peeked in on him around eleven-thirty," Delphine offered meekly.

We both looked at her. "How can you be so sure of the time?" I asked.

Confusion reigned on the old woman's face for a moment before she replied with a little more assurance, "It was shortly before Pastor Henley came, remember, Ivy? You were rushing to finish the potstickers for them to sample. Otto was upstairs with Maynard while we were frying the first batch."

"That's right," Mrs. Duncan remembered, explaining to me: "I wanted them to be as fresh as possible for Pastor."

"Was Mr. Duncan a smoker?"

Their faces registered surprise. "Not after he was diagnosed with cancer," Mrs. Duncan replied.

"Then why was a lighter found in his room—inscribed 'To My Pilgrim Soul'?"

Mrs. Giles coughed while Duncan's widow explained, "Maynard thought he'd lost that some time ago."

"No chance he was sharing a smoke with Mr. Randall?"

"Otto doesn't smoke," Mrs. Duncan replied with a frown at Mrs. Giles.

I made a note to follow up on that question with Mrs. Giles when we were alone. "Who else visited your husband that day?"

In addition to Randall, Mrs. Duncan confirmed Pastor Henley and one other visitor that day—Victor "Skip" Sheffield, Jr., CEO of Urban Contemporary Network, a black-owned cable network and film studio headquartered in Burbank.

"Was Mr. Sheffield interested in *Stormy Weather* for UCN?"

Ivy Duncan snorted, her mouth pulled down in distaste. "That cheap-ass Negro? Hardly!"

"Now, sister, let's not be crabs in a barrel," Mrs. Giles whispered urgently, glancing at me out of the side of her eyeglasses. "I don't think Detective Justice needs to hear your low opinion of Mr. Sheffield—"

"No, please." I bit back a smile while Mrs. Duncan gave her sister-in-law an exasperated look. "Go ahead."

"I know the papers reported he just got some big-time venture capitalists interested in helping him take the company public, but I tell you the man is slime!" Mrs. Duncan insisted. "My husband and Mr. Sheffield served on the Still We Rise board down at Peaceful Shepherd together. Maynard wasn't very impressed with some of Mr. Sheffield's ideas for economic development, so I know what I'm talking about!"

"And don't forget about Dolores," Mrs. Giles interrupted nervously. "Dolores Amargosa's our housekeeper," she explained. She helpfully spelled the last name. "She came for part of the day to help us with the prep and cleanup in the kitchen before Otto took her up to Hollywood to catch a bus for the airport at two-thirty."

"Didn't you say something earlier about having lost her?"

"I'm sorry, Detective, I've been so beside myself lately," Mrs. Giles replied, embarrassment showing on her weathered face. "We *have* lost her, but not in the way it sounded. Dolores called to say her baby took sick while they were down in Puerto Rico for Thanksgiving. She's been stuck down there ever since."

"My sister-in-law doesn't want to believe this," Mrs. Duncan began, bristling on the sofa, "but I think that ditzy heifer is just trying to get out of doing an honest day's work."

"Now, sister!" Delphine Giles scolded, saying to me, "God knows how we'll get along without her."

"Hmph! Semiskilled labor comes a dime a dozen," Duncan's widow muttered under her breath. "Pick it up on any street corner."

"Shame on you!" Mrs. Giles chastised her sister-in-law. "You know we did not pick up Dolores on a corner. Maynard said she was the best."

"You have her address or phone number in Puerto Rico?" I broke in.

Mrs. Giles shook her head. "They live in a very remote area near some jungle. Her husband's family doesn't even have a phone—Dolores had to call us from a pay phone with a terrible connection."

"Any other visitors?"

Ivy Duncan said, "There was that young FedEx woman, and our driver who dropped off some supplies, but they didn't come upstairs."

"Who was the FedEx package for?"

"My husband. Dolores took it up to him."

"What's this all about, Detective?" Mrs. Giles wanted to know, her voice quavering again. "Why do you need to talk to all of these people?"

"Perhaps we could speak privately for a moment, ma'am." I glanced at Mrs. Duncan, hoping she'd catch the hint and excuse herself.

Instead the other woman blurted out, "The police seem to feel there's something fishy about Maynard's death, Del. He may have died from a drug overdose."

Mrs. Giles's head jerked around from her sister-in-law to me. "Is that true?" she demanded, her eyes obscured by the reflection off her glasses from the lights in the living room.

"It could be any number of things, Mrs. Giles," I explained, trying to cover my annoyance at Ivy Duncan for ruining my opportunity to tell Mrs. Giles in private and gauge her reaction. "It's a little early to say just yet. If you'd excuse us for a moment, Mrs. Duncan, I'd like to speak with Mrs. Giles privately—"

"What are you saying?" Delphine Giles's voice took on a strident quality as she reached out for Ivy Duncan's steadying arm. "That my brother either committed suicide or was *murdered?*" She teared up again as she looked at her sister-in-law. "Dear God in heaven, give me strength!" She looked over at me, fear in her eyes and her voice breaking hard. "If . . . if there was something amiss about the way Maynard died, Detective, please, I need to know!"

I watched the older woman's shoulders tremble with emotion, and her sister-in-law moved closer to comfort her. After ten minutes of her becoming progressively more agitated, Ivy Duncan had to give her another tranquilizer and take her upstairs. As she led her sister-in-law up the polished staircase, I remembered Mrs. Duncan's comment about their years in show business. *We all acted,* she'd said. As I let myself out, I wondered if either—or both—of them were acting now.

CHAPTER 6

No Black
Jack
Kevorkians

Going over my list of potential suspects, I called Skip Sheffield's office, but he was out of town; Otto Randall was nowhere to be found. Scanning the rest of the names, I started my car and headed south, deciding maybe it was time I got some religion. Or at least an edu-mo-cation in black church politics.

Although he had to compete with the more venerable and visible of L.A.'s black churches, Peaceful Shepherd Missionary Baptist's minister, Pastor Clayton Henley, was doing everything in his power to step out of the giants' shadows and make a name for his Crenshaw District church and for himself as a mover and shaker in post-Uprising Los Angeles. His latest coup was an extensive article in the current issue of *Los Angeles Magazine,* prominently hanging on a wall and displayed on a coffee table in his office, where I was deposited by an assistant to await an audience with the Head Shepherd himself.

The article noted that the fifty-six-year-old smooth-talking Henley, a former program director for a black radio station in Baltimore before being called to the ministry, had set a score of church stalwarts' tongues to wagging when he arrived in Los Angeles in 1985. But those same critics, the magazine noted, had been forced to bite their tongues after he tripled the size of the congregation by creating a series of avant-garde outreach ministries while simultaneously expanding the church's popularity among middle-aged and older black parishioners turned off by the politics of some of the bigger establishments. He'd even managed to steal some of city-backed Rebuild L.A.'s rah-rah thunder when he led a coalition of smaller black churches in establishing Still We Rise, a post-riot rebuilding effort that was supported vociferously by a number of black community activists and entertainers who felt disenfranchised by the Olympic-sized Peter Ueberroth-led venture, and surreptitiously by several city council members, including Her Royal Divaness Earnestine Moore, in whose district Peaceful Shepherd sat.

A picture of the silk-suited pastor and Councilwoman Moore held a place of honor in the middle of the wall behind Pastor Henley's aircraft-carrier-sized desk, along with photos of everyone from movie stars to the president-elect, who had made two highly publicized visits to Peaceful Shepherd during the campaign to discuss his economic development plans. As I waited for Pastor Henley's assistant to fetch him from a meeting, I wondered whose picture would be on the wall if the Republicans had won.

Not that one party or the other could have affected Pastor Henley's appeal. With his good looks and skunk's stripe of white highlighting his otherwise ink-black hair (plus the fact that he was a widower), Pastor Henley moved easily in both grassroots and country-club circles and was particularly attractive to another key, bipartisan group—single women between the ages of twenty-five to the day before death, all looking to be the second Mrs. Pastor Henley. Or at least his mother-in-law. Not to mention the married women who could squirm—moved by the Holy Spirit and certain baser fantasies about their handsome pastor—while positioned safely in the front pews next to their husbands at one of Peaceful Shepherd's numerous Sunday-morning services.

I was just reading a message from Pastor Henley in the church newsletter about AIDS in the black community when I was interrupted by the man himself. He strode into his office wearing a conservative yet expensive navy-blue suit, custom-made shirt, silk kente cloth tie, and shoes shiny enough to see yourself in. "You're a far sight prettier than the first set of detectives I talked to," he crooned, extending a manicured hand, a smile twitching about his mustache-topped lips. "How can I be of service to the LAPD?"

Pastor Henley got serious, though, when I told him I wanted to talk about Maynard Duncan's death. "Brother Duncan's passing is a mighty blow, a tremendous loss to our congregation." His face grew pensive, and he motioned me to sit. "Maynard was a visionary, extremely generous in spite of the personal burden he was carrying—as are many members of our congregation from the entertainment community."

That last bit was a line straight out of the magazine profile, which had hinted at Pastor Henley's reputation for kissing up to members of the black entertainment community, many of whom in turn had become strong financial supporters of the church and its programs. Their favorite was reported to be the Green Pastures Nursing Home, named after the old Rex Ingram movie. The church opened it a few years ago to care for the community's elderly, with a special emphasis on the Hollywood stars and lesser lights who felt geographically and culturally isolated at the industry-subsidized Motion Picture and Television Home out in the San Fernando Valley.

"Was the entertainment community shaken by the Little Angel of Mercy murders?"

"They were at first, but, praise God, they remained foursquare behind us until that devil was arrested and the regular staff cleared."

"And I hear the Green Pastures staff, in turn, continues to be supportive of HealthMates, the agency where Mr. Clemenza worked. I understand they even referred Mrs. Duncan to them for home health care of her husband."

He nodded vigorously. "From what the nursing home staff tells me, HealthMates is a fine agency. It would have been unchristian to punish them for the actions of one deranged employee."

"You visited Mr. Duncan on the day he died."

"I visited him three days a week," he corrected. "Brother Duncan was a strong man, fought his disease every step of the way, but I sensed that last day that his spirit was getting weary."

"Weary enough to want to speed the process along?"

Pastor Henley warded me off with a neatly manicured hand. "Now, I've heard about your suspicions, Detective—"

"From whom . . . Delphine Giles or Ivy Duncan?"

Ignoring the question, he continued, "—but Maynard Duncan would not have taken his own life. The Almighty God"—he sounded as if he was talking underwater, the Lord's name coming out something like *Ga-u-u-u-u-d* in his officious mouth—"was his rock and he knew only *God* has the power to determine the length of our travels and travails on this earthly plane."

"That is, until man steps in to alter the plan." I watched the good pastor do a slow burn at my words. "What time did you arrive at the Duncan home?"

"About noon. Brother Duncan and I broke bread together in his room, talked a little business, and then we prayed."

"What kind of business?"

"Brother Duncan had been our church's treasurer before his illness forced him to turn the reins over to one of the other officers. But because he remained chairman of Still We Rise, there was concern that he was no longer able to fulfill the demands of that position, either. So I asked him to consider turning over the chairmanship to one of the other board members."

"How did he take it?"

"He was very disappointed, of course, but Brother Duncan couldn't argue with the facts—he was a very sick man." Pastor Henley's mustache gave another little twitch. "And, despite his personal feelings, he knew how important vibrant leadership would be to our plans."

"Plans?" I echoed.

"To redevelop South Central real estate destroyed in the Uprising," he replied and gestured to the *Los Angeles Magazine* article, as if to scold me for not reading it closely enough. "It's been six months, Rebuild L.A.'s board has only had two meetings, and we're still looking at burned-out lots in most of our community. Maynard and I firmly believed those vacant lots on Florence and Normandie, just a few miles south of here, and other flashpoints from the Uprising could be developed into animation studios, special-effects houses, soundstages, and more." His delivery had taken on the tone and cadence of a sermon, his hands virtually creating in the air the buildings he was describing. "With the right backing, we can create jobs right here in our community. Jobs that can transform our young people from gangbangers to taxpayers, from gun toters to new voters. Excuse me." He snatched up a pad at his elbow and began to scribble furiously. "I think I'll use that in my next sermon," he noted.

"That sounds like a pretty ambitious objective."

Henley paused to grace me with a blissful smile. "I prefer to call it divinely inspired, Detective. We've been blessed to have some mighty powerful angels in our corner."

"And Mr. Duncan didn't have any problems stepping aside?"

"His ego was a little bruised, but Brother Duncan knew how important it was to bring jobs into our community, and with aerospace practically nonexistent these days, entertainment is the number one industry in Los Angeles. An industry that has conspired, with a few notable exceptions, to keep our people on the outside looking in. So Brother Duncan was willing to do whatever it took to move Hollywood off their butts to do their fair share, even if it meant giving up something he dearly loved. In that respect, Brother Duncan was truly a generous, selfless man."

"How long did the two of you talk that day?"

According to Pastor Henley, he had left the house a little after one, right after Duncan's home health nurse arrived. "And not a moment too soon," he added, gathering up his notes and passing them to a secretary who had magically appeared. "The Lord was Brother Duncan's strength, but his earthly vessel was so racked with pain, he was just hanging by a thread."

While I made a note, Pastor Henley went on to say there was only one other interruption during his visit with Maynard Duncan. "Around twelve-thirty, her usual time, Sister Ivy brought up a few appetizers for us to sample from a party they were preparing for downstairs," he remembered. "That day it was sweet potato potstickers." He licked his lips at the memory.

"I understand Mr. Duncan had been having trouble with his appetite. Did he eat that day?"

"Not much, as I recall." He smiled lamely and added, "I'm afraid I ate most of them."

I ducked my head to suppress a smile; like every other clergyman I'd ever known, Pastor Clayton Henley was loath to miss a free meal, as his ample paunch could attest. "How did his family cope with his illness?" I asked.

"Sister Ivy and Sister Del are strong in the Lord, Detective," he replied a little too quickly. "They were angels, there for Brother Duncan every step of the way, especially Sister Ivy. Every step of the way," he repeated more to himself than me.

"Could they have helped him 'step' to the other side?"

Pastor Henley gathered himself up to his full height behind his desk and gave me a stern, thou-shalt-not look. "I don't know what kind of Christless horrors you see in your line of work, Detective Justice, but in my experience *our* elders are generally not prone to suicide, assisted or otherwise. There are no black Jack Kevorkians seducing our people to end it all." Pastor Henley spread his hands wide and intoned, "The Scripture says, 'The Lord giveth, and the *Lord* taketh away.'" He brought his hands together suddenly, clapping the very thought of anything else into oblivion. "Besides," he confided, leaning toward me conspiratorially, "you know as well as I do that as hard as most of our people fight to survive in this world from day to day, we're generally clinging to the very last thread of life."

While I was inclined to agree, I was neither willing to admit it nor dismiss the possibility that someone, angelic or otherwise, had had a hand in ending Maynard Duncan's suffering.

I called Cassie Reynolds from my car and informed her I expected the motion to quash to be dropped and Duncan's medical records to be made available Tuesday. "When do you think you can get to the autopsy?"

"Assuming we actually get the records tomorrow like you say, maybe Thursday. We're not too backed up right now, but you know how quickly that can change."

"Then let's pray for the health and safety of the city's residents."

It took me half an hour to get back to the PAB from Peaceful Shepherd through traffic that had slowed to a crawl, as it will in L.A. for no particular reason. I checked in the evidence I'd picked up at the coroner's shop and Ivy Duncan's, and went up to my office on three to listen to my messages. The manufacturer's rep hadn't called back yet about the pump, so I left another message and turned my attention to catching up on my paperwork.

After spending almost two hours refining the new crime scene diagram and summarizing the day's interviews, I spent another hour catching up on the paperwork on the home invasion cases, and another half hour beyond that nursing my struggle buggy through the mist-dampened streets before I pulled into the driveway of my house in L.A.'s Fairfax District. I was met at the chain-link fence by Beast, my fawn-and-white Boxer, who started wiggling his stump and barking out a welcome as if we hadn't seen each other in a week instead of just since this morning. Beast and I had been a team for two and a half years, ever since I'd found him at the scene of a double homicide of a mother and daughter. The T-shirt worn by the dead girl had his and her photo Xeroxed on the front and "Beauty and the Beast" printed underneath. And although he had personality plus, there was no chance that the broad-muzzled canine with a serious underbite was ever called Beauty. So I had christened him Beast by default that night at the crime scene, and the name had stuck. But, as the saying goes, no matter how ugly a child is, he's always beautiful to his mother. And

over the years since I'd "adopted" him, Beast had become as handsome to me as Lassie was to Timmy, and he'd helped me out of just
as many jams.

I changed into sweats and a windbreaker and leashed up the
dog for a power walk in the neighborhood. We wiggle-walked our
way up to Wilshire Boulevard and the Los Angeles County
Museum of Art, then around the perimeter of Park La Brea, a towering collection of forties-era apartment buildings that housed a
multiculti mix of residents behind its recently erected iron gates.
Too bad they didn't realize gates keep the evil inside as well as out.

In less than an hour we were hustling our way back home,
Beast beating me to the door as the hesitant mist turned to stinging
rain. Once in the kitchen, I toweled him off, filled up his kibble dish,
and headed for the shower, passing the closed door of the bedroom
that had served as the office/nursery for my husband and daughter.

Even though it had been over twelve years since their murders, I hardly ever ventured into the office/nursery I still considered Keith and Erica's room. And even though I'd made a stab at it
in the spring, I'd never been able to finish cleaning it out, despite
offers of help from my family, friends, even my housekeeper. But
since Aubrey had stepped into my life, that door and the task
behind it loomed larger than the Great Wall of China.

Aubrey Scott had been the first man who made me even want
to think about making some changes in my life, breaking down the
protective barriers I'd erected around myself and sweeping out the
cobwebbed past. He and I had fallen into a frighteningly comfortable routine since our chance encounter during the riots. Perhaps
the stress of those days and the deaths we were both trying to assim-
ilate contributed to the speed with which we had become intimate.
While it's never been my MO, I know some folks just need somebody warm to hold on to, and any somebody's warmth would do.
But that didn't seem to be the case with Aubrey either, so try as I
might to explain it away, there was something going on between us
that transcended the darkness of those early days.

But whatever that something was had been scaring the hell
out of me. After I'd endured more than a decade of almost total

celibacy, Aubrey Scott stormed into my life like Sidney Poitier stormed into Esther Anderson's in *A Warm December*—he was caring, supportive, intelligent, and good-looking. He was even a doctor like Poitier in that old movie—which, while it meant less than nothing to me, placed him just below God and Sir Sidney in the eyes of that status-seeking missile known as Joymarie Curry Justice. But every time my mother tried to tell me how perfect Aubrey was, despite the fact that he'd been divorced, the cop voice in my head warned: *It's just the calm before the storm.*

It didn't help that the man was spoiling me rotten. That night I was going up to his house in Los Feliz, lured by the promise of a home-cooked dinner followed by a lavender-oil massage. Now God knows food I didn't have to cook was enough of an inducement, but the thought of dinner plus a massage administered by those wonderfully long, sensuous fingers of Aubrey's almost had me running my ancient Volkswagen Rabbit off the winding road to his house, and leaning on the doorbell like a sugar-starved trick-or-treater.

When Aubrey opened the door and gave me a hug, I could smell something spicy clinging to his black cashmere sweater that wasn't attributable to his cologne, while his kiss—full lips brushing sensuously against mine—was enhanced by a definite twang. "I'm making chicken enchiladas," he explained as he broke the embrace and moved into the kitchen, long muscled legs sending subtle messages beneath his soft wool pants.

It was the same outfit he'd worn on our first date. The memory of the good parts of that night gave me a hot rush somewhere below my navel, which I tried to ignore by saying, "You know, I've gained five pounds since we've been dating."

He gave my hips a calculating glance. "And it looks good on you, too," he decided aloud, his lips puckered deliciously. He poured me a glass of Chardonnay and a Corona for himself. "There's Key lime soufflé for dessert."

"Here's to you keeping current with your CPR," I said, laughing as we clinked glasses, "because I swear I'm gonna have a heart attack the way you've been feeding me."

Aubrey was the chief executive officer of a medical group that provided emergency physicians for hospitals up and down the state. And while he was more of an administrator than a practicing physician, he still knew enough medicine to be able to help out a sister in need. And tonight I needed his help in more ways than one. So while I had made it a policy since we'd been dating not to talk shop, tonight I sipped my wine and filled him in on the Duncan case, concluding by asking what he knew about HealthMates, the home health agency that cared for the victim.

"One of the partners in our firm knows them. They've had a good reputation," he said, an uncommon edge in his voice, "or did until the Little Angel of Mercy scandal sent their business into a tailspin."

I could see how Aubrey would empathize with the agency's position. The sensational murder of one of his partners last spring had put the medical group Aubrey headed in the limelight, too, effectively deep-sixing a buy-out he'd worked months to negotiate. "You hear of anything out of the ordinary going down at HealthMates before the Little Angel of Mercy case?" I asked.

He shook his head as he moved to his next task, mixing a pale green batter. "Not until those murders hit the news. You think HealthMates is somehow involved in the case you're working?"

"Too early to tell," I replied cautiously. "But I would appreciate it if you didn't repeat any of this to your colleagues. I don't want word to get back."

Aubrey looked up from the batter he was pouring into a soufflé dish, a frown on his face. "Char, I can't believe you'd say some shit like that!"

"Well, this is an ongoing investigation . . ."

"Damn your investigation, I'm talking about you and me!" He exhaled sharply, carefully put the soufflé in the oven, then snatched up some potholders and grabbed an earthenware casserole dish. *"You're* the one I'm having a relationship with, not the owners of some home health agency. Who do you think comes first with me?"

I looked away, feeling like two cents for mistrusting Aubrey even for a moment. "I'm sorry, honey," I mumbled, "but I had to say it, even though I knew the answer."

Aubrey stared at me like I'd sprouted horns, then shook his head and strode into the dining room with the casserole. "I don't want to talk about this," he muttered.

Even though I eventually cajoled him into a better mood, I could tell from the set of his mouth and the dullness in his honey-colored eyes that my remark had struck a nerve. And for the first time in over six months of lovemaking that was usually steamy enough to peel the wallpaper off the walls, put the kink back in my hair, and have me speaking in tongues, there was a tension between us in bed that night that was not of a sexual nature. After a lackluster massage and not much else, Aubrey got up, saying he had some work to do, leaving me alone in his huge bed to wonder if what I heard outside was the sound of thunder or something more ominous.

HealthMates International was located in the South Bay suburb of Hawthorne, fifteen miles southwest of L.A. One of the cities my parents had avoided when they were young because of its reputed Ku Klux Klan connections, Hawthorne had rewritten its past quicker than a Hollywood starlet, and was touted now as a city whose biggest claim to fame—other than being the home of Barbie—was being named after the author of *The Scarlet Letter.*

I'd say Rita Eddinger's face turned about that color when I showed up in the HealthMate's lobby late Tuesday morning. Underneath the anger and makeup, the agency's executive director was pale, her body soft in a way that suggested health, at home or elsewhere, was pretty low on her list of priorities.

As expected, she wasn't exactly jumping for joy when I explained why I was there. "Of course, we're very sorry to hear about Mr. Duncan's death, but we've been prohibited from releasing those records by the family's—"

"The family's motion to quash is being withdrawn, Mrs. Eddinger," I broke in. I watched her eyes disappear in the folds of her wide face and her mouth compress into an angry red slash. "You can call Mrs. Duncan if you'd like confirmation."

Which she slipped into her office to do, showing me a seat outside her door to wait. I sat in the outer office, smiling at her assistant and pretending to look at a magazine while I eavesdropped on the conversation as best I could through a closed door.

Mrs. Duncan must not have been too helpful, because I heard Eddinger hang up abruptly, speed-dial another number, and talk to someone else in hushed and fearful tones. She emerged a few minutes later, looking frightened but resolved. "Mrs. Duncan wasn't available. But I spoke to my attorney, who advises me not to release any records without seeing the paperwork."

"We *will* get those records, Mrs. Eddinger. You're just delaying the inevitable."

She shrugged, arms crossed over her bulky bosom. "It may seem that way to you, but I can't afford a lawsuit from a patient's family on top of everything else we've been dealing with."

"Well, can you at least give me the master key to the pump and the code to open it so we can get on with the investigation?"

"Well," she said slowly, uncrossing her arms, "I don't see what harm that would do." She extended one hand toward her office by way of invitation.

Walking by, I added, "And some background information on Alice Thomas?"

I caught a glimpse of her lips disappearing again, but she led me into her office anyway, which was awash in files and computer printouts. "Yuki," she called to her assistant, "go downstairs and get one of the keys to the continuous fusion pumps in the equipment room, then pull a copy of Alice Thomas's personnel file. It may still be listed under her married name."

Her last comment made something prick at the edge of my consciousness, but I couldn't quite bring it into focus. Eddinger cleaned a stack of files off one of the guest chairs and motioned me to sit. She lit a cigarette without asking me if I minded the smoke. "What do you want to know?"

"How long has Alice Thomas worked for you?"

She exhaled smoke in my direction. "Seven years."

"What kind of employee is she?"

"A little fragile as a personality, but she's an excellent nurse. Very competent, very caring, very committed to her patients."

"Has she ever seemed unduly stressed about the nature of her work?"

"You mean working with people who usually die?" she asked, a penciled eyebrow raised as she took in another lungful of poison. "There is a certain amount of burnout among our hospice workers, but not as much as you'd think. Most of our employees see their jobs as a calling. Alice is one of those people."

I wanted to say, *So was Angelo Clemenza, and look how that turned out,* but decided to look for a more natural segue. I tried, "Was she friendly with the staff?"

And got another wave of smoke. "Alice was very shy, but since so much of our staff's work is out in the field, they rarely see each other. I understand she's totally different with patients."

"Did she have much interaction with Angelo Clemenza?"

As smoothly as I tried to slip the question in, Eddinger took offense anyway. Stubbing out her cigarette, she said, "They attended staff meetings together because they occasionally backed each other up on their cases," her voice terse. "But they never seemed to be any closer than that. Don't tell me you think Alice was somehow involved in those murders Angelo committed?"

"We don't think anything yet, Mrs. Eddinger."

There was an uncomfortable silence until Eddinger's assistant returned with the key, and a manila folder that must have been Thomas's personnel file. As Eddinger angrily gave the key to me, something started nagging at me again, something Billie had mentioned over lunch.

"Like all of our continuous fusion pumps, the code to open the machine is four-four-nine-one, the address of our offices," she explained. "Press that and the 'enter' key and you'll have access to the programming feature on the pump."

As I wrote down the instructions, it suddenly came to me. "You mentioned earlier that Ms. Thomas was divorced."

The little angry slash of red reappeared. "Yes, the decree was final just recently."

"You look like you didn't think much of her ex."

She shook her head, and her lips compressed again. "He was a real loser, if you ask me. Just about drove poor Alice mad. But the real tragedy was, Alice was always making excuses for him, even when he didn't deserve it. But to quit her job . . ."

My pen stopped over the notes I was making. "When did this happen?"

"Yesterday. She left on vacation last Wednesday, then called from Hawaii yesterday afternoon to say she had decided to resign." Her eyes reluctantly met mine. "I know she was devastated by the divorce and all, but this is so out of character for Alice. She's usually so dedicated to her patients. But she's determined to resign, make what she calls a fresh start. Told me she's coming back tomorrow to start packing up her stuff, and in two weeks she's moving to Maui permanently."

I searched the notes I'd made when I had lunch with Billie, finally finding what I was after. "Is Thomas her married or her maiden name?"

"Maiden. But she started using it a couple of years before her divorce was final."

About the time Clemenza was most actively killing those patients. "And her married name was . . ."

She frowned and consulted Thomas's personnel file. "Carver. Why do you ask?"

Billie had said Clemenza's diary entries and letters about "the Twin" had been written off by the South Bureau detectives and the D.A.'s office as delusional ranting when his case was brought to trial a year ago. Now I was looking at the first possible link between Angelo Clemenza and the twin of whom he wrote—a coworker named Alice Carver who shared his initials and some of his patients.

Did she, I wondered, also share his penchant for dispensing narcotics overdoses?

CHAPTER 7

YOU'VE
REALLY GOT
A HOLD ON
ME

I hurried downtown to the PAB, calling ahead to Herman Wozniak in Latent Prints, who Neidisch said had been assigned to the case. "Hey, Woz, what's up?"

"Same old, same old," the fingerprint technician replied cautiously. "What can I do for you, Justice?"

I replied, "We're taking over from Wilshire Division on the Duncan case," and gave him the background. "I've got something from the scene I want you to sprinkle some of that juju dust on."

"We dusted everything in sight," he said a little defensively. "Even the bathroom and parts of the kitchen. We miss something?"

"Not really. I just got the key to the morphine pump you dusted at the scene, so now we can open it up and give you a shot at the keypad."

"You're gonna hafta come to me," he demanded. "I'm swamped."

When I got to the office, I went directly to the Property Room and checked out the pump, and took it to Woz's office on the second floor.

And was surprised to see he'd lost a small child, at least thirty pounds, since I'd worked with him during the riots. And while he was still wearing his old clothes with the belts cinched, he had a new haircut, and was wearing something other than the black-framed glasses that looked like they'd come from Nerdcrafters. Seeing my reaction, he explained, "Weight Watchers," and showed me a treasure trove of low-fat, low-cal cheese curls in the top drawer of his desk.

"After my mother's Thanksgiving dinner last week, I may have to join you." I followed him to a workstation in the back, set the pump on the desk, and extracted some gloves from a box nearby.

I used the key I'd gotten from Mrs. Eddinger to open the machine while Wozniak donned a pair of goggles and handed me a pair. He went into a cabinet for a portable laser and killed the lights. "The laser is much less likely to damage the pump's inner workings than the powders we used on the outside," he explained.

I gave Wozniak the access code and watched him as he passed the apparatus slowly over the keypad of the machine. And was rewarded with a clear print on the enter key. He left the room and returned with a camera to make a photograph of the print. "I'll run this with the others taken at the scene."

"We don't have a card on the vic's nurse yet."

"Not to worry. Nurses are fingerprinted at the time they apply for their licenses, so it oughta be in one of our databases."

"There's a set missing for the housekeeper and the caterer, too." I read off their names. "I don't have a lot of time on this one—Lieutenant Stobaugh wants a full report on Friday, and this nurse is due back from vacation tomorrow. If she's my girl, I want to alert my boss sooner rather than later. So whatever you can do to rush it . . ."

"Is there ever a time when you people aren't in a rush?" he grumbled.

"I'll bring you a month's supply of those cheese curls."

His eyes lit up. "I'm gonna hold you to that."

"No problem. Tomorrow afternoon, then?"

He cinched up his pants. "I'll see what I can do."

put the pump back into evidence and went to check for messages on my desk. Instead I found one of those white records boxes, a note taped on top.

It was from Steve Firestone. He and Detective Rudolph were out in the field, the note read, but Firestone had left me a present— the lovely box on my desk, full of more reports and field interviews from the task force's work—along with instructions to incorporate them into the corresponding murder books ASAP and to see him first thing Wednesday morning.

I dropped the box on the floor, crumpled the note into my pocket, and headed over to my lieutenant's desk to bring him up to speed on the Duncan investigation. As Stobaugh listened to my recap, his fingers formed a familiar steeple in front of his chest, his face thrown upward as if in prayer. "So I imagine you'll want to go to Maui and bring this nurse back," he said to the acoustic ceiling tiles.

I was about to cop an attitude when I noticed a smile flirting with the corners of my lieutenant's mouth, and realized he was just messing with me. "I wish, sir," I said, smiling back, "but there's no need for that—she's due back tomorrow. I don't think she suspects anything, but just in case, I'm going to call the local PD over there, see if they can shadow her discreetly, be sure she gets on that plane. In the meantime, I'm going to get busy on a search warrant. But I could use some help."

"You talk to Firestone?"

I fingered the wad of paper in my jacket pocket. "He was out."

Stobaugh nodded, came around to sit on the edge of his desk, and spoke to me in a strangely offhand voice, his eyes on his one swinging foot. "Chief Youngblood spoke at a training program today . . ."

I knew he was referring to Henry Youngblood—my father's best friend and my godfather—who was still called chief, even though he held the rank of deputy. "Where was this?"

"At the Academy," he began, head still down. "The department's undertaking a concerted effort to let sworn and civilian staff know that the LAPD will not tolerate sexual harassment."

Suddenly I felt the back of my throat close up and heard my blood coursing through my ears. For a moment I could see my lieutenant's lips moving but no sound was coming from them. "By way of example," I finally heard him say, "the chief was telling us a story about a number of female officers being harassed on the job by their superiors. 'Hit on,' he called it. The way it usually goes down, he was saying, was if the females wouldn't give in to the demands—if they refused to date, perform sex acts, or sleep with their superiors—they were given menial tasks or substandard performance reviews until they transferred out. And while he didn't call any names"—he raised his head, scanning my face for a reaction—"it got me to thinking about why you've pulled the assignment you did on the Home Invasion Task Force and some of our other investigations these last few months."

Was Kenneth Stobaugh a better detective than I thought? As much as I was tempted, I could never trust my ambitious lieutenant enough to confide in him about my troubles with Firestone, and I knew Billie wouldn't put my career at risk by snitching me out. But how else could he have known?

As I tried to hold a steady gaze on my lieutenant's face, a painful knowledge was taking hold in me, the knowledge that the most likely source of my lieutenant's information was me, the minute I slipped and mentioned something about my problems to my father. But Matt had always been the soul of discretion, one of the few people in my family I could confide in and know it wouldn't go anywhere. And besides, that conversation had happened a month ago, plenty of time for Uncle Henry to take action, unless . . .

That busybody Joymarie, I thought, my stomach lurching.

My mother probably could barely wait until I left the Nut House on Thanksgiving Day to call Uncle Henry, giving him a good piece of her narrow little mind. And while it was disastrous for me, I was sure that for my mother it was all in a day's work of trying to get me to quit a job she'd always felt was unsuitable for a member of the upwardly mobile Curry/Justice clan.

"I don't know what you're talking about, Lieutenant," I lied to my shoes. "And even if I did, I wouldn't be cowardly enough to run tattling to you like some kind of kid who's afraid of the schoolyard bully."

Stobaugh peered at me over his glasses. "It's not about being seen as a coward, Detective, it's about our personnel being able to do their jobs."

I shifted uneasily in my chair. "I understand that, sir. But I can handle myself just fine. I'm not the kind of person who needs anybody interceding on her behalf."

Stobaugh sighed in what sounded like relief. "That's what I said to Chief Youngblood. 'I maintain an open-door policy with all of my detectives. If the females in my unit haven't seen fit to come to me with any concerns, I have to assume they're not that significant'—those were my words, or something to that effect."

A convenient rationalization.

"I was correct in making that statement, wasn't I? There isn't any significant problem between you and Detective Firestone, is there?"

Whether he intended it or not, the way he phrased his question gave me an easy out. "Significant? Absolutely not, sir," I said, finally able to meet his gaze.

His eyes narrowed. "But just remember, when I see our resources on a case as important as the home invasions being inefficiently deployed, I'm going to take action, whether you think I need to 'intercede on your behalf' or not."

Lieutenant Stobaugh looked genuinely concerned, so much so that I was tempted to spill my guts right then and there. But while it might make me feel better in the short term, the long-term consequences for my career—being branded a traitor for ratting out my team leader, the resulting isolation, or worse—just wouldn't be worth it. "I appreciate your concern, sir," I assured him. "About that help on the Duncan case . . ."

He moved back behind his desk and sat down, apparently as

relieved as I was that I had signaled the end of the matter. "Cortez can work it with you when she gets back tomorrow. I'll square it with Steve."

Badly shaken but trying not to show it, I made it back over to my desk. I sat down and stared at the phone, wanting more than anything to call up my mother and ream her out. I could feel the cool plastic in my hand, hear the phone ringing, hear Joymarie's shocked gasp when I told her just what I thought of her constant carping about my job.

It took a count of thirty before the impulse passed and I called the Maui County PD. There I talked to a detective who graciously agreed to have Alice Thomas kept under surveillance on Maui and coordinate with Honolulu until she was safely on her flight back to Los Angeles on Wednesday morning. After arranging for photos of the nurse to be faxed to PDs on both islands for identification purposes, my next step was preparing a warrant to search Thomas's home, car, and work area at HealthMates.

I ignored most of what Neidisch and O'Donoughue had documented in the original murder book and gave the Duncan case a new spin, highlighting as probable cause Thomas's close working relationship with Clemenza (including my suspicion that she was the twin to whom he addressed entries in his diary), her close contact with the current victim, the results of our check of the machine, and what I believed to be her exclusive access to the death-dealing device.

After I walked the warrant over to the Criminal Courts Building for a signature, I went back to the PAB, where I dialed Billie Truesdale's digits. When I ran down my suspicions about the Alice Carver/Angelo Clemenza connection, she offered to accompany me on a visit to the senior deputy DA who had prosecuted Clemenza. By five-thirty that evening I was back in the Temple Street building, sitting with her and Mark Ikehara in a conference room on the eighteenth floor, surrounded by a dozen file boxes of evidence in the Clemenza case.

"Ike" Ikehara had been in the DA's office for fifteen years. An unusually tall, good-looking sansei—grandchild of Japanese immigrants—with an intensity he tried to mask with a shy smile and self-effacing demeanor, Ike had started out as a filing deputy, but was too sharp and too ambitious to remain at the bottom of the DA's food chain for long. And he hadn't, parlaying his faux humility, his hard work, and his political connections into second chair, then cochair of some high-profile trials and finally into first chair on the Clemenza case.

The trial had been televised on Court TV and covered in everything from *People* to *Parade*. It had also catapulted Ike to a new level of fame and a promotion to supervisor of the Serial Crimes Unit, one of the then DA's last-ditch efforts to regain some of the prosecutorial luster lost in the embarrassing string of high-profile defeats sustained on his watch. But it was too little, too late—the bad press attached to the Twilight Zone, McMartin preschool, and Rodney King cases was a politician's nightmare, and had contributed to the incumbent dropping out of a hotly contested reelection race almost two months before the votes were cast.

His successor, a longtime senior deputy in the department, had zero tolerance for prosecutorial missteps of any kind. Everyone knew that Ikehara, with his slick suits and even slicker moves, and his Serial Crimes Unit were on the death watch, the plug likely to be pulled at the first whiff of anything that smelled like the heavy-handed tactics of the previous administration.

But Ike Ikehara was hungry—hungry for another score, maybe even a run at the DA's job when the time was right. "The press haven't gotten wind of this, have they?" he wanted to know, drumming a stack of files with an expensive fountain pen while he stared out the window to his right.

I shook my head, thinking, *Don't worry, Ike, no one knows you may have screwed up.* "Not yet, but we've got a pretty big blanket over this one."

He turned to face us, the pen working overtime now. I could practically see him rehearsing his statement to the press. "If it is twinning killers," he speculated, his words keeping time with his pen, "it'll be the biggest case this office has seen since the Hillside Strangler." He tossed the pen on top of a stack of files. "I'd like to join you for the search, but I've gotta show face at a mixer for the boss at seven. Can we make it tomorrow?"

Like I'd invited him. But there was little I could do to keep him away. "Our potential suspect's out of town until late tomorrow morning. Why don't we make it a little before seven?"

"In the morning?" Out of the corner of my eye I could see Billie's lips curve inward as she swallowed a smile.

But Ike surprised us both by agreeing to the early hour, writing down the address and promising on his way out the door that he'd be there. As soon as he was safely out of the office, Billie said, "From the minute Mikki Alexander called me from the coroner's shop, I've had a bad feeling in my gut about this case." She kicked off her loafers and reached for one of the file boxes Ike had indicated would be of most interest to this new investigation. "Now you've got that glory grabber underfoot."

"Like I really want to be bothered with some senior deputy looking for another notch in his Hermès belt," I agreed. "Although I must admit, it feels good to be working with you again. It's like Teddy was saying the other day—'Truesdale, Justice, and the American Way.'"

Billie had removed the lid on a second box of files. "I don't see what's so American about a serial killer," she mumbled irritably.

"Why do you think those slasher movies make all that money? Or why they'd give what's-his-face an Oscar for *Silence of the Lambs?* And if that liver-and-fava-bean-eating freak of nature isn't enough to get people going, on the real side they can tune in to Jeffrey Dahmer or Aileen Wuornos on Court TV or *20/20,* and that's only here in the States. I'm not even going to get into the coverage the papers gave to that Russian who dismembered his victims alive! Sad to say, but following serial killers has probably surpassed baseball as the new national pastime, despite the small number of murders they actually account for."

My outburst conjured a silence over the boxes on the conference table thick as the rain clouds I could see massing outside. While Billie grimly worked her way through the files, I went to the phone and left a message on Aubrey's service, then stood for a minute looking out the window. The lights at the top of the Library Tower, glowing ruby and emerald in honor of the Christmas season, seemed to make more of an Afrocentric Kwanzaa statement in the heightened darkness. "Do you remember what Eldridge Cleaver once said about violence?"

Billie thought for a moment. "Something like 'It's as American as cherry pie?'"

I turned back to the window in time to see the rain start up again. "And where do you think those pies got baked? Right there at home, with Mom and Sis and maybe Grandma, too. Remember how Jeffrey Dahmer's family saw him hanging roadkill in the backyard when he was a kid and didn't think much of it?"

"You think Dahmer's family was a mess." I heard the schuss of a file slide across the table. "You ain't seen nothing yet."

It was a deposition taken from Angelo Clemenza's mother, and it filled in a lot of blanks that had never been explained in the news accounts of the trial. Born in New York in 1954, as a boy little Angelo alleged he had been molested by a priest in their Bronx neighborhood. A few months after the accusation, small birds and animals began showing up poisoned on the front steps of the church. No one connected the dots until quiet little Angelo was caught in the act, forcing his parents to move in the mid-sixties from their home in the Bronx to the relative peacefulness of suburban New Jersey, finally ending up in Orange County, California, in the early seventies, where Angelo settled down to become a model student and entered nursing school.

Angelo's father died in 1982 after a long battle with cancer. A few months later, the family's elderly priest succumbed to emphysema in a nursing home down in Laguna Beach. No one save Mrs. Clemenza knew Angelo had attended both men's final days or could have known that the Laguna Beach priest bore an uncanny physical resemblance to Angelo's childhood molester. But, according to her deposition, not even Mrs. Clemenza put two and two together at the time.

She was forced to do so when Billie and her partner showed up at her front door ten years later, armed with evidence and a list of victims that included a retired assistant pastor from Peaceful Shepherd and another elderly parishioner, both of whom had died at the church-operated Green Pastures Nursing Home. While the South Bureau detectives were eventually able to definitively link Clemenza to twelve other killings, his diary and trophies from his victims confiscated in the search of his home had convinced the detectives and the DA's office that he'd been responsible for many more, even if they couldn't prove it.

"This is the kind of stuff he wrote." Billie passed a spiral binder my way. The pages were filled with a compact, tiny scrawl. Billie had paper-clipped one page in particular, dedicated to "the Twin." *Beware the sanctified, sweet one!* it read. *The hands that grab, the mouths that press. Beware the white-haired men and shun what's 'neath their holy dress.* "What do you make of that?" she asked.

"Other than his obvious obsession with the clergy?"

"Yeah, we got that."

"Well, for one thing it's a piss-poor imitation of 'Jabberwocky.' "

"Jabber-what?"

" 'Jabberwocky.' It's a poem from *Alice in Wonderland* or one of those Lewis Carroll books."

"Ain't that a blipty!" Billie's palm slapped the conference table. "I *told* my lieutenant and the D-III on the case we needed to have copies of those diaries sent to one of the profilers we use, but they just blew me off. Had we known, we might have made the connection between Alice Thomas and Clemenza sooner."

Another box contained the transcripts from the trial. The defense psychiatrist's testimony was that Clemenza was a victim of multiple personality disorder, probably stemming back to his childhood trauma. The prosecution countered with their own psychiatrist, who portrayed Clemenza as an evil, cold-blooded killer who plotted the murder of each elderly victim out of a misplaced desire for revenge, fully aware of the consequences of his actions.

The jury wasn't buying the wolf ticket Clemenza's attorney was selling and found the defendant sane and guilty as hell on all twelve counts. "Evil, yes—evil twin, no," a *Times* article stuck in the file quoted one juror saying after the trial. The trial judge concurred, handing down the death penalty, and remanded him to San Quentin's Death Row.

Among the news clippings was a photo of the slightly built Clemenza, taken as he was leaving the courtroom after his conviction. His black hair and luminous eyes were enhanced by a dark fringe of lash that made him look like butter wouldn't melt in his mouth. "What do you want to bet they're negotiating the movie deal right now?" I got to my feet, checked my watch. "Speaking of which, I've gotta go."

"You're negotiating a movie deal without me?"

"No, I'm *going* to the movies."

"With Dr. Scott?" she inquired in a teasing voice.

"I'm not telling."

"You don't have to—that goofy smile you're wearing is doing it for you. You're really into him, aren't you?"

"As much as I can be, given what's been going on at the job."

"Jobs come and go, girl. Relationships are what get us through the night."

"Sounds like you're speaking from experience."

"I'm not telling." Billie mocked me with a sly smile. "You go ahead. I'll have these files copied and sent over to you tomorrow."

It took me longer than I expected to get home, power-walk with Beast, and get changed, and even longer to make my way under a pitch-black sky to meet Aubrey for our date. I was relieved to find him still in his Infiniti, his tall frame hunched over his cell phone. I got out of my car, rapped on the window, said, "Sir, would you put the phone down and step out of the car?" in my best Robocop imitation.

He threw me a crooked smile, held up a slender finger while he finished his call. I waited until he got out of the car and moved toward him, needing a hug, which seemed to be returned a little too quickly. Before I could explain why I was delayed, Aubrey was pulling me along by the hand, grumbling, "Let's get inside. We've probably already missed the previews."

"Like you're dying to see the trailer for *House Party III,*" I teased.

"That's not the point." He paid for our tickets and hustled me past the concession stand and into a seat in the back half of the nearly empty theater.

My seat squeaked as I sat down and my stomach let out a bass rumble in reply. "I'll be right back." I went to the lobby to buy some nachos and Snapple, then remembered where I was, or rather wasn't. Although the Baldwin had been around probably for more years than I had, no one had put any money into the theater for years, and it showed in everything from the lobby to the quality of the concessions. So much so that its mostly black clientele had fled to the better-appointed yet overcrowded helleplexes in Westwood, Marina del Rey, and Century City. Looking at the Baldwin's paltry selection of snacks, I understood why.

But I remained doggedly loyal nonetheless. I'd had my first real date at the Baldwin in 1968, so I had asked Aubrey to meet me there out of a sense of nostalgia. That and a desire to support the black, nonprofit developers who were trying to get funding to build a new multiscreen complex on the site. But I was sacrificing to do it—no nachos, a decade of gum coating the floor, and a date who looked like he'd rather be somewhere else. By the time I sat down, the movie had started, and I settled in to watch Whitney and Kevin throw smoldering looks at each other. And even though the music was okay, for me neither it nor the chemistry between the stars could compare to the heat generated between Abbey Lincoln and Sidney Poitier in *For Love of Ivy,* or Sidney and Elizabeth Anderson in *A Warm December.*

I said as much as we were leaving. Aubrey only grunted, which was just enough to egg me on. "And folks need to stop acting like these R&B soundtracks are something new and give some props to Berry Gordy and Motown for all that music in *Nothing but a Man.* Remember the bar scene with Ivan Dixon and Abbey Lincoln and Smokey's 'You've Really Got a Hold on Me' playing in the background?"

As I blathered on, I felt as if something had a hold on me, forcing me to hold up both ends of the conversation. But I couldn't help myself, because Aubrey was pretty much quiet, the look in his eyes saying he wasn't paying any more attention to me than the man in the moon. I grabbed the sleeve of his jacket as we were leaving the lobby. "Are you okay, honey?"

And got shrugged off: "I'm just tired, that's all."

"Long day?"

The working of his jaw muscles told me that the "Too long" response I got was about more than his workload.

Oops, there it was. Seven months almost to the day since Aubrey Scott and I started seeing each other and there it was—full-blown, I-don't-want-to-talk-about-it, tight-jawed brother-with-a-'tude. "So what did you think of the movie?"

"I'd rather see *Boomerang* again than that mess."

"It wasn't *that* bad."

Another shrug: "I guess sisters knocking boots with white boys is not my favorite thing to watch."

There seemed to be a particular barb in Aubrey's voice that caught my attention. "What's that got to do with anything?"

"Never mind," he said, a little too quickly.

Wondering if Aubrey had been talking to my mother, I said, "Look, if this is about me being late, I'm sorry, but I got caught up with some paperwork— "

And got cut off: "This isn't the first time, Char."

It was almost midnight and threatening to rain again. Did I really want to have what was turning into another unpleasant conversation about my job?

Not!

The first splat of rain, big as a silver dollar, hit me on the top of the head. I tried to keep up with Aubrey, who had lengthened his already long stride to the point where I had to trot to keep up. We reached his car first. He said, "I gotta go," his hand on the door handle. "I've got an early meeting in the morning."

"Me, too." I leaned close, rested my hand on his forearm, and whispered, "Let me make this up to you. Why don't you come over and spend the night with me? We could give each other early wake-up calls."

It had turned chilly, the rain coming down in earnest now. Aubrey shuddered and mumbled something about not being a ghostbuster.

"What the hell is that supposed to mean?" I asked.

He broke away from my touch and opened his door. "Look, I'm tired and I've got a lot of reading to do. I wouldn't be very good company."

You always see these things clearly in retrospect. Had I been able to step outside of myself, outside of my anxiety and my weariness, I would have let it go, would have cut my tongue out, gotten out a needle and thread and sewn my lips shut to keep from making matters worse.

But I couldn't, and I didn't. What I did was open my big mouth and say, "Like last night at your house?" Wrong as I could be, but I just had to say it anyway.

For his part, Aubrey acted as if he didn't hear me, but I knew he did because he gave me a thin-lipped kiss that was drier than the Mojave Desert, muttered a "See ya," and drove off with barely a wave.

CHAPTER 8

A SERIOUS TIME WARP

Needless to say, I wasn't in the best of moods when I pulled up to a side street near Alice Thomas's apartment at oh-dark-hundred hours Wednesday morning. Even though it was her first day back after vacation, Cortez was there before me, shivering under the canvas awning in front of the building, drinking from a Starbucks cup and clutching a large briefcase. I had called her at home after my abbreviated date with Aubrey to bring her up to speed on the Duncan investigation thus far and have her join Billie and me at Thomas's apartment for the search.

Wherever she'd been on vacation, Cortez hadn't gotten much sun. In fact, her otherwise richly colored Latin skin looked a little pale, what my Grandmama Cile calls "peaked." Her pallor was intensified by the dullness of her usually glossy black hair, which she'd pulled into a haphazard bun at the nape of her neck.

She saw me pull up and gave me a perfunctory nod. Cortez and I had gotten off to a rocky start when she first joined RHD as an entry-level detective trainee, but I had decided to forgive, if not forget, her ambitious naiveté and blatant brown-nosing among the males in the department. And since I'd straightened her out, we'd maintained a cordial, although distant, relationship that went no farther than the lobby of the Parker Administrative Building.

Although she and I had been de facto partners during the riots, Cortez was primarily assigned to Firestone, as part of an experimental three-person-team concept the department was testing. As such she spent most of her time trying to learn the ropes and build a reputation for herself as a solid detective. As for the rest of her reputation—fueled by whispers I'd heard in the coffee room or in the PAB's gym—I turned a deaf ear, knowing how the rumor mill can churn against a woman trying to make her mark.

I joined her under the awning with my cup of tea, and made room again when Billie arrived at seven. The three of us spent another ten minutes waiting for Ike Ikehara, who didn't show.

"Let's get on with this," Billie urged, mumbling, "There's no sense in waiting for that grandstanding son of a sea cook."

Hollywood Tower was a seven-story, indecisive gray building at the corner of Franklin and Vista del Mar in Hollywood. The faux French Normandy apartment building was so old it probably had had a view of the sea when it was built and dwarfed the burgeoning studios to the south as well. Back then it would have been surpassed in height by only a few offices on the Boulevard and the Hollywoodland sign to the north, the latter erected by developers to promote the hillside lots they were trying to unload on sunseeking suckers from back East. Somewhere along the way the LAND part of the sign disappeared, as did most of those smaller studios and vacant land, gobbled up by the Hollywood Freeway, a slew of now-deteriorating buildings along the Boulevard, and Spanish-language billboards that overran the place like weeds.

Hollywood Tower, though, was a last vestige of an earlier era. You could tell by the way the planting in the front was kept neatly trimmed and the lobby smelled Spic-and-Span clean. That probably had a lot to do with the Old World diva who managed the place. As we studied the card she handed us, I wished I could have bought a couple of vowels to add to her name. For her part, I could tell by the way Mrs. Szczesny studied the search warrant she was wishing she could be doing anything except helping "ze police."

"Zis is quality buildink," she asserted as she hastily cinched up her robe and put a scarf over thinning, pincurled hair. "Vas built in ze twenties by George Raft, ze beeg movie star, as hotel for his friends. Anybody could kem here and haf complete privacy."

As she escorted us through the lobby, she explained, "Since I been ze manager, ve naivah hed no problimz vit our tenants. Und zat Miss Alice iss doll—been here fifteen jeers, live very quiet, naivah bother livink soul." She stopped to fumble with the lock. "She don't deserve zis, after all ze trouble zat nogoodnik cause her."

"Who's that, ma'am?" I noticed with some amusement that Cortez wasn't about to try pronouncing her name either.

Vowelless pulled her lips inward and shook her head violently. She tapped at the door, waited a very short count of three before opening it and sending an exploratory "yoo-hoo" into the empty apartment. She positioned herself between us and Alice Thomas's threshold. "She's not beck yet. Can't ju wait until later?"

We assured her we could not, and eased her aside.

Thomas's apartment windows faced south. I could see the top of the record-stack-shaped Capitol Building through the half-closed venetian blinds, its spindly sundial a lightning rod in the thundering sky. What little natural light there was from the windows and the hallway, which threw the smallish living room into slatted relief, shadowed the fake mantel on the left and the poster of Bogie and Bacall in *To Have and Have Not* above it.

They weren't the only actors enshrined there. Thomas had taken the faded glory of the building's history and morphed it into a tribute to Hollywood love. In addition to the Bogie and Bacall poster was one of Clark Gable and Carole Lombard swapping spit in *No Man of Her Own,* a signed publicity still of Burt Lancaster and Deborah Kerr in that famous sand-in-their-swimsuits scene in *From Here to Eternity,* even Paul Newman and Joanne Woodward in a romantic clinch in *Paris Blues.*

Yet for all of its showiness, there was a pathetic sadness in the place. "Looks like someone's in a serious time warp up in here," Billie observed.

"Alice loves the h'old movies," Vowelless explained, and sighed.

"No shit, Sherlock," I mumbled under my breath and threw the vowel-challenged manager a courtesy smile. "You've been very helpful, ma'am, but you'll have to excuse us while we get to work."

"Don't break nothink," she warned, and would have said more if Cortez hadn't firmly closed the door in her face.

We began our initial walk-through of the apartment, getting the general lay of the land and identifying any areas we'd concentrate on later. Cortez had extracted a camera from her briefcase and was taking Polaroids of every room in the apartment from different angles, in case they were needed later on. "She's got more old movie stuff than some of the shops on Hollywood Boulevard," she exclaimed. "Wait till the guys in the office see this."

Billy pointed to the liplocked Woodward and Newman, grousing, "It was fairy tales like this that made me think I'd never fit in," and flipped a finger in their direction.

"Roger that," I added. "I spent most of my adolescence wondering why I couldn't be as thin as Diahann Carroll or as sexy as Pam Grier."

Cortez added, "How about having every man you meet confuse you with 'Mexican spitfires' like Rita Moreno and Chita Rivera and trying to cop a feel?" There was a beat of silent acknowledgment in the room before she added, "You get tired of fighting them off sometimes."

Our collective mood worsened as we donned gloves and spent the next four hours combing through every movie book and magazine, drawer and closet, cereal box and tampon box for vials of morphine or any other evidence that Thomas had more on her mind than "the h'old movies." We were almost convinced we were barking up the wrong tree when I came across a tooled leather scrapbook in Thomas's bedroom, propped up against a low wooden bench by the window. In a bookcase nearby were several well-worn volumes on death and dying, including books by Elisabeth Kübler-Ross and Jack Kevorkian.

"Now we're cooking." Cortez took some Polaroids of the area as well as a close-up of a silver-framed photo of Maynard Duncan and other elderly people, surrounded by candles, incense, and molding oranges that had been arranged in the middle of the bench.

While Cortez examined and catalogued the photos and Billie examined the scrapbook, I slipped on some gloves to leaf through Thomas's books and found passages in the Kübler-Ross and Kevorkian books marked with exclamation points and notes scribbled in the margins. I stacked them by the door to examine more closely back at the office.

"This scrapbbook's got articles and photos of every film Maynard Duncan ever acted in or directed," Billie called out. She showed me old newspaper clippings of a younger, debonair Maynard Duncan posing with two men. The caption of the first, dated June 5, 1939, from the black-owned *California Eagle,* read: "FAMED POET LANGSTON HUGHES AND ACTOR CLARENCE MUSE CONFER WITH ACTOR AND FLEDGLING DIRECTOR MAYNARD DUNCAN ON *WAY DOWN SOUTH.*" A later one, from a mid-September 1941 edition of *The Hollywood Reporter,* blared, "BRIT BIOPIC DIRECTOR TRISTAN CAVENDER GIVES TIPS TO NEGRO NEWCOMER MAYNARD DUNCAN," and was a group shot taken in front of the old Cocoanut Grove, Duncan's sister and brother-in-law standing off to one side while in the foreground, wearing a white coat and black fedora, was Maynard Duncan cheesing for the camera and lighting a filtered cigarette for a dashingly tall and handsome fellow who must have been Cavender.

"I'd say this belongs to your vic," Billie observed.

"His widow probably hasn't even realized it was missing," I replied as I sat at the foot of the bed and examined the pages more carefully. "You think it could be some kind of trophy from the kill, like Clemenza collected from his victims?"

"I wouldn't rule it out," Billie said from behind me.

My reading was interrupted by an exclamation from Billie, who was going through a pile of mail on the nightstand. She handed me an opened letter that had been sent to Alice Thomas at her work address. It was written in a familiar scribble and was postmarked from San Quentin two weeks before Maynard Duncan's death. "From Clemenza?" I asked, my heart in my mouth.

Billie nodded and looked on while I read the first line aloud. "'You heartless cunt. You're as much responsible for this as we are.'"

"Is he using the royal 'we,' or were a group of them doing these old men together?" Cortez asked.

I read on. "'If you had only listened to me, you wouldn't have old men's blood on your hands, you bitch.'" Clemenza then described in sordid detail several murders he'd committed, the joy he'd felt in making each man pay for his crimes against man and God. "Now maybe you'll understand," the letter concluded, "why we did it, why it had to happen this way."

I turned to Billie. "You know this scumbag. What do you make of it?"

"It's consistent with the multiple personality disorder angle the defense tried to work in the trial," she admitted reluctantly.

"From the looks of this, it may have been more than just an angle."

"Yeah, but is he blaming Alice for *his* actions," Billie wondered, "or implying the two of them were in it together?"

I folded up the letter, slipped it into an evidence envelope. "With all these books she's got lying around on death and dying," I replied, "it makes you wonder."

Our debate was cut short by a key in the lock. Expecting Mrs. Vowelless, Cortez and I went into the living room to intercept her and were surprised to be confronted by a fiftyish, whisper-thin brunette weighed down by suitcases, beads around her neck, and huge black-framed sunglasses "Who are you?" she asked in a tremulous voice.

"Ms. Thomas, I'm Detective Justice of the Robbery-Homicide Division of the LAPD, and this is Detective Cortez. We have a warrant to search the premises."

Alice Thomas peered hesitantly into the disarray that was her apartment. "What's this all about?" she demanded. "Did someone break in?" She set down her suitcase in the hallway, entered the apartment, and removed her sunglasses to examine the warrant I handed her. Something in her crumpled when she came to

Maynard Duncan's name. "Oh, dear," she whispered, and turned abruptly back into the hallway.

I could see Cortez tense up, ready to run Thomas down if she bolted, but she relaxed when the home health nurse tearfully asked for some help with her things. In the hallway beyond her I could see a number of flattened boxes and a roll of bubble wrap propped up against the wall. I called out to Billie in the bedroom to give Cortez a hand with the packing material while I stood back to be sure she didn't try anything.

Their hands full, my colleagues waited for Thomas to drag the large suitcase into the apartment. "Although you always expect these things, I'm a little surprised at the timing of Mr. Duncan's passing," she said as she struggled with the bag. "He seemed to be doing better at home, and his pain was being well managed. But if the police are involved, you must suspect foul play."

"We're calling it a suspicious death for now."

Thomas put down the suitcase inside the door, and after a deep breath, straightened up to face us. "Why do you think his death was suspicious?"

I pulled out my notebook. "There are several factors we're looking into," I assured her with a noncommittal smile, "but mainly we're just covering our bases by talking to his caregivers."

"And you think because I was administering his morphine, *I* might have something to do with his death?" Thomas put her left hand to her chest for emphasis, revealing a pale band of skin on her ring finger that a few days in the sun had not completely erased. "I'm not the only one who had access to that pump, you know. The nurse who relieved me could have made a mistake. Besides, I've been in Hawaii since last Wednesday!"

"But you *were* at the house last Tuesday afternoon, correct?"

"Sure. I got there at one to replenish the morphine in Mr. Duncan's pump, but I was there only a few minutes." Fresh alarm widened Thomas's eyes. "Why didn't Mrs. Eddinger tell me any of this when I called yesterday?" Her distraught gaze fell on

Cortez unzipping her suitcase. "Hey, she can't do that! That's my personal property."

"The warrant covers the contents of the apartment, including your luggage," I informed her, glad we had made sure Thomas brought the suitcase inside herself. Had she left it in the hall, it would have been excluded from our search, or been considered tainted had any of us touched it. "It's all explained in the paperwork."

Thomas eased into a battered club chair to read the warrant more carefully. "This is unbelievable." Tears slid down her cheeks, and her voice quavered more noticeably. "Just because I was his nurse is no reason to suspect me! Everyone in that household—even Mr. Duncan himself—saw me program that pump. Are they suspects, too?"

"How well did you know Angelo Clemenza?"

My question caught her off guard. She fell back in her chair, a slender hand cupped over her mouth. "Only from work, not that well at all," came her muffled voice.

"What about this?" I asked, extending Clemenza's letter.

Thomas seemed to recoil, one hand held up as if to ward off an evil spirit. "When I got that letter a couple of weeks ago, it was just too creepy." Her pale green eyes searched ours. "Aren't there laws against inmates sending disgusting letters like that?"

"So why didn't you notify the DA's office or the police when you received it?"

"I thought if they saw that thing, they might suspect me of being involved with those murders," she replied, pointing at Clemenza's letter as if it were a squirming insect. Her voice grew more agitated, her eyes filling with tears. She reached into her purse for a handkerchief, shaking her head. "I should have quit the agency as soon as that whole Angel of Mercy mess started. And I would have, if it hadn't been for patients like Mr. Duncan."

I folded up Clemenza's letter, put it back in its envelope, and removed my gloves. "We'll just hold on to this for now."

"Be my guest," she said, wiping her eyes.

"Did Clemenza ever show you his diaries?" I asked.

"He used to bring these spiral notebooks to the staff meetings, but he never let anyone read them. I explained that to the DA's investigator when he interviewed me."

I stopped writing in mid-sentence as Billie asked, "You were interviewed by the DA's office but were never called to testify?"

"Mr. Ikehara picked Mrs. Eddinger to testify over me. I really didn't know the man."

Billie caught my eye over Thomas's head as if to say, *No wonder Ike was a no-show this morning.* This way he could put us on the scent as his personal bloodhounds by proxy, yet keep the Serial Killer Unit at arm's length if the search turned out to be a bust.

I knew there was a reason I didn't like Ike.

"I saw you have a scrapbook on Mr. Duncan," Billie was saying.

"That's not mine. Mr. Duncan loaned it to me a couple of weeks ago. He knew how much I was a fan of Hollywood's golden era, and he gave it to me thinking it would cheer me up."

"Was something bothering you?"

"My divorce, that letter. But Maynard—Mr. Duncan—told me I couldn't let myself be shackled by the past."

"So Mr. Duncan was aware of your connection to Clemenza?" Billie pressed.

Thomas dropped her head and said softly, "Mr. Duncan and I shared a lot of things. It happens sometimes with terminally ill patients."

"I'm sure it does." Billie murmured, then added: "It's just that we found the scrapbook in kind of an unusual place."

Thomas began, "If you're referring to my altar . . ." but was distracted again by Cortez, who had finished checking the suitcase and stood up, giving us the all-clear signal. ". . . I put the scrapbook there so I wouldn't forget to return it to him."

"That's convenient," Cortez muttered under her breath.

"Makes perfect sense to me," Billie agreed, her voice carrying a subtle warning to our less experienced colleague. "Who are the other people on the altar?"

"Relatives, patients, people I include in my daily practice," she replied, a little more easily.

I made another note while Cortez pressed, "What's this daily practice you're into? Buddhism? Taoism?"

"I'm into everything-ism, Detective," she replied, an indulgent smile accentuating her words. "All faiths can answer your prayers if you're willing to open yourself to the presence of God. You should try it sometime. You might learn something."

Cortez's face flushed a deep red, but she held her tongue. I positioned my body to address the home health nurse directly. "I'm hoping we might actually learn something from you, Ms. Thomas."

"Such as?"

"Such as what you think really happened to Mr. Duncan."

Asking potential suspects how they think a crime was committed is often a way to not only defuse a tense situation but also find out how their minds work, giving detectives some clue to motives or thought patterns that can be pursued later in the investigation. I could tell Alice, like most, was flattered, by the way she readjusted herself in her chair. "Well, I must tell you I honestly don't think Mr. Duncan was capable of taking his own life," she replied firmly. "I've treated a number of dying patients in my career, and he did not exhibit any of the classical signs. He was vibrant, engaged, connected to life. He reminded me of Kirk Douglas's character in *Lust for Life*. He had the same kind of passion for his craft, the same determination to somehow capture it all, that Van Gogh did."

"But," Cortez interrupted, "Van Gogh committed suicide, didn't he?"

"You're missing the point, Detective. Every day was a gift to Mr. Duncan, a gift to be savored and used to complete his dream."

"And what was that?" Cortez asked.

"*Stormy Weather.* He worked on that documentary almost every day, no matter how much pain he was in. And the days he couldn't, he talked about it. What I saw of it was a revelation to me. See, I was raised in a little town in Montana where the only black people we saw were in Shirley Temple movies or on *Good Times.*

When Mr. Duncan heard that, I became his official test audience. He believed if he could show people like me a more complete vision of the African-American experience through film, he'd have accomplished his mission. And from what I saw, he was getting there."

"So as far as you're concerned, suicide was out of the question?" I pressed.

Her head bobbed emphatically. "Most patients who come to hospice care like Mr. Duncan don't live for more than a few weeks. Mr. Duncan lived for three months. I think it was because he had something to live for." Thomas removed the necklace from around her neck and said in her wispy voice, "Excuse me for saying so, Detective Justice, but I think you're looking in the wrong direction." She coiled the necklace onto an end table and folded her tiny hands in her lap. "I had no reason to harm Mr. Duncan, and I don't think he killed himself. If there was something suspicious about the way he died, I'd start by talking to that minister of his."

"Pastor Henley? Why him?"

"He was on fire to get Mr. Duncan to sign a new will the last time I was there, asked me to be a witness. But since the agency doesn't allow us to get involved in our patients's legal matters, he got the housekeeper and another man working there to do it."

"Why didn't Pastor Henley witness it himself?"

"He said he couldn't—something about the church having a conflict."

"Conflict?"

"I'm pretty sure that's the word he used. Plus, soon as they finished the paperwork, he scooped up the document from Mr. Duncan and said something like 'And not a moment too soon.'"

While I was digesting this information, Billie hefted the books we'd found in Thomas's bedroom and Cortez went into the bedroom, returning with the scrapbook and photos from the altar. "We appreciate your cooperation, ma'am," I said. "But we'll need to take these with us."

"I use those books in my work!" she complained in a fretful voice. "And the scrapbook belongs to Mr. Duncan's family."

"We'll be sure Mrs. Duncan gets it back when we're finished."

She was also reluctant to accompany Cortez downtown to have her prints taken and give a written statement, even after we explained it was merely a formality. "I promise not to keep you long." Cortez's voice was reassuring. "I know you have a lot of packing to do."

"Not as much as you'd think." She gazed wistfully at the collection on her walls. "When I first separated from my husband, I would sit staring at all this stuff for hours, wondering what was wrong with me, why couldn't I have a relationship like the ones I'd seen in the movies. But that was as much of a pipe dream as thinking my ex-husband was going to come to his senses and stop slapping me around when he got drunk. Worshiping all this old memorabilia was blinding me to what was going on in my own life, right here and right now."

"Even so, you've got a lot of great things here," I noted, wondering how she could even begin to pack up a whole apartment full of memories when I was having trouble with just that one room in my house.

"Things can't keep you warm at night, Detective." She got to her feet and gathered up her purse and keys. "So I'm putting the whole kit and caboodle up for sale. It's time I got a life of my own."

CHAPTER 9

LYING LIPS

It was close to noon when we finally left the apartment, although you couldn't tell by the sun's hesitant appearance through a pewter-colored sky. Billie considered Thomas as she got into Cortez's car. "You think she showed the wife or the sister how to reprogram the pump, then split town so she couldn't be directly linked to the killing?"

"Could be. But I'm also wondering if Maynard Duncan innocently told someone about Thomas's connection to Clemenza, someone who then decided to kill him and set her up to take the fall."

"Who'd you have in mind?" Billie asked.

"The wife, the sister, even Pastor Henley, depending on the size of that bequest."

Cortez was silent through this exchange, in fact seemed to be having trouble following our conversation, and her color hadn't improved from earlier in the morning. "Are you sure you feel up to taking Thomas's statement?" I peered at her carefully. "You don't look so good."

"It's nothing." She shook her head as if to clear it. "What else do you need me to do?"

"See if you can get someone from the manufacturer into the office to tell us how that pump was programmed. Their number's in the murder book. By now you should also be able to get Duncan's medical records from the coroner's shop for comparison purposes."

I watched as Cortez got in her car and pulled slowly away from the curb, wondered what was going on with her. I turned to Billie. "I'm going to go over to Duncan's house. I know the funeral's today, but I think I'd better check into this will business ASAP."

"I can back you up," Billie offered. "I've got a court appearance later this afternoon, but I could use a good lunch."

Billie's comment wasn't an idle one. She knew, as I did, that no matter if you're rich or poor, black folks put on the dog when it comes to repasts. Even if they can't afford anything better than a felt-covered box for the casket, the food our people serve at the post-funeral repast will be the best of the best, demonstrating through the TLC they put into the fried chicken or the macaroni and cheese what they sometimes couldn't convey to the deceased in life.

I wasn't sure if it was the director's death or the possibility that Soulful Celebrations was doing the catering that drew the crowd that was in attendance at the Duncan residence, but the joint was jumping like a down-home Saturday-night fish fry by the time Billie and I pulled up in our unmarkeds. Maybe not as many cars as Hattie McDaniel's fabled funeral procession, but at least a hundred luxury vehicles were crammed onto Duncan's street, and spilled over to the others behind Fremont Place's gates. Not to mention the limos, complete with a gaggle of multiculti drivers standing a short distance from the house, talking and eating from plates provided by the catering staff. Watching them as I slipped some equipment into my purse, I was reminded of an Elmore Leonard novel in which the drivers waited outside a country club for their wealthy employers, trading stock tips. With this group it would be scooping the inside poop on who was knocking boots with whom, or swapping the names of the baby barracudas at the big talent agencies willing to take a chance on selling the scripts they were probably writing in their spare time.

They all hopped to attention when the door of the house opened, scrambling to appear as if they'd been waiting patiently all along. When a tall, slightly built white man—smartly dressed in a black suit, silver-gray hair combed back from a high widow's peak—emerged onto the front porch, the chauffeurs relaxed. Obviously, he was not one of theirs.

Maybe the old guy was just a gate crasher, because he was trailed outside by Delphine Giles, who gave him a tight-lipped, eyeball-to-eyeball dressing-down before she abruptly turned away, slamming the door behind her. The man stood uncertainly for a moment between the concrete lions, then reached into his breast pocket for a pack of cigarettes. Further searching yielded a book of matches, one of which he was struggling to light as we walked up the long path to the steps.

He was exhaling his first long drag by the time we reached him, the smell of mentholated tobacco mixed with the aroma of a heady cologne. His gaunt, lined face looked familiar, though oddly out of context, like seeing your dry cleaner at a jazz concert. But his simple "Pardon me," uttered as he stepped aside to let us pass, was delivered in an accent that was unmistakably English. Once I heard it, I realized I'd seen a younger version of this man in Maynard Duncan's album.

Noticing him about to falter, I grabbed him by the elbow. "Are you all right, Mr. Cavender?"

He squinted at me uncertainly. "Have we met?"

"No, sir, we haven't, but I know who you are. Were you a friend of Mr. Duncan's?"

"Not if you go by the reception his sister just gave me," he replied uneasily, dragging again on his cigarette.

"What's her problem?"

He exhaled, ground out the half-smoked cigarette on the steps. "Just a misunderstanding, that's all." He gave us a courtly little bow. "Good day, ladies."

"What do you make of that?" Billie asked as she rang the doorbell.

I watched Cavender feel his way down the steps and carefully navigate the long walk to the street. "Duncan's sister had a real pinecone up her butt when I first interviewed her about white directors getting recognition her brother didn't. Maybe Tristan Cavender's at the top of her hit list."

A brown-skinned young man, attired in a stylish black suit, black silk T-shirt, and bottle-blond ponytail, greeted us at the door and encouraged us to sign the guest book in the foyer. I scanned the book's open pages, noting, in addition to Cavender's, the names of black and white directors, actors of both sexes, and entertainment executives I'd seen in the *Times'* Calendar section, in the pages of *Jet,* or on *Entertainment Tonight.* Even the Urban Contemporary Network's CEO, Skip Sheffield, who'd visited Duncan on the day he died, had made it back into town in time for the funeral, the spiky flourish of his signature obliterating several others.

As Billie signed in, she ran her finger along the names of the old and new Hollywood guard. " Daa-yumm! If I'da known I was coming over here, I'd've brought Turquoise's autograph book."

I steered her past a full bar set up in one corner of the foyer and down into the crowded living room. "Your daughter's autograph collection will have to wait. We've got work to do."

Apparently we weren't the only ones. Listening to the animated hum of voices, I was surprised some of them hadn't brought headshots and résumés to place on the table in the foyer. A group of young black women near the fireplace were sipping eggnog and bemoaning the fact that NBC and the other "nets" weren't developing quality programming to fill the gap left by the departure of *The Cosby Show.* Over at a second bar, a group of well-known black actors were debating whether the guilt-ridden promises made by studio execs at some hastily convened post-riot industry summit at the American Film Institute were for real. A third group nearby argued that the NAACP's more recent threats of a boycott probably wouldn't increase the number of minority production executives or result in even *one* black person who could greenlight a film. "Man, it's gonna be the same thugs, slugs, and jitterbugs as usual," one of them predicted, and took another draw on his beer.

I was growing weary of the chatter and wearier still of trying to find Duncan's widow in the crush of lushly scented, designer-clad bodies. Billie, on the other hand, was lapping it all up like a kitten at a dish of cream. She was particularly impressed at seeing a veteran black actress from her favorite sitcom talking to a dread-headed young man who had cornered her near the fireplace. "I just got the green light today from HBO," I heard him congratulate himself. "Although it's my first feature, it was the heat offa that last Salt-N-Pepa video I helmed that got me over. So I know you're gonna wanna be in the mix on this one."

Her voice almost reverential, Billie wondered aloud, "Is that the brother who directed *To Sleep with Anger?*" Then she corrected herself: "No, I remember now—he's that young brother from the projects caught a break doing music videos after the riots. There was an article on him in the paper."

Like I cared. But everyone else seemed to be vitally concerned, about that or some other self-absorbed conversation. I saw bald-headed young actors who probably went to the Yale School of Drama bragging about their breakout roles as Carjacker #2 in the Knit Cap in the latest *Boyz N the Hood* clone. And directors who worked those same wretched films pretending they were "artistic expression" and not just a way to maintain the leases on their Mercedes or keep their kids in private school.

And thoughts of Maynard Duncan, the pioneering actor and filmmaker, on whose giant shoulders these midgets stood? Lost in the liquored-up aria of "me, me, me, me, me" bouncing off the walls all around us.

I found a waiter passing a tray of hors d'oeuvres and asked if he knew where Mrs. Duncan might be. He pointed us toward an area off the dining room. "Her and Miz Giles was in the sunroom talkin' to Mr. Sheffield," he said, his voice betraying his origins as somewhere between South Carolina and South Central. But by the time we walked to the back of the house, the women weren't there, only Victor "Skip" Sheffield holding court in the persistent afternoon gloom.

And court it was—a line of supplicants stood in the archway

leading to the room, hoping for a word with the West Coast's most successful black cable executive. Sheffield was being sheltered by a giant redwood masquerading as a human being whose sole duty seemed to be keeping everyone behind an invisible line drawn in the carpeting. On the other side, seated in an overstuffed bamboo chaise longue, his shoes dripping on the upholstery, the great man accepted a crystal cup of eggnog from the blond ponytailed man who met us at the door while the other hand encircled the knee of an aging white woman sporting a precision-cut, professionally streaked chestnut bob and a skirted suit intended for a woman half her age.

Sheffield and the woman were loudly discussing the financing of some film he had written and UCN was producing. "*Caddyshack meets Boyz N the Hood,*" I overheard him bragging. As we got nearer, Tree Trunk planted itself in our way.

"And you are?" it bristled nastily.

"Your worst nightmare if you don't move out of my way," I replied sweetly, reaching for my shield.

Before I could get it out, Tree Trunk made a grab for my wrist. "Bitch, nobody gets to see the boss unless I say so!"

I twisted toward Billie, my voice light. "Don't you just hate the 'B' word?" Swinging back around quickly to put my elbow in Tree Trunk's leather-clad gut and plant a high heel in its instep, I murmured, "You really need to work on your manners," as I flashed it my badge and shouldered past it into the sunroom.

Skip Sheffield's eyes, momentarily distracted from the thigh he was kneading, noted my approach, a bemused smile on his lined face. I caught myself thinking how he could be mistaken for a model, one of those distinguished, gray-browed seniors the department stores seemed to have only recently discovered. At first glance, he would seem perfect for the high-end catalogs my mother studies like the Bible—with that expensive Swiss watch on his wrist, his beautifully knotted silk tie, and a sparkler on his left ring finger some underpaid South African probably sweated blood to excavate.

But it was all wasted, because once he opened his mouth, you might as well have hung a marquee over his head announcing "Ghetto Fabulous," because that was exactly how the media man of the moment sounded.

"Yo, yo, yo, yo, yo, Kamau, my man!" He laughed heartily, flashing a set of cheaply capped, frighteningly white teeth. "Let the ladies through!"

As if we weren't already standing in front of him. But perhaps that was Sheffield's way of helping his pitiful excuse for a bodyguard save face.

"You'll have to excuse us, ma'am," I informed the woman. "This is police business." On my nod, Billie steered her by the elbow to the other side of the still-hobbling Kamau. I caught Sheffield following the woman's retreat with his nasty eyes, running his tongue over his headlight-white teeth. What a lech. Made me want to pull that tongue out of his head and tie it in a knot next to that got-to-be-Italian number around his neck.

We introduced ourselves and gave him our cards. "We need to talk to you about your meeting with Mr. Duncan last Tuesday," I explained as I got out my notebook.

Sheffield's gaze drifted unwillingly back to me. "This is a terrible loss to the black film community. Why would Maynard Duncan want to take his own life?"

"We didn't say he did, Mr. Sheffield."

"But why else would you be here?" he asked. "Unless you expect foul play . . . or you're writing an MOW on Maynard Duncan's career in your spare time." He gave us another peek at those teeth. "In which case I hope you pitch it to UCN before any of the other nets."

I knew from hanging around my father and uncle that an MOW was a movie-of-the-week, but there was no way in hell that I'd let on to this self-important asshole that I knew.

"Just answer Detective Justice's question, Mr. Sheffield," Billie snapped, her voice conveying the exasperation I was feeling.

"Yes, of course." He frowned as if trying to recall the question, took a slurping sip of his eggnog as if to aid his memory. "Let's see. When I got on the horn with Maynard last Monday morning, he invited me over to discuss the rebuilding proposal being presented to the Still We Rise board. You have heard about our plans?"

"Why don't you bring us up to speed," I replied blandly.

"Our vision is for a low-rise, multitenant office complex that would appeal to smaller postproduction companies—the mini Industrial Light and Magics of the business, if you will. While George Lucas can afford to locate his company up in Marin County, a lot of the smaller outfits who create special effects for films need to be closer to their studio clients. The Santa Barbara Plaza property would be ideal."

Without even consulting my notes, I was certain Pastor Henley had mentioned sites in South Central when I spoke with him at the church on Monday, not the collection of shabby but prime-for-development properties situated at the foot of the upper-middle-class houses of Baldwin Hills. When I said as much to Sheffield, he smiled indulgently. "Pastor had been worried about what some of the church's members in the 'hood would think, but I convinced him somebody had to be realistic about this thing."

"But wasn't the whole idea behind the project to create jobs for inner-city youth?"

"It is, but putting that studio in the heart of the riot zone is like letting the homies run the asylum," he added, chuckling at his own disparaging joke. "Look, if we locate the Still We Rise development in an area with better proximity to middle-class neighborhoods and a couple of freeways, we'll have a slam dunk. Fox, Warner Brothers, Disney, all the big studios will want to play on our team."

"You didn't include UCN in that lineup."

"Urban Contemporary Network is just a benchwarmer compared to those superstars," he replied, his smile dialed down to humbly demure this time. "Ours is just a minor part of the plan."

"What was Mr. Duncan's reaction to your proposal?"

"He knew it was the right thing to do." Sheffield beamed with satisfaction. "Supported it one hundred percent. He just wasn't sure he'd be able to make the board meeting on the first to vote for it, given the up-and-down nature of his health, so he asked me to bring over a proxy for him to sign that I could take to the meeting."

"He was alert enough to sign it?"

"He seemed fine to me."

"Did the two of you discuss anything else the day you saw him?"

"He mentioned he was ready to talk a distribution deal for *Stormy Weather.* Maynard knew UCN had gotten a substantial round of venture capital to start a theatrical film division plus an original programming unit on the cable side, so naturally he wanted to talk to us first about a combined theatrical/cable deal."

"Mrs. Duncan stated her husband had already talked to and been turned down by BET and Turner."

Sheffield's gray eyebrows came together as he wiped a cocktail napkin across his mustache. "Technically that may be true, but Maynard had always wanted UCN to be involved from the beginning. But given the historical significance of the film, I wanted him to get as wide a distribution as possible. So I encouraged him to pitch it to some of the bigger outfits first."

I watched his lips move, thinking, *What a lying sack of shit.* Ivy Duncan's initial reaction to Sheffield when I interviewed her had only reinforced what I already knew about UCN and its CEO's reputation. And while I imagined UCN's cable programming might improve with that new venture capital, I was sure Skip Sheffield *had* told Maynard Duncan to pitch his film elsewhere— with female Jell-O wrestling leading his network's prime-time lineup and a spin-off movie rumored to be in the works, Skip Sheffield wouldn't know what to do with a serious documentary if it bit him in the behind.

"Not that I wasn't more than willing to negotiate with him," Sheffield was saying, "but . . ." He let his voice trail off.

"But what?"

"Between you and me, *Stormy Weather* wasn't very commercial, at least not for our target demographic. Full of old movies clips, dull interviews with a bunch of over-the-hill stars, and Duncan's personal ramblings. It was like he'd called it in instead of doing the work that was necessary to craft a coherent, marketable product."

Like this fool would know, I thought.

"I don't want to speak ill of the dead," he whispered, "but I'd noticed before, on the Still We Rise board, how erratic and unfocused Maynard was at times. What with the painkillers he was taking and all, I'm sure it was understandable, but I can tell you from an industry viewpoint that Maynard's illness wasn't helping his chances of getting that documentary sold. People in this town will drop you like a hot potato if they suspect you're ill. And Maynard was *very* ill."

"I appreciate your candid assessment of Mr. Duncan's health, Mr. Sheffield." *You backstabber.* "But let's get back to your activities on the afternoon of his death."

Sheffield said he'd arrived at the house at one forty-five and left before two, a fact that Kamau confirmed from a safe distance by the archway. "Dolores had warned me he was wiped out, so I didn't stay long," Sheffield explained.

"Can anyone not in your employ corroborate the times you entered and left Mr. Duncan's room?"

"Ask Dolores. She walked me up there." He drained his glass and handed it to Billie. "And tell her to bring me some more of that eggnog, will you, doll?" He smacked his lips appreciatively as a scowling Billie and I moved toward the kitchen. "It's got it goin' on!"

Although Dolores Amargosa had gotten back into town the night before, she looked like she hadn't slept since the plane landed. A petite Hispanic with quite a bit of Africa in her blood, she was about forty, but looked older—her hooded eyes were bloodshot and her eyelids sagged at the corners, an effect that was underscored by circles under her eyes that showed like soot. Her broad face looked like ten miles of bad road.

We found her in the kitchen, talking softly on the phone in

Spanish. She ended the call, tried to compose herself, and started arranging hors d'oeuvres on china platters while Blondie and the drawling waiter, their backs to us, were comparing notes collected on their serving rounds. "Can you imagine the gall of those two, cutting a deal right here at the repast?" Blondie whispered his indignation.

"Who d'ya think they'll get to distribute it?" the Drawler asked. "Universal? Disney?"

Blondie gave a derisive half-snort. "Those big studios won't get involved in a film these days unless they can make a ride out of it!" Billie set Sheffield's cup on the countertop, causing the men to turn around just as Blondie was saying, "A cross between *Caddyshack* and *Boyz N the Hood?* He needs his ass whupped!"

Something shattered on the floor, drawing everyone's attention to the housekeeper. A platter full of hors d'oeuvres was scattered in pieces at her feet "*Con cuidado,* Dolores!" Blondie exclaimed. "You don't want Mrs. D. on your ass again for breaking her good china!"

Her eyes flashed angrily. "*Mi 'jo* is in the hospital and all these people care about is . . ." She caught herself, mumbled an apology, and hurried, red-faced, to the utility room. "I'll try to be more careful," she said when she returned with a hand broom and dustpan.

While the housekeeper began to frantically wipe the mess from the floor, the two men readied themselves to go back into the fray. "Man, why would a black man in a position of power like Sheffield make a dumb-ass movie like that?" the other man asked, picking up a platter of stuffed mushrooms.

Blondie shook his head sadly. "Believe you me, I've been catering these Hollywood events for years, and I can tell you it ain't got nothing to do with this"—he pointed to his brown skin—"it's all about this," and he rubbed a thumb and two forefingers together before hoisting a platter.

Billie snagged a potsticker as he went by. "Mmm . . . sweet potato," she murmured, oblivious of the flicker of annoyance that crossed Mrs. Amargosa's face.

"Excuse me, ma'am," I said to the housekeeper. "Is the man with the blond ponytail Otto Randall, Mrs. Duncan's catering manager?"

The woman nodded and frowned, fingering a religious medallion and locket on a thin gold chain. Her frown was transformed into a nervous smile, however, when we flashed her our ID. She immediately rushed to fix Billie a plate, an offer my sister detective readily accepted. "Something for ju, missus?" she asked me in a heavier accent than I'd noticed before, her eyes averted.

I declined, telling her why we were there. While the news seemed to surprise her, Amargosa readily complied when I took her into the utility room to get her prints. While she was washing her hands at the sink, I handed Billie a couple of kits and whispered, "Talk with Mr. Randall about his movements the day Duncan died. And get a set of prints from him and Sheffield for me while you're at it." In response to her look of mock indignation, I added, "Randall's the one with the potstickers."

Billie hopped off the stool and headed for the living room, licking her fingers as she went. "All I needed was an incentive."

Amargosa led me outside to a bricked-in side patio filled with stacked-up, tarp-covered tables and chairs. The rain had slacked off to a fine drizzle that whispered on the rusted aluminum awnings and made the backyard appear more desolate than ever. I helped her pull back a mildewed tarp, lift a couple of chairs from one of the stacks, and drag them across the worn bricks to a spot not far from the kitchen door. From where I sat I could smell the dead leaves in the backyard and see through the sunroom window that a new group of acolytes and wannabes were practically kissing Skip Sheffield's ring and whatever else he might have wanted.

Amargosa waited for me to sit before perching on the edge of her own seat. "Ju sure ju don't want something to eat, missus?" she asked, poised as if to flit off to the kitchen at my command.

"Don't worry about me, ma'am. You seem to have enough on your mind already." She stared ahead vacantly. "Mrs. Giles tells me your child is ill."

Her fingers found the locket around her neck. "Very ill."

I gestured toward the locket. "You carry a picture of him? May I?"

She reluctantly removed the locket from the chain and opened it with a trembling hand. One side held a lock of blond hair, the other a worn color photo of a solemn-looking toddler with piercing, slate-colored eyes. "He's beautiful," I said, handing the locket back to her and pulling out my notebook.

"He's my baby," she whispered, her voice thick.

Although she acknowledged my interest in her child, her jitteriness seemed to increase, especially when she saw the notebook.

"It's just to help me remember, Mrs. Amargosa," I explained, elaborating in my poor Spanish: *"Yo tengo mucho olvido."*

My reasoning did little to calm her, so I put the notebook away, pulled my chair closer, and patted her hand. Her exhausted eyes were on the verge of spouting tears. "I'm so tired but I can't stop," she murmured wearily. "There's still so much to do."

I patted her hand again, noticed its coldness. "The quicker we get this over with, Mrs. Amargosa, the quicker you can get back to work. *¿Comprende?*"

Dolores Amargosa had been busy in the Duncan household the day she left town, too. She had arrived before seven, thoroughly cleaned and vacuumed Duncan's sickroom and bath, and done a cursory hit-or-miss of the rest of the house before pitching in at nine to help the women and Randall with preparation for a Thanksgiving dinner party they were catering.

"Were there any deliveries during the time you were there?"

"Only the catering man for Señora Duncan."

I checked my notes from my interview with Mrs. Duncan and her sister-in-law. "What about FedEx? Didn't you accept a package for Mr. Duncan?"

Dolores Amargosa's eyes went blank for a minute, then she said, "Oh, jes, I forgot! The FedEx lady, she come around ten but she no go *arriba*. I take the package up to Señor Duncan myself."

"You know what was in it?"

She shook her head, her eyes blank again.

"Or who it was addressed to?"

"No missus," she said quickly, and dropped her head. "I no read so good."

"How were Mr. Duncan's spirits when you were upstairs cleaning the room or delivering the package?"

"He was acting kinda funny."

"Funny how?"

"Señor Duncan he say Otto and me have to—*¿como se dice?*—witness his signature on a paper from his lawyer. When he tell me it was his, eh, new will, I didna want to do it."

"Why was that?"

She dropped her head and started fiddling with the locket again. "I feel kinda funny about it, ju know? Liken it meant Señor Duncan was going to die or something. But when his *padre* come, he say Otto and I should do it, too."

"What time did his pastor arrive?"

"Eh was noon, I think, when I taken him upstairs."

"And that's when he talked to you about witnessing Mr. Duncan's will?"

"No, it was after I took up their lunch. Señor Duncan tell the *padre* I was being difficult and his *padre* said I would be a good Christian iffen I help Señor Duncan out."

"What time did you serve Mr. Duncan and his *padre* lunch?"

"Twelve-thirty, Señor Duncan's regular lunchtime. Señora Duncan and I took, eh, the trays upstairs."

"Did both men eat?"

"Their plates was clean, but the señora want me be sure Señor Duncan get enough, so she have me given Missus Alice some of the *coquito* to taken to him."

"*Coquito?*"

"*Sí,* es Puerto Rican eggnog my eh husband's *familia* make. I was teaching Señora Duncan how to make it for their Christmas parties. After she written down the recipe, she say let's given it for Señor Duncan. 'Maybe it make, eh, him eat,' she say. But he say he no wanna drink it without the rum, so when his nurse come she take it and say she given it to, eh, him later."

"When did you and Mr. Randall witness the will?"

Amargosa's eyes teared up. She clearly remembered the time as one-fifteen, "Because I had to leave in a hour to catch the bus to the airport, and I still have to, eh, finish washing the dishes for the party."

"How did Mr. Duncan seem when he signed the will?"

She looked at me and blinked. "He was awake, if that's what you mean."

"And what time did Ms. Thomas leave?"

"One-thirty maybe? I let her out maybe twenty, thirty minutes before Otto and I left." Her eyes went to the crowd visible in the sunroom. "Can I go now? I've got to get back to work."

"Just a few more questions, Mrs. Amargosa. Did you see what happened to the will after it was signed?"

"The minister, he took it," she said, a hint of sadness in her voice.

"Was that the last time you saw Mr. Duncan?"

"No," she responded to her hands. "I go in there to say Happy Thanksgiving before I leave at two-thirty, but he was asleeping by then."

So far, the times she gave me for the arrival and departure of the various visitors and guests were consistent with the statements Ivy Duncan and her sister-in-law had given to Neidisch and O'Donoughue. I made a few more mental notes, acutely aware that pulling out a notebook would spoil the casual atmosphere I wanted to maintain for this interview.

But nothing I did, or didn't do, seemed to calm the Duncans' servant. "Is there something else you want to tell me, Mrs. Amargosa?"

She leaned forward in her chair, eyes back on her hands. She turned slightly in her chair, glancing toward the sunroom. *"Yo no sé."*

" 'I don't know' is not an answer, Mrs. Amargosa."

She twisted her hands in her lap as if washing them before blurting out, "I think that nurse that coming here was wanting Señor Duncan's money. I would come into the room and she was always there, always talking, talking, talking to him."

"Talking about what?"

"Everything. Old movies, some crazy guy on her job, but mostly how he should think about leaving his money where it was going to do the most good."

"And this was before Pastor Henley asked you to witness the will?"

"Jes, missus. Weeks before." Amargosa began to cry again, but there was anger mixed with her tears this time. "Even his nurse asked me that day. I no want to do it, but they make me."

I listened to the rain whispering on the awnings, and waited to see if there was anything else Mrs. Amargosa had to tell me. After a few more moments of the rain doing all the talking, I asked about Sheffield's visit and found out it was just as he'd said—he arrived at one forty-five, shortly after Pastor Henley and Alice Thomas had left, spent a few minutes with Duncan alone, and departed shortly before Otto Randall and Amargosa left at two-thirty.

"And you let Mr. Sheffield in and escorted him out that day?"

She looked to the French windows. "Jes."

"And Mr. Duncan was awake on both occasions?"

"Sí." She said, nodding more vigorously.

I was sure something was being left unspoken, but I was equally sure Dolores Amargosa wasn't about to tell me. Thinking maybe I was missing some cultural nuance that Cortez would pick up, I explained my partner would need to get her written statement, which she could come to our offices downtown to complete. At that she just about jumped out of her skin, and made some flimsy excuse that her duties at the Duncan household would keep her too busy.

"We can do it this evening after you leave work. It will only take a few minutes, and you would be helping us find Mr. Duncan's killer."

She complained she didn't have a car.

"That's no problem—I'll send Detective Cortez over to pick you up."

She still protested, looking so fearful it dawned on me to ask, "What you told Mrs. Duncan and her sister about being from Puerto Rico wasn't true, was it, Dolores?" Her startled reaction was all the answer I needed. "I'm only interested in Mr. Duncan's death," I reassured her, "not your immigration status." I patted her still-cold hand again, saw the relief flicker in her eyes. "You can come downtown and talk freely without worrying about *la inmigración*."

Just then Ivy Duncan appeared in the sunroom doorway. "Dolores, Mr. Sheffield is upstairs asking for more *coquito*," she said sharply.

The little woman practically knocked her chair over in her haste to get back to the kitchen. "I'm very sorry, missus. I have to go back to work."

Ivy Duncan stood looming in the kitchen, tapping her foot as the housekeeper hurried to pull premixed ingredients from the large refrigerator. "We don't pay you to sit around lollygagging while there are guests in the house, Dolores," she chided the woman. "You know how hard Mr. Maynard's death has been on us. We're depending on you to be there, not off somewhere putting our business in the street!"

Billie had taken up residence on one of the stools at the kitchen counter, and was wreaking havoc on what looked like a second helping of appetizers. She cut her eyes in my direction as Duncan's widow continued haranguing Amargosa, the black woman's assault so relentless that I finally had to step in and remind her that her housekeeper was assisting us in a police investigation.

That slowed Ivy Duncan's roll long enough for Amargosa to finish stirring the *coquito* and struggle out of the kitchen with the punch bowl. And Mrs. Duncan's ranting came to a complete standstill when I informed her we would need the name and number of the family's attorney. "Why do you need to talk to Mr. Pressman?" she asked curtly. "Haven't you people done enough already?"

"I'm sorry, I'm not sure what you mean."

"Because of that coroner woman's morbid determination to violate my husband's body, they couldn't get the autopsy done until tomorrow. And what was I supposed to do? I'd already notified his friends, colleagues, and the press about the funeral services. I was forced to have Maynard's funeral with a closed casket. Do you know how embarrassing that was for me?"

"I'm sure no one even noticed."

"People in this town notice *everything*," she spat back, her voice indignant, "especially at funerals. They're probably in this house right now, drinking my liquor, eating my food, and gossiping about why the casket was closed."

At least she got two out of three right.

Billie walked over to the distraught woman, put a calming hand on her arm. "You're getting yourself all worked up, Mrs. Duncan. Perhaps we could find somewhere quiet we can talk."

She eyed us both dubiously, then dragged a hand across a face that was showing the strain. "Come with me," she said, a note of resignation in her voice.

I let Mrs. Duncan walk ahead while I filled Billie in on my interview with the housekeeper. By the time we caught up with Ivy Duncan on the second-floor landing, I could just make out another group of people gathered down the hall in a room at the front of the house, in the opposite corner from Maynard's sickroom. Excusing herself, Ivy Duncan said: "Let me just check on Del. This whole ordeal has upset her so badly she's taken to her bed."

While Ivy Duncan ducked into the bedroom overlooking the rose garden, my attention was drawn to a muffled burst of deep-voiced laughter coming from the other room, followed by a voice I was surprised to recognize.

HERE'S TO MAYNARD DUNCAN

"**N**egro, please!" my Uncle Syl exclaimed as he moved into view through the French doors that separated the sitting room from the rest of the house. "Just because you and Maynard was born and raised in Harlem and Herb Jeffries's film was called *Harlem on the Prairie* didn't mean either of you Negroes should have been in it!"

"You are so right about *that!*" another male voice chimed in good-naturedly. "Maynard and I hadn't even *seen* a live horse, much less ridden one, until they carted us out to that dude ranch in Victorville."

"And it showed, too!" my uncle retorted, to peals of masculine laughter.

I turned my back on the doorway, trying to shield myself behind Billie. I had almost succeeded when my uncle's voice reached out to me across the open hallway. "Charlotte, is that you?"

Caught. While Billie excused herself to go to the rest room, I went to face the music.

Uncle Syl was dressed to the nines, the heather-gray sweater and matching flannel slacks he wore accentuating his silver hair and gray-rimmed brown eyes. He grabbed me by the elbows and shook my arms as if I was a kid. "Baby Girl, what are you doing here?"

Before I could ask him the same question, my uncle was dragging me toward the sitting room saying something about wanting
me to "meet the boys." We were halfway down the hall when I dug
in my heels. "Just don't introduce me as a cop, okay?"

His eyebrows arched with surprise. "So your interest in
Maynard Duncan on Thanksgiving *was* more than just curiosity."

I started walking. "Let's meet your friends."

He pulled me to a stop. "On one condition. Come by and
help me trim my tree tonight." I was about to decline when I saw
the sadness cloud his eyes. "After a day like today, I don't think I
can do it alone."

My heart swelled in response. I knew he was thinking of his
lover, Jackie, who'd been buried only a few months earlier. "What
time do you want me there?"

"How's six? I'll even cook us some dinner, how's that?"

By the time we'd struck the bargain we had entered a grand
salon that took up most of the north side of the second floor. The
room was filled with rose- and sea-green-colored chintz-covered
sofas and a variety of green velvet chairs grouped in small conver-
sational settings.

Between two banks of windows on the south wall hung the
still photo from the Tarzan movie that Uncle Syl had shown us on
Thanksgiving, six young men swaddled in a Hollywood nightmare
of African attire. The picture was flanked by a quartet of shrunken
but smiling replicas of the young men pictured on the wall. Uncle
Syl took his place on the left while another elderly gentleman in a
gold-buttoned blazer, silk shirt, and Kangol cap prepared to take
their picture. "Man, I wish Maynard could see you now!" he said in
a tremulous voice, the camera wobbling up to his eye.

His words caused the men being photographed to deflate, the
room falling silent until Uncle Syl raised his cup of eggnog and
shouted, "Here's to Maynard Duncan!" stimulating a sea of various-
shaped glasses to rise on a tide of voices carrying the sentiment.

"This is my niece, Charlotte, fellas," my uncle said after the shot
was taken. "I thought I'd show her what some *real* stars look like."

An assortment of gray and Grecian Formulaed heads turned

in my direction, and a group of elders in a corner on the opposite side of the room raised their eggnog cups and double old-fashioned glasses in salute. As the introductions were made, my eyes scanned the array of carefully dressed seniors in the room, noting the faces and voices of men I'd seen in everything from Tarzan movies to blaxploitation flicks, from *Cabin in the Sky* to the latest commercials, until they fell on Pastor Henley, who was engaged in a private tête-à-tête with Skip Sheffield, Kamau the Pitiful not far away.

Sheffield saw me first and stuck out his hand, giving me one of those toothy greetings as if we'd known each other for years. Pastor Henley looked on, beaming. "I see you've met our new chairman."

"Of what?" *The Dirty Old Men's Usher Board?* I wanted to ask.

"The Still We Rise board," Henley replied, still smiling. "Mr. Sheffield was unanimously elected to the post by the board of trustees yesterday."

"What about the South Central redevelopment project?"

"Santa Barbara Plaza, Detective," Sheffield corrected me, a broad smile on his face. "The vote was six-five in favor, wasn't it, Pastor?"

Clayton Henley smiled back, the two men doing a vigorous soul brother handshake as if to reaffirm the deal. As Sheffield and his roughneck bodyguard departed, I wondered if this was the "vibrant leadership" Henley had mentioned to me that day in his office, willing to sell out the poorest of the poor for a deal that would appease those too nervous to park their Porsches in a 'hood parking lot.

Henley got to his feet, drained his eggnog cup, and headed for the door. "You two talk. I've got a Bible study group back at the church."

I stopped him in midstep. "Pastor Henley, perhaps we can chat for a minute before you go."

It was more like ten minutes before I released Henley to scurry down the hall. "I'll have that document waiting for you at my office today, Detective," he said over his shoulder, avoiding so much as a glance at Ivy Duncan, who was standing in the hallway.

And asserting to Billie as she handed her a card, "I don't know where you got your information, but I certainly don't know anything about my husband signing a revised will," that familiar indignation threading through her voice.

"I'm sure there's just been a mix-up," Billie replied noncommittally, handing the business card over to me.

"Mrs. Duncan, why don't you join Detective Truesdale and me in here for a moment." I led her to her husband's darkened sickroom, flipped on the light, and closed the door behind us. I indicated a spot on the stripped hospital bed for her to sit. She sat gingerly, as if afraid to occupy the space where her husband had lain. Noting but ignoring her discomfort, I positioned myself above her and only a few feet away, arms crossed over my chest.

Before long, Ivy Duncan's steely gaze faltered, and she started squirming as if sitting on a bed of hot coals. She looked from the orchid at the bedside to Billie, then to me. "Why are you two just standing there, staring at me?" she demanded, her quivering chin thrust high in defiance. "I haven't done anything wrong!"

"The problem, Mrs. Duncan," I took my time saying, "is I think you've been lying to me. And that really irritates me. So I'm just standing here trying to figure out—am I irritated because I resent my elders lying to me or am I irritated because you thought all your talk about the old days in Hollywood could bamboozle me into forgetting to do my job?"

"Why should I lie?"

Billie said, "People lie for a lot of reasons." I was pleased she had deliberately made her voice gentle, going along for the good cop/bitch cop ride even if she didn't know exactly where we were headed. "They lie to cover themselves. They lie to cover for someone they love."

"In your case," I added more caustically, "I think it's a little bit of both."

Ivy Duncan had grown quite still, but her eyes held a spark of anger I was curious to see if I could ignite into something more. I turned to address Billie. "And what's so sad is she continues to protect him. From my standpoint, he didn't do right by her. Siphoned off funds they'd worked years to amass, making a film no one wanted to buy, knowing he was about to die and saddle her with the debt. But that's the way it always is . . . men putting their interests ahead of their obligations to their wives."

"I don't have to sit here and let my husband's memory be insulted by the likes of you!" Ivy Duncan sat stock still, the hiss in her voice and the growing spark in her eyes the only thing letting me know I had struck a nerve. "You have no idea of what you're talking about, young lady!"

"Then maybe you should set her straight," Billie replied.

The old woman pursed her lips in disgust, then shivered slightly as if rousing herself to speak. "He didn't have to die like that," she began, her eyes cast downward. "We had talked it all out, and I had forgiven him."

"Forgiven him for what?" Billie asked.

Ivy Duncan's narrowed eyes fixed themselves on my face. "You already know."

"Pastor Henley gave me the general outline. But I have a feeling there are some things he left out."

"Not left out, Detective. Doesn't know." She reached into her pocket for a handkerchief, which she placed carefully in her lap. She toyed with it for a while, turning it this way and that, as if trying out which angle suited her best.

"About a year ago," she began, "a young man name Philippe Baptiste called me from the airport with a sob story that his mother had died the year before and he had come out here to be with his father. With Maynard. Philippe was only twenty-five at the time, so if he was Maynard's son, that meant . . ."

She dropped her head, took in an uneven breath. "I'd never seen my husband so upset," she whispered. "Tried to tell me at first the boy was lying, that he'd never slept with another woman. But when Philippe came to the house, he had pictures of himself and my husband in New York, starting when he was nineteen, the year he claimed his mother reestablished contact with my husband. And then there were pictures from trips to Paris and London, when Maynard took the boy when he did interviews for *Stormy Weather*."

Her head came up, her eyes full of bitter tears. "What was I supposed to do? Turn the boy out and have him take those pictures to the press? Of course, it marked the end of Maynard's and my relationship, such as it was." She was off the bed now, pacing about the room and dabbing furiously at her eyes. "Maynard never had—how do you young people put it?—the hots for me. Ours was more of an intellectual relationship. Oh, things were okay in the beginning, but later there wasn't time, what with his career or mine to consider."

She came up for air, looked directly at me. "I've searched my soul many a night after Philippe Baptiste disrupted our lives, and I think I know how it could have happened. If you will allow me to explain a little about the old days, Detective, I promise I won't try to bamboozle you. And it may help you understand."

She continued pacing about the room as if the activity would help her resurrect the story she felt compelled to tell. She paused at the bed, then turned and walked toward a bookcase of awards. "Back in the mid-fifties to early sixties, things started opening up for black actors. They were stepping out of the shadows, away from the Mammy and Stepin Fetchit roles. Dorothy Dandridge had gotten that Oscar nomination, and Sidney Poitier and Harry Belafonte were beginning to get substantial roles opposite white women for the first time. Maynard was getting acting jobs, too, but more important, the chance to be an assistant director on some major motion pictures being filmed back East and overseas. And even though the sleeping and eating accommodations were still segregated, there *was* intermingling between black and white."

She took one of the awards off the shelf, turned it slowly in her hands. "So, the more I thought about it, the more I could understand how Maynard, after months of those French hussies throwing themselves at him, could have been seduced by that girl. I could understand how she'd try to prolong the relationship by following him to the States, even try and trap him into marriage by throwing a baby up in his face."

I felt the blades of the fan above me, stirring up the stale air in the room. "Whose existence your husband hid from you all these years."

"Maynard knew me well enough to know that if I had learned the truth, I would have left him. Can you imagine the headlines ... Maynard Duncan, noted black filmmaker, divorced by his wife because of a knocked-up *white* girl? And if he had married her, it would have been the kiss of death at that point in his career, I don't care if she was a foreigner or not."

"But interracial marriages weren't unheard-of by that time," Billie blurted out, to my surprise. "Lena Horne had been married to a white man for some time by then. And Sammy Davis, Jr., and Sidney Poitier were married to white women, too."

"And Maynard always said none of them got the recognition they deserved afterward, too," Ivy Duncan replied. "You girls are too young to remember, but there was a time when keeping the races apart romantically was a big deal. Lena Horne had to sneak off to Paris back in 'forty-six to marry Lenny Hayton because of California's laws against mixed marriages. And a couple of years later the Hollywood gossip columnists almost *ruined* Dorothy Dandridge's career for just *dancing* with Anthony Quinn at an Actors Lab mixer, and he was half Mexican himself! So although the laws eventually changed, Maynard knew people's hearts and minds hadn't, even by the time this little French floozy came along."

Getting her back on track, I asked, "So how did this woman contact your husband after all those years?"

"Maynard said she showed up on a shoot he was on in New York, claiming she and the boy needed help. Of course, she timed it for just when Maynard was finally getting some recognition from his peers for all the years he struggled in this business. So he did the right thing—paid for the boy's schooling, but only through under-grad at NYU. That was their agreement back in 'eighty-six. But just before she died two years ago, Philippe's mother turned around and lied to the boy, told him Maynard wouldn't pay for his graduate schooling because he didn't believe he was really Philippe's father."

"Which brought the boy to your doorstep?"

Her eyes reflected the remembered pain of that first meeting, and it took her a moment before she could continue. "Soon as I saw him, I knew."

"The physical resemblance was that strong?"

"Not so much physically. My husband was dark-complected with dark eyes. Philippe's eyes were gray, and he had that sandy-colored hair and creamy complexion you see when the races mix. What made me see the connection was the way Philippe carried himself, the aloofness. It was like seeing Maynard all over again when he was young."

She dabbed at her eyes. "And in addition to the photos he had, he could quote dates Maynard had made trips to New York from the mid-eighties onward or had flown him out here. Time they'd spent together when I thought my husband was on location somewhere interviewing people or doing research for the documentary."

"You must have been devastated," Billie said softly.

"I'm not going to lie to you, I almost divorced him," she agreed, "but I prayed on it and, with counseling from Pastor Henley, finally found a way to forgive him." She sat back down on the bed, wiping away the last of her tears and balling up the handkerchief in her fist. "But sometimes I think that boy invading this house was the beginning of a nightmare that has never ended. That spring we learned Maynard had cancer, but he had the lung removed and underwent radiation and we thought we were home free. Then it spread to his spine and he had to undergo chemotherapy, which didn't help. Yet, through it all, Maynard always had his faith; I just can't accept he was so depressed that he would take his own life."

But she flatly denied her or her sister-in-law's involvement in her husband's death. "There's no way Del and I could live with ourselves if we did something like that. It's against everything we believe in as Christians, Detective Justice. I don't care if Maynard had begged us all day long, we wouldn't have helped him end his life."

Nor did she believe anyone else was involved, reasoning, "Alice Thomas was too much of a professional, and Pastor Henley would be the last person to break God's commandment."

I wondered whether she'd say the same thing if she knew

about the bequest to Peaceful Shepherd that was allegedly included in her husband's will, or whether she might be covering for her younger lover. "What about the staff in the house that day? Could either of them have been involved?"

She shook her head. "Otto and Maynard were very close. And Dolores?" She laughed derisively. "The woman can barely read or write English. How could she know enough to give my husband a morphine overdose?"

"What about Skip Sheffield?"

At the mention of his name, Ivy Duncan's nose crinkled as if she'd smelled something disagreeable. Her voice dropped an octave. "Skip Sheffield wanted my husband alive and working on that film. How could Maynard repay the money he owed Skip if he was dead?"

Billie and I exchanged a look. "Mr. Sheffield didn't mention your husband owing him any money," I said.

"That figures," she replied with a sneer. "In June, Skip Sheffield loaned my husband a considerable sum to finish postproduction work on *Stormy Weather*—a hundred thousand dollars. We wanted to make it an unsecured loan, but Sheffield insisted that we put up some collateral. Maynard didn't want to make him a producing partner in the documentary and there wasn't enough equity in Soulful Celebrations, so we had to pledge the house. It was foolish, I know, but Maynard said we had no other choice." She paused and took a deep breath. "The note was due on the first of this month. And if we didn't pay it off, Skip Sheffield could have either put a lien on the house and forced a sale or taken possession of the film."

It sounded like the kind of bargain a shark like Sheffield would strike. "But the first was yesterday. Had you or your husband talked to Sheffield about what he's going to do?"

"He's not *doing* anything," she proclaimed, a note of icy triumph in her voice. "Maynard came into some money just before he died. And while it's not a fortune, it's enough to get that nickel-slick Negro out of our lives once and for all."

In spite of the professional distance I had to keep, I couldn't help but think, *Good for you, Ivy.* "Does Mr. Sheffield know this?"

"He does now. I told him a few minutes ago that he'd have his principal plus interest as soon as I could write the check."

"What about Philippe Baptiste?" Billie asked. "Has he been around lately?"

Ivy Duncan turned her chilly gaze from me to my colleague. "Philippe moved out the beginning of this year."

"Why?" I asked.

"He'd come out here desperate to get into the business, and although Maynard introduced him to his friends, we weren't sufficiently 'in the mix,' as Philippe put it, to do him any good. Once Maynard was diagnosed with the cancer, Philippe started running with what he called a 'better' crowd, trying to establish his own contacts. It got to the point he wouldn't look for a real a job, just wanted to hang out until all hours 'networking.' When his behavior got more out of control, and valuables started disappearing around Christmas last year, I put my foot down, told Maynard no matter how he felt about Philippe, he had to go."

"And you haven't heard from him since?"

"They still stayed in touch until Philippe called here one night during the Uprising, talking crazy, demanding we give him twenty-five thousand dollars so he could support himself while he finished and registered with the Writers Guild a screenplay some producer wanted to option. When Maynard told him we didn't have the money, Philippe cursed him out and just dropped off the face of the earth. That hurt Maynard, I think, more than anything else. He truly loved that boy, tried to do the right thing by him."

I watched her face closely and asked: "Would doing right by Philippe include naming him in his will?"

And saw the coldness in her eyes intensify. "Since the day Philippe first showed up, Maynard had talked about making the boy a bequest in his will. But as things worsened for us financially and Philippe's behavior became more and more erratic, Pastor counseled Maynard that his primary obligation was to me and his sister. So although Maynard did change his will to leave Philippe something, a much smaller portion of the estate went to him than he was originally supposed to get."

I wondered if, in the will Dolores and Otto witnessed, that was still the case.

"Where did Mr. Duncan keep his will?"

"I haven't been able to find it, but why should that concern you?"

"Does the boy know of his father's death?"

She shook her head. "We don't know how to get in touch with him."

I wondered how hard she'd tried.

The toilet flushed in the bathroom next door, causing Ivy Duncan to lower her voice. "I'm truly sorry, Detective, I wasn't more forthcoming with you earlier," she whispered urgently, "but I couldn't be sure what you'd do with the information. Saddity society Negroes in this town—got their noses so far up in the air—think entertainers are all trash anyway. If the press had gotten wind of Philippe, they would have had it and gone. I didn't want that kind of thing tarnishing my husband's legacy, or what's left of my and Delphine's lives. Surely you understand that."

I studied the apprehensive woman before me, framed by shelves bulging with row after row of films and awards—the tangible, crowning achievements of her husband's barrier-breaking, creative life. I considered Ivy Duncan's thriving business and her fastidiously preserved clothes, the jewelry she wore like talismans and her expertly made-up face. Saw the pain-etched creases between her perfectly plucked brows, sensed what it was this beautiful but shallow woman feared. Humiliated by her husband's secret, could she take her place among L.A.'s black elite as the widow of a distinguished director and a success in her own right, or would she be seen merely as a done-wrong old juke joint singer, not fit to cater, much less attend, the political fund-raisers or A-list parties of my mother and her class-conscious friends?

But, as I excused her to get back to the repast, there was something else troubling me, a wisp of something that irritated me as persistently as corn silk trapped between my teeth. Interviewing Philippe Baptiste might help—if I could find him.

Billie closed the bedroom door behind Mrs. Duncan and

shook her head in disbelief. "Girl, the lives of the rich and famous are a mess, aren't they?"

"You sure seemed to be into it."

"Sorry." She shrugged and sat on the bed in Mrs. Duncan's spot. "I guess I did overdo it a bit with the Lena Horne comment. How much of this did you know?"

"Not as much as she thought I did. Pastor Henley made some vague comment about trying to undo some foolish notions of Maynard Duncan's before he passed, so given what Alice Thomas told us, I figured it must have had something to do with the will. I just pushed the right button. Mrs. Duncan spilled the beans herself."

"I can't ever imagine a woman like that telling even her pastor any of that mess."

"I can, if she was desperate enough to get the will changed before Duncan died."

"Did Henley say if the church was a beneficiary?"

"It is, but he claimed he never so much as peeked at the will to see the amount. And if you believe that wolf ticket, I've got some beachfront property in Watts I want to sell you."

Billie half-laughed. "Ain't that the truth!"

The blades of the fan cast slow-moving shadows in the room, making the patterned scarf around my neck flutter. "But I kept getting the feeling there's more shit in this game than what Mrs. Duncan is letting on."

"Like what?"

"Like Duncan's son, Philippe Baptiste. How could someone be that close to his father and then just up and disappear? Surely if he'd seen Duncan's obituary in the paper or heard it on the news, he would've shown up for the funeral. Especially if Mrs. Duncan's characterization was accurate and he thought there was some money to be had."

"So where do you think he could be?" Billie asked.

"At the rate he was going? On the streets or gone back to New York probably. But if he registered that screenplay, he ought to be traceable through the Writers Guild."

I made a few notes. "Then there's Mrs. Duncan herself. For one, she's lying about that will. I heard her tell you right outside her sister-in-law's bedroom that she only knew of one will, then she admitted to us later she knew about a later version. I wouldn't be surprised if she encouraged Pastor Henley to help her get her husband's son's portion reduced. And she knows where it is—she just doesn't want us to see her dirty work."

"You may be reading too much into the situation, Charlotte. Maybe she just said that because she thought her sister-in-law would overhear us from her bedroom."

"I think there's more to it than that. And there's a discrepancy about Duncan's last meal. Ivy Duncan specifically said her husband hadn't eaten all day, yet his minister and the housekeeper indicated he did."

"Maybe Mrs. Duncan just wasn't aware of whether he'd eaten or not."

"I don't think so. Amargosa was pretty adamant that Mrs. Duncan wanted to be sure her husband ate. So much so she had the woman take up some of that *coquito* Ivy made for him to drink. Ivy Duncan *wanted* him fed, and I'm betting there's something in her husband's stomach contents that will tell us why."

"You've really got a bee in your bonnet about Ivy Duncan, don't you?"

"I just know she had a lot to gain by her husband's death—revenge for his affair, not to mention stemming the outflow of funds from her bank account. You should have heard the woman going on when I met her about how much money they had spent on her husband's care. She was definitely counting her pennies."

"But if Ivy Duncan's hooked up for murder, her husband's life insurance wouldn't pay off, and the will would probably be contested by the other heirs, Philippe Baptiste included. She's got to be smart enough to know that."

I walked over to the window, looked out onto the quiet street below. "You'd think so, but you never know what people will do when pushed by greed or revenge. And we both know either one can be a good enough motive for murder." I turned back to face her. "What did Otto Randall have to say? Any problems getting him to cooperate?"

"Nah, he was afraid I'd eat up all the potstickers if he didn't."

Even with Billie's threats, Randall had had little to contribute to what we already knew. The Soulful Celebrations catering manager had arrived at nine and had seen Duncan only twice—once when he looked in on him when he first arrived and again when he was summoned upstairs to witness the will. Other than that he was in the kitchen with Ivy Duncan and Dolores Amargosa, in the backyard getting the chairs cleaned, or helping unload the provision truck. "Randall did say Duncan seemed pretty coherent when he signed the will," Billie noted as she handed over the prints.

"That's what Mrs. Amargosa said, too. We'll see what the autopsy shows." I looked at the single set of prints. "Where are Sheffield's?"

"He's already gone."

"He was upstairs just a minute ago."

"He must've slipped by me when I was in the head. Sorry."

"No biggie. I'll take care of it later."

Billie gathered up her purse, said, "I'd love to tag along with you if my plate wasn't so full," and burped. "I gotta get downtown to the courthouse," she added a little sheepishly. Let me know how everything turns out. Today was quite a floor show."

I remained behind in Duncan's sickroom, standing in a corner and waiting for the four walls surrounding me to reveal their secrets. But instead of them telling me what had happened in Maynard Duncan's last hours, I found Ivy Duncan's assessment of what had become of her passion for her husband echoing in my head.

Things were okay in the beginning, but later there wasn't time, what with his career or mine to consider. Maybe that's what drove them apart, drove Maynard Duncan into the arms of another woman, and set up the anger and hatred between them that led his wife to kill him.

But another thought struck me—Ivy Duncan could just as well have been talking about Aubrey and me. Hot and heavy at first, "things" had gotten downright frigid between us lately, and I wasn't entirely sure why. What was it that had Aubrey giving me the cold shoulder and me worrying over his every word?

The ceiling fan continued to circulate the stale air around me. I moved away from the windows, feeling colder than the rain outside warranted. I wandered over to the desk, saw some of the bits of pink paper nearby, and realized none of the pages from the script I'd taken into custody were pink. On closer examination, the bits of paper looked like they were from a FedEx multicopy shipping label. But Dolores hadn't mentioned Duncan sending a package, just receiving one.

I copied the tracking numbers from the blank FedEx shipping labels on the desk, then dropped to my knees to look under the desk, hoping to find the pink receipt from a package that may have been sent. But the crime scene techs had already been under there, had found Duncan's lighter under the desk. If a FedEx receipt had been there, surely it would have been collected, too.

I wandered over to the metal table on the other side of the doorway, but other than a note pad, I found nothing of any significance. Even the wastepaper basket was empty. I went to the bed, where my eye fell on the stack of newspapers below me. A few bits of that pink paper were there, too. I dropped to my knees to search for the receipt, but only found a videocassette, buried under the magazines, bearing the title *Stormy Weather: Black America's Turbulent Relationship with the Movies*. I smiled, sure my father and uncle would approve of that phrase.

Like a kid about to snoop in the closets for Christmas presents, I listened for voices on the other side of the door. Hearing none, I turned on the VCR and slid in the tape.

It started with Lena Horne, wearing that gorgeous, diaphanous gown from the movie and singing:

Don't know why
There's no sun up in the sky . . .

Lena's image faded into a montage of actors, restored to their proper glory. The bit actors in maid's or chauffeur's uniforms who would light up the screen for a nanosecond in some thirties screw-ball comedy or Charlie Chan mystery, the ones as a kid I'd follow off-camera with my eyes, thinking, *I want to go with her!* The black stars I knew and loved from television and the movies, dates at the Baldwin and drive-ins with my family, my father's business calendars and the Justice Family Film Nights. A montage of clips from dozens of musical shorts and full-length features—from *St. Louis Blues* to *Carmen Jones, Stormy Weather* to *Black Orpheus*—flashed across the screen along with heart-wrenching, Oscar-winning performances by Hattie and Sidney, Louis Gossett and Denzel Washington, too. And there was Sidney Poitier introducing clips of the dramas that made me proud to be black—*A Raisin in the Sun* and *Cooley High, Nothing but a Man* and *Malcolm X.* A little counter in the lower right corner, captioned "Episode One," ticked away the seconds that marked almost a century of black faces and fantasies. Faces of the women my father had made up and my uncle had costumed. The dream men Grandmama Cile swooned over and the ones I prayed as a teenager could maybe love a fat girl like me.

Excerpts from Episode Two featured an interview with Judith Jameson preceding clips of the dancers. Bill "Bojangles" Robinson dancing like a gentleman in top hat and tails and Katherine Dunham moving like a queen to a pseudo-African drumbeat. The Nicholas Brothers defying gravity and Del and Mo Giles burning up a soundstage, strutting their stuff and hoofing it up for all they were worth in musicals Hollywood would never make again.

What I saw of Duncan's documentary was magnificent. If no one else in the world saw *Stormy Weather,* it must have been of tremendous comfort to the dying director. If I had just played those few minutes over again and again, let the images overtake me, maybe I would have been comforted, too. I could have stayed in the fantasy world Maynard Duncan inhabited in his last days, a world where black people had dignity and pride, where no one pulled back the dirty curtain on the ugly side of life. But a veil of static descending over the screen intruded on my private Shangri-la, and the video moved on to show a side of Hollywood I didn't realize existed.

The third episode was called "Hidden Hollywood" and was the shortest. Lena's voiceover introduced the segment:

Life is bare,
Gloom and misery everywhere
Stormy weather . . .

But this time the images were of black rapists in D. W. Griffith's *Birth of a Nation,* and headlines from the first of what would become a series of NAACP protest campaigns. Then the segment moved on to an offensive thirties cartoon called *Coal Black and the Seben Dwarves* and even a stereotypical black character from what looked like Walt Disney's *Fantasia* who must have been cut from the version I saw as a child. Black maids bucking their eyes, black men dancing like fools in movies I otherwise loved. And there were newspaper headlines bemoaning the tragic deaths of Dorothy Dandridge and Stepin Fetchit, and the equally sad deaths of other black actors and directors I never knew.

Then Maynard Duncan himself appeared on the screen, in an interview that evidently had been shot in this very room. The film quality was horrible and the sound was practically nonexistent. Duncan looked drawn and frail, but his eyes burned with a passion that practically leaped off the screen, and his hands moved about freely as he talked. I understood what Alice Thomas had meant when she spoke of his lust for life and desire to finish his film. This was not the face of a man who committed suicide.

I had just ejected the tape from the machine and slipped it into my purse to take to the office when my pager started vibrating at my side.

T W O   B I R D S
W I T H   O N E
S T O N E

It was Cortez, relaying a message from Wozniak in Latent Prints. "That partial on the morphine pump's keypad belongs to Alice Thomas. Matched a right index fingerprint taken when she applied for her nursing license."

"What about the other prints he lifted from the house? Any of them found near the drugs or on the pump?"

"Nothing yet. But he's still working on it."

"Well, tell him I'm dropping off a couple more sets of elimination prints for him."

I proceeded to fill Cortez in on my interviews at the Duncan house. She listened politely, but seemed distracted. "What's wrong, Cortez?"

"Steve talked to the manufacturer's rep from the company that makes the pump. He had her come up from Irvine to verify how the thing was programmed. She says the machine was programmed at twice the level for a man the size of our vic."

"But, based on the info I got from Dr. Reynolds, that could be perfectly normal for a patient in the advanced stages of cancer."

"Well, it got Steve's attention to the extent he called Mark Ikehara. They're interviewing Thomas now."

"How the hell did Firestone get in the middle of this? I told you we were to report directly to Lieutenant Stobaugh on this one."

"Steve said he was just pitching in to help with the rep," she explained, the weariness in her voice coming through the wire. "But after he heard the results from Woz, he went to the lieutenant himself."

"But we expected the print to be Thomas's. She was the only one at the scene who should've had a key. So, without the medical records to confirm the dosage the doctor prescribed, that alone shouldn't be enough to have Firestone and Ike sweating the woman."

"I think with the other evidence we found at the scene, Steve and Ikehara felt they had enough of a profile on Thomas to move ahead."

"Hold up! You mean to tell me you *showed* him the books and stuff we got from Thomas's apartment before we even had a chance to evaluate it *ourselves?*"

"Don't go getting all loud with me." Cortez's tone was uncharacteristically abrupt. "What could I do, once Ikehara came over here and started breathing down everybody's neck?"

"Tell him to step off, for one thing."

"Just get down here as fast as you can, okay? Steve says he's got something for us."

"Fine," I replied, trying to get my anger in check. "In the meantime, I need you to call FedEx on a package they delivered to Maynard Duncan's house last Tuesday." I gave her the tracking numbers I had copied from the blank FedEx labels in Duncan's room. "There may also have been a package sent from the house, with an airbill number somewhere within those sequences. If so, I want to know where it was going. And try to keep Firestone and Ikehara out of this until I can get there, okay?"

Cortez hung up without a word.

Even though I swung by Pastor Henley's church to pick up a copy of the proxy statement Duncan had signed for the Still We Rise board meeting, it only took me half an hour to get to the

PAB. Ikehara and Firestone were still interrogating Thomas, "not to be disturbed," so I killed some time making copies of the proxy for our use in the investigation and then booking it and the video-tape I'd taken from the house into evidence. Then I made another detour to give Amargosa's and Randall's print cards to Wozniak. But I still ended up summarizing my notes into the Duncan murder book for almost an hour before I finally saw Steve Firestone emerging from the interview room with the unliked Ike. The senior deputy DA was wreathed in smiles, as if he'd just won the lottery. Or hooked up a high-profile suspect for murder.

"What are you two up to?"

"What do you mean?" Firestone asked, looking like a kid with his hand caught in the cookie jar.

"For one thing," I said to Firestone, "you're all over a case you didn't have time for two days ago." I turned to Ikehara. "And here you are this afternoon, interrogating Thomas, when you couldn't even meet us for the search of her apartment this morning!"

Ikehara's face flushed. "Some things have changed since then."

"What things?"

"We're developing a profile on her," Ikehara explained. "She's a highly intelligent but passive white woman, raised in some mountainman redneck town, enraged over the failure of her marriage, lack of job opportunities, fixated on old films. Whether she was in this with Clemenza or not, a black director like Duncan's success may have represented an insult to her psyche so profound that killing him became the only way to regain control over her life."

I looked at Firestone. "Did he get this from some course he took at Quantico or is he making it up as he goes along?"

"We've got this under control, Justice." Ikehara smiled conde-scendingly. "We don't need to call in the FBI."

"So she confessed?"

Firestone raised a hand to calm me down. "Not yet."

Ikehara held up a well-manicured thumb and index finger. "But we're *that* close."

"Her lawyer cut you short?"

"She hasn't asked for one yet." Firestone exchanged a smug look with the senior deputy DA.

"We told her she's only helping us in hooking up the minister," Ikehara explained, looking quite pleased with himself.

"Smooth move, Ike." It was a tactic I'd used myself in interrogations—enlisting a suspect's "help" in determining a killer's method in the hope he would incriminate himself in the process—but somehow the thought of these two pulling it on my case left a bad taste in my mouth. "You ask her about the dosage of morphine programmed into the pump?"

"Not yet," Firestone replied. "Ikehara here doesn't want to scare her into demanding an attorney just yet."

"Well, you would have embarrassed yourselves if you had," I replied. "Reynolds said on Monday that twice the dosage wouldn't be enough to kill someone accustomed to taking morphine. And without Duncan's chart, you don't even know what her doctor prescribed. So I wouldn't be so quick to hook her up just yet."

Firestone shot Ikehara an uneasy look. "She's got a point, Mark."

Ikehara's jaw clenched and unclenched slowly. "Fine. Cut her loose for now. Better to let her think we're looking in another direction while we dig into her background, check out the medical record on this vic and all her other cases plus the ones she and Clemenza worked together." Ikehara shook Firestone's hand. "Call us if you run into any trouble with the warrants."

Raking his fingers through his mass of kinked curls, Firestone watched Ikehara's retreating form. "He's really balls to the wall on this one," he said, half to himself. "Nice way to jump-start a career."

I cleared my throat. "Can we talk?"

Firestone seemed almost surprised by my presence. "Sure, Justice." He led me to his desk while he went to get some coffee. "You want something?"

"Tea's fine," I said, surprised he would even ask.

He returned with two Styrofoam cups and a tea bag. "Good work on the Thomas search." He looked up at me and drew his lips back over his gums in what was a fairly good imitation of a smile.

It was an expression I rarely saw on Steve Firestone's face. I felt reluctant to upset this rare moment of peace, even though I was mad enough to spit nails over the stunt he'd pulled with Ikehara. I took a calming breath before saying, "I know the evidence is pointing to Thomas, but I'm not so willing to draw a conclusion just yet."

He slurped at his coffee. "Why not?"

"Well, when I talked to Dr. Reynolds over at the morgue, she indicated the dosage would have to be maybe four times over the rate prescribed to kill a man who'd built up as much of a tolerance for narcotics as Duncan." Seeing the blank look on his face, I asked, "Have you had a chance to read the murder book Neidisch over at Wilshire put together?"

"Not yet," he admitted a little uneasily.

"Well, you should. According to his wife, he'd been taking oral narcotics for pain for months. Medicine cabinet full of Demerol, Vicodin, that kind of stuff. His doctor had just recently put him on that IV pump so he could control his own dosage."

"So he was shooting up, like a junkie?"

"That's probably overstating it, but you've got the general idea. Point is, who knows what all he had in his bloodstream? And if the rep from the pump manufacturer says the dosage programmed into pump was only twice the normal level, according to Dr. Reynolds, that alone shouldn't have been enough to kill him. His nurse would know that."

I flipped through my notes, bringing him up to speed on the other interviews, the unaccounted-for prints found in Duncan's sickroom, trying as I explained to make him see the murderer could have been Duncan's wife, his pastor, even his yet-to-be-found son. "There are just a lot of unanswered questions in my mind."

"So what are you suggesting?" he demanded, his voice edged with sarcasm. "That we halt our investigation of our primary suspect while you go chasing down leads on vengeful wives, greedy preachers, and missing heirs?"

"Of course not, but I think we should examine all of the evidence collected, dig a little deeper into everybody's backgrounds and verify their alibis and motives, before you and Ikehara go tooth and nail after Alice Thomas."

Firestone's benevolent smile returned. "Look, Justice," he said, his tone more conciliatory. "I know you're gung ho about other possibilities, but you uncovered some facts that I think are significant—Clemenza had been in communication with Thomas, she's heavily into reading books on dying and assisted suicide, and then there's her oddball religious practice."

"You mean the altar in her bedroom? There are millions of Buddhists in the world, Steve."

His smile dimmed a little. "Sorry, I didn't mean to insult your religion, Justice." As the hairs on my neck stood on end, he added, "We do know from the housekeeper that this Thomas woman encouraged Duncan to change his will and a few hours after he signs it, he's histo." He returned his attention to his paperwork. "And I have a feeling that will is going to shed even more light on her motives."

I saw an opening and ran for it. "I agree. I'll call Duncan's attorney right now, go over and pick it up. And if it doesn't shed any light on Thomas's motives, it'll certainly tell us how big a stake his pastor had in Duncan's death. Plus, I need to call the coroner's office to find out the time for the autopsy tomorrow."

Firestone held up his hand. "Before you go charging off, I've something much more urgent for you." Head still down while he combed through the pile of papers, he said, "Lieutenant Stobaugh seems to think I've been keeping you too much under wraps on the Home Invasion Task Force." His voice took on a forced casualness as he looked up at me, his smile fainter this time. "Maybe I *have* been keeping you buried in the office and not giving you a chance to do enough fieldwork," he admitted. "After all, look what you came up with on the Thomas search—a great lead in the case. . . ."

I was momentarily struck dumb. Firestone had never admitted he was wrong in his behavior toward me in the four years I'd been in RHD. "Ah, here it is." He indicated a bunch of computerized sheets, saying, "Let's see what you can do with this."

I frowned at the stack of papers. "What's this got to do with Duncan?"

"Nothing. It's the lead I've been developing on the home invasion cases, specifically the murder that went down in Pacific Palisades. Seems some ghetto Galahad was dropping off his girl-friend at her house in the Highlands and witnessed a seventies Toyota Celica, gold with California plates, peeling off from a drive-way a few doors down. Same house, same night an elderly couple were bludgeoned to death."

"That was six weeks ago. Why didn't this wit come forward sooner?"

"Had a bad auto accident on his way back home," Firestone explained hurriedly. "Was laid up in a coma at UCLA. He didn't hear about the murders till he got home, caught one of the news bulletins one night, and remembered seeing the car. But he and the girlfriend were afraid to come forward. His mother was the one who tipped us." He barked out an odd-sounding laugh. "Seems the girl's parents don't know their honor student's been swinging from the rafters with Mandingo."

I breathed deeply, tried to ignore the racial slur from a man who was half black himself. "And the printout is?"

"Results of the ten twenty-eight request I made to the DMV. A list of seventies-era Toyota Celicas in Los Angeles County. One of these cars belongs to the killers of that couple in the Palisades.

"So I want you and Gena to go to the wit's house with one of the model books. If you can get him to narrow down the year on the Toyota from the grille or tailgate configuration, then you can winnow down this list and run some license plates by him, see if that'll jog his memory. If not, we'll put a couple of teams of uni-forms on the plates and narrow it down to the most likely suspects that way. This is the best lead we've had in months in catching this gang, and I want you two on it right away."

"Why don't we just have this kid come in instead of schlep-ping all this stuff to him?"

"Got no choice there." He sipped his coffee again, and

shrugged. "He's immobilized at home, in a full body cast. You'll have to go to him."

"But what about the Duncan case? You have no right to pull me off when I'm beginning to make some headway. I report directly to Lieutenant Stobaugh on this one!"

"Not anymore. Stobaugh asked me to step in as team leader. I'm putting a joint team together now with us and some guys from the DA's Serial Crimes Unit." Firestone saw the storm brewing on my face and waved his hand in dismissal. "Nobody's trying to cut you out of the case, Charlotte. You did good work bringing us to this point."

"Why are you doing this, Steve? You know as well as I do the Duncan case may not have anything to do with Clemenza."

Ignoring me, he continued, "When you and Gena get back from down south, you can pick up the will and start preparing the search warrants for the medical records of Thomas's other cases so we can see if any of those other deaths seem suspicious." He twisted his mouth and added, "That is, if you don't mind doing the paperwork."

I grabbed my cup, sloshing tea onto my scarf. "I never said I objected to paperwork. I just don't want to be riding the paper all the time."

He smiled again. "There's probably going to be a lot of fol-low-up work on this case, Justice. You'll *still* be an integral part of the team, all right?"

I reached for a napkin to blot the tea stain on my scarf. "Then let me work up the warrants for Thomas's patients' medical records, get a lead on the whereabouts of the Baptiste boy, go and pick up the will from the attorney, maybe even re-interview Duncan's pastor—"

"There's just no winning with you, is there, Justice?" he said in exasperation. "I give you the primary responsibility of keeping the paper on the biggest case of our careers, and you complain about not doing more fieldwork. So I give you important field-work, and you want to sit here and do paperwork!"

"The Duncan case is important!"

"Important to whom, Justice?" His hazel eyes narrowed as he studied my face. "Look at you. I warned you from the get-go that you'd get so caught up with those Hollywood types that you wouldn't be able to maintain your objectivity."

"That's ridiculous!" I insisted, feeling the barb nonetheless. "I'm just saying Gena can handle interviewing this kid without me. Let her take one of the uniforms with her."

"Well, she's not, 'cause you're going with her. Like it or not, Gena Cortez is part of our team. Ever since we've been experimenting with this three-person-team concept, she's been up under me because the two of you have some kind of female thing going on that I don't even *pretend* to understand. But I'm not her baby-sitter. She's been out of the office a week, she needs to get back in the loop, and all I ask is that you go with her on this call. Am I being unreasonable, or do we have to take this to Stobaugh?"

"Of course not," I mumbled.

"Good. You go down south with Gena," he repeated, sliding the printout my way. "You bond, you map out a plan of attack on the Duncan case, you deal with this kid. We kill two birds with one stone."

And dismissed me with another rare smile.

As I went to find Cortez, I thought, *That's three birds, you nitwit.*

CHAPTER 12

THE MEXICAN
SPITFIRE

Cortez was about as happy with our change of plans as I was, even happier to be stuck with carrying the printout and metal binder that held photos and catalogs of Toyotas dating back to Woodstock. "What's going to happen to the Duncan investigation?" she asked as we got into the elevator.

I balled up my stained scarf and shoved it in my pocket. "Firestone's taking it over himself. And he's pulling in Ikehara's Serial Crimes Unit to assist us in building a case against Alice Thomas."

"What about the legwork we still need to do on the FedEx package, the will, Philippe Baptiste?"

We emerged at the lobby level and headed outside. "Oh, I'm sure he'll let us squeeze that in between reviewing hundreds of patients' medical records."

"It's not my fault he picked up the phone while we were out," she said, her voice rising an octave.

"You could have told him to back off. I would have."

"I guess I'm not as assertive as the fabled Detective Justice."

The car door opened, I paused to ask: "Did you say something to Firestone about us not getting along?"

"I didn't *intend* to say anything to him," she mumbled as she put the paperwork in the backseat and got in. "It just came up."

"Came up *when?*" I started the car and eased out of the lot, unwilling to trust myself to say more. I was silent until we were headed south on the Harbor Freeway. "What is it with you, Cortez? Do you have no sense of loyalty to your partner whatsoever?"

"*Partner?*" She whipped around to confront me, dark eyes flashing lightning in her pallid face. "You've got your nerve! When I first came into this department, I was scared shitless. There I was, only four years a detective, a year in Homicide at South Bureau before being called up to RHD, the big leagues. The first Latina in the department, a credit to *la raza,* but all the while I was hearing whispers in the hallways that all *el jefe* wanted to do was have a little more 'color' around the PAB when the press came calling. Like I didn't earn this spot by busting my ass all that time!"

There was an edge in Cortez's voice I'd never heard before.

"So there I was, all by myself, the Latina token. And the detective I looked forward to working with the most, the one who broke the glass ceiling for females of all colors in RHD, turns out to have more walls and barbed wire built around herself than a federal pen, and not an ounce of sympathy for a sister detective from her old stomping grounds!" She snorted derisively. "Hell, after that first case we worked, you even stopped calling me by my first name!"

"That's not true!" I protested, quickly replaying my words and thoughts to see if it was. "I call everybody I work with by their last name! Most cops do."

"But you're not most cops. And you *don't* do it with Billie Truesdale," she replied a little petulantly. "Or is that because she's black and I'm not?"

I could feel the fire rising in my cheeks. "This is not a black/Latino thing, and you know it! And you can say what you want now, but you never did come correct to me when you first arrived in RHD, never did treat me with any of that sisterhood you're talking about. And you didn't exactly show yourself to be a model of partnership on our first case together, either!"

"As if having your back on the street during that riot wasn't enough!" she shot back. "And if you dare mention the *one* report I ever wrote that wasn't one hundred percent in agreement with yours, I'll get out of this car right now!"

She put her hand on the door handle. And pulled.

"Shit!" I grabbed her arm to pull her away from the open door, swerving out of my lane and almost sideswiping a truck on my right. I slowed down enough for her to be able to close the door. "What's wrong with you? You trying to live up to that Mexican spitfire rep you were talking about this morning?"

Gena Cortez was trembling, but she had not lost her grip on the door handle. She turned to face me. "I'm just tired of being pressured to fit in, tired of getting second-guessed or screwed by everyone I turn to for support."

I'd often felt the same way myself, but had never shared those feelings outside of a few close associates and family members, the female in this car not among them. We rode along in silence for several miles. It wasn't until we'd gotten off the freeway at Century Boulevard and gone several more blocks that I reached out and touched her arm again, more gently this time. "Look, Cort—Gena, I'm sorry we got off on the wrong foot. But if the job is getting next to you, if you need to talk . . ."

She brushed my hand away. "Forget it. We're here."

We had pulled up to a run-down California bungalow on Ninety-fifth Street near Avalon. It was painted a halfhearted green, peeling paint revealing gold and Pepto-Bismol pink colors underneath. There was a larger bay window on the left—which I assumed was the living room—and a smaller window for what must be a bedroom. Black burglar bars adorned them both and were visible on one side of the house as well. Positioned in the front yard were three cars in various states of disrepair, a zigzag of rusted lightning. "You sure this is the address?"

"I wrote it down just the way Firestone gave it to me."

"Just checking." I held up my hands in mock surrender, then got out of the car and stood in the middle of the potholed, practically deserted street. "Man, I remember when this neighborhood used to get down with Christmas decorations for the holidays. This whole block'd be nothing but lights, fake snow, Nativity scenes, the whole nine. My parents used to drive us through here when I was little, just to sightsee."

Gena shifted the printout and metal-bound binder to one hip. "The Three Wise Men are looking just a little tired," she said, gesturing to the rusted car bodies in the yard.

We walked around the cars, kicking aside the occasional forty-ounce bottle as we went. "Kinda reminds me of my old neighborhood in East L.A.," Gena noted, a twinge of sadness in her voice.

"And look how well you turned out," I replied.

She cut her eyes at me, then realized I meant it as a compliment, and gave me a wary half-smile.

It was four when we approached the house, me first, Gena bringing up the rear, the binder and printout securely under her right arm. "Does the boy—what's his name—know we're coming?"

Gena moved to my left and read from her notes. "Demarcus Tolliver. Firestone said he called the house in advance to tell the boy's mother to expect us."

"And the mother's name?"

"Bernita Tolliver."

"Nice to see Mrs. Tolliver tidied up for us," I joked, gesturing at the yard.

We made our way past an overgrown holly bush on the right and gingerly stepped up onto the falling-down porch. The heavy-gauge metal of the screen door made a hollow sound as I knocked.

"Who is it?" a young-sounding male voice called out.

"Who the fuck you got coming up in here, man?" said another male voice, low and suspicious, from behind the door.

Something in that voice made me reach for my holstered gun and step to the right of the door. I motioned Gena to do the same on the other side, saw her turn away as she struggled to get her gun hand free.

"Who is it?" the higher-pitched voice repeated, this time a little louder.

Gena, her back to me, still wasn't in position.

"Fuck it, man," the other one said, agitated now. "What you want?" he yelled, his voice moving away from the door.

Fear swelled my tongue, making it hard for me to speak. I swallowed hard and said, "Demarcus Tolliver? LAPD, Detectives Justice and Cortez. Your mother thinks you might be able to help us with a case—"

"That crackhead ho' mama of yours ratted us out!" the deeper-voiced one yelled.

Then I heard it—the unmistakable sound of the slide on a semiautomatic, coming from my left. "Gun!" was all I had time to yell before my voice was drowned out by the blast through the living-room window.

Gena stumbled backward across the doorway toward me. Together we dove off the porch, into the holly bush. My heart in my mouth, I slammed past the scratchy leaves and pressed my body against the foundation of the house, my head doing close to a three-sixty, looking all around us for signs of any other assailants.

I tightened my grip on my gun, my mind and heart racing. What in the hell had just happened? Was I going to go down like this? I looked around, saw nothing coming at us from any direction. I tried to remember the psalm I used to carry in my wallet for protection. *Unto thee I cry, oh God my rock . . . Those aren't the right words say anything, just pray, Baby Girl, pray. . . . Please please God let me live long enough to solve the Duncan case and tell Aubrey how sorry I am for ever doubting him and please God let me live long enough to get things straight with my mother and please God give me another chance to be the kind of partner to Gena I'd want her to be to me and please God . . .*

I filled my lungs and tried to still my mind. Listened for sounds inside the house. My blood pulsing in my ears and my own ragged exhalation were the only sounds I could hear.

It was then that my mind froze, discarding all but the most important information.

I could hear my own breathing, but not my partner's.

Gena was still on her back, tangled in the holly bush. Still clutching in her left arm a piece of that computer printout and the metal-clad binder. An ominous-looking hole penetrated the latter. Blood coming from her side and her left cheek. I felt her neck for a pulse, found a faint irregular beat beneath my fingers. I dug my scarf out of my pocket, pressed it to the wound in her side.

She was still alive, but I had no way of knowing how long she could last trapped out here. My impulse was to move her, but I knew doing so might worsen her condition. But I couldn't leave her there, a sitting duck for these shitheads. "Gena?" I rasped. "Gena? You all right?"

Her eyes fluttered open. Her right hand moved aimlessly in the direction of her left side. Her eyes were glazed and her left cheek was badly scratched. "I couldn't get . . . I couldn't get to my . . . what happened?"

"I don't know, but we've got to get to some cover. Can you make it over to those old cars?"

"I don't have much choice, do I?"

I helped her up, my head under her right arm. Together we struggled until we made it behind the rear fender of the closest car. Safe. We crouched in the car's empty wheel well, me checking in all directions for shooters. Ninety-fifth Street was completely empty. Neighbors crouching in their bathtubs for protection, no doubt. Had they had the presence of mind to call the police once they were out of harm's way?

I held Gena's cold hand in mine and looked her hard in the eyes. "I'm going to radio for some help. Can you cover for me?"

"Like I said," she replied, this time with more of a wince than a smile, "I've got no choice."

A tinkling of glass came from the house. I peeped through the car's broken windows in time to see the barrel of a semiautomatic being used to break out the rest of the glass in the living-room window. A curtain moved at the bedroom window. Behind me the other two cars stood like sentries, blocking easy access to my car and radio.

There were at least two of them, one of them armed for sure, probably better than we were. My partner was down, maybe seriously injured, and we were trapped like two dogs in a pen. If I kept low to the ground and moved in an erratic pattern, I might be able to get to our car and call for help without drawing any fire.

Might. What if I didn't? *Stop it, Baby Girl, just breathe.*

I leaned over and whispered to Gena, "Can you get a bead on the bay window? I think he's our main concern."

"No problemo," she said, but her Beretta shook like a leaf in her hand, whether from panic or pain I couldn't tell.

I put my hand lightly on her shoulder. "You can do this, Gena. On my signal." I moved to the car's rear bumper, crouching down, slowly easing backward. *O Lord, my rock.* When I gave her the hand signal, she hauled herself up to peek through the car's broken window at the shooter on the left. When she was in position, she nodded readiness.

I counted to three, offered up one last prayer, and ran backward, drawing fire from the living room. Bullets whizzed by me, pitting one car near my shoulder, another somewhere too close to my knee. Gena and I returned fire in the direction of the bay window. Where was the other shooter? Dead?

I heard bullets pinging off metal as I scrambled around the next car's fender, and the next, until I was on the street and safely behind our car. Still crouching, I opened the door, switched to the Southeast Division's freek, and pulled the receiver of the radio out with me behind the front wheel. "Officers need help. I repeat, officers need help," I yelled to the RTO. "I've got shots fired and an officer down, repeat, officer down!"

The radio telephone operator was cool, getting our exact location, the potential number of assailants, and their location in the house, reassuring me all the while that help was already on the way. I tried to get back to Gena, but was pinned down by shots fired from the house.

It seemed like forever but it couldn't have been more than two minutes before more black-and-whites rolled up than you could shake a stick at. Among the officers was Mike Cooper, a wisecracking CRASH detective I'd worked with from South

Bureau on gang cases and his partner, followed close on by a sergeant. They wasted no time in sealing off the area and calling out to Demarcus and his buddy to come out. When they got more shots fired at them in response, the order went out for six of our guys to pepper open windows with tear gas canisters.

It took only a minute before the two assailants threw out their weapons and emerged with their hands on their heads. I saw blood tricking from a wound in one of the suspect's legs. As the uniforms closed in to make the arrests and sweep the interior, I raced to Gena—who'd taken cover on the ground during the gun-fire—realizing in midflight that neither of the young men standing on that porch was wearing a full body cast as Firestone had led me to believe.

Cooper and his partner got to Gena before I did. When Cooper realized it was Gena and me, he muttered something under his breath I didn't quite catch. But snide remarks aside, he ordered his partner to get the paramedics from down the street while I continued to apply pressure to her side, using my scarf.

"You're gonna be fine, Gena, just fine," I said a little too loud-ly. She nodded, face paler than ever, eyes shutting back the tears. "You hear me?" I felt as if I was shouting through water. "Just fine!"

We walked to the ambulance, watched them close the door and pull away. It wasn't ten seconds before Cooper turned to me, all up in my face. "Just because the new chief disbanded the Gang Task Force is no reason to send a couple of Red Hot Dogs down here like Annie Oakley!" he thundered, his small eyes flashing. "Why would you two come down here half-cocked instead of letting us coordinate back up with Southeast Division like we'd discussed?"

"'Discussed'?" I could feel the hairs on the back of my neck rising for the third time that day. "What the hell are you talking about, Mike?"

When he calmed down enough to explain, I felt like a storm cloud had passed over my head, momentarily letting in the light. I could see what was now a crime scene, see the significance behind the troubled look on Mike Cooper's face, and see the meaning of the bloody scarf in my hand. "You're absolutely sure about this, Mike?"

"Why the hell wouldn't I be?" he snapped.

But then the clouds massed again as we were separated by the newly arrived watch commander, a black lieutenant named Stallings, who had us wait in apprehensive silence along with the other officers on the scene until the three-person Officer-Involved Shooting team pulled up in separate unmarked cars.

Although they were a part of RHD, and therefore reported to Captain MIA, everyone knew the Officer-Involved Shooting team really served the chief of police, circumventing the regular chain of command to report directly to him on any officer-involved shootings or uses of force. And while some critics of the department derisively called them the chief's lapdogs, I knew and had to give props to the sensitive role the OIS team played—even though being in their presence in a professional capacity scared me half to death.

Not everyone, though, respected their work. Ever since Eulia Love, a black woman who was shot by LAPD officers back in 1979 over an unpaid gas bill, there'd been persistent allegations of police brutality heaped on the department, too many of them deemed regrettably true. And OIS was increasingly seen as part of the problem, not the solution. Even Amnesty International had gotten into the act, issuing a report on human rights violations by the LAPD against the citizens of the city, as if atrocities in Haiti and Rwanda weren't keeping them busy enough.

All of which only put more pressure on the chief to ensure that every deadly use of force was appropriate and within procedure. Hence the three-person OIS team's timely arrival at Demarcus Tolliver's house.

Hence my fear.

The OIS team moved quickly, a D-III named John Davenport establishing control of the crime scene while a second detective named Banks began to catalog and photograph the evidence around the house. The third member of the team was another D-II named Marie Grundzien, who transported us to the Southeast Division while her partners processed the scene. I was installed in the empty watch commander's office, where I filled out reams of required paperwork, plotted revenge, and threw up twice in the bathroom.

Then, about half an hour later, it was back to the scene, to walk through each step we took, review each shot we fired, while Grundzien and Banks took copious notes and more pictures from my vantage point. We returned again to Southeast for a formal, tape-recorded interview—them probing for tactical errors, procedural missteps, and excessive uses of force, me trying to keep them focused strictly on the shooting and not on the whos, hows, and whys of Gena's and my being sent out there in the first place.

When they finally let me go—revealing little about the report they would make to the chief but admonishing me not to discuss the shooting with anyone—I headed in fury to the hospital, knowing my partner and I had something even more important than Demarcus Tolliver and Ninety-fifth Street to discuss.

CHAPTER 13

BREAKING
THE CODE

Aubrey once said every major city has one—the usually large, usually county-run, usually woefully underfunded hospital that catches the fallout from man's innate desire to stab and shoot his fellow man. In L.A., it was Killer King—aka Martin Luther King, Jr., Medical Center—nicknamed for its poor patient survival statistics, brought on, no doubt, by the number of gunshot wounds and assorted physical mayhem it treated on a daily basis.

But according to Mike Cooper, the Killer King staff, led by a chief resident named DiStefano, hopped to it when they realized an ambulance was bringing in a cop, hustling Gena into a major trauma room and getting to work right away.

But there'd been little word from Dr. DiStefano, Cooper informed me, after Gena had been brought in, causing the sea of blue churning about in the emergency waiting room and hallways—the extended LAPD family of colleagues and well-wishers that always showed up whenever they heard a cop had been shot—to get restless.

"Let me try something," I suggested, and stepped a few feet away from the crowd to call Aubrey.

The receptionist at his office put me right though. After I

explained where I was and why, he said, "It's not one of our con-
tracts, so I don't know anyone down there personally, but I can
make a couple of calls."

"Would you?"

"Sure. Who's the chief resident?" I heard him take down the
name I gave him, then pause on the line. "What about you, Char?
You don't sound so good."

My hand went to the scratches on my face. "I'm fine," I insisted, and hid my trembling hand in my pocket.

"What happened?"

I whispered a brief synopsis of what had happened on
Ninety-fifth Street. "If he'd had his way, we'd both be dead now."

"Who?"

Just then Mike Cooper arrived with a cup of hot tea. I nodded thanks, whispered to Aubrey, "I gotta go."

I heard a drawer slam on the other end of the line. "Look, I'm
coming down there—"

"No. It's rush hour, it'd take you forever. I've got to call in
anyway, talk to my lieutenant."

There was a long silence on the phone, then Aubrey's muffled
voice: "You want me to call Matt and Joymarie?"

"And have my mother down here raising sand about me
leaving the department? I don't think so!"

"What can I do then?" His voice filled with exasperation.

"Why don't you call your high school running buddy?"

God love him, Aubrey picked up my coded talk right away.
"You want me to call Perris. And tell him what?"

An Asian woman in blood-spattered scrubs, her cherub face
grave, came around the corner, and mouthed, *Are you Detective
Justice?* Her badge read *Dr. J. DiStefano.* I nodded and she
motioned me to come with her. "I gotta go, Aubrey. The doctor is
signaling me. Tell your friend I'll be available by cell phone in half
an hour."

"Okay, but call me when you're done, you hear?" he shouted.
"Better yet, why don't you come by later? I want to check you out
for myself."

A smile crept to my lips. "Okay."

"Hurry up," he said. "I love you."

I hung up the phone—surprised at Aubrey's admission but grateful that the snit he had been in last night had blown over—and fell in behind the doctor's retreating form.

Dr. DiStefano led me through a knot of uniformed officers, from both the sheriff's department and the LAPD, until we came to one imposing young bull blocking the door, his buzz cut sharp enough to cut glass. "Detective Davenport doesn't want any LAPD personnel talking to Detective Cortez until he's had a chance to interview her," he informed Dr. DiStefano, his voice gruff.

"Bullshit!" Dr. DiStefano shot back, and stood on tiptoe to point at his chest. "I've got to calm my patient down, and she won't until she can see for herself that her partner is okay. Do you want to be responsible for losing that detective in there?"

"After thirteen years on the job, I think I know the drill, Officer . . . Walters," I added, glancing at his name badge. "Keep it light, no talking about the shooting." I spread my arms wide in invitation. "You can listen in if you want."

Walters backed down and let us pass. "Your partner said I might have to get rough to get you by the deputy," DiStefano whispered once we had closed the door. "Did I do a good job?"

"You did just fine," I whispered back.

Inside, a nurse stood by helplessly while Gena tried to sit up on a gurney. "I gotta get out of here," she insisted, struggling up on an elbow.

"Can you talk to her?" Dr. DiStefano pleaded. "She wants to leave."

"You said it was just a superficial wound," Gena protested.

"I'd still prefer to keep you a few hours for observation," the doctor reasoned.

"No way, nohow. I'm outta here." She looked to me for confirmation. "Right?"

"I don't know, Gena. If the doctor thinks you should stay—"

"Where are my clothes?" She made a vague motion with her left hand, winced from the effort.

"Give us a minute?" I asked Dr. DiStefano.

"I'll give you ten if you can talk some sense into her." She motioned to the nurse, who followed her out of the room.

I stood at the edge of the gurney, blocking the door. "The OIS team's gonna be here any minute. Talk to me, Gena."

Tears had accumulated in my partner's eyes but did not fall. "You know what happened?"

"I know we got pulled off the Duncan case and almost got killed for our trouble, but I'm not sure why."

She sat with a pained expression on her face, as if trying to sort out what to say. I moved a little closer, reached out for her hand. "Why don't you lie down and chill out a minute before we get you out of here."

She nodded, let me help her lie back on the gurney, but kept one anxious eye on the door. "After he . . . I . . . I told him I was going to . . . I threatened to file a complaint with IAD," she whispered. "I just . . . I couldn't let him keep . . . I had to do *something* . . ." She turned away, winced again.

"Are we talking about Firestone here?"

Gena looked at me fearfully, then turned away. "Maybe I shouldn't be telling you this."

"Then let me tell you." I ran down what Mike Cooper had told me on the street. About how Manny Rudolph, the Robbery detective assigned to the Home Invasion Task Force, had responded to a phone tip of a witness's ID of the gold seventies Toyota. How he'd called around among the CRASH detectives in the field until he got to Cooper. How Cooper had immediately made the car and given him the name and address of Demarcus Tolliver, a young ex-con and gangbanger on parole for armed robbery, who drove a similar make and model.

"It was a *suspect's* address Firestone gave us, not a wit's," I concluded. "Cooper had offered to have one of their CRASH units surveil the house and report back on how much backup would be needed to go in. But Rudolph told him Firestone nixed the idea, said he'd handle it himself."

Gena's eyes grew wide as she took in a shaky breath. "So he set us up." It was a statement, not a question. "But why you?"

The memory of my conversation with Lieutenant Stobaugh about sexual harassment, Firestone's fake smile, and the irony of his words made my stomach churn. *Kill two birds with one stone* was what he had said. "I broke the code."

"And I threatened to," she whispered, the panic returning to her eyes. "I gotta get out of here."

Gena shifted noisily on the gurney, letting out a sudden moan as she clutched at her side. Dr. DiStefano and the nurse came running, the doctor elbowing me aside. "Excuse me, Detective."

I wandered back to the nurse's station to find Cooper had left a message to page him with any news. I took the slip of paper from the clerk and crumpled it up in my pocket. What else was there to say?

In about fifteen minutes, Dr. DiStefano joined me. "Let's go somewhere where we can talk."

"Somewhere" was a shabby family conference room, filled with half-empty coffee cups and the fear of words not yet spoken. "Is she gonna be all right?" I asked.

"The injury she sustained in her right side is superficial," she began, "but we've called for a OB/GYN consult, just to be on the safe side."

"OB/GYN?"

Dr. DiStefano's angelic face froze in place, then bloomed bright red. "Oh, dear, I'm sorry. When she said you were partners, I guess I assumed . . ."

Now Gena's paleness, the outbursts, and the rest made sense. My partner was pregnant. And, as far as I knew, hadn't been dating anyone for months. What had she said? *I threatened to file a complaint with IAD.*

My cell phone rang. I answered it, heard my brother's voice on the other end. I excused myself from the embarrassed doctor, left the conference room, and started giving Perris the rundown as I walked down the hall.

And ran smack dab into Steve Firestone, Lieutenant Stobaugh, and Captain MIA.

"**C**harlotte, are you all right?" Firestone rushed forward and attempted to put an arm around me. I clicked off the phone and used it to hold him at bay, wishing I was holding a gun in my hand instead.

Lieutenant Stobaugh and Captain MIA hung back, their faces creased with concern. "Have you seen her yet, Detective?" MIA asked, his voice grave. He stood ramrod-straight, every hair in place, as if he was receiving a report on the troops in battle.

Or waiting for the news cameras to show up.

"Just briefly, sir," I could barely say through my rage.

"What'd she say?" Firestone asked.

"Just that she wanted to get the hell out of here." I tried not to choke on the part left unspoken and added, "But I think they're going to keep her a little longer."

"I should talk to her . . ." Firestone began, but I noticed he did not move.

"Not until OIS interviews her. Besides, the doctor says she needs to rest, sir," I said, addressing our lieutenant. "She's been through quite a lot. I think it would be a good idea to leave the uniforms outside her door, be sure there's no retaliation from anyone carrying a grudge over what happened on Ninety-fifth Street."

I said this last bit, to my credit, without so much as a glance in Firestone's direction. But I could see him bristling out of the corner of my eye anyway. "I don't think that's necessary—" he began.

"Consider it done," MIA cut in, with a "see to it" glance at Stobaugh, who was already heading down the hall to make the arrangements.

"And no visitors for a while—except for the OIS team," I told the other two. "Give her a chance to collect her thoughts."

With a nod of his silver head and a wave of a manicured hand, MIA replied, "Of course, of course. We wouldn't want to interfere with the OIS investigation." He glanced at Firestone. "We can hold off until then."

There was an uneasy silence I felt no obligation to fill. Finally, Firestone tried: "We would have been here sooner—"

"We've been interrogating the suspects on Ninety-fifth," our captain started to explain, then looked around and whispered, "Let's go outside."

The three of us ended up outside the ambulance entrance to the ER, amid cigarette butts and a darkening sky. "You and Detective Cortez should be quite proud of yourselves, Detective Justice," MIA began, his patrician mouth widening into a smile.

"For what?" I asked bitterly and turned to see Stobaugh approaching us. "Almost getting myself and my partner killed?"

"On the contrary," MIA replied. "One of those boys confessed."

My head whipped around. "What? Which one?"

"Bobby Fluornoy," Stobaugh said from my side. "He was the wheelman for most of the home invasion robberies. He had used the Tolliver kid's car for the one we got the tip on in the Palisades."

"Then there never was a girlfriend in the Palisades Highlands," I said, more for MIA's and Stobaugh's benefit than my own.

"Apparently not," Stobaugh replied.

"So we were sent out to a *suspect's* house instead of a wit ness's," I replied slowly, hoping the illogic of it all would dawn on my superior officers. "How could that happen?"

My lieutenant turned to Firestone. "Steve, why don't you explain."

I turned to him too, thinking, *Yeah, Steve, let me see you wiggle your way out of this one.*

But Firestone had evidently been working the lie out in his head, because the words rolled off his lips as effortlessly as water off a duck's back. "Near as I can piece it together, Bernita Tolliver wasn't completely straight with us when she called in the tip. From what I gleaned from our interview with Demarcus, his mother had suspected he was involved somehow in the robberies, ever since she saw the bulletins on TV. But rather than turn him in, we think, she just steers us in the right direction by making up the story about us needing to interview the boy as a witness, figuring we'd get to the truth of it ourselves."

Something about Firestone's explanation sounded odd to me. "This is fact or conjecture on your part?"

"Instinct," he replied sharply, "but I think it'll be corroborated by Mrs. Tolliver, if we find her."

" 'If' you find her? Why can't you find her?"

"She's in the wind. Probably afraid her son's homies will put a cap in her ass."

"I'd be in the wind, too, 'cause if someone set me up like that, I'd sure 'nough put a cap in their ass," I said, watching Firestone's eyes for some sign that he was lying.

But Firestone's gaze was on Kenneth Stobaugh, no doubt wondering if our lieutenant was buying the wolf ticket he was selling. Stobaugh's eyes, in turn, were on me. "But we didn't tell Tolliver's friend Fluornoy that," my lieutenant explained. "Let him think we had a signed statement from Mrs. Tolliver fingering him for the robberies and those murders. By the time he was through cursing her ancestors, we'd gotten Fluornoy to confess to six of the robberies and roll over on two of his accomplices."

"So we won't even need the Tolliver woman's statement," Firestone said.

Before I could reply, Captain MIA was clapping me on the back and walking me back into the ER. "Be proud of yourselves, Detective Justice," he boomed. "You and Cortez broke this case. Tonight we can chalk up one for the good guys."

I was still looking over my shoulder at Firestone, who looked as if he wanted to throttle me for stealing his glory. I felt as if I was choking on lies, as if the only relief would be to throw up again. "Thank you, sir," I managed to say.

"Of course, you'll have to ride a desk for a couple of days until you're cleared by the use-of-force review board," MIA went on. "But you did exemplary work, Detective. It's another proud day for Robbery-Homicide."

And another notch in your belt, I felt like saying. "Can I go now, sir?" I asked Stobaugh.

"We need you to sit down with a couple of our guys to go over what happened," my lieutenant replied.

"Lieutenant, I'm asking IAD to handle this one, since it's one of our own," MIA corrected.

While I knew RHD usually investigated officer shootings in the LAPD, the thought of facing two Internal Affairs detectives made me nauseous. "Begging your pardon, sir, but I'm exhausted. I've already told everything I can remember to OIS plus completed all of the necessary incident and use-of-force paperwork at the station. I've got to get some rest."

And figure out my next move.

"Go on home, Detective." Stobaugh put a surprisingly gentle hand on my shoulder. "It can wait until tomorrow."

"Thank you, sir," I replied, and headed out into the cloudy night.

CHAPTER 14

UP IN THE
KOOL-AID

By the time I entered Lafayette Square and pulled up to my Uncle Syl's large Mediterranean-style house, I was so furious I could barely enjoy the quiet of the tree-lined streets or appreciate the icicle lights that hung from my uncle's roof. The residents of Lafayette Square, an upper-middle-class, mostly black neighborhood southwest of Hancock Park in the Mid-City district, had received permission three years before to erect barriers to stop wholesale cruising down their stately tree-lined streets—and, according to their detractors, to separate themselves from the hoi polloi just outside the square's half-dozen or so blocks. The riots had made Sylvester Curry and his neighbors look incredibly farsighted—even though they, like the thousands of other Angelenos doing the same thing all over the city, had to bear the brunt of public opinion and the cost of installing and maintaining the barricades they so desperately wanted.

Habit, and the day's events, made me eye the bushes and parked cars carefully before hurrying up the flagstone walkway. Perris stood outlined in the glow of my uncle's open doorway, watching Beast investigate a bush. He looked as if he'd picked up the dog from my house without going home to change, his white dress shirt standing out in stark contrast to the darkness of his suit. When we talked earlier, I had insisted on meeting my brother at an out-of-the-way location, one, because going home gave me the heebie-jeebies, and two, I wasn't too sure Perris's office wasn't under surveillance, too, given his ongoing civil lawsuits against the department.

"You look like you ran through a briar patch," Perris noted, one hand on his hip, his tie loosely knotted around his neck.

"That's not too far from wrong," I agreed, touching my cheek.

"Where's the Rabbit?"

I looked over my shoulder. "I left it downtown, just in case anyone was waiting for me there."

He leaned down to give me a quick kiss as I whistled for the dog. "Don't you think you're being a little paranoid? From your phone call I thought you'd talked to Firestone and Lieutenant Stobaugh and everything was cool."

I dropped to my knees to scratch Beast, who snuffled at me carefully. "You know from experience, Perris, you can't be too cautious about something like this."

He closed the door behind me. "Sure I do, but use your common sense, Char." He leaned down to whisper, "Firestone wouldn't be stupid enough to follow you here!"

"That's easy for you to say!" I hissed back, the fear I'd seen in Gena's eyes a few hours ago playing before me like a movie. I got to my feet. "I just hope you didn't let anyone tail you over here."

"Don't insult my intelligence! I used to work with those clowns. I think I know enough to be able to spot a tail."

Uncle Syl stepped up behind my brother, his unruly gray eyebrows knitted in warning. "You two kids are gonna have to stop all this fussing in my house. You're raining on the Santa Claus parade!" It was then that I caught the scent of a burning fireplace and fresh pine in the air, noticed the forest-green blazer my uncle wore over a red turtleneck and green plaid trousers.

Uncle Syl put his arm around me while he led me upstairs. "I've drawn you a bath so you can freshen up. There's some peroxide in the medicine cabinet and"—he lowered his voice—"some of that single-malt Scotch you gave Jackie last Christmas."

Perris added from behind us, "Louise and I ran by your place to get you some clean clothes. They're hanging on the back of the bathroom door. She says you're welcome to stay with us tonight if you want."

"No, thanks. I promised Aubrey I'd go by there."

Uncle Syl opened the door to the master suite, releasing a strong fragrance of oranges, which Beast sniffed curiously. While he and my brother went downstairs, Beast and I entered the master bathroom, an aqua-and-black-tiled refuge with a gleaming white clawfoot tub against the far wall. Soon I was comfortably settled into the warm water, complete with scented bubbles and rubber ducky, sipping the Ledaig my uncle had thoughtfully set out, trying to drown out the world.

There was a knock at the door. "You decent?"

"Up to my neck in bubbles."

Perris eased past Beast into the room and sat on a black-velvet-covered chair positioned before a vanity straight out of a forties movie set. From either side of the mirror, glamour shots of Lena Horne and the three Di's—Diana Ross, Diahann Carroll, and the vastly underrated actress Diana Sands—all wearing my uncle's creations, looked down on us regally. The only male presence in the room, other than Perris, was a black-lacquer-framed photo of Uncle Syl's beloved Jackie, a sweetheart of a man who had died earlier in the year of a massive coronary.

His back to me, Perris pulled his tie off over his head and started working furiously at the knot while talking to my reflection in the mirror. "So what kind of lie did that asshole come up with?"

My brother had been shot in the line of duty years ago and it had left him bitter about policing and the department.

"This is strictly between us chickens," I warned him. "No running and blabbing to the folks or trying to use this in any of your civil cases against the department."

"Just last week I took on the case of a woman in the department who could really benefit from knowing about your situation . . ." he began.

"There's no *situation* here, Perris!"

"Don't worry, I won't say anything to anybody."

"Not even Joymarie?" I watched him shake his head in the mirror's reflection. "Justice Family Oath of Silence?"

He turned to face me. "Come on, Char! I *said* I wouldn't say anything."

"*Swear!*"

To humor me, he listlessly made the familiar sign—an imaginary key turned over his lips—that we kids used when we wanted something to be top secret from our parents. "You want it sealed in blood?"

"No, thanks," I replied, "I've seen enough of that today," and I filled him in on my misadventures on Ninety-fifth Street.

"And your lieutenant bought Firestone's weak ass story about the suspect's mother?" he asked when I paused to take a sip of the Ledaig.

Lena was staring over at me, a knowing smile playing about her lips. "Without any other information to the contrary, what's he supposed to do?"

"And so you're just going to let him get away with it?" he asked incredulously.

"Of course not, but what was I going to do right then? Confront Firestone with Lieutenant Stobaugh and my captain standing right there in the emergency room?"

"It would have been a good start."

"Come on! You *know* how these guys are. He would've tried to turn it right back on me: 'I told you all along to wait for backup. You and Cortez were just trying to make a name for yourselves.'"

"You should have said *something*. At least that way your superior officers would have been put on notice."

"Shoulda, woulda, coulda." I set down my glass, sank back into the bubbles. "The good news is, Captain Armstrong is walking around crediting Gena and me with breaking the case. You shoulda seen the look on Steve Firestone's face."

"Question is, is your captain's approval worth risking your life for? You could have gotten killed!"

"Gena almost did," I reminded him, and solemnly raised my

glass again. "But instead—thanks to Firestone's botched attempt to set us up—we're fucking heroes. Us and Mike Cooper. You remember Cooper, don't you?"

"I sure do," Perris replied hotly. "You realize it's possible Cooper could have had a hand in setting you up."

"I'll admit, he was pissed enough at me during the riots. But, odd as it sounds, I think Cooper's basically a decent guy. I find it hard to believe he'd be the type to hold a grudge all this time. After all, he didn't hesitate to come to my assistance out there today."

"I used to work with cops like Cooper, so I'd keep my eye on him regardless."

"It's Firestone I'm more concerned about."

"How's your partner?"

"She's okay, but they're keeping her overnight for observation, with a couple of deputies from the sheriff's department stationed outside her room. They've got strict instructions—no one can get in to see her but her immediate family and the hospital staff."

"Is that enough to keep Firestone at bay?"

"I don't think he's man enough to try something overt, plus you know those sheriff's deputies don't play. Besides, he doesn't really know how much Gena's told me, so if he messes with her at this point, I could make it that much worse for him."

Perris turned away, suddenly busying himself with the bottles on the vanity, and examining the old scar above his eye. It was a few long moments before he asked: "Charlotte, how much longer do you think you can hang on to that job?"

How long, the divas seemed to echo. "With the changing of the guard, I'm encouraged enough to think I can do my twenty-five. Did I tell you I met the new chief at a luncheon some of the females in the department gave for him and his wife? He made all the right noises. He might be able to turn things around."

"See?" he said, slapping his palms on his knees. "Now you're sounding like Uncle Henry, the eternal LAPD optimist. I know from my years on the job those old boys running the department aren't *about* to let an outsider mess up their good thing!"

"But things have changed a lot since you got out. What about the seven new captains he just appointed? One of them is a female!"

"Who I remember as being a damn good cop. But do you think they're going to let her be chief?"

"Why not? She's got the skills!"

"She'll never break through that Kevlar barrier," my brother shot back.

"But you've got to admit having more females in senior command positions is a beginning. Sometimes I think I could do a lot of good in a command position myself. Did you know there's never been a black female in the LAPD to make it above the rank of lieutenant?"

"Get real, Char! For a lot of those old boys on the force, women are *still* way down on the totem pole, below the men—white, black, or otherwise."

"Well, I'm not about to let Firestone and his kind derail my career. There's got to be a silver lining in this mess somewhere, a way I can expose him for what he tried to do to us." I reached for the soap. "Now take the dog and get out of here so I can wash up."

Perris and Beast were waiting for me in the living room. "What I don't get is how your partner could be so naive as to get tangled up with a jerk like Firestone."

"He probably pulled the same thing on her that he used to try with me—dropping by her house after hours to discuss cases, feeding her that 'my wife doesn't understand me' line of bullshit, then making his move on her in her own home." I shook my head wearily. "And all this time I thought it was *her* coming on to *him.*"

I suddenly felt cold, even though we had just passed the fireplace and I was wearing the sweats Perris had brought from my house. I took another sip of Scotch and tried to throw off the feeling as we walked into the kitchen. I could see Uncle Syl over by the sink, foot tapping as he hummed some Christmas tune.

"Way I see it, you've got three options," Perris said, ticking them off on his fingers. "You can file a complaint and let Internal Affairs look into it—"

"You know if I ratted out Firestone, it'd be the end of my career! Besides, IAD's going to be all over this case because of Gena's getting shot."

"Anybody talk to you yet?"

"Just the Officer-Involved Shooting team." I paused while Uncle Syl put hot sauce on the table. As he walked away, I whispered, "I've got a formal sit-down with a couple of IAD suits tomorrow. In the meantime, maybe they'll stumble onto Firestone's little plot themselves."

"Not if they aren't pointed in the right direction," he replied, eyeing me pointedly before moving on to another finger. "Two, you can lay this out for Uncle Henry. He is in charge of personnel matters on the job, you know."

"Not a good idea," I said emphatically. "Thanks to *your* meddling mother, that little talk Uncle Henry gave to my lieutenant is what I think got me into this mess in the first place."

"But you can't let this kind of bullshit go unanswered!"

I shined Perris on, took another sip of Scotch, and gazed at the ceiling. "Is this black Santa border new?" I called out to Uncle Syl.

Busy mounding salad onto a plate next to a slab of ribs big enough to feed the whole neighborhood, my uncle paused, obviously pleased I had noticed. "Picked it up in the Design Mart last week."

Perris's head was tilted up to the ceiling, too, but not in admiration of Uncle Syl's latest purchase. "Your third option is to quit," he muttered out of the corner of his mouth. "You could make a lot more money as a PI."

I snapped open a black Santa napkin, draped it across my lap. "You know, big brother, you are all up in my Kool-Aid and don't even know the flavor!" I drained my glass. "There's gotta be a fourth option. I just don't know what it is yet."

Uncle Syl padded toward us, his leather mules making a soft thwapping sound on the tile floor, bearing a plate for me. "You want something to eat, nephew?"

Perris rose from the table. "Louise has probably cooked something."

"You could have brought her and the kids for dinner. There's always plenty."

"I don't want to give her any ideas by bringing her over here. She's been so afraid of her own shadow since the Uprising, she wants us to move to some gated community where she'll feel 'safe.'"

"There's nothing wrong with gated communities, per se," Uncle Syl muttered a bit defensively from his spot next to me.

"There is if you end up cutting yourself off from reality and your roots. I don't want that for my kids."

"All gated communities aren't the same. Lafayette Square is a great community. And we're predominantly black, unlike Fremont Place or some of the others."

"Speaking of Fremont Place, Uncle Syl," I interrupted, "what were you doing at Maynard Duncan's repast today?"

"I could ask you the same thing, not that I object to seeing a good detective like you investigating *whatever* it is—"

"You're avoiding the question, Uncle Syl."

He made a noncommittal face and airily waved a hand in my direction. "I *told* you I knew the man."

"Uh-uh, what you said Thanksgiving Day was you were in a Tarzan movie with him." I looked to Perris, who nodded in vigorous affirmation. "You didn't say you knew him."

"How could we not know each other and work in the same industry? There aren't *that* many of us in Hollywood, you know."

My brother shot me one of those pure cop looks that implied we both knew my usually tell-it-like-it-is uncle was holding back. "I think I will get me one of those ribs," Perris said, and crossed the room to the stove. I went about eating my food in silence, keeping my eyes on my plate the whole time.

We kept up the act for a while, Perris and I eating quietly, Uncle Syl looking from one of us to the other in increasing exasperation. "You two can forget it. I am *not* putting that man's business in the street!" he insisted. "Don't you know it's bad luck to speak ill of the dead?"

"It's equally bad luck to let a man's murder go unsolved," I countered.

My uncle mulled that over for a bit. "Maybe we can talk about this later," he whispered, throwing a brief glance in the direction of my brother.

Who took the hint, polished off the rest of his rib. "I'm outta here. Louise gets freaked if I'm not home by nine."

"She afraid you'll turn into a werewolf?" I teased, falling in behind Uncle Syl as he saw Perris to the door.

"No, afraid I'll get Rodney Kinged by one of your boys in blue," my brother replied with a laugh that wasn't funny at all.

Uncle Syl closed the door behind my brother, deposited his glass in the kitchen, then thwapped his way over to a turntable built into one wall. He switched it on and pulled out an album, and soon Nat King Cole's "The Christmas Song" was doing its best to put the two of us in the holiday mood. He then moved to the coffee table, where several large boxes held the collection of Christmas ornaments he and Jackie had made over the years. "I'm not really in the mood to do this tonight." His hands hesitated over the gold-foil boxes as if they might electrocute him. "Jackie made most of these ornaments himself. He loved Christmas so much, I don't think I can bear to look at them without remembering him, remembering how alone I am."

I moved beside him and put an arm around his stooped shoulders. "You're not alone right now. And you won't be alone Christmas Day, either. We'll all be here."

His brimming eyes searched mine. "But what happens when you all leave and I'm alone in this house full of memories? What do I do then?"

"You get used to it, I guess."

"Have you?" he asked, eyes still locked with mine.

I felt a pang, not unlike the one I felt when I used to wander around alone in the house Keith and I bought all those years ago, dusting and cleaning as if I expected them home any minute. "I don't know. I guess so. I'm still there."

"Not for long." He wiped his eyes and patted my hand reassuringly. "You mark my words."

Uncle Syl's comment stirred an uneasiness in me, which must have shown on my face, because he asked, "You *are* bringing Aubrey to Matt and Joymarie's tree-trimming party on Sunday, aren't you?"

"I don't understand why my whole goddam family is so gung ho on Aubrey Scott!" I went into the kitchen to retrieve my drink. "He's nothing but a man."

"Oh, really?"

Back in the living room, I mumbled, "Can't we talk about something else?" and opened one of the boxes.

We unwrapped ornaments for several minutes before I asked my uncle what it was about Maynard Duncan he had been reluctant to say in front of Perris.

"Nothing, really." A veil fell over his eyes, which he kept focused resolutely on his work. It took a couple of minutes of enforced silence before he broke. "Oh, all right," he said, popping a bit of bubble wrap between his fingers in irritation, his brows a tangle of wild gray, his mustache puckered tightly over his lip. "But I'm telling you, I don't condone gossip, especially when it comes to people's personal lives."

The look on his face reminded me of the one he'd worn when my grandmother sighed over Duncan. Which in turn reminded me of the pain on Ivy Duncan's face as she whispered her fears for her husband's memory. "Maynard Duncan was closeted, wasn't he?"

"Says who?" he asked sharply.

"No one. It's just that everyone associated with this case has been so secretive, and then some of the men you introduced me to at the house today seemed . . ."

"I wouldn't go spreading that rumor around," he warned, his voice lowered as if the walls had ears. "People have a right to their privacy, you know. Besides, it's not the kind of thing some of the fellas at the repast would want out in the street."

"You should have heard his wife the other day, giving me this song and dance about falling in love with him from the minute he walked into some nightclub where she was singing."

"That would have been Brothers, this club run by a couple of goyas—what you call transvestites now. But Ivy was fresh out of the South and kinda innocent back then, so she might not have known."

"Ivy Duncan sang in a transvestite club and didn't think the men she met there might be gay?"

"I'm sure all Ivy was thinking about was that Maynard was a couple of steps higher up on the social ladder."

"She seemed so devoted to him."

My uncle had counted the ornaments on the coffee table, and moved now to the tree and the strings of lights jumbled at its base. "Ivy *was* devoted to Maynard, and she was even more devoted to keeping up appearances after they got married, especially around that Bible-thumping sister of his. But if you want my opinion, she'd have to be deaf, dumb, and blind not to have figured out what Maynard was up to, much as he used to show up at Brothers with this white fella we worked with in that Tarzan film."

The photos in Duncan's scrapbook and the scene Billie and I had witnessed on the front steps of his house at the repast came to mind. "Are you referring to Tristan Cavender?"

"That's the one! He used to show up with Maynard at the black clubs that were off the beaten track, places he could go slumming without Hedda Hopper or Louella Parsons reporting on the number of drinks he had. Or who he left with. He and Maynard were the talk of the Eastside for years until Miss Ivy came on the scene."

"What was the talk?"

"That Maynard had made a deal with the devil—he was Cavender's personal guide for those walks on the wild side and Cavender was Maynard's ticket out of bit parts and into directing."

"So were Duncan and Cavender lovers?"

I could tell I'd struck that "I don't condone gossip" nerve by the way my uncle tightened his lips. "You'd have to talk to Tristan Cavender about that. Although I doubt if you'd get close enough to even ask these days."

"Why's that?"

"Oh, he's big-time now. A retrospective of his films aired on one of the cable stations this summer, he's getting a star on the Walk of Fame, and the Directors Guild is giving him a lifetime achievement award in February." Uncle Syl went to the kitchen and returned with a copy of *Variety*, which he held out to me. "He's come a long way from his days of ripping and running the streets with Maynard Duncan."

On the front page of last week's issue was an article about Cavender's DGA award, the schedule for the star ceremony tomorrow, and more. Accompanying the story was a color photo of the man I'd encountered in front of Duncan's house, flanked by a white-haired industry type while a handsome young blond stood behind them, gazing at the director with a proprietary gleam in his eye. The hairs stood up on my neck as I read the caption under the picture: "TRISTAN CAVENDER, JOINED BY INDUSTRY PALS AND WELLWISHERS, AT ACTOR'S HANCOCK PARK HOME LAST JULY."

I went upstairs to get my purse, Beast dutifully trailing me. I returned to the living room, tore out the article, and made a note in the margin. "I wonder how Ivy Duncan felt living so close to her husband's old running buddy."

"I'm sure she adjusted, given the directing jobs her husband was able to get based on his friendship with Cavender. And remember, for a Southern girl with Hollywood aspirations, making money can cover a multitude of sins."

The light strings were connected now, and Uncle Syl tested them at a nearby plug. Tiny luminescent globes of lights cast a warm glow on my uncle's lined face, but caused my dog to take a few cautious steps back. I took the end of the string Uncle Syl handed to me, weaving it through the branches of the Douglas fir, Beast watching from the safety of the boxes on the floor. "Even if it was like you say, I have a hard time believing an old diva like Ivy Duncan would go along with that kind of charade."

"Don't make the mistake of looking at the forties and fifties through nineties–colored glasses. It was easier to turn a blind eye to the truth back then because the closet was very big and very dark. The Hollywood publicity machines saw to that."

"Like with Rock Hudson?"

My uncle laughed heartily. "Remember *Pillow Talk?* There was Rock Hudson, a gay man in real life, acting like a straight man pretending to be a gay man to get Doris Day into bed. I almost felt sorry for him until I remembered he was white, which meant he and the studios stood to make a lot more money off his little charade than a black man ever would. Another one of those deals with the devil, see what I'm saying?"

"Did you and your friends have to go through those kinds of gyrations, too?"

His laugh turned scornful. "Not as much when we were in our own community, but some people didn't have a choice." He took another string of lights, started working them through the branches on his side of the tree. "It was easier if you weren't in the limelight. Ruby Dandridge's mother lived with this woman and her daughters like it wasn't nothin' and got away with it because it was Dorothy, not her, whose face was front and center. And Billy Strayhorn made no bones about who he was, but nobody messed with him because he had Duke Ellington's protection.

"But if you had high visibility in the business, with all the preachers and gossip columnists and tell-all rags, you pretty much stayed in the closet, and a segregated one at that. And as far as a lot of gays in Hollywood and the press are concerned, the only difference between then and now is the segregation part."

"Is that what Maynard Duncan did?"

"Maynard was in a tough spot, trying to make it as an actor *and* a director. As an actor, getting married was more of a necessity for him than it ever was for me. But after he switched to working exclusively behind the camera, I suspect he had a little more freedom, too."

Now I could make sense of my uneasiness about Ivy Duncan—her description of Duncan's hesitancy to marry, his frequent trips on location. But she had played it off like a pro, even mustered up tears when the occasion demanded.

"So can I assume the story I heard about Maynard fathering a child out of wedlock isn't true?"

"Who told you that—Ivy?" Uncle Syl gave me a withering, tight-lipped look and went back to hanging ornaments on the tree. "All I've got to say is: 'Skim milk masquerades as cream, things ain't always what they seem.'"

"Meaning?"

"Meaning if Maynard fathered a child—which is *not* impossible, even if a man is gay—it would have been a convenient excuse for Ivy, wouldn't it?"

"Excuse for what?"

"Now, far be it from me to be—what did you call it?—up in that woman's Kool-Aid, but acknowledging that young man as Maynard's 'son' would allow her to go on with her life and ignore what was going on right under her own roof."

He moved to put on another record while I digested the information he'd just dropped on me. When we had finished decorating the tree, we stood arm in arm to admire our handiwork. "It looks mighty fine, Uncle Syl."

"I couldn't have done it without your help." My uncle turned to look me in the eye. "I wasn't trying to eavesdrop or anything, but I couldn't help but hear when you and Perris came downstairs. . . . Are they giving you the blues at work?"

"Nothing I can't handle." I disengaged my arm and looked around for my drink. "And *please,* don't say anything to my parents about Perris meeting me here. Especially to your busybody sister."

"Have I ever told one of your secrets? Ever?"

I felt a momentary flush of embarrassment. Uncle Syl had always been more of a friend and confidant to me than an uncle, the one I could go to when my mother's aloofness or, conversely, her driving me to succeed became unbearable. His unconditional affection and his protectiveness of me were the only things that made me believe there was any hope for the color-struck, social-climbing Curry side of my family.

"What gives with you and Joymarie?" he demanded. "You two have been awfully short-tempered around each other lately."

I started gathering up my things. "I'm just sick and tired of her meddling in my business. She's just about had me married off to Aubrey since our third date, and I'm pretty sure she snitched me out to Uncle Henry about a situation I've been dealing with on the job."

"What kind of situation?" Uncle Syl's mouth became fixed in a grim line as I ran down my problems with Steve Firestone and his failed ambush-by-proxy attempt. "You need to talk to your mother, Baby Girl. I'm sure she just thought she was being helpful."

"That kind of help I don't need. Her interference could have gotten me killed."

It had started raining again, and from the way it was coming down, it looked like we were in for quite a drenching. My uncle held out his arms for a goodbye hug. "Do tell that nice young man of yours hello for me, would you? And tell him I may ask him to bring a dish for Christmas dinner."

"We'll see," I said vaguely, and broke the embrace.

"What's the matter? I thought you two were getting serious."

"Aubrey's been acting kind of strange lately. Besides, I don't know if I'm ready to be serious about anybody right now."

"If not now, when? I know you probably don't want to hear this, but your personal life has been in limbo since Keith and Erica were killed. And while I'd never make light of your pain . . ."

"I know, Uncle Syl," I whispered to the floor. "But I don't know . . . don't know if I can let myself feel that strongly about anyone again."

"Don't be no fool and make a good man like that wait too long, Baby Girl." He kissed me carefully on the cheek and shooed Beast and me into the car.

A   C O L D
D E C E M B E R

Up the hill from Aubrey's house in Los Feliz, someone was throwing a party in a low-slung modern house set precariously atop thirty-foot steel columns. Through the rain-streaked windshield of my copmobile I could see the backlit, elongated silhouettes of people holding stemware and balancing plates. I drove past a pack of black-clad fashion ninjas closing in on the party house. They looked like the same crowd who'd attended the Duncan repast that afternoon—they all had that well-groomed, on-the-hustle look I had come to associate with entertainment people.

Aubrey intercepted me in front of his house. As I rolled down the window, I saw him frown at the scratches on my face. "I'd let you park in my garage, but somebody's blocking my driveway," he shouted through the rain.

He went around to the passenger side to let Beast out and grab my bag. I found a parking space several houses away and began the process of fighting my way up the hill, needles of cold water stinging my face and soaking my sweats. Aubrey met me midway, carrying an umbrella and a slicker, which he threw over me and held me close.

"Are you all right?"

I nodded into his chest, and sneezed. "Just achy and wet."

"Come on." He led me inside the dimly lit house. Beast was already tongue-drying himself before the warmth of the massive stone fireplace in the living room. The windows facing the street were shuttered against the party hearty crowd, while the ones facing the canyon and mountains beyond bared themselves to the pelting rain. I sat huddled next to the dog, shivering, while Aubrey ran downstairs, returning with a towel partially draped over a big, gold-wrapped box.

"It's too early to exchange gifts!" I protested weakly, wondering at the same time if this would be the only time I would see him until after the New Year.

He thrust the package down at me. "I was going to give it to you at Christmas, but I think maybe you can use it now."

Beast helped me wade through an ocean of tissue paper until I found a dark green bathrobe nestled inside. I pulled it out of the box, the softness of what had to be cashmere startling my unsuspecting fingers. "Oh, my God. You shouldn't have!"

He squatted next to me and reached for the package. "I can return it if you don't like it."

I pulled it back. "Don't you dare!"

"Here," he said, smiling, "let me help you." He was sitting next to me now, pulling my sweatshirt over my head and toweling me off. He concluded my torture by wrapping me in the lushness of my new robe, walking me over to the sofa, and enfolding me in his arms. "Let's just chill for a minute."

Lying with one ear against Aubrey's chest, I listened to the rain outside and the rise and fall of Aubrey's steady breathing, felt the fireplace's valiant attempt to warm us. I rose up a little and, opening the top button of his flannel shirt, kissed his chest, the tightly curled hairs there tickling my lips.

"You're pretty frisky for someone who almost got shot," he said.

I kissed his palm. "Is there something wrong with that?"

He put a restraining hand on my shoulder. "How are you feeling?"

"I'm not the one you should be concerned about. Gena's the one who could've died out there. And all because of that asshole Firestone!"

"*He's* the one who set you up?" I could see Aubrey's jaw working and the sparks of anger in his eyes; he'd met and had an unpleasant experience with Firestone himself some months ago. "Why didn't you say so on the phone?"

"There were people around."

After I recounted the rest of it, he was still fuming. "That man needs his ass whipped!"

"Believe me, that's on the top of my list, too, but I've got enough on my mind with Gena in the hospital."

"I wouldn't worry about your partner. I called the hospital and talked to her doctor. She was doing well enough for them to discharge her. She's going to be fine."

I exhaled in relief, my head in my hands. "I feel like this is my fault. I should have warned her a long time ago that Firestone would try and hit on her. That's been his MO from the day he joined RHD."

"Even if he tried, how were you to know that it would escalate to this, or that she wouldn't know how to handle it?"

"There were signs, Aubrey. How she responded to pressure during the riots. Her eagerness to please. She's always been afraid of going up against the boys."

"That's a far sight from letting yourself be forced into sex with a superior."

"Not as far as you might think."

There was an uneasy silence before he said, "Be that as it may, she was the one who chose to keep it to herself. Had she reached out it would have been different." He moved to the stereo, slipped in a jazz piano CD, and rejoined me on the sofa. "How are you feeling?" he repeated softly.

I moved away a little. "I already told you . . . guilty about how I treated my partner."

"That's about Gena. I'm wondering how you're feeling about *your* situation. Your ass was on the line out there, too."

I squirmed in the expensive robe, frowned, tried to feel something. And came up empty. I was so used to cutting myself off from my emotions while I was working, so used to wearing protective armor to keep from losing it at some of the more horrific crime scenes I investigated, that here, when I was being given the space to express an uncensored feeling, I couldn't. The realization made me shudder, made me want to withdraw even farther into a protective cocoon, made me wish Aubrey had some Scotch.

He put a hand on my shoulder: "Just let it go, Char. You're safe here."

As hard as I fought against it, I felt my body losing the battle to the exhaustion and the fear. "If I'm so safe," I said, "why does it feel like my world is coming apart?"

"It isn't." He took me into his arms. "Come here."

There had been few people or places where I'd felt safe in my life, where I could let my guard down. Despite the department's motto—to protect and to serve—the LAPD's politics and perils had always made going to work an adrenaline-pumping, heart-thumping experience. And now I felt my life was on the line in more ways than one, and there was nowhere I could go for help. Not to my lieutenant, who meant well but who I was certain didn't want to get involved in an intradepartmental beef if he could avoid it. Not to Uncle Henry, who, if he took some kind of direct action, could be accused of playing favorites, which could jeopardize his position as well as mine.

The home front wasn't much better. There was no comfort to be found in the way my mother held herself apart from me, the way she fought with me, either directly or behind the scenes, her constant criticism of everything I'd ever done in my career. And my brother, while he had his better moments, always seemed to be sparring with me, too, always after me to get out of the department, get on with the life he thought I should lead. It was only with my father, Matt, with Uncle Syl, and for a too-brief time with my husband, Keith, that I'd felt that open-hearted acceptance I craved like water.

And here I was experiencing it again, in the form of this wonderfully generous man who was taking me, not to mention my dog, in, practically rescuing us out of the rain. No "I-told-you-so's" or "what-you-should-do's." But my mind was racing so fast, I couldn't enjoy it.

After a few minutes, Aubrey led Beast and me downstairs to his bedroom, where he gave me an oversized T-shirt to wear. "Not very sexy." I tried on a smile that didn't fit either.

"I've said this before—I don't mind your leaving some clothes here. Now maybe you'll take me up on my offer." Aubrey lit a candle on the nightstand. "I'll be right back."

While he was gone, I tiptoed upstairs to check my pager and saw a message to phone the coroner's office. I retreated downstairs to Aubrey's office to place the call and was informed the Duncan autopsy was scheduled for nine the next morning. While I was at it, I called home to check for messages. My blood ran cold to hear Steve Firestone's voice among the others on the machine, wondering where I was and telling me the chief of police wanted to meet with us on the home invasion case at four the next day.

I jumped back into bed moments before Aubrey reappeared, a heavy mug in his hand. "Drink this." It was chamomile tea, spiked with honey and lemon and not much else. "And take these."

I scooped two brown caplets. "Tranquilizers?"

"Echinacea with Vitamin C." He stretched out beside me. "Just in case."

The warmth of him next to me reawakened the urges I had stifled upstairs, made me overcome my exhaustion and self-consciousness and reach out again. "You can't stop making me want you by lying here fully clothed."

He captured my fingers, kissing them this time, and held them on his chest. "Take your pills and drink your tea."

I drank, feeling a storm of anger surging inside of me. I was furious at Aubrey for rejecting me, at my mother for interfering, at Steve Firestone for betraying me, but most of all furious at myself for trusting anyone or anything other my own instincts. Watching the condensation on the bedroom windows, I shuddered just thinking how I'd get through the next few days without doing bodily harm to myself. Or someone else.

I awoke Thursday morning to a clock that read seven-twenty and an empty space in the bed next to me. The rain clouds had cleared away, leaving the sky unnaturally clear but cold.

I grabbed my robe and went down the hall to Aubrey's office to make a few phone calls. That done, I climbed the back stairs, guided by smells that made my stomach growl. I found Aubrey with his back to me, standing at the window by the kitchen sink, his long fingers cradling a mug of tea. The sun rose weakly over the mountains in the distance, casting a sliver of light on Beast, who was sleeping under the breakfast-room table. "Early meeting today?" I asked.

He turned to greet me, his sensuous mouth stretching into an easy smile. "I'm taking the day off," he said, moving toward the microwave with a plate of bacon. "Got some errands to run. I could use some company."

"I wish I could, but I've got a lot of work to do today on the Duncan case and the home invasion robberies. I can't let what that ass Firestone tried to do slow me down."

"Sometimes slowing down isn't necessarily a bad thing."

I went to a cabinet for a mug, poured hot water into it from the kettle, and got a tea bag from the canister nearby, glad to busy myself while I avoided answering the underlying challenge in Aubrey's invitation. I took the mug to the table, let it steep while I scratched Beast's ears. "Last time we were in this kitchen, I seem to remember putting my foot in my mouth."

"Yeah, you did."

"You're not supposed to agree that easily!"

"Just being honest," he said with a roll of his shoulders, and opened the oven, letting the smell of cinnamon and calories escape into the room. Beast click-clacked his way over to investigate for himself, was rewarded with a piece of bacon.

"What I wanted to say, Aubrey, is that my job gets very intense sometimes."

"Yours isn't the only one," he reminded me.

"I'm not saying it is. Just let me get this out, okay?" I took in a breath and began again. "And sometimes it makes me a little pre-occupied, a little . . ."

"Insensitive?" he helpfully offered, his full lips compressed into a tight smile.

"That, too. The bottom line is, even though we've been see-ing each other for a while, old habits die hard with me."

"Tell me about it," he agreed, not quite under his breath.

"I beg your pardon?" But Aubrey had already gone back to his cooking, Beast his ever-present sous chef. I walked over to him, grabbed his arm. "What was that supposed to mean?"

A few seconds passed before he put down his tea and crossed his arms over his chest. "It means that I've been dating you a little over six months, Charlotte, and I still feel like I'm on the outside looking in, like there's something or someone between us!"

I could see the anger and pain on Aubrey's face, felt my chest tighten in response. "I really can't handle this right now," I mut-tered, heading for the back stairs and down to the bedroom. "I've got a bunch of loose ends to tie up before a big meeting with the chief this afternoon."

"All you've talked about since Thanksgiving has been this damned Duncan case or some other aspect of your job!" he hollered after me. "You're knocking yourself out for people who'd just as soon see you get yourself killed. You'd better step back and think about it, Char!"

That brought me thundering back up the stairs. "Aubrey, I explained when we started dating that my job could get pretty intense. I thought you were cool with that."

His look was withering. "You don't get it, do you? I'm not talking about you having an intense job. I've got one of those too, remember? I'm talking about you living and breathing it every waking and sleeping moment of your life, even when it threatens to kill you, even when it creates a barrier between you and me!"

"I hear this shit all the time from Perris and Joymarie," I shot back, my voice growing loud. "Why do you think I'd stand here and take it from you?"

"Because maybe your mother and brother have a point," he said, more than matching me in volume. "I'm the closest thing you've had to a normal life in years! Problem is, you don't know how to handle it! And the minute I begin to get closer to you, you start shutting me out, treating me like I can't be trusted! Tell me—did *I* do something to you that makes you treat me like shit?"

The timer on the oven went off. As soon as he bent to remove the pan, I was in the living room snatching up my clothes and overnight bag. I was down the stairs and halfway into my sweats before he and Beast caught up with me.

"Running away from me isn't going to make this go away, Charlotte," he warned.

I bundled up the robe, tried stuffing it in the bag, but it wouldn't fit. I threw it on the bed. "Well, please tell me what will, because I'm definitely *not* into having this conversation!"

He stopped and stared at the robe. "Not having it today or ever?"

I glared at him. "Why don't you just say what you mean?"

He picked up the robe, folded it over his arm. "Okay," he said, voice tight. "Clearly, we're in different places in our lives, Charlotte. You're into erecting these elaborate walls of mistrust and suspicion that are just too hard for me to break through. I don't know where or why this started with you—maybe it's just the nature of your job, or maybe it's got something to do with your losing your husband the way you did. All I know is I want you in my life, but not if I've got to do battle with you, the ghosts up in that house of yours, and the whole damn LAPD to do it!"

"If you don't want to be with me, fine!" I motioned to the dog. "Come on, Beast."

My Boxer hesitated for a moment, then ducked his head and slunk reluctantly toward me. I snatched him by the collar, hauled him up the stairs, and grabbed my purse.

Aubrey was already at the door, blocking my way out. "Think about what I'm saying to you, Char."

I could feel my jaw tighten. "Would you *please* move?"

He stepped aside. As I opened the door and hurried down the rain-soaked sidewalk, I could hear him shout, "You're the one who's pushing me away, Char. You've got to decide. It's your choice, not mine."

CHAPTER 16

ALL IN DUE TIME

Twenty minutes later I stormed into my house, flung some kibble at my traitorous dog, and took a quick shower.

My cell phone rang as I was getting dressed. It was Gena, responding to the page I had left for her when I was at Aubrey's. "What's up? I'm on my way downtown."

"How're you doing?" I asked, as I pulled on a wool skirt.

"Good enough to get back to work. You?"

I dodged the question, not wanting to get into my battle with Aubrey, noting instead the forced cheerfulness in my partner's voice. "You know you won't be able to get a clearance to return to duty that fast."

"Why the fuck not?" she demanded, surprising me with her profanity. "Bullet just grazed my side, didn't do any real damage."

There was an awkward silence on the line. As much as I wanted Gena to take care of herself, I understood the anger she was feeling, understood channeling it into work was the only way she could cope.

"I'm on my way to the doctor now," she was saying, as if reading my mind. "The sooner I get a clearance, the sooner we can get back to the Duncan case."

I buttoned my blouse, the phone cradled against one ear. "Given your injury and my administrative duty status, there'll be precious little for us to do."

"They've got you riding a desk?"

"Until the review board meets on the case and determines if the use of force on Ninety-fifth Street was within policy. You know the drill."

"Like I give a shit at this point," she said.

"Well, you'd better, unless you want to get disciplined," I warned. "And all that would do is undermine your case against Firestone—if and when you choose to file one."

I could hear Gena's breathing slow over the line as if she was trying to control her fury. "But I can't stand by and let him ride roughshod over this case, Charlotte. He and Ikehara are practically lynching the Thomas woman."

"I know, and it's bugging me, too. There's way too much about this case and the vic's relationships that we still don't understand."

"That's because we haven't been allowed to complete our investigation!"

Slipping on my shoes, I took a moment to consider the implications of what my partner was saying, and felt a shiver of apprehension mixed with excitement. "Look, Gena, much as I wanted to rub Steve Firestone's nose in his mistakes, make him pay for what he tried to do to us, I don't want to blow off my career in the process. If Firestone or Lieutenant Stobaugh finds out I'm going off on some rogue investigation while I'm supposed to be on administrative duty, that's just another reason to consider me a liability in the department."

I heard her snort. "Firestone's already ruined what little career I had," she said in a tone that cut right through me. "Way I see it, I've got nothing to lose."

In her rage against Steve Firestone, Gena had gone to a mental place that I knew could impair her judgment. Knew because I was having those thoughts, too, and was fighting to keep them at bay.

But despite her anger, Gena was right about Thomas, right about the fact that Ikehara in particular seemed intent on building his career on her back—using the LAPD as his muscle. But the case he and Firestone had cooked up against the home health nurse was so far-fetched I couldn't imagine it holding up in court. They were going to look like fools—or, since we were the investigating detectives assigned to the case, maybe that would be how they'd tag Gena and me if their case against Thomas fell apart.

And there was no way I was taking the fall for those idiots' bad judgment. Or let the wrong person get hooked up for a crime they didn't commit. I'd just have to find a way to rein Gena in, make sure she didn't let her personal animosity toward Firestone jeopardize us or the investigation.

So I brought her up to speed on what I'd learned from my conversation with my uncle and then tentatively laid out what needed to be done. "Most of this I can handle from my desk in the next couple of days," I assured her.

"But someone ought to be at the coroner's office when they make the cut," Gena countered. "Plus you said you wanted me to have another go at interviewing the Duncans' housekeeper."

"Don't worry about that—you've got your doctor's appointment. Plus you've got paperwork to complete on the shooting. And there's a meeting with the Chief on the Home Invasion at four."

"I slipped into the office and did most of the Ninety-fifth Street paperwork last night." In response to my silence, she pleaded: "Just hear me out, okay? Since the doctor's office is downtown, I can attend the autopsy afterward and then talk to the Amargosa woman in plenty of time to get to the office, finish the paperwork, and get ready for the meeting with the chief. If anybody tries to jack me up about it later, I'll say I was just trying to tie up some loose ends, trying to be a team player."

"That *would* free me to pick up the will from Duncan's attorney," I admitted. "Firestone thinks it might provide us with a motive for Alice Thomas, so I know he won't sweat me about that." I went through the pockets of the suit I'd worn yesterday until I found the card Billie had gotten from Ivy Duncan. "Cy Pressman's the attorney. His office is in Mid-Wilshire. I can go by there on my way to the office to pick up the will. And if he just so happens to want to talk about Duncan and his wife, all the better."

"What about the housekeeper?" Gena asked. "How do we explain going to Duncan's residence and interviewing Amargosa?"

I thought for a moment, then said: "I decided we needed to double-check the guest book from the repast, see if Philippe Baptiste might have slipped in there at some point and left a forwarding address. You offered to pick it up for me on your way to the office."

"But you forgot you'd asked me to do it and we both arrived there at the same time."

I considered the lie, turning it over in my mind. "I still don't think it'll play."

"Not if we both stick to the story."

"Don't forget, Gena—Firestone may be a vindictive bastard, but he's no fool. And with that injury of yours, and him riding your bra strap anyway, it's going to be much harder for you to slip anything by him for more than a day."

"But at least I've got a day to make some headway. I just don't want to see them botch the whole Duncan investigation. We deserve better."

As do Alice Thomas and the victim's memory.

There was a pause on the line, then Gena's muted voice "More than anything I want to hurt him, Charlotte. Hurt him bad for what he's done to me, what he tried to do to us."

I felt a chill run through my body. "All in due time, Gena." I said, trying to reassure her, not knowing yet how or when we'd get the opportunity to even the score. "All in due time."

I called Latent Prints from home, thanked my lucky stars I got Wozniak on the line so early in the morning instead of his division's answering machine. He put me on hold while he pulled the file. "There are two sets of prints I can't tie back to the print cards of the people in the house that day," he said when he got back on the line.

Assuming one set was Skip Sheffield's, that left one set unaccounted for. "Where'd you find them?"

"The vic's room. There were several finger and palm prints from one person on the metal table. And a separate set of fingerprints showed up on the bedstand matching those on that lighter that the team from Wilshire found under the desk."

My ears pricked up. "No one else's?"

"I'm afraid not."

So, contrary to what Ivy Duncan had told Detective Neidisch, the lighter probably wasn't Maynard Duncan's after all, nor did it belong to anyone she and Ivy said was present in the house that day.

Maybe it belonged to the elusive Philippe Baptiste. I checked my notes. The inscription on the lighter—*My Pilgrim Soul*—would make sense as a gift from a son to a father. I asked Wozniak if he'd gotten any hits when he ran the prints through the databases.

"I tried AFIS, NCIC, California DOJ, the works. Nothing."

"Any prints on the IV tubing the vic was hooked up to?"

"Just Alice Thomas's."

"Where else did you find her prints?"

"The bed, the desk, and the phone."

"What about the housekeeper's?"

"Hers were primarily in the bathroom—toilet, sink, and tub."

Which would have been consistent with her cleaning ritual, but I made a note of it anyway. "Anybody's prints on the medicine cabinet or the narcotics bottles inside?"

"Wiped clean."

Which suggested that if the drugs that killed Duncan came from his own supply, the killer was methodical enough to wipe away the prints.

Wozniak cleared his throat significantly. "You'll notice it's just Thursday, a full day earlier than you said you needed this." His voice rose expectantly. "I think I've held up *my* end of the bargain."

"Don't worry, Woz," I said with a laugh. "You'll have your cheese curls by the end of the day."

I was sitting and thinking about medicine cabinets and cigarette lighters, old films and new ones, when I realized, with a knotting of my stomach, that I probably should check in with Firestone. Much as I hated the thought, I knew he would try to make something of it if I didn't return his call. I compromised by calling over to the Robbery bullpen instead, under the presumption that Firestone might be there talking with Manny Rudolph and the other guys from the task force.

Or at least that's what I'd say if asked after the fact.

"He's not here, but I talked to him earlier," Detective Rudolph informed me. "He and Lieutenant Stobaugh want to see you and Cortez, if she's able, at one. Somethin' about wantin' to go over a few things before the meeting with the chief at four."

"I'm sure."

"Hey, Justice." Rudolph's drawling voice held a note of hesitation. "I heard about the crossed wires out there on Ninety-fifth. You and Cortez made the best of a bad situation."

"If you want to call it that."

There was a deafening silence on the line. "I hope y'all don't think . . . I want you to know . . ."

"Know what, Manny?"

More silence, then: "The suspect's mother, Bernita Tolliver . . . what Firestone said she . . . I didn't know anything about it."

My heartbeat quickened. "What are you trying to say, Manny?"

"Nothing," he said too quickly. "I just don't want you to think—"

"I don't think anything, Manny," I said carefully. *Yet.* "I'm just glad no one got hurt."

"Yeah," he said, the relief apparent in his voice. "Me, too."

I hung up the phone, thinking, *Weak-kneed son of a bitch. Firestone's got him jumping at his own shadow.*

I threw some waffles into the toaster and sat down with my notebook. Gena's and my fury at Firestone aside, I was sticking my neck out on this case because I believed he and Ikehara had everything bass ackwards, focusing on Alice Thomas so early in the investigation. What they were doing made no sense considering what we all knew was routine police procedure and their years of experience on the job. And while the facts could be interpreted to point in Alice Thomas's direction, experience had taught me that when half a dozen other possibilities existed, they all had to be thoroughly checked out and excluded before the primary focus should fall on any one suspect. So I made a page in my notebook for each potential suspect, and began to transfer notes gleaned from my interviews and observations.

If I set aside Thomas's largely circumstantial ties to Clemenza and the housekeeper's unsubstantiated allegations against her for the moment, I couldn't ignore Maynard Duncan's widow as a likely suspect. She had been furious over Duncan's illegitimate son, furious enough to get his portion of her husband's estate reduced. And she had obviously been working on Pastor Henley behind the scenes, getting him to advocate the changing of her husband's will, perhaps even coaching him on what to say when I interviewed him at Peaceful Shepherd. I had a partner once who said that if given a chance, people will paint a picture of themselves more telling than anything you could ever imagine. The picture I was getting of Ivy Duncan was of a grasping, avaricious woman who'd do anything to, as my uncle put in, keep up appearances. The question was whether her husband's transgressions were so embarrassing, so unforgivable, that murder was the only option she felt she had left to make things right in her world.

Then there was the Duncans' minister, Pastor Henley. Maybe he wasn't aware of the extent of the couple's financial straits and figured Peaceful Shepherd was in line for a big bequest that could form the basis of Still We Rise's redevelopment plans. Maybe the good pastor had used his close relationship with the couple to ensure the bequest was made, through friendly persuasion of the husband or emotional manipulation of the wife. Then it would have been only a matter of biding his time before Maynard Duncan shuffled off his mortal coil and Henley had free rein over the director's bequest—and maybe, through his relationship with Duncan's wife, over the rest of the estate too.

But maybe Henley took it a step further and obtained a key for the morphine pump from the church-owned Green Pastures Nursing Home. He could have given it to Ivy Duncan. It was possible she'd seen Alice Thomas program the dosage in the pump enough to be able to do it herself. Or maybe Henley wasn't the predator here at all—maybe Ivy Duncan had sought him out and seduced him into being an accomplice to her plan.

As I put the finished waffles on a plate, I ran through the other names on my list. Although I could be mistaken, Delphine Giles seemed too out of it to be able to plan and execute a murder like Duncan's, and from the look of the crime scene and the lack of substantial clues, I was pretty sure the murder had been planned carefully, and in advance. I just needed to know more about her to determine if, born-again Christian or not, she had that kind of devious mind—and a motive compelling enough to kill a brother whom she so obviously idolized.

Then there was nickel-slick Skip Sheffield. From his exploitive programming on UCN to selling out the city's poorest residents on the development deal, it was clear the man had no social conscience. But setting his reputation and my personal dislike for him aside, it wouldn't make sense for Sheffield to kill a man like Duncan over what was probably for him no more than a chump-change debt, especially when they had so many other, more important business dealings together. But still, he'd neglected to mention the loan he'd made Duncan to Billie and me when we interviewed him, which was leading me to believe there was more to it than met the eye. So, aside from getting that set of elimination prints, a more formal interview to see how Sheffield would react to my knowledge of his more direct connection to Duncan's *Stormy Weather* project seemed the way to go.

I also didn't have a clear read yet of the Duncans' hired help, especially Dolores Amargosa. She'd seemed jumpy during our interview, but that could be attributed to her uncertain immigration status or to being brow-beaten by Ivy Duncan, aka the Employer from Hell. I hoped Gena's interview with her would give us a better read.

I intended to ask Amargosa and Randall if they'd seen the two visitors whose prints were all over Duncan's sickroom. The fact the prints had shown up despite Dolores Amargosa's cleaning early that day suggested that whoever they were, they had been there and had most likely dropped the lighter *after* the housekeeper had finished her upstairs chores. Flipping through my notes, I realized the time would have to have been after nine, when Randall arrived and Amargosa went downstairs to begin food preparation for Ivy and Del's Thanksgiving client, and before noon, when Duncan began to receive a steady stream of visitors. Not that the visitors in question couldn't have arrived before or after, but given the information I'd gotten from the coroner's office about time of death and the time it would take for any number of narcotics to do their job, I doubted it. Especially if one of the visitors was Duncan's killer.

Which brought me back to the mysterious Philippe Baptiste. Could he have been tipped to the change in Duncan's will *before* it was signed and gotten someone to let him into the house? But if he had, there would have been a record of his visit at the development's gatehouse. Nevertheless I made a note to myself to double-check the logs the Wilshire detectives had obtained when I got to the office.

But if I could just find Baptiste, I could question him first-hand. There had to be some record of his whereabouts. I called my contacts at the phone company and utility companies to see if they had any service registered in Baptiste's name and came up empty. Ditto for the Writers Guild, which wouldn't give me an address for Baptiste nor even verify his membership without a search warrant.

I felt as if I was going in circles, a ship lost in the storm. Maybe some food would help.

The waffles smelled and tasted like cardboard, especially after the seductive scent coming from Aubrey's oven earlier that morning. As I drenched the pale squares with syrup, I was struck by a thought: Was what I had been doing all morning, going over the Duncan case, just good work ethics, or a way to avoid just what

Aubrey had accused me of doing—avoiding the more turbulent aspects of my life? Like, why wasn't I going after Firestone for the hornets' nest he'd sent us into, instead of working out the details of the Duncan case? Why hadn't I pressed Manny Rudolph harder about what he was trying *not* to tell me? And more germane to the point—was I afraid to even admit to the *possibility* of a life with Aubrey, afraid the pleasure he brought me might be taken away as it had been with Keith?

I dismissed the thought as ridiculous, until I looked down at my plate, saw syrup spreading from my plate all over the counter-top. As I ran for a sponge to wipe up the mess I'd made, I wondered if maybe Aubrey wasn't right after all.

I was on my way out the door when my cell phone rang. It was Firestone. "Where are you? It's almost nine o'clock."

The sound of his voice made my stomach lurch. "On my way to pick up Duncan's will." I forced myself to remain calm, felt my breakfast threaten to make an unscheduled reappearance. "Remember, we talked about it just before Gena and I went to Ninety-fifth Street?"

"I remember, but I want you to remember you're supposed to be on administrative duty, not out in the field doing interviews."

"I'm only going to pick up the document. It's on my way to the office anyway."

"Well, don't be all day," he said gruffly. "I want to review that will this afternoon."

"What's the rush?"

"Ikehara's just chomping at the bit to get started on Thomas."

"That man is trouble if you ask me."

"Not if he's right about Thomas. You talk to Detective Cortez?"

So it was *Detective* Cortez now. "Just briefly," I lied.

"She say anything in particular?"

"Like what?"

"I don't know . . . about Ninety-fifth Street?"

"Not really."

"Where is she?"

Where you can't find her. "I think on the way to the doctor's for a medical clearance. Haven't you talked to her?"

"She hasn't been home," he said, then added hastily, as if covering his tracks, "or wasn't answering her phone. How are you two getting along?"

"No better, no worse," I lied, declining to tell him how remarkable it was how almost getting killed could bring two people together, could bind them together in a common cause.

The line was dead for a moment, then: "Cortez has a lot of issues, Charlotte. It's one of the reasons I needed to get her out from under me. It wasn't a healthy situation."

Certainly not for her, I wanted to say, but bit my tongue again. "Yeah, well, if there's nothing else, I gotta run."

"I'll see you in the office."

I hung up the phone, thinking, *Not if I see you coming first.*

CHAPTER 17

A PIECE OF WORK

Cy Pressman's offices were located on Law Lane, a stretch of high rises on Wilshire Boulevard near Normandie that used to house hundreds of attorneys who enjoyed both the proximity to the downtown courts and the nearby watering holes/pick-up bars. There was a time that a bomb dropped on Law Lane would have wiped out half the lawyers in Los Angeles, which, with few exceptions, would be no great loss in my book.

As I circled the block looking for a parking space, I passed the abandoned and fenced-off Ambassador Hotel, known to successive generations as the site of either the famous Cocoanut Grove or the infamous Bobby Kennedy assassination. But notoriety had long since bypassed this part of the city, which was struggling to accomodate a hodgepodge of Korean-owned restaurants, past-their-prime churches, and run-down hotels. The fact that Cy Pressman clung to offices here while the powerhouse entertainment law firms were either headquartered in Beverly Hills or Century City told me more about Duncan's attorney than any background check.

Meeting him only confirmed my theory. Cy Pressman was a carefully dressed, precise man whose receding chin was more than

compensated for by a snow-white, five-star comb-over and a slop-
ing nose with a bump on its bridge the size of a mogul at
Mammoth. Gold-rimmed eyeglasses held together by masking tape
struggled for a place on that promontory, giving him the appearance of an aged, slightly threadbare anteater.

After going through the usual pleasantries, I stated my purpose and asked how long he'd known the Duncans. "Since the late
forties," he replied. "I was legal counsel to the Actors Lab when
Maynard was apprenticing there as a director. Some years later I
represented him and Ivy in the purchase of their house."

"I thought real estate brokers did that in California."

"They usually do. But in this case, I was the intermediary
between Maynard and Ivy and a straw buyer inside Fremont Place
who was helping them purchase a home in the development. After
the purchase was complete, I drew up the paperwork for the buyer
to deed the property over to the Duncans as well as set up private
financing through this individual's friends."

"Why go through all those changes? Was it because the
Duncans were famous?"

"It was because they were *Negroes,* Detective Justice, although
that wasn't the term his neighbors-to-be used in the fifties. You
must remember, this was not long after the Supreme Court struck
down California's restricted housing covenants and some other
'neighbors' burned a cross in Nat and Maria Cole's front yard
when they bought just a few blocks from Maynard and Ivy."

"You and that straw buyer were pretty courageous, busting
the block like that."

"We were both good friends of the Duncans, plus we were
committed to breaking the stranglehold those prejudiced WASPs
had on the neighborhood."

Pressman went on to explain how the experience cemented
his relationship with the couple, which extended to his preparing
all of their wills. "You say that like there were several," I noted. "Do
you have copies I could review?"

"I've got the duplicate originals right here." He fumbled
under his desk until he unearthed a thick Pendaflex file from a

stack of papers. "There were, let me see . . . four in all. Ivy's has never changed; it leaves her interest in the catering business to her sister-in-law, Mrs. Giles. Maynard's had three over the years."

He flipped through some manila folders until he found one yellowed with age. "The first one was executed in the fifties, not long after he and Ivy moved into Fremont Place," he explained, scanning the pages. "The house, of course, was joint tenancy and excluded from the will, but Maynard left his production company to Ivy, and an annuity to his sister and her husband. Then, two summers ago, he had a second will executed that left his business to his wife, a smaller cash gift to his newly widowed sister, and the annuity and a co-op in Manhattan to a friend by the name of Philippe Baptiste."

I felt the hairs on my neck rise at the mention of Baptiste's name. "Was the co-op solely in Mr. Duncan's name?"

Pressman nodded. "Maynard purchased it many years ago when he was doing a lot of television and film work in New York and overseas in Europe. He used it as his East Coast base of business."

More like monkey business, from what Uncle Syl had told me. "Why wasn't title to the co-op held in joint tenancy like the house here?"

My question caused something to shift in the old man's face, which he tried to disguise by swiveling his chair around to study the traffic inching its way east on Wilshire toward downtown. There was an awkward silence before he spoke, his voice barely above a whisper: "Because Ivy didn't know about the co-op at first. She didn't learn of it until about a year after the second will was executed."

"That was about the same time Mr. Baptiste moved out here from New York."

He turned back to face me. "I wouldn't know about that," he demurred, eyes darting behind his glasses. "All I know is Maynard needed to take out a second against the New York property to pay the expenses on his documentary but the lender insisted Mrs. Duncan be on title and cosign the note. That's when I got involved."

I let the silence linger a little before saying: "I'm sure you'd never pry into your clients' personal lives, Mr. Pressman, but there's a possibility that Philippe Baptiste was more than your client's friend—he may have been Mr. Duncan's son, even his lover. Could either of those possibilities have influenced Mr. Duncan's generosity in the development of his second will?"

The lawyer's lips twisted disdainfully, which he tried to disguise with a dry cough and a bony fist over his mouth. He removed his glasses and put them carefully in his pocket. "I wouldn't know about that, but let me just say this—there's a certain class of person in this world who preys on decent people's sense of guilt and obligation. And when these decent people come to me in their anguish, I must advise them of what I think is fair and equitable to all parties concerned, especially when I represent multiple interests."

"So when Mr. Duncan came to you about executing a second will, you felt you had to protect Mrs. Duncan's interests as well as carry out Mr. Duncan's wishes in regard to Mr. Baptiste."

"That's correct, although I'm sorry to say I wasn't as successful as I would have liked."

"Why do you say that?"

"Maynard called the Friday before he died, said he'd had a change of heart. But when he gave me his instructions over the phone, I realized he'd just exchanged one folly for another."

"How do you mean?"

He extended the heavy folder in his frail hands. "See for yourself."

I worked my way through the individual files until I got to the third will, which had some notable differences from the first two. For one thing, it scaled back the bequest to Baptiste, but still left the young man a healthy twenty-five thousand dollars—the same amount he'd called and asked Maynard and Ivy for in the spring. Duncan's sister, Delphine Giles, got her annuity back—and Alice Thomas was bequeathed Duncan's entire film and memorabilia collection, which, while the home health nurse might not appreciate it given her new outlook on life, I imagined would have been a coveted addition to any of a dozen film archives across the country.

But what was most interesting to me was the cash bequest to Peaceful Shepherd Missionary Baptist Church—one hundred thousand dollars provided it be used to establish a specialized hospice program at Green Pastures Nursing Home in Duncan's name. As Pressman buzzed his assistant and gave her the documents to copy for me, I asked, "When did Mr. Duncan receive the revised will?"

"I had it messengered over there Monday morning."

"And we know he signed it on Tuesday. When did you get it back?"

"Wednesday morning. Of course, by then, Ivy had called me with the news of Maynard's death."

"Pastor Henley made out pretty well in that last version."

"Like a bandit," he said, shrugging in apology for his candor. "But Mr. Duncan had strong feelings about Pastor Henley and his work at Peaceful Shepherd."

"Which you didn't share?"

"Have you met the man? Well, then you'll probably understand why I think he's a little too slick."

"Did you share your reservations with Mr. Duncan?"

He nodded his head, his lips thinned. "I tried. But Maynard and Ivy clung to that man like a life raft in a stormy sea. And I'm sorry to say I believe he capitalized on it."

Based on the size of the bequest to the church, I tended to agree. I made a note and moved on. "I also noticed there was no mention of the co-op in the third will."

The attorney put on his glasses to scan some pages in the folder on his desk. "It was sold last spring to repay some debts and raise cash for Maynard's nursing home care."

"Speaking of cash, is Mr. Duncan's estate large enough to provide for all of those named in the will?"

"Maynard had a life insurance policy that was made payable to the estate to specifically cover the cash gifts. He purchased the annuity many years ago."

I read over my notes, trying to make sense of the logic behind the dead man's actions. "Wouldn't it have been simpler and less costly to have designated an individual or a charity as beneficiary of his life insurance policy rather than have it made payable to the estate and have to go through probate?"

Pressman's eyes narrowed behind his glasses with something akin to frustration.

"His accountant and I told him that, but Maynard believed this way gave him more control."

"Control from the grave? Over who, or what?"

"He wouldn't elaborate."

"Then tell me this—why didn't Mr. Duncan get cash from the annuity rather than tie up his property making that documentary? And even if he did it to preserve the annuity, why go to Skip Sheffield for financing instead of UCN directly or a commercial lender?"

Pressman held up his hands in supplication. "His accountant and I tried to dissuade him from that course of action, too, even referred him to some of our contacts in banking, but he and Ivy were so overextended by that point that neither UCN nor the banks would take the risk."

"So in rides Skip Sheffield, bearing one hundred thousand dollars, to save the day."

"If that's what you want to call it," Pressman mumbled, his lips bunched.

"You don't sound like a big fan of Mr. Sheffield's."

The old man's mouth twisted into a full sneer, the pressure behind his lips building until he couldn't hold it any longer. "The terms of that loan were two percent per month interest only, with the principal due and payable the first of December this year. Far as I was concerned, Skip Sheffield was no better than a *gonif,* a common thief, but given the Duncans' precarious credit situation, he had them convinced he was being quite generous."

Even as I wrote it down, the words "generous" and "Skip Sheffield" didn't seem to belong in the same sentence. "Other than interest rates higher than my credit cards, what else was in it for Mr. Sheffield?"

"Plenty. Typically a package like *Stormy Weather*—five hours of original programming with rights to first-run and two rebroadcasts—would be worth a minimum of two hundred and fifty thousand dollars on the open market, and that's with the filmmaker retaining world and video rights. But Sheffield knew that Maynard had gone way over budget making the film, so when Maynard first approached UCN, he instructed his people to offer him only one hundred and twenty-five, with UCN retaining all the ancillary rights."

"Which would barely cover the loan Sheffield made to Duncan."

"That's correct. And given the lack of response from other potential buyers, Maynard was worried sick that he'd be forced to take UCN's lowball offer, sell the house to repay Sheffield, or lose the film to him entirely. Assuming it was the latter, Sheffield could turn around and sell *Stormy Weather* to UCN through one of his dummy corporations at the going rate and later resell the rebroadcast rights to another network or recut it and release it theatrically. Sheffield would be getting five hours' worth of quality programming for his network while making a tidy profit for himself on the side."

"He's quite a piece of work."

"That's the least of it."

"What else is there—stealing from the church collection plate?"

Pressman smiled grimly. "You're not too far off, Detective. Maynard and Sheffield had a major difference of opinion over where Still We Rise should locate a postproduction complex designed to attract film companies to the area. Maynard wanted it to be in the heart of South Central and was suspicious of Sheffield's counterproposal, so he had me look into the property Sheffield wanted to target for development."

"This was the property at Santa Barbara Plaza?" I asked.

He nodded. "A contact of mine over at Angeles Crest Title did a property profile on about two dozen parcels in the proposed redevelopment area. Lo and behold, they're owned by several dummy corporations that are controlled by either Skip Sheffield, one of his business associates, or his relatives."

"When did you find this out?"

"The title company called me with the results on Monday afternoon. I asked them to send the documents overnight to Maynard."

"But Mr. Duncan allegedly signed a proxy on Tuesday to approve the Santa Barbara Plaza project."

"Then he must not have seen the report."

I quickly skimmed my notes. "There was no record of it being in the papers found at the house." My mind went to the FedEx package Dolores couldn't identify as a thought occurred to me. "Or maybe his vote in favor of the Santa Barbara Plaza plan was a *quid pro quo* for getting the money to repay Sheffield." I backtracked to explain Maynard and Ivy Duncan's unexpected windfall. "One of Sheffield's dummy corporations or business associates could have deposited the funds into the Duncans' account."

Pressman disagreed. "Maynard hated Sheffield way too much to have let himself be bought off like that. He would have exposed Sheffield and gone down fighting to keep the house rather than take a nickel of bribe money from that man or his cronies."

Pressman was writing down the name of his contact at the title company when his assistant returned and gave him the copies, which he in turn passed to me. I noticed Duncan's shaky signature on the third will, making a mental note to have our Questioned Documents unit compare it against the others and the proxy Duncan signed for Sheffield the day he died.

I waited until I was gathering up my things to ask my last question. "Why did Mrs. Duncan file that motion to prevent the autopsy on her husband? What was she trying to hide?"

"I haven't a clue." He shook my hand and returned to his paperwork. "You'll have to ask her that yourself."

As it turned out, I didn't have to.

I was getting into my car when I got a call from Gena, who'd just left the morgue. "I feel I've had a full day already, and it's only nine-thirty," she complained.

I brought her up to date on my interview with Cy Pressman. She told me what she'd learned from FedEx. "They traced the package that was delivered to Duncan's house."

"Was it from Angeles Crest Title Company?"

"How'd you know that?"

"They were supposed to send Duncan the results of some profiles they did on the Santa Barbara Plaza properties, but Pressman wasn't sure it arrived." And since we now knew it had arrived, yet we hadn't found it among Duncan's things, someone must have walked out of the house with it. Based on the delivery time, it could have been any of Duncan's visitors—even Sheffield himself. Or . . .

"Did you find out if FedEx picked up anything from the house that day?"

"Yeah. Even though it's against FedEx's policies to pick up packages without the customer scheduling it in advance, the regular driver on Duncan's route knew how sick he was and bent the rules for him. So after she delivered the package, she waited outside while Duncan filled out a slip from that sequence and then dropped the package off at a collection box on Wilshire."

"Who was the addressee?"

"Skip Sheffield," she replied, and read off an address in Laughlin Park.

"That makes no sense. Why would Duncan send a package to a man he was going to see that same day?"

"Maybe Duncan forgot Sheffield was coming."

"Sheffield was bringing a proxy for Duncan to sign for the vote on Still We Rise's development project. Even if he was groggy from the pain medication, I couldn't imagine Duncan forgetting something that important. I also can't imagine him signing the proxy if he knew Sheffield was up to no good on that development deal. Now I'm even more convinced Duncan didn't see that property profile."

"Or maybe he did and figured he could parlay his information into a nice payday."

"That's what I suggested to Pressman, but he insists Duncan

wouldn't have gone down that easy. And if he wouldn't, maybe that was reason enough for Sheffield to kill him."

"So how do we flush him out?"

"I want to revisit the Duncan residence first. I've always felt Dolores Amargosa knew more than she was letting on about Duncan's last day, so let's hope your interview with her gives us some new information. Plus it'll give me an opportunity to follow up with Mrs. Duncan regarding her husband's dealings with Sheffield on the Still We Rise board."

"You should also follow up with her about her husband's illness."

"Why?"

"Dr. Reynolds finally got the vic's medical record. Maynard Duncan was HIV-positive."

CHAPTER 18

WITHIN
THEIR GATES

I felt that sudden jolt of recognition, like when a fragment of a jigsaw puzzle that has made no sense is suddenly revealed to be part of a familiar landscape.

"Of course—'an ugly way to die!' Mrs. Duncan used the phrase to describe her husband's illness, but I assumed she was talking about his cancer." Other pieces were falling into place, patterns arranging and rearranging themselves almost faster than I could keep up with them. "So the motion to quash, Ivy Duncan's whole response to the autopsy make perfect sense. But why didn't the coroner's shop pick up on any signs of the disease when they first saw the body in Processing?"

"Because there weren't any physical manifestations they could detect on a visual examination of the body," Gena explained. "And since no medications were found at the scene, Alexander and Dr. Reynolds couldn't know until they reviewed the chart from his doctor."

"When was he diagnosed?"

"Beginning of August. They put him on a couple of oral medications, including AZT, the treatment they've got Magic Johnson on."

"The *expensive* treatment," I said. I brought the car up to the Fremont Place gatehouse and flashed the black female on duty my ID. Something Pressman had told me sparked an idea, so I wedged the phone between my ear and shoulder as I fished through my bag for the *Variety* article I'd picked up at my uncle's and showed her the photo as well. "Have you seen this man in the development?"

The guard shoved a bookmark in the paperback she was reading to take a peek. "Ms. Thing's moved out, but Mr. Cavender still lives here."

I looked at the photo again. " 'Ms. Thing'?"

"That's what I called him."

"You know his real name?"

"Philippe Baptiste."

I felt a chill come over me. "Maynard Duncan's son?"

"Right," she replied with a twist of her mouth.

"How long since you've seen him around?"

"Not since the beginning of the year, except for a few weeks in the summer when he was visiting Mr. Cavender."

I stared at the photo of the handsome young man, wondering whether his relationship with the British director was more than the obvious. Realizing I still had the phone in my hand, I asked Gena to call me back in five, then returned my attention to the guard: "So you haven't seen Mr. Baptiste since this summer?"

"He came around here a few weeks ago, looking all pale and pitiful, whining about how everyone had turned their backs on him and he had nowhere else to go. I kinda felt sorry for him, but I had instructions not to admit him."

"From whom?

"Mr. Cavender *and* Mrs. Duncan. They froze him out like he stole sum'n."

While I knew Baptiste had allegedly stolen from the Duncans, what was his offense against Tristan Cavender? "Where does Mr. Cavender live?"

She indicated a house in the direction of the Duncan residence. "One block down, the bright-colored house on the left with the bougainvillea."

"You seen him this morning?"

"Not yet, but it's still a little early for him to be out. He usually takes a walk around the development between eleven and twelve. Always stops by to bend my ear, like I don't have more important things to do."

I looked at the curled edges of the romance she was reading. "Did he take a walk last Tuesday?"

"Unh-uh," she replied. "Only day last week I got any reading done."

Hearing another piece fall into place, I thanked her and was on my way toward Cavender's when Gena called me back. "From what I heard, sounds like that Baptiste kid really got around."

"You ain't said nothing but a word," I replied and quickly recounted the rest. "Where were we?"

"Duncan's HIV drugs."

"Right. Ivy Duncan said something when I first interviewed her about Medicare not paying for her husband's medication and it costing the family thousands of dollars per month. So if Duncan was taking those HIV medications along with the cancer-related drugs, that would have only intensified their cash crunch."

I stopped the car in front of the salmon-and-green drop-dead gorgeous Spanish hacienda the guard had ID'd as Cavender's. It sat a block away from the Duncan address. "Did you tell Dr. Reynolds what the manufacturer's rep said about the dosage programmed into the pump?"

"Yeah, I did," Gena replied, " but the medical record indicated the dosage was consistent with a change his doctor called in to HealthMates shortly before Duncan died. And, according to Dr. Reynolds, the new dosage was still within the normal limits for a man in his condition."

"So if the morphine dispensed from the pump didn't kill him, it had to be some other form of narcotic either ingested or injected."

"And unfortunately," Gena added, "Reynolds says we won't

know what or how much until the tox screens come back on the body and tubing in a couple of weeks."

And as much as I might not like it, there was little I could do to speed it along.

I studied the facade of Cavender's magnificent mansion. By comparison, Maynard and Ivy Duncan's slightly shabby spread in the next block was just a poor relation. But both houses, insulated as they might seem by the gates and guards and money, still festered with secrets that fairly oozed out their front doors. And while I now knew what some of them were, the thought of exposing the rest gave me no particular joy.

"Tell me something, Gena—how do you think a woman of Ivy Duncan's generation would react to discovering, after a half century of sacrifice and struggle, that her husband's so-called son was really his lover, that he'd been diverting money to this boy in New York while she and his sister's family struggled to make ends meet at home, and that on top of it all this 'son' may have transmitted the HIV virus to her husband?"

"I think she'd come completely unglued."

"Me too. So the question is whether knowing about her husband's secret life and condition so unglued her that murder became the only solution."

"So what's our plan?"

"I want to see how much of this Ivy Duncan gives up voluntarily, before we have to advise her and that lawyer Pressman gets involved."

"Maybe she'll roll over on that minister of hers. Maybe he sweet-talked her into offing her old man."

"That thought ran across my mind when I read about the bequest to Peaceful Shepherd," I conceded, pulling away from Cavender's house. "But the more we learn about our guy's secret life, the more I think whoever did him had a lot more to gain than a bequest in a will. Where are you?"

"On Wilshire, a few blocks from the Duncan address. I was just going by there to pick up that guest book you wanted, remember? Just trying to be a team player."

"And here I just pulled up in front of the house to do the same thing myself."

"Then I guess we'll be bumping into each other pretty soon."

It was a little before ten by the time Gena pulled up behind me. As she got out of her car, I noticed how slowly she walked despite the chill in the air, how she gingerly eased herself into the passenger's seat of my car, a seat she'd almost jumped out of less than twenty-four hours before. "You look like death warmed over."

"Same thing the doctor said, only in more clinical terms," she replied with a tense smile.

"Go on home, Gena. This case isn't worth your health. How long did the doctor say you're supposed to be off?"

Her response was slow in coming, and when it came, it was barely above a whisper. "Another week minimum."

" 'Another'?"

"I had a little surgery over the holiday," she admitted softly, "but the doctor says I came back too soon. I was just trying to keep it quiet . . . I didn't want him to know. . . ."

I scrutinized my partner's pale face, understanding finally that she wasn't pregnant when I saw her at King Hospital. She *had been* pregnant. The knowledge caused my jaw to tighten in anger. "Firestone."

Gena's eyes were heavy with tears, but she maintained her silence. I put a hand on her shoulder. "I'm not here to judge you."

"He *raped* me. A tear slid down her cheek. "I'm Catholic, I've got a brother who's a priest. Do you know how hard this has been for me?"

"I'm so sorry, Gena. Are you gonna be all right?"

"I will be," she said softly, pressing her palms over her eyes. "I am. Truly. Let's go on in there and get these interviews over with."

Ivy Duncan answered the door herself. The timeless beauty I'd admired a few days ago had completely vanished, leaving in her place a pinched and angry old woman, a black sweater pulled about her shoulders like a shroud of pain. "What is it now, Detective

Justice?" she asked through the partially opened door. "Come to gloat over the autopsy results?"

"No, ma'am. This is Detective Cortez." Gena stepped forward, but Ivy Duncan declined to shake her outstretched hand. "May we come in?"

Duncan's widow continued to block the doorway with her body. "I suppose you're here for the sideshow, so you can run back and blab to the *Star.*"

"We wouldn't do that, ma'am."

"Well, somebody's been talking. We've had a corporate cancellation already this morning."

"That wouldn't be from anything leaked by our offices," I assured her.

Ivy Duncan's eyes narrowed in thought. "Perhaps you're right," she said slowly.

"We need to examine the guest book from the repast."

She seemed distracted. "Why would you want to do that?"

I eased closer, Gena behind me. "We just need to see who came to the repast, check it against the visitor list at the gatehouse for the day your husband died."

She held the door open reluctantly and we crossed the foyer. I headed down to the living-room sofas, while Gena took up a position at the foot of the stairs. Ivy Duncan stood above her, fists tightly clenching her sweater.

"Before you get the book," I began, "let me reassure you, Mrs. Duncan, that our investigation is under a strict press embargo. No one from the LAPD is going to talk to the *Star* or anyone else about the details of this case."

I sat on the sofa to the left of the fireplace, encouraging her to do the same. "Unless you're suggesting your husband's condition—"

"No need to spare my feelings at this late date," she said stiffly. "You mean his HIV?"

"Yes, ma'am. If his HIV—or other factors—had something to do with the reason for his death."

I was relieved she'd opened the door voluntarily on the subject of her husband's illness. Now stepping through it and discover-

ing what I needed to know without pressing her too far and causing her to call Cy Pressman was going to be the trick.

"Isn't that what these muckrakers will make of it, regardless
of the truth?" Ivy Duncan's eyes swelled with angry tears that
threatened to savage the grief-worn contours of her face. She
moved down the stairs and sat heavily on the sofa opposite me. "I
saw what they did to Rock Hudson, and that poor young man
who was in *Midnight Express,* even Magic Johnson. Someone in
Maynard's position wouldn't stand a chance." She looked at me
with a fierceness I'd not seen in her before. "That kind of rampant
speculation would overshadow everything my husband ever tried
to achieve in his career. There was no way I could let the world
know about his condition. I would have done anything to keep
that from happening."

"Would 'anything' include hiding his medication?"

Embarrassment fought with anger on her face, and she
looked away. "I admit I flushed his HIV pills down the toilet before
the paramedics arrived, but that's all."

"I hate to bring this up," I said, digging out my notebook and
pretending to search my notes. "But a question has been raised
about the *coquito,* too."

Mrs. Duncan looked at me sharply, her face almost crimson.
"Did that lying heifer Dolores insinuate I tried to poison my husband? She knows damn well I was just trying to get some nour-
ishment into him, for God's sake! I wouldn't have hurt him. You
may not believe this, but I *loved* Maynard, and in his own way, he
loved me."

"Even after Philippe Baptiste showed up at your door? Even
after you discovered your husband had secretly purchased a co-op
in New York, and that he probably took the boy there, or others
like him?"

"You're twisting the truth. It wasn't like that at all!"

"I'm sure it wasn't, ma'am," I said, rising suddenly to my feet.
"But I think we'd better end this interview right now, or we'll have
to advise you of your rights and take you downtown for a more
formal interrogation." I waited for my words to sink in before

delivering the final blow. "And of course, you'd be allowed to call Mr. Pressman."

Previous experience with Ivy Duncan had taught me that, for her, maintaining appearances was more important than anything. But the threat of going to a police station on the one hand and the chance that truth might come out on the other may have finally broken something loose, because Ivy Duncan's eyes widened in panic.

"That won't be necessary." She quickly brushed tears from the corners of her eyes. "I'll tell you what you want to know."

I got out my notebook, feeling a twinge of guilt that I was somehow stripping an old woman of what little illusion she had left. But despite my feelings, I let Ivy Duncan's emotions run their course, waiting patiently to see whether they were real or part of another act, whether breaking her down would lead to an affirmative statement of her guilt on charges more serious than interfering with a police investigation.

"I had an inkling from the beginning that Maynard was different somehow," she said, sniffling. "But when I was growing up, there weren't any words for that kind of thing—or at least none you could use in mixed company. When I broached the subject with Del, she told me Maynard was just sowing his wild oats, that he needed a good woman to put him on the right track. And he *tried* to please me. But by the time we'd been married a few years, and the whole truth came out, I'd resigned myself that physicality of marriage wasn't as important as the companionship. We had built so much together, why destroy it all over an occasional fling?"

"So you never did believe the story that Philippe was your husband's son," I said softly.

She shook her head briefly, the tears collecting in her eyes again. "But I had to act like I did, or people would have started talking! When I went up to Maynard's sickroom last week and found him dead among all that AIDS medication, I realized what we had built would be destroyed if the truth got out! Maynard was gone—Del and I were the ones who'd have to put up with the snickering in church, have to endure clients who'd hire us just to be able to ask embarrassing questions." The look on her face was desperate. "I called Pastor Henley and he counseled me that throwing away Maynard's medication was for the best. Surely you can understand my motives!"

"What I understand is that because of your desire to whitewash the truth, you've tampered with evidence and implicated yourself and perhaps others in your husband's—"

"Ivy?" Delphine Giles, a white flowering orchid plant in her hand, stood gripping the banister at the top of the living-room steps. Seeing the anguish on her sister-in-law's tear-streaked face, her own hardened in response. "What's the matter?"

Struggling to regain control of herself, Ivy said, "This doesn't concern you, Del. Why don't you go up to your room and get some rest?"

"I don't need to rest," the older woman replied testily. "And if it's about my brother, it most certainly *does* concern me!"

"We were just clearing up some things with your sister-in-law," I explained.

Mrs. Giles looked to Ivy Duncan, who blurted out: "They're trying to say Pastor Henley and I conspired to kill Maynard!"

Before I could correct her, Mrs. Giles cut in, "That's ridiculous! Leave her alone," and angrily descended the stairs. She set the orchid on a side table and moved to a telephone. "Don't say another word, Ivy. We're calling Mr. Pressman right now. Ivy and Pastor Henley didn't have anything to do with it!"

"Don't do that, Del! I . . . don't want Cy dragged into this," Ivy Duncan stuttered through her tears, then turned to us. "Yes, I tried to hide the fact that Maynard was"—she shot me a worried look—"sicker than he appeared, but I didn't have anything to do with killing him, and neither did Pastor Henley!"

Mrs. Giles joined her sister-in-law on the sofa, gently taking her trembling hand. "She's telling you the truth, Detective. I know who gave my brother that overdose."

"Who was it, Mrs. Giles? Tristan Cavender?"

Ivy Duncan's face went crimson again with rage, and she snatched her hand away from her sister-in-law's. "That's impossible! Del, tell them they're mistaken."

"They're not mistaken, Sister," Mrs. Giles said out of the corner of her mouth, her eyes still on me. "I left the door open for him myself. But how did you find out?"

"Mr. Cavender lives right here in Fremont Place, just one block over—"

"But that doesn't mean he was here that day," Ivy Duncan insisted to no one in particular.

"The guard at the gatehouse reported Mr. Cavender didn't take his usual walk on Tuesday. Plus, we found an item in Mr. Duncan's room with Mr. Cavender's prints on it."

Luckily, my bluff worked; Ivy Duncan joined me in staring at her sister-in-law, who had pulled in her lips and averted her eyes. "That lighter wasn't Maynard's at all, was it, Del?" she asked accusingly.

The other woman shook her head slightly. "It belongs to Cavender," she whispered. "He and Maynard had a matched pair made up years ago."

Delphine Giles's admission caused something to derail in Ivy Duncan's brain. "How—why in God's name would you let Tristan Cavender into our home?" she asked, her eyes glazed. "You've always said you loathed the man, and you know I've always been uncomfortable around him."

There was a heavy silence as Delphine Giles surveyed the room's crowded furnishings and mementos. "We were drowning financially trying to help Maynard finish *Stormy Weather,*" Mrs. Giles explained to me as if her sister-in-law hadn't spoken at all. "When I walked in on my brother Monday morning, he was having a big argument with Skip Sheffield on the telephone. When he got off the phone, he was livid, vowed he was going to get out from under Sheffield's thumb once and for all. I suggested he call Tristan Cavender for help." She stole a guilty glance at her sister-in-law. "I knew how . . . close they were when they were younger, the secrets they shared."

"You *knew,* and you still pushed me into marrying him," Ivy Duncan said numbly.

"You can't be as close to someone as I was to Maynard and

not know something like that," Mrs. Giles said to me. "But I made my brother promise to accept the Lord into his life, and renounce from his sinful ways. If he didn't, and the truth had gotten out, it would have been the end of us all."

I looked at the emotions working the old woman's face and wondered if it was concern for her brother's eternal soul or for his bank balance that motivated her. Yet I knew there was truth in her argument. A rumor back then about someone's sexuality would have become the main topic of conversation at church socials and beauty parlors all over black Los Angeles within a week. I guess in those days nobody ever really listened to the lyrics of that old Billie Holiday song "Ain't Nobody's Business If I Do." As if they ever have.

Ivy Duncan shook her head in disbelief. "But, sister . . . if you knew about Maynard and Cavender, why disrespect me by allowing the man into *my* house?"

"What choice did we have, Ivy? Even though I knew Tristan Cavender was a godforsaken son of Sodom, I had to admit his behavior has been nothing but aboveboard since you and Maynard married. And he's always been Johnny-on-the-spot whenever you needed him —introducing Maynard to producers and studio heads, helping you two buy this house you just *had* to have."

Ivy Duncan's mouth formed words, but no sound came out.

"And since Mr. Cavender had helped out his old friend before," I said, "you were counting on him to do it again."

Mrs. Giles nodded quickly, took a deep breath before plunging ahead. "Just as I predicted to Maynard, Cavender agreed to help. They set up a meeting for eleven-thirty the next day. My job was to make sure everybody was occupied out back and to leave the front door unlocked."

Thinking back to the *Variety* picture, I asked Mrs. Giles if Cavender had come alone and discovered that although she thought he had, she hadn't seen him arrive.

Cavender's visit threw a new light on the investigation, one that meant rethinking our assumptions about the killer's motive and opportunity, and directing our attention to a potential suspect who might not be as accommodating of our questions as two elderly women.

And maybe that was just what Delphine Giles wanted. "Why didn't you tell me about Tristan Cavender from the beginning, Mrs. Giles? Don't you realize you could be arrested for interfering with a police investigation?"

"I started to," she admitted nervously, "but given how generous he's been to us . . ." She hung her head. "I guess I didn't want to go off half-cocked and jeopardize the man's career."

What she meant was she didn't want to jeopardize her and Ivy's seats on the Cavender-financed gravy train. I glanced over at Ivy Duncan, whose blank stare told me she was still in shock. "But now you're convinced Mr. Cavender gave your brother an overdose?" I watched skeptically as Mrs. Giles nodded. "Why the sudden change of heart?"

"When you came around on Monday talking about a drug overdose, it all began to make sense. And when I confronted Cavender at the repast, he called me a conniving shark, but he didn't outright deny it."

Staring dully at her sister-in-law, Ivy Duncan echoed, "Cavender at the repast?"

"I swear I threw him out, Ivy, soon as I saw him signing the guest book! He said he came to pay his respects, but I think he was returning to the scene of the crime!"

"Why do you say that?"

"He just looked so devastated, I knew he was guilty!"

I knew there could be any number of reasons for Cavender's appearance and demeanor at the repast—from genuine shock to wanting to cover any traces of his presence at the crime scene.

"How was your brother after Mr. Cavender left last Tuesday?"

"Maynard seemed serene, resolved somehow. Told me, with Cavender's help, everything was going to work out for the best. But I thought at the time he was referring to our money situation, not about ending his life."

I couldn't help but wonder if Maynard Duncan's newfound serenity stemmed from getting the money he needed to repay

Sheffield, from the drugs he might have gotten from Cavender, or from something else entirely. I turned to Mrs. Duncan. "You mentioned when we first spoke about your husband's not being impressed with Mr. Sheffield's ideas for economic development. Was there something specific he objected to?"

"The more Maynard saw of Skip Sheffield's business practices, the more disgusted he became," Mrs. Duncan explained. "My husband used to say that Skip Sheffield wouldn't bother to give you change for a dollar if he couldn't get five quarters back on the deal. But it wasn't just about the loan Sheffield made to us. Maynard suspected there was more, and he was bound and determined to expose him no matter what."

Two new lines of investigation and possible motives were opening up—Tristan Cavender's relationship with Duncan and Skip Sheffield's business dealings with the dead man—neither of which would be easy to pursue without word getting back to the office. Nevertheless, I made notes on them both, then, thinking of the proxy Duncan had signed that day, asked if we could speak with Dolores Amargosa.

"We let Dolores go," Ivy Duncan said. "I just couldn't tolerate her breaking things and her odd behavior. I dismissed her yesterday, right after the repast."

"Where did she go?"

"Probably back to that nickel-slick piece of trash where we got her Skip Sheffield!"

Mrs. Duncan's revelation took me by surprise, until I recalled how Sheffield, in offering the housekeeper as his alibi, had referred to her by her first name. Why hadn't I noticed it before?

I was so busy beating myself up, I almost didn't realize Mrs. Giles was speaking. "Maynard suggested we give her a try after Skip Sheffield kept raving about how good she was at making those Latin dishes that are in such demand these days."

"She's probably at his house now," Ivy sneered, "cooking for that party we were supposed to cater until UCN called this morning canceling our contract. I guess Sheffield figured why buy the cow when he can get the milk for free."

Realizing Gena and I had a lot of ground to cover in a short period of time, I closed my notebook to signal the end of the interview. Catching the hint, Gena asked again about the guest book. Seeing Ivy Duncan hesitate, I added: "We can come back with a search warrant for it if you'd prefer."

"That won't be necessary," Mrs. Giles replied quickly. "I'll get it."

Go with her, Gena, I motioned with a jerk of my head. While they were gone, I asked Mrs. Duncan if there was anything else she needed to tell me.

"Just don't be too hard on Pastor Henley," she begged, her voice quavering. "He's been a rock to me during this ordeal. And his motives were pure—he was just trying to keep two old ladies' names from being dragged through the mud." Mrs. Duncan's voice caught in her throat. "But I don't see there's any way we can avoid it now. The truth always has a way of getting out, hard as we might try to hide it."

"Got it," Gena said a few moments later from the stairs, the black satin guest book in a plastic pouch.

Rising to leave, I thanked the women for their time.

"You're not going to arrest us, Detective Justice?" Delphine Giles asked anxiously from the top of the living room stairs.

"No, we're not, but we may need you to come to our offices tomorrow so we can get a formal statement. Until you hear from us, don't talk to anyone about the case and don't allow any visitors into the house. And neither of you should stray too far from home."

"Don't worry," Ivy Duncan replied bitterly, surveying the faded opulence of her surroundings. "Once word of this leaks out, I don't know that I'll ever be able to show my face outside Fremont Place again."

CHAPTER 19

TERMS OF ENDEARMENT

I stood with Gena between the concrete lions, feeling the damp threat of rain. "You buying the sister's story?" she asked.

"Maybe. Based on her statement, Cavender had the opportunity to poison Duncan that day, and he was there within the time frame we got from the coroner's office. His connection to Baptiste may be significant, too, but something is missing."

"Yeah—why give someone you purportedly once loved a hundred thousand dollars and then a fatal dose of narcotics?"

"Exactly."

"So, how do you want to handle this?" she asked. "Should we question Cavender before we head up to Sheffield's?"

"You know the first thing Hollywood types like Cavender and Sheffield will do when we show up is call their lawyers," I replied, giving voice to my earlier concern. "And when the lawyers call Lieutenant Stobaugh, and he finds out we're still actively working the Duncan case, he'll have us up on insubordination charges quicker than you can count to ten."

"So what's the alternative?" Gena shot back. "Lay all of this out for Firestone, and have him rat us out anyway? All he'll do is yank us off the case, and wrap it up for a notch on his own belt. Way I see it, we're in for a penny, in for a pound."

I had to agree with her. Either way, we were dead meat. I dragged a hand over my face, suddenly feeling very tired. I was tired of Senior Deputy DA Mark Ikehara and his high-handed methods. I was tired of Firestone and his dirty tricks. And I was equally tired of the layers of secrets every person associated with this case had been keeping. Skim milk masquerading as cream, as Uncle Syl put it. But could I cut to the core of this case, finish the investigation, and still manage to keep my job?

I started rummaging through my purse. "What time is it?"

"Ten forty-five. Why?"

"I have an idea how we can at least put ourselves in Cavender's path before we have to meet with the chief." I found the article from my uncle's house, scanned it while I reasoned aloud: "It'd take more time to brief the detectives they assign to this case than it will to interview Cavender ourselves. At least that's what we'll say when they pop us for insubordination."

Gena's head tilted upward as she considered the shifting clouds. "You want to chance it walking to Cavender's from here?"

"He should be gone by now." I trotted to my car and unlocked it, "You can follow me over there. The ceremony should be over, but if we get a speed on, we can probably still catch him."

"Catch him where?" she asked.

"The Hollywood Roosevelt Hotel. We're going to see a star."

Thousands of them was more like it, terrazzo-and-bronze novas streaming down Hollywood Boulevard and dotting the sidewalks of Vine Street. We were heading for the Walk of Fame, which drew more people into Hollywood's orbit than its dizzying array of tattoo parlors, lingerie stores, and prostitutes ever would.

My father had taken us kids to Hollywood dozens of times. He would point out the Max Factor building, where he had worked as a janitor during the war, or let us put our hands in the cement at Grauman's Chinese Theatre, or buy us a sundae at C. C.

Brown's, or take us to see the too few stars awarded to "our people." For Matt Justice and a lot of black folks like him, seeing a black entertainer's star on the Walk of Fame really meant something, confirmed the hard-won achievements of a show-business career and went down in the unofficial record books of memory that got dusted off when the race's progress was charted at the local barbershop or at holiday dinners.

I imagined getting a star was a big deal for Cavender, too—bigger than snagging an invitation to a super-exclusive post-Oscar bash or the waiters knowing your name at Musso & Frank Grill. It was a big deal, too, to the three hundred or so fans who'd braved the light rain to gather around the podium erected in front of the Hollywood Roosevelt Hotel.

As we got out of our cars, I could see an official-looking little man from the Hollywood Chamber of Commerce conferring with a young woman who I assumed was Cavender's publicist, if the cellular telephone sprouting out of her ear, miniskirt riding up her ass, and cutting-edge designer shoulder bag slung over her shoulder were any indication. Next to her stood Cavender, frail but looking every bit the stereotypical Hollywood elder statesman—silver-gray hair rising over a high forehead, this time wearing a soft black wool blazer, dark red turtleneck, and dark gray wool slacks.

"Get out your notebook and a pen."

"For what?" Gena asked.

I already had mine in hand. "Mr. Cavender," I called out, trotting up to the podium, extending my card. "May we speak with you for a moment?"

Cavender ignored the card, automatically nudging the Miniskirted One. Like a robot, his young handler stepped forward, reciting: "Thank you so much for coming," and thrusting glossy photos and folders in our direction. "Unfortunately Mr. Cavender can't grant individual interviews right now, but everything you need to know is in the press kit. And don't forget to mention in your articles the televised DGA awards show, February tenth at nine."

"That's very nice, miss," I said, handing them back, "but we were hoping Mr. Cavender could give us a comment about Maynard Duncan."

Hearing the dead man's name stopped Cavender in his tracks, his face flushing a color almost as deep as his sweater. He peered at me closely. "You're not a reporter. Where did we meet?"

"At Mr. Duncan's repast."

He had already begun to turn away. "I'm sure you're mistaken."

I eased up behind him and whispered, "You barely had time to sign the guest book before Duncan's sister threw you out. I've got it in the car if you'd like proof."

He regarded me cautiously. "Who are you?"

"LAPD." I offered him my card again.

He took a good look at it this time, his shoulders slumping, then gestured toward the hotel entrance. "Let's get out of the bloody rain."

Leaving his publicist to pass out the photos, Cavender guided us unsteadily through the hotel's entrance hall, which was dominated by a trio of paintings of old Hollywood stars and a garish full-scale statue of Charles Chaplin. He slowly led us up the main staircase to the mezzanine, past a photomural on Hollywood history, and to the Academy Room, where in the back stood a display table of videocassettes of some of Cavender's films in a special collector's edition and an unattended bar. Cavender grabbed an ashtray from the bar and led us to the front of the room, where tables had been set up for a luncheon, fifteen rounds of ten awaiting the guests' arrival.

The director dropped into one of the chairs, one hand cradling his head, his blue eyes staring moodily into the empty place setting before him. "What's this all about, young woman?"

"Mr. Duncan's sister said you visited him at his home last Tuesday," I began. "What was the purpose of the visit?"

Cavender thrust an unsteady hand inside his breast pocket. "Maynard Duncan was an old friend and colleague," he said, his voice carefully measured. He took out a cigarette, felt in his pockets until he found some matches, and fired up. "He called me last Monday, in a bit of a pinch over a loan he'd taken out to complete his latest—his last—film project. I'd heard him talking about the project at a DGA meeting and since I'd given him a little help from time to time in situations like this, I offered to advance him the money to pay off the loan."

I flipped through my notes, searching for something. "A hundred thousand dollars is more than a *little* help, sir."

His eyelids flickered a moment amid the smoke curling around his white mane of hair. "As I said, we'd known each other a long time. We were . . ."

I found my notes from my initial review of the murder book with Neidisch. "Pilgrim Souls?"

Cavender brought the cigarette to his pursed lips with a trembling hand. "I see you found my lighter. I'd appreciate having it back."

"What does it mean, 'pilgrim souls'?"

"It was a pet term," he said tersely, taking a drag on his cigarette. "From a W. B. Yeats poem."

"I'm afraid I'm not familiar with Yeats."

Cavender exhaled, looking away as he flicked an ash into the tray, and recited:

> *"How many loved your moment of glad grace,*
> *And loved your beauty with love false or true,*
> *But one man loved the pilgrim soul in you,*
> *And loved the sorrow of your changing face."*

He watched the cigarette smoke float on the air in a pained silence. I put down my pen and said carefully: "While I understand that you and Mr. Duncan must have been very close, sir, business is business—even among close friends. Surely there were some sort of terms to the loan."

Cavender took a sip of water to compose himself. "Maynard insisted on giving me a fifty-one percent stake in *Stormy Weather,* which wouldn't amount to—excuse the expression—a piss in the wind unless it could be sold. But I agreed he could attach my name to it as executive producer, see if that stimulated any interest."

"How did the money change hands?"

"He asked me to have my bank wire the funds directly into his and Ivy's personal savings account. From the way he put it, I assumed he needed access to the funds straightaway."

Given his wife's antipathy for the Englishman, I knew that wasn't the only reason Duncan didn't want his ex-lover's check lying around the house. "Did you have any kind of an agreement drawn up to delineate your interest in the documentary?"

"Maynard insisted I get something typed up, so we could both sign it and make it official."

Thinking of the fingerprints Wozniak lifted from the metal table in Duncan's sickroom, and my own observation of the signature and other writings embedded on the notepad nearby, I asked if either of them had made any additions to the contract.

"No, Maynard just read it and signed it on the spot."

"Where was Mr. Duncan when he signed the agreement?"

"In bed. He was in too much pain to get up, so we put it on top of some old newspapers for him to sign."

Which would account for the disheveled stack of newspapers I'd seen on the sickroom floor the day I examined the scene—and the prints on the nightstand that matched those on the lighter. But to be sure, I took a print kit out of my bag and asked Cavender if I could take a set of elimination prints.

"Is that really necessary?" he asked anxiously, looking over his shoulder toward the door. "My DGA colleagues will be here any minute."

"Better to do it now than have them see us escorting you out of the building and into a police car."

A few minutes later, Cavender was wiping his hands on a napkin while I asked if he'd actually seen Duncan's *Stormy Weather.* "We watched a demo tape that day," he replied. "Maynard showed it and the shooting script to me."

"Friendship aside, a documentary about blacks in Hollywood from a little-known director would hardly seem something you'd get behind."

"That's where you're wrong!" he retorted, jabbing his cigarette in my direction. "It's a remarkable film. And it will prove Maynard

Duncan's an important force in filmmaking. *Stormy Weather* will be of enormous significance to the film industry and his community."

"I'm impressed you'd take time from your own work to champion it."

He waved his cigarette. "Although I don't try and make a big show of it, I've always tried to help those less fortunate than I make their mark in this business. Black, white, straight, queer, it doesn't matter as long as they have the talent and strength of character to tell their stories honestly."

It seemed that last bit was offered almost as a challenge, Tristan Cavender's rising voice seeming to dare us to mention sexuality—Maynard's, his, or anyone else's. When I didn't take the bait he added, "Come on, Detective, there's no need to be coy. If that sanctimonious sister of Maynard's told you I was at the house the day he died, surely she told you we were once lovers?"

"We're not here to pry into your personal life, sir," I murmured, feeling my face burn nonetheless.

"It wouldn't matter to me if you were—my sexuality is no longer a secret," he said, exhaling a cloud of smoke. "Hasn't been since I came out in support of Sir Ian McKellen's knighthood in the *Guardian* last year." His laugh was sarcastic. "It got a little ridiculous, after four failed marriages, to continue telling the press 'I'm a hopeless romantic' or 'I'm a serial monogamist' when questioned about my love life."

He drank deeply from the water glass before continuing, "Don't let anyone tell you any differently, Detective—the closet can kill. If it doesn't drive you to suicide, or break your spirit, it'll have you abusing alcohol, drugs, the people around you, or all three. If you don't believe me, ask my ex-wives. Ask Ivy Duncan."

Cavender drained his water glass. "Naturally, one doesn't go about this homophobic town shouting 'I am queer' from the rooftops, not if you want to continue working. In Hollywood's myopic moral ledger, open homosexuality equals AIDS equals box-office risk equals your phone stops ringing. But I finally decided I'd better stop living a lie before it was all over, and anyone who didn't like it could very well sod off!"

"Too bad Mr. Duncan didn't get that opportunity."

He leaned forward eagerly. "But, don't you see, that was the beauty of it! The money I loaned Maynard was, in part, to help him tell the *truth* of his life and that of a lot of other black gay pioneers in Hollywood. He thought my support would give additional credence to his efforts and at the same time allow him to get out from under that awful man who was trying to control his film and his life."

So Duncan was going to come out of the closet, and on film no less. Suddenly the title of the third segment of *Stormy Weather* made sense. "Hidden Hollywood" wasn't just about negative images of blacks in Hollywood—it was about all the ways black lives, both straight and gay, were distorted and marginalized on film. "Is that why Mr. Duncan gave you a controlling interest in the project?"

"He wanted to be sure the paperwork was in order, so there'd be no misunderstandings with that cable fellow or with his family after the fact. He said he'd worked too hard and too long to have his film butchered if he didn't live long enough to complete it."

"That's why his wife and sister hadn't seen the film."

"He was so paranoid he kept the 'Hidden Hollywood' segment locked away in his desk. He gave it, the manuscript pages related to it, even the diskette containing the script, to me for safekeeping."

Which accounted for the ten pages missing from the *Stormy Weather* script in Duncan's office, and the absence of any diskettes containing the screenplay as well. No wonder he was so peaceful when he saw his sister afterward. "Sounds like a man who knew he was going to die," I said.

Cavender dropped his head and whispered: "It'd been a long battle for Maynard. Between the cancer eating away at him and the HIV diagnosis, he knew he didn't have long. That's why he was so obsessed with finishing that film."

"It must have been hard for you to see him suffering like that," I said, observing his thin face for an inappropriate response.

"I should say so," he replied crisply, "especially knowing how he'd contracted the virus."

"You mean unsafe sex?" Gena asked.

He turned to her. "I mean unsafe sex with that little liar Philippe Baptiste."

"Is this the little liar you're talking about?" I showed him the *Variety* photo of him with Duncan's lover. "You seem to know him pretty well yourself," I noted.

"I knew him all right." He nodded at the photo, his face a hardened mask. "But not in the Biblical sense."

"Then how?"

"I met Philippe with Duncan at a DGA event late last year. When he figured out who I was and that we were neighbors, he undertook this campaign to get a job with my production company. I finally relented and hired him to provide coverage—synopses," he added, seeing the uncomprehending look on our faces, "of scripts we were considering optioning."

In the *Variety* photo before me, Baptiste's intense gaze was fixed on the back of Cavender's head. "How well did you get to know him?"

"Well enough to hear his whole life story—how he was raised by an overly religious single mother who beat him regularly, then threw him out of the house at thirteen when she learned of his homosexuality. How he was forced to hustle the streets until he met Poppy Maynard when he was nineteen."

"Was that the *exact* term Mr. Baptiste used to describe Mr. Duncan?" Gena asked.

Cavender drew himself up disdainfully. "It's certainly not a term I would have used."

Eyebrows knitted together, Gena mouthed something I couldn't understand. "The story Mr. Baptiste told you is quite different from what he told Mrs. Duncan," I said to Cavender.

"I'm sure it was, if Ivy Duncan allowed the boy into that fortress she erected around her husband," he noted dryly. "But Philippe was a very pretty liar."

"Even so, that's no reason to accuse him of infecting Mr. Duncan with the HIV virus."

"*I'm* not the one making the accusation. Maynard called me

himself when he was diagnosed in August. Knowing I'd met the boy—and what a weakness I had for a pretty face and a hard-luck story—he called not only to tell me about his condition but to warn me to be careful."

From Cavender's appearance, I wondered if perhaps it was too late for that. I also wondered whether, by virtue of knowing about his sexuality, I was as guilty of making the same kind of wrong-headed assumption as the people he criticized in the film industry. Or as he was making about Baptiste.

"How could Mr. Duncan have known for sure it was Mr. Baptiste who infected him and not some other partner?"

His lips pursed, Cavender said, "I can't possibly know what was in Maynard's mind at the time he called me, or his entire sexual history, for that matter. But if you'd ever met that thieving gold digger, you'd know he was the one."

Ignoring the raw hatred beneath Cavender's words, I flipped back in my notes to an earlier interview. "It was our understanding that Mr. Baptiste and Mr. Duncan weren't even speaking by August. Why would Mr. Duncan think to call and warn you about Mr. Baptiste when he was diagnosed?"

"Maynard said that when they last spoke, Philippe told him that I'd admired a screenplay he'd written. Of course, the little shit was lying, trying to use my name to extort money out of Maynard and Ivy. But it was a moot point by the time Maynard called me— my producing partner had caught Philippe trying to forge some checks, so we'd already given him the boot."

"Where did he go?"

"I don't know and I don't care." Cavender spat the words out with considerable force. "Maybe someone bought that wretched screenplay. I encouraged him to write something more personal, more character-driven, but he insisted on that piece of stereotypical drivel."

"It was that bad?"

"It was one of those vile comedies the studios are shoving at what they euphemistically call 'the urban market' these days— *Blaxploitation: The Sequel,* was what Maynard had called them. Well,

Philippe had penned one called *Teed Off,* about a group of home-boys invading some posh country club, but I can't imagine who would have bought it."

I could. I shoved the article back in my pocket, flipped my notebook closed, and rose to shake his hand. "Thank you for your assistance, Mr. Cavender. We'll let you know when you can pick up your lighter."

"**D**uncan sure took enough precautions to ensure his film remained intact," Gena noted as she trailed me down the steps and past a tour guide talking about the hotel's famous ghosts. "But watching his wife and sister go after each other, I don't think the man was too far wrong. And can you believe the nerve of that kid Baptiste? First he worms his way into Duncan's life here in L.A., then he steps over his broken body to get to Cavender."

I paused at the corner to watch a group of Japanese tourists across the street, oblivious to the spitting rain, take turns stepping into some star's shoeprints at what was now Mann's Chinese Theatre. "But what goes around comes around," I said, backtracking to describe Skip Sheffield bragging at the repast about the screenplay he'd written. "*Caddyshack* meets *Boyz N the Hood,* he called it. But now it appears he didn't write it at all—he stole it from Duncan's lover."

"Maybe that's what Duncan was referring to when he vowed to expose Sheffield."

"It was either that or the shady deal Sheffield was trying to force through the Still We Rise board of directors. Either way, it might have been enough to get Maynard Duncan killed for his trouble."

We were headed for our cars when I remembered to ask Gena what she had been trying to say to me during the Cavender interview.

"It just struck me as odd that Baptiste would call Duncan 'Poppy,'" she said.

"Why?"

"It's just so close to the Spanish term *papí,* and with Baptiste's mother being French and all, I was just wondering where he picked it up. On the streets of New York City, I imagine."

I pulled out the *Variety* photo and considered the blond-haired young man closely. "But given he lied about his family history, maybe he lied about his mother's nationality, too."

"Cavender *did* call him a pretty liar," Gena noted.

While "pretty" wouldn't be a term I'd apply to a man, I had to admit Baptiste was striking—the photo captured a solemn mystery about him that I could imagine being alluring to both men and women. Except for those gray eyes, which held an edgy hunger that made me uneasy.

My uneasiness gave way to a chill. "I think I've seen this kid before."

"Where?"

"I'm pretty sure his mother showed me his picture, right there at Maynard Duncan's repast. But when she called him her baby, I thought she meant it literally, not just a term of endearment for a sick child."

My interview on the patio with Dolores Amargosa came flooding back to me, reframed by what I now suspected were her ties to Philippe Baptiste. Her sudden clumsiness in the kitchen when Otto Randall was complaining about Sheffield's movie, her vacant stares during our interview, her lament that she still had so much work to do.

I asked Gena for the address FedEx had on Skip Sheffield. She flipped through her notes, read off a location in Laughlin Park. I got in my car, started the engine, and rolled down the window. "Call Mrs. Duncan and Mrs. Giles. Tell them if Dolores Amargosa tries to get back into Fremont Place, they're to have the guard at the gatehouse call the police. And find Skip Sheffield over at UCN, tell him to stay put and not to meet with Amargosa until we can get there. We've got to get to him before she can finish her job."

I was cursing the rain-slowed traffic on Highland when Gena called me back. "Sheffield's not at the office. His assistant said he was working from home today."

I pulled out my siren and stuck it on top of the car. "We'd better hurry."

CHAPTER 20

ANOTHER
WEALTHY,
GATED
ENCLAVE

We hustled over to Laughlin Park, another wealthy, gated enclave, this one nestled in the hills between Franklin Avenue and Los Feliz Boulevard, just south of Aubrey's. But the security gates were wide open, courtesy of a broker's open house being held somewhere inside the development. A young man, huddled beneath an umbrella near the real estate agent's dripping flag, waved in every car that passed without signing it in, checking ID or destination. As we skidded up the winding, rain-slicked street, I wondered whether Dolores Amargosa had already slipped through.

When Sheffield's bodyguard, Kamau, threw open the front door of the two-story Italianate mansion, I had my answer. "Shit, it took you long enough!" he exclaimed, breathing hard. "Where are the paramedics?"

Behind a roll of thunder, I could hear the wail of a siren. "Where is he?"

He motioned us down an Oriental-carpeted hallway: "In the office."

Skip Sheffield was laid out on the carpeted floor of his mahogany-paneled office, white foam at the edges of his mouth and blood coming from a wound in his shoulder. Around him were the signs of a struggle—he'd pulled down some papers and a letter opener from his desk; the latter did not appear to have caused his wound. "I just left him and Dolores here for a few minutes while I went to the bank," Kamau said from a spot by the door. "I found him slumped over the desk when I got back, so I called nine-one-one and started CPR, but he ain't comin' around."

I knelt beside Sheffield, checked his pulse, and pulled back his eyelids. Seeing the telltale signs in his eyes, I motioned Gena over to take a look and hurried to get my briefcase. "Mr. Sheffield got any drug habits, Kamau?" I asked on my way out.

"Other than a little recreational blow, I 'on't know," the bodyguard said hesitantly.

Returning with my crime scene briefcase, I took out a plastic mouth protector and resumed CPR as the siren in the background grew louder and more distinct, then abruptly died away, replaced by a thumping at the front door. Kamau ran for the door, returning with a team of paramedics and followed close on by a couple of uniforms from Northeast Division who must've caught the call. I stood back, told Kamau to wait in the hallway where we could see him, and began briefing the patrol officers, whose names were Coan and Hayes, on who we were and what we'd found.

Meanwhile, Gena had pulled on a pair of gloves and had started searching the office for a weapon. "Found something," she said, holding up an empty glass coated with a white liquid. "You know what was in this glass?" she called out to Kamau. She sniffed at it carefully. "Smells like coconut."

"Must be the *coquito*. Dolores was supposed to make some for Mr. Duncan's party tomorrow night."

"How did Mrs. Amargosa get here today?" I demanded.

"Bus, I guess."

"Could someone have driven her?"

"Maybe."

"Where is she now?"

"Hell if I know."

"How long were you gone?"

"Forty-five minutes, an hour tops."

Long enough. I took the uniform named Coan aside. The salt and pepper in his mustache and four stripes on his sleeve told me I wasn't dealing with a baby. "Check with the young man at the front gate, see if he saw a Latina—forties, petite, brown-skinned— leave the development by car or on foot in the last hour. She may have been alone or with a blond-haired young man, slender, in his twenties." I turned to the female, Hayes. "Take Kamau here to the living room and start taking down his statement."

Gena and I were with the paramedics, waiting to see if Sheffield would regain consciousness, when Coan returned. "The kid didn't see anyone fitting those descriptions coming or going," he informed us. "But he said either one of them could have exited one of the other gates on the west or the south side of the development without his seeing them."

Or they could even be hiding somewhere in the house. "Okay, Coan, we're going to search the house, room by room."

We went together to the entryway. "Anyone else live on the property?" I called to Kamau in the living room.

"I got a spot out in the apartment out back."

"Do we have your permission to search your living quarters, Kamau?"

He hesitated for a moment, mind working behind his eyes. "Sure, if it'll help you find that bitch."

"How many rooms are there in the main house?"

"Six bedrooms, nine baths. There's also an office on this floor and a home theater and a gym in the basement."

All of which Coan and I checked thoroughly, in addition to the cabana by the pool and a few enlightening minutes spent in Kamau's quarters at the rear of the property. I warned Coan to keep quiet about our discovery, and we returned to the main house just as they were loading Sheffield into the paramedic's van. "He's unconscious but alive," Gena told me as they pulled away. "They're transporting him to Hollywood Presbyterian's ER."

Thunder again, followed by a crack of lightning. "Is he going to make it?"

"They aren't sure." Gena started unfurling the crime scene tape across the driveway. "I take it you didn't find Amargosa."

"She's in the wind."

"Well, there's something in the kitchen you'll want to see."

"Is it the weapon?"

"Better than that."

While Coan finished establishing the crime scene, Gena led me into a lavishly appointed kitchen. A stone mortar and pestle sat on the granite counter, and in the open trash compactor lay an amber pill bottle atop of a pile of eggshells and empty cans of coconut and condensed milk.

"The bottle contained Oramorph, which I assume is some kind of morphine," she whispered. "The prescription was filled for Philippe Baptiste."

"When?"

"November nineteenth."

Just five days before Duncan was murdered. I reached into my pocket for a pen, bent over, and carefully rotated the bottle around it. The prescription, filled at Hollywood Memorial Medical Center, was for sixty tablets. Reading the recommended dosage, I calculated that if Baptiste had been taking the medication as directed since the nineteenth, there should have been over forty pills left in the bottle. "Can we get an address on Baptiste from the hospital?"

"Better than that. I called over there and found out he's a patient on the fifth floor."

We'd finally run Philippe Baptiste to ground. I felt a rush of exhilaration as I examined the mortar and pestle, noticed the powdery residue in the bottom of the bowl. "Probably the same way she got the morphine into Duncan's *coquito*," I noted. "But she was much more careful then. This time she didn't even bother to clean up behind herself here."

"Which suggests to me she's pretty far around the bend."

"To say the least." I straightened up and looked my partner in the eye. "I know you aren't going to like what I'm going to say, Gena, but I don't think we have any choice but to call the office ASAP."

"But we're so close! We can't let Firestone pull us off the case now!"

Talking over her protest, I said: "There's no point in arguing. You know Hayes or Coan has already called in to Northeast's watch commander to report our presence. If they're cooperating so readily, you can bet it's because they've been told to by their WC, which means he's probably called RHD by now, which means it's only a matter of time before Stobaugh tracks us down. So let's save ourselves the heartache and call in now, tell him what we've found and that we need a team of detectives from RHD to back us up."

"Then let me make the call," Gena offered. "It'll give me a chance to rehearse the story we worked up earlier, plus it'll free you up to interview Kamau before they pull the plug on us."

"You sure?"

"Yeah, I'm sure." Gena looked scared, but there was a resolve in her voice that told me she would be all right.

"And tell the lieutenant we'll probably need a surveillance unit sent down to Dolores Amargosa's place in South Central, in case she turns up there. Her address is in the murder book on my desk."

While Gena made the call, I went to the living room to confront Kamau, who was sitting opposite Officers Coan and Hayes on a white leather sofa, huge hands covering his restless knees. His knees picked up their pace when he saw me, and for good reason.

Hayes handed me her notes on Kamau's statement, which turned out to be as worthless as I'd thought. Knowing I had an advantage, I dropped the statement on the coffee table and slowly and deliberately got out my notebook. I told Hayes to start on the house-to-house with the neighbors, leaving Kamau with just Coan and me.

"How much can you tell us about Mrs. Amargosa?"

"Not much. She's worked for the boss off and on since October."

"How'd she get the job?"

The big man hiked his shoulders. "I 'on't know," he mumbled, his jittery knees racing each other for some unseen finish line.

"Does the name Baptiste ring a bell?"

His eyes flickered a moment and his knees grew still. "Not in particular."

"Well, your boss has a bottle of Baptiste's narcotics medication in his trash can. You got any ideas how it happened to get there?"

"Dolores must have brought it."

"But you've never met this man Baptiste?"

"Why you sweatin' me about Philippe Baptiste when the bitch that attacked the boss is runnin' 'round loose?"

"I don't recall saying what Mr. Baptiste's first name was."

The big man faltered, his eyes going dead for a moment. "You musta."

"Did you hear me mention a first name, Officer Coan?"

Coan looked at Kamau like he was a juicy steak. "No, ma'am, I didn't."

"I want my attorney!" Kamau bellowed.

"People in hell want ice water!" Coan shouted back, his lips twitching beneath his salt-and-pepper mustache. I could see I was going to like working with Officer Coan.

"You're not under arrest or even suspicion of hurting Mr. Sheffield, so why would you want an attorney?" I asked innocently.

The bodyguard's eyes skittered from Coan to me. He got a hopeful look on his face. "I—"

"What bank did you go to?"

The shift in my line of questioning caught him off guard. "The Glendale Federal branch over in Silver Lake."

"You sure?"

" 'Course I'm sure!"

"How do we know you're not lying like you lied about not knowing Philippe Baptiste?" Coan shouted.

"I got a receipt!"

"Show me."

"Carefully!" Coan warned, unsnapping his holster.

Kamau nervously reached into his pocket, produced a piece of paper. "They got them surveillance cameras at the bank, too, you don't believe me."

"I believe you, Kamau," I said, examining the receipt. It was a withdrawal slip for five thousand dollars, date and time stamped for forty minutes before. Although it was just a piece of paper, it felt more valuable than the Rosetta Stone in my hand. "I'm just wondering why you needed so much money."

"I was cashing a check for the boss."

"Why'd *he* need so much money?"

Again the dead eyes. "I 'on't know."

I saw Gena join us out of the corner of my eye, knew the meaning of the grim look on her face. I rubbed a hand over my mouth, feeling the events of the last twenty-four hours weighing on my mind, knowing I didn't have much time before the case would be snatched away from us.

"Officer Coan, would you mind closing your eyes for a moment?"

Coan stared straight ahead. "They're already closed, ma'am."

I stepped up and quickly slapped Kamau upside the head. "I'm tired of you lying to me, Kamau. Why'd your boss need the money?"

The big man surged to his feet, was stopped by Coan's hand on his weapon. "What do you people want from me?" he demanded, nostrils flaring.

"The truth, Kamau. How do you and your boss know Philippe Baptiste?"

"It wasn't me what knew him, it was the boss. They met at the AFI industry summit in June. A couple of months later, the boss hired him to work on *Teed Off*."

"Was this the screenplay I heard Mr. Sheffield saying at the repast that *he'd* written?"

"It was the boss's *idea,*" Kamau corrected me. "He hired Philippe to develop it into a script—let him live in the cabana rent-free for most of August and September while he worked on it—but he ended up havin' to shit-can him when he couldn't deliver the pages."

I made note of, but didn't debate, the fact that Cavender had said Baptiste had been working on that same screenplay in the spring, long before Sheffield supposedly gave him the idea. "And so what did Mr. Sheffield do at that point? Take Baptiste's name off of it and substitute his own?"

"I 'on't know," Kamau said, rolling his eyes away with a shrug.

"Bullshit!" I shot back, reaching out my hand as if to strike him again. "You know everything else about Mr. Sheffield's business, but you don't know that? I'm tired of you lying to me, Kamau!" I stood up and started to walk away. "Advise him of his rights, Officer Coan. And let him make that call to his attorney."

"Why you bustin' me?" he demanded. "I thought you said I ain't done nothin'."

I turned to face him. "Because you obviously don't know how to cooperate." I produced the glassine packet we'd found in Kamau's room, bagged and marked as evidence. "And because we found this in your room."

The bodyguard's eyes grew wide. "Th- that's not mine!" he stammered. "I told you Mr. Sheffield did blow!"

"And he leaves it on your bathroom counter for safekeeping?"

His eyes started twitching as he glanced around the room, resting finally at his feet.

I turned my back on him again. "Advise him, Officer Coan. He makes me sick."

"Look, lady, I can't afford to get popped again!" Kamau wailed.

"Then let's start again. How did Dolores Amargosa get the job, and why did Mr. Sheffield need five thousand dollars?"

"Okay, okay! Just give me a minute to recollect." As intended, my scattershot method of questioning had gotten to Sheffield's bodyguard. He started fidgeting again, his hands gripping his knees to hide his nervousness. "This woman rings at the gate one Friday a couple of months ago, sayin' Philippe told her Mr. Sheffield needed a cook and housekeeper. I tell her the boss eats out, and we already got a housekeeper. She goes away, but shows up again Saturday mornin' with the same story. I was gonna go down to the street and drop-kick her to the curb, but the boss tells me to let her in. They go to his office and close the door and the next thing I know, she's cookin' for him."

"Did Mr. Sheffield ever say why he hired her?"

"Just that it was temporary. Sure enough, a few weeks later he gets her hooked up with the Duncans. Told me he couldn't wait to get her out of here."

And into the Duncans' employ. "Why'd he let her come back?"

"She shows up today, kinda weird-actin', says she's finished her work at the Duncans' and needs her old job back."

"And Mr. Sheffield rehired her, just like that?"

"Not exactly. He told her he'd pay her to make some *coquito* for a party he's hosting, then he sent me to the bank for some money to get rid of her."

It was apparent from the empty glass and Sheffield's condition that Dolores Amargosa had a similar plan in mind. "Five thousand's a lot of money just to make some *coquito*. What were Mrs. Amargosa and Mr. Sheffield doing when you left them?"

"Mr. Sheffield was in his office and Dolores was in the kitchen opening cans for the *coquito*. She was such a—I 'on't know—a zero, I didn't think she'd try somethin' like this. But that bitch is crazy!"

Crazy like a fox. Crazy like the slaves who ground up glass in massa's food and served it with a smile. I concluded the interview and pulled Gena into the kitchen. "What did the lieutenant say?"

"After he got through cutting me a new one, he promised to call the watch commander over at the Seventy-seventh to send a car by Amargosa's house. He's also sending Ted Goddard and Nick Terjanian up here to relieve us so we can attend the briefing with the chief."

I ignored Gena's last remark, not wanting to think about the home invasion case for a moment. Searching through my pockets, I found Cy Pressman's card. "The woman whose name is on the back of this card is the title agent who ran the profile on the Santa Barbara Plaza properties. Call and see if she can fax a copy of it over to the office so Goddard and Terjanian can use it to prepare a search warrant. I want to be sure we hook up this asshole by the book."

"You think Sheffield planted Amargosa in Duncan's house to intercept the document?"

"That's exactly what I think. My hunch is when Amargosa saw that package arrive from Angeles Crest Title, she had instructions to smuggle it out of the house. So she did it via a cooperative FedEx driver, then either gave Duncan the overdose of narcotics herself after Alice Thomas left or looked the other way while Sheffield did the deed. Whichever way it went, I've got a feeling our little zero of a housekeeper is knee-deep in this mess."

I returned to the living room to talk to Coan. "Go through the house with Mr. Kamau, see if anything has been stolen. And until Detectives Goddard and Terjanian from RHD and the crime scene techs from SID show up, Detective Cortez is in charge."

Gena was on my heels as I headed for the door. "What are you doing?"

"Trying to help you salvage your career. Stay here and coordinate the hand-off to Goddard and Terjanian. Be that team player you were talking about earlier today."

"And where are you going?"

I turned up my collar against the rain. "Over to Hollywood Memorial. Everywhere I turn in this case, Philippe Baptiste's been hovering on the horizon like a mirage. But until today, I had only an inkling of how central he is to breaking this case. It's high time I confront him myself, see if he's the manipulating conniver everyone associated with this case makes him out to be."

"What about the meeting with the chief?"

"I can't sit in front of him, nodding and smiling like we're big heroes, when the only reason we're there in the first place is that we were set up to be ambushed by our own team leader."

"It'd be sweet revenge for Firestone to have to watch us get the credit for breaking a case he's spent months spearheading," Cortez pointed out.

"Sweet as it'd be, I'd rather turn in my badge than take credit for something so rotten."

"From the way Lieutenant Stobaugh was sounding, we may have to turn in our badges anyway."

"I don't care. The Duncan case is *ours* and I want to follow it through to the end."

"Let me go with you." I saw the hurt and disappointment on my partner's face, realized she was as invested in seeing this case through as I.

"Join me as soon as you can. But just know it's not going to win you any brownie points with the brass."

"In for a penny, in for a pound," she said, her face breaking out into a wide grin.

CHAPTER 21

TO SLEEP
WITH ANGER

Though only a few blocks from the starry scene at the Roosevelt Hotel, Hollywood Memorial Medical Center might as well have been in another galaxy. A rain-soaked concrete-block facility off Vine Street, it didn't have the shabby glamour of the Roosevelt nor the urgent bustle of King Hospital, where I'd visited Gena the day before. At Hollywood Memorial, there was hollow dread on the faces of the families I saw huddled in the lobby or the hallways, as if they were waiting for the downpour outside to break down the doors and overtake them in a furious, inevitable torrent.

The volunteer at the information desk looked up Philippe Baptiste's name and directed me to the fifth floor and something called the Immune Suppressed Unit. The head nurse up there referred me to the unit social worker, a sad-eyed African whose name badge read Irene Mugerwa. She in turn ushered me into a small office adjacent to the nurses' station.

Mugerwa listened patiently as I made my request and then crisply informed me that patient confidentiality prevented her from sharing the nature of Mr. Baptiste's condition. "But he *is* a patient here?" I pressed. "And 'immune suppressed' is a euphemism for AIDS, isn't it?"

"It's a lot more complex than that, Detective," she said in a somber, English-inflected accent.

"I understand if you can't discuss the nature of Mr. Baptiste's illness, but can you at least tell me when he was admitted?"

"You mean this last time?" Seeing my surprise, she pulled one of the charts from a rack and placed it unopened on the table between us. "Philippe has been here several times, which is not unusual for someone in the advanced stages of . . . well, his disease."

"Is that common?"

"In the first couple of years of this war—and make no mistake, this disease is becoming just that, especially for people of color in Africa and the Americas—patients used to be admitted with a high fever or seizures, and we'd lose them within days. But we've learned a lot over the past few years fighting this battle, and Philippe has benefited from our advances."

"Don't misinterpret my reaction, Ms. Mugerwa. I wasn't making a value judgment."

"Forgive me for lecturing, Detective. It's just that we see so much ignorance among our people about HIV and AIDS." Embarrassed, she focused her attention on the thick chart, thumbing through the pages. "The first time Philippe was admitted was for three days during the riots, May first to the third."

Right around the time he called Maynard and Ivy Duncan, asking for money allegedly to finish his screenplay. Now I understood why he'd asked for so much, why he'd been so insistent about his need. "And the next time?"

"The middle of June. Then we didn't see him here for a while after that—which can happen when patients are being managed successfully on an outpatient basis."

Or maybe Philippe was being gainfully employed by Tristan Cavender and could afford his medications. As if to confirm my suspicions, Mugerwa added: "But then Philippe ran into a bad patch in the summer. We couldn't qualify him fast enough for the state's Medicaid program, so he had to stop taking his medication."

Which would have coincided with losing his job with Cavender and his no-pay scriptwriting assignment for Skip

Sheffield. The thought turned my stomach, but I fought back my revulsion to listen to what Mugerwa was saying.

"Not surprisingly, his T-cells plunged to dangerously low levels, and he ended up back in the unit for two weeks in October with an opportunistic infection. He was homeless by that time and very ill. That's when he agreed to let us contact his mother in New York."

"And his mother's name is . . ."

"Dolores Amargosa."

My suspicions confirmed, I finally felt the clouds were clearing around this case. "What happened when you called her?"

"She was much more supportive than Philippe assumed she'd be. Took a leave of absence from her job and came out here immediately. Rented an apartment for herself and Philippe down in South Central and tried to care for him at home. We tried to connect them to some support services, but there aren't that many for people with HIV or AIDS in that part of town, so she was forced to readmit him in November."

I peered at the upside-down chart, trying to decipher the scribbling on the page. "When in November?"

Mugerwa flipped a couple of pages. "The twenty-second."

Two days before Duncan was killed. "And he's been here ever since?"

"Oh, yes. Philippe's much too sick to be discharged."

"Why did he wait so long to tell his mother about his condition?"

"Many of our patients won't tell their families about their status for fear of being judged harshly or abandoned. For some, to reveal they're HIV-positive is to acknowledge their sexuality to their families for the first time. It was even harder for Philippe, because of his mother's occupation."

"Was he concerned she couldn't afford the trip on a housekeeper's salary?"

Mugerwa looked at me strangely. "Mrs. Amargosa isn't a housekeeper, Detective—she's a registered nurse. Philippe was worried she'd try to get him to come back to New York, where she'd wear herself out trying to care for him herself."

So that was how Amargosa knew how much morphine to give Duncan. Mugerwa's revelation made my head hurt and my ears start to roar as if I was in the middle of a hurricane. Uncle Syl's prophetic saying came back to haunt me: *Skim milk masquerades as cream, things ain't always what they seem.*

"Based on some old family history," she was saying, "Philippe felt he needed to prove to her that he could make it on his own. But his situation had grown so desperate, I advised him it was best to call her."

Trying to get my bearings, I asked what was the family history.

"I don't know the whole story," Mugerwa confessed, "but I do know that up until his condition worsened and he was forced to call his mother, she was under the impression that he'd made it big as a Hollywood screenwriter."

Which is probably what Philippe Baptiste had told her he'd be when he left New York with photos of himself and his older, married lover as his entrée into the inner sanctum of Maynard Duncan's life and career. Or perhaps I was being too cynical. Perhaps Baptiste was in an authentic May–December romance and came to L.A. to be close to the man who'd been his lover since he was nineteen. Or maybe part of what he told Ivy Duncan was true and Maynard had paid for the young man's film school training and he came out here with high hopes, sent even higher when Skip Sheffield showed an interest in his screenplay.

Or maybe it was a little bit of all three. But whatever his assumptions, I could only begin to imagine Philippe Baptiste's shock and disappointment when his dreams came crashing down around him, and he found himself homeless, penniless, and sick. And what a bigger shock it must have been to his mother to come to Hollywood, only to find her son living in vastly different circumstances from what she'd been led to believe. "How did Mrs. Amargosa cope with her son's condition?"

Mugerwa's hands made some vague movement over Baptiste's medical record. "Frankly, I'm not sure. When she first moved to L.A., she joined one of our caregiver support groups. But no matter how much we talked about AIDS being a disease and not some sort of Biblical punishment, Mrs. Amargosa was consumed with rage at the injustices she believed her son had suffered out here. Frankly, given her training, I was taken aback by her reaction. But by the time she had Philippe admitted to the unit this last time, she'd done a complete one-eighty—she'd made peace about his condition, said God's will would be done. I must admit I was a little surprised, but I assumed she was going through the process of letting him go."

Evidently not without taking out some of those she felt injured her son along the way. I rubbed my aching temples, feeling the toll of the last twenty-four hours in my head, my shoulders, my soul. "Has Mrs. Amargosa been here today?"

"Not yet, but she usually doesn't come to visit until after she gets off work, around five."

I checked my watch. It was a little after two. "Where is Mr. Baptiste's room?"

"He's in five-fourteen, but I hope you won't upset him."

"I'll do my best not to."

As Mugerwa was walking me out of her office, I saw Gena rush up to the nurses' station and look expectantly in my direction. "Have you questioned him yet?"

"I'm on my way to Mr. Baptiste's room now."

"I wouldn't expect too much, Detective," Mugerwa warned, indicating a room midway down the hall. "He drifts in and out a lot at this point." Then she asked uneasily, "Should I tell Mrs. Amargosa you want to see her when she arrives?"

My lips formed a smile my heart did not feel. "I'd prefer that you didn't."

"I do hope she's not in any trouble."

"It's nothing like that," I replied, forcing that lying smile. "She's just assisting us with an investigation."

"Well," she replied, releasing a tense sigh, "try not to raise your voice. Philippe is extremely sensitive to sound. And please read the instructions on the door before you go in. Even at Mr. Baptiste's stage of the disease, we can't be too careful."

"What's the status on Sheffield?" I asked as soon as we were alone.

"Cardiac arrest in the ER. He's gone."

I felt the first twinge of guilt. "Damn! If we had gotten to Sheffield's earlier, this wouldn't have happened."

"But it was the information from Cavender that led us pointed clearly to Sheffield."

"But I knew something was off about Amargosa before we interviewed Cavender. I should have listened to my gut."

I was still blaming myself as we approached the door to Philippe Baptiste's room. "What's the deal here?" Gena asked. "Why was that woman so skittish about us interviewing him?"

There was a note attached to the door of room 514, in three languages. The English read:

> Our patients' immune systems are compromised, which means they can become gravely ill from the slightest infection or fever transmitted by an unsuspecting friend or family member. If you have any type of illness, virus, or fever, PLEASE COME BACK ANOTHER DAY. If not, please take a few minutes to THOROUGHLY WASH your hands, and put on the gown, gloves, and mask provided in the boxes near the sink to your right. Thank You.

"I think you've got your answer."

Sobered, we followed the directions carefully, and were soon inside a dimly lit room. A single hospital bed sat just beyond the bathroom to my left, a curtain partially pulled between it and the window. A series of monitors were positioned nearby, their leads and wires converging on a small shape huddled in the narrow bed. Through the window beyond, I could see thunderclouds stacked up over the Hollywood sign like jets over LAX.

As we inched forward, a whisper-thin husk of a man turned

his head our way. Although I knew it had to be Baptiste, he looked nothing like the photo I'd seen, his once handsome face now spotted with boils. "Mamí?" he said listlessly, looking beyond us to the door.

"No, Philippe, it's Detective Justice of the LAPD," I whispered as I showed him my ID. "Detective Cortez and I are here to talk to you about Skip Sheffield."

Baptiste tried to speak, but his voice was lost in a gurgling, strangled sound. "Mamí called you?" he managed to get out, his watery eyes focused somewhere over Gena's left shoulder. "You came to help me . . . get . . . my money?"

"If we can," Gena said.

"Who owes you money, Philippe?"

"Skip Sheffield!" The cardiac monitor spiked green lines, and the numbers went up slightly as Baptiste gasped for air. "Fifty thousand!"

Baptiste's left hand groped the air in front of him. Gena grabbed a cup of water from the tray by the bed and guided the straw to his lips. With a start I realized Philippe Baptiste had gone blind.

"Did you send your mother to talk to Mr. Sheffield about your money?" I asked.

He shook his head, drew the water through the straw slowly, moistened his lips. "I told her . . . the Writers Guild handles disputes . . . but she insisted. But when she went to Skip, he said . . . no . . . unless she helped . . . another project."

Gena stared at me over Baptiste's head.

"Helped him how?"

"She didn't say. But she promised . . . get me what I needed come hell or high water."

Even if it involved spying on, maybe even killing, Maynard Duncan? Regardless of Sheffield's intentions, it must have seemed like the chance of a lifetime to Philippe Baptiste's grieving, vengeful mother.

I was just about to ask him that question when he said, "She was . . . getting . . . money today," then was consumed by a coughing spell that turned to gasps.

I thought of the paltry five thousand Kamau had gotten from the bank and wondered how far that would go to pay for Philippe's repeated hospitalizations, drugs, and doctors' visits. "Don't trouble yourself about that right now," Gena soothed, putting her hand behind his back to support him as she offered him more water.

I was about to ask another question when Baptiste's torso jerked away from Gena's hand, and the green lines on the monitor spiked again, then plunged. We stood in shock as numbers on the right side of the monitor plummeted to 70, 50, 40, 20. The alarm sounded, but no one came. Panicked, I skidded into the hall and raced to the nurses' station. "The man in five-fourteen's in cardiac arrest!" I shouted to the nurses behind the desk.

Their eyes averted, one of them murmured, "Yes, ma'am, we know," but did not move.

Flashbacks of my own terror, of screaming for help for my husband and child as they lay dying in the streets all those years ago, threatened to overpower me. "Well do something, goddamnit!"

Gena joined me at the desk, her face pale. She shook her head slowly.

Mugerwa emerged from her office. "He's DNR, Detective. 'Do not resuscitate'."

"I know what it means, but why?"

"Because my son's suffered enough." Wearing a raincoat, knee-high rubber boots, and no hat, Dolores Amargosa stood dripping by the elevator. Her voice was clear and precise, the Spanglish accent she'd adopted to throw me off during our first interview magically gone.

Skim milk masquerades as cream.

She approached the nurses' station, her face streaming water, her eyes dull. Gena and I automatically moved toward her. "Dolores Amargosa, you're under arrest for the murders of Maynard Duncan and Skip Sheffield."

I heard the sharp intake of breath from Mugerwa and the nurses behind the desk. I grabbed one arm to turn Amargosa around, then cuffed her swiftly while Gena patted her down. She did not resist.

After Gena advised her, I asked if she wanted an attorney to meet us downtown. "With my baby gone, I don't care about any of that," she said mechanically. "I'll sign anything you want admitting I killed them both. Just let me say goodbye to my son first."

The cop in me objected, but the mother I once was hesitated. The look on Gena's face told me she shared my feelings. So we waited until a doctor from the ER pronounced Philippe dead, then let Amargosa precede us into her son's room. Gena took up a position just inside the doorway and I escorted her to the bedside.

Hands cuffed behind her back, Amargosa approached the bed as if it were a shrine. "He looks like he's sleeping." She turned and looked at me, gesturing plaintively with her bound hands. "May I touch him, please?"

I hesitated for just a moment before walking over and undoing the cuffs. She rotated her wrists for a moment, then lovingly reached out and smoothed her son's hair. "We had our differences, but Felipe never hurt a soul. It is Felipe, by the way, not that phony French name he used on the streets. Were you here when he died?"

"Yes, ma'am, I was."

"Did he go peacefully?"

I saw the anguish in her eyes, knew I couldn't tell her the truth. "Yes, he did."

Amargosa nodded with satisfaction as she stroked her son's lifeless face. "I didn't want my baby dying with the evil those men did to him preying on his mind. That's why I had to take the burden off his shoulders."

"It was the *coquito,* wasn't it?"

She gave her son a sad smile. "Felipe loved my recipe, so I figured it would be only right that they enjoy it, too. Of course, theirs had a generous dose of Felipe's morphine added. I called it giving them a taste of their own medicine for what they did to my child, although I had to force Sheffield to swallow his at knifepoint." She turned those anguished eyes on me. "But they deserved it for how they used my boy. And tried to use me to get at each other."

"How so?"

"Duncan was trying to get dirt he could use on Sheffield—that's why he was so interested in his wife's hiring me. Every day, he tried to pump me for information on Sheffield's business dealings. And Sheffield sent me over there to steal whatever documents Duncan had collected to fight the Santa Barbara Plaza project, tried to get me to cooperate by telling me that it was Duncan who was responsible for my son's condition. But I knew they were both to blame. Felipe didn't stand a chance between those two sharks. My baby was an innocent until they corrupted him!"

It must have been easier for Amargosa to blame Duncan and Sheffield than to look at her own role in forcing her son onto the streets. Forcing him to make his living off the chicken hawks who preyed on young boys instead of being accepted and nurtured at home for who he was. And while I also believed from talking to others that there was a darker side of Philippe Baptiste's personality, there was no use arguing any of these points with Baptiste's mother now. Besides, the only person who could know the whole truth was laid out before us, long past truth, or pain, or anger.

I watched Dolores Amargosa throw back the covers. "What are you doing?" I demanded, stepping forward.

"I gave him his first bath," she explained tearfully. "Please let me give him his last."

She went into the bathroom and ran water into a metal basin. She returned with a washcloth and the basin, which she set on the bedside table. Crossing herself, she carefully started removing her son's perspiration-soaked hospital gown.

I felt a catch at the back of my throat, and realized I couldn't watch this. I cuffed her left wrist to the metal bed railing and asked Gena to keep an eye on her. Stepping into the hall, I figured I could use the time to make a call. A passing nurse told me I couldn't use my cell phone inside the hospital, so I went back to the nurses' station to use theirs, keeping my eye on the doorway to room 514 the whole time.

I called Lieutenant Stobaugh, expecting to get blessed out for violating department policy in pursuing the case and for missing our briefing before meeting with the chief. He did not disappoint. As he ranted and raved, I realized it was the first time I'd ever heard Kenneth Stobaugh shout or curse.

"I understand, sir, but I've arrested the Duncans' housekeeper for his murder and Skip Sheffield's. She's confessed, so all we've got to do is get her to complete and sign a statement. It's going to be at least a couple of hours of paperwork. Can't we put the chief off until tomorrow?"

"Goddammit, Justice, don't argue with me, just get in here!" he growled and slammed down the phone.

Seeing my career going up in flames, I went back to Baptiste's room in time to see Dolores Amargosa slumped in the chair beside her son's bed. Gena stood over her, frantically pressing her hands into the woman's neck.

"I just turned away for a moment," Gena said, her panicked voice going up an octave. "It seemed so private—saying goodbye to a child."

Amargosa's right arm dangled by her side, blood dripping from it forming a pool on the floor. A kitchen knife clattered to the floor, probably the same knife she'd used on Sheffield.

"I-I searched her after you cuffed her," Gena stammered. "It must have been in her boot."

I ran into the hall again, yelling for nurses, who this time called the ER and announced a Code Blue over the intercom system. Sick to my stomach, I went back to room 514, saw the fixed smile on Amargosa's face, the deep slash across her throat that was no longer pumping blood. "My God, Dolores, what have we done?" I murmured, uncuffing her from the bed as the emergency room team shouldered past me.

S E T T I N G   T H E   H O O K

Two hours later, Lieutenant Stobaugh glowered at Gena and me from behind his desk. "I'm so disappointed with the two of you I don't know where to begin," he said.

I could feel my face grow warm. "Let me explain, sir—"

"Letting an arrestee out of your direct control for even a minute is neglect of duty and violates every tenet of good policing going back to the Academy," he exclaimed, pointing. "And while I can understand your having some empathy because her son just died, your duty is to secure the arrestee, first and foremost."

"It's my fault, sir," Gena said. "Detective Justice had cuffed her and asked me to watch her while she went to call you. I was the negligent one. I let my emotions get in the way and then let her out of my sight."

"Not to mention your failure to properly search her to begin with!"

"I was in charge, sir, so if you've got to blame someone—"

"Justice, you weren't *supposed* to be in charge of anything. You know damn well I'd turned the case over to Firestone. What you and Cortez have done amounts to gross insubordination!"

"But Firestone was so caught up in riding on Ikehara's coat-tails, he was willing to pursue hooking up an innocent woman to the exclusion of everything else!"

"If you had a concern about the way the investigation was being conducted, you should have taken it up with Firestone, or come to me. My job is to administer the work of this unit and to protect my personnel. I can't do that if you won't trust me."

There was that word again, "trust." The accusation, so similar to the one I'd heard from Aubrey the night before, brought me up short. Although I couldn't see it at the time, Stobaugh *had* reached out to me just the day before when he tried to feel me out about the demeaning assignments Firestone had been giving me. Had I frozen him out not because he couldn't be trusted, but because I didn't know how to trust? Would I have been in this predicament now if I had opened up, if I had trusted him then?

"It's my job," he was saying, "not yours, to ensure that our investigations explore every avenue, every possibility, before an arrest is made."

"We were on that page, too, sir," I said eagerly. "So when Detective Firestone had me pick up Duncan's will from his attorney—"

A fleeting frown crossed my boss's face. "Steve sent you to pick up the will?"

"Absolutely! And while I was there, the attorney's comments suggested some angles that I thought I could pursue with Duncan's widow more effectively than by sending in a third team to interview her. I had every intention of coming back to start the paperwork to get the medical records for Thomas's patients as ordered by Detective Firestone, but one thing led to another and pretty soon we were hot on Amargosa's trail."

I checked Stobaugh's reaction, noted his face was no longer red and his fingers had formed the familiar steeple that indicated he was at least willing to listen to my argument. I took a breath and plunged ahead. "Frankly, sir, much as I might have wanted to—"

Which you really didn't, the little voice inside reminded me.

"—there wasn't time to come back to the office for a round-table to discuss our options. I honestly thought there were lives at stake."

Stobaugh was quiet for a moment, looking at us over the tops of his fingers. "Put it any way you want, Justice," he finally said, "but the bottom line is that after Ninety-fifth Street, you were supposed to be on administrative duty and Cortez on sick leave, not free-lancing the Duncan case on your own." He looked at us wearily from behind his gold-rimmed glasses. "You should have called Firestone as soon as there was any chance of your crossing the line and let him decide how to proceed, not gone charging off like a couple of gunslingers at the OK Corral."

He took off his glasses and massaged his temples. "Look, I know you two have been through a traumatic experience, but what in the hell have you been thinking the last twenty-four hours? You have both violated an explicit command by actively pursuing an investigation. Your neglect of duty has resulted in a sus-pect's death, an arrestee's killing herself, as well as drawing the attention of a chief with a personal vendetta against rogue cops."

He turned to Gena, fixing her with those green eyes of his. "And while I *might* be able to pull the chief off your ass . . ."

His eyes now drilled me. "Justice, you've been on thin ice for doing this kind of thing before."

"Hold up!" I complained "If you're referring to that case dur-ing the riots, I pursued that under extraordinary circumstances!"

"But it's still sitting as a question mark in your personnel jacket, and now I've got Firestone outside that door, recommend-ing we discharge the both of you!"

Nothing Stobaugh could say to me was worse than what I was saying to myself. The threat to my job aside, nothing anyone could say or do could absolve me of the fact that had I acted on my instincts, we would have gotten to Skip Sheffield's sooner and he and Dolores Amargosa might still be alive. But guilty as I felt, there was no way I was going to let Steve Firestone use their fallen bodies or our misconduct to cover his own dirty tricks. Yet exposing our team leader's little plot wasn't solely my call to make.

I had said as much to Gena when we were closing out the crime scene at Hollywood Memorial and preparing to come into the office. "You know, you've got a lot more to lose in some ways than I do, if we pull all the stops out against Firestone," I'd told her.

"But I'll get back my self-esteem, and that's more important," she had replied.

My partner's comment had made me stop and study her profile. Gena had been through a lot in the last few days, more than I had in many ways, and it had showed. But her jaw had been firm, her gaze resolute as she had looked into my eyes. "I'm with you to the bitter end on this one."

I glanced over at her now to be sure she was still down with the plan, and saw her doing a slow burn. She gave me an imperceptible nod to confirm our agreement.

I looked my lieutenant in the eye. "I don't think Detective Firestone is in a position to recommend discharging anyone, sir."

"Other than himself," Gena added forcefully.

"What are you two talking about?" Stobaugh demanded with a frown.

"Let's start with Ninety-fifth Street," I said.

An hour—and a few strategically placed phone calls—later, Lieutenant Stobaugh, Gena, and I had hammered out a tentative agreement and a plan to set the record straight.

"I don't want to hear another peep out of the two of you until you've worked with Terjanian and Goddard to complete the murder books on Duncan and Sheffield and the Home Invasion Task Force paperwork is complete!" he bellowed as he opened his door. "And you can expect to hear from IAD before the day is out."

Firestone couldn't contain his glee as we trudged back to our desks. "IAD, huh? I guess this time you aren't going to get away with your slipshod police work. I told you both it would catch up with you one day."

I had to place a restraining hand on Gena's arm to keep her from jumping down his throat. "Can we just table this for now?" I asked. "We've got a lot of work to do before that meeting with the chief tomorrow, so I'd rather just focus on that."

"The chief's still willing to talk to the two of you?" He snorted incredulously. "I'm surprised."

Her back turned, Gena muttered something under her breath. Firestone stepped forward. "What did you say?"

"Ignore her." I stepped in to referee. "She's still pissed at the reaming-out we got from Stobaugh. What do you need us to do to wrap up the home invasion case?"

For the rest of Thursday afternoon and into the night, Gena and I worked diligently to tie up the loose ends on the cases that had threatened to end our careers and our lives. I also tried to call Aubrey a couple of times, to tell him something, I wasn't sure what. Or maybe I just wanted to hear his voice and reassurance that all this would turn out all right.

I finally caught him at his office while I was reading over Gena's summaries of the interview with Baptiste as well as Amargosa's confession and subsequent suicide. "Aubrey, I—"

"What do you want?"

Although I was on his speakerphone, the distance in his voice was more than just a poor connection. "I—we're wrapping up the Duncan investigation."

I heard the rustling of papers. "So?"

"Can we talk?"

"Aren't we talking now?"

"I mean later."

He was silent for a beat. "That depends. How much later?"

I handed Gena the documents back, giving her a thumbs-up. "I've got a lot of paperwork to do right now, and then we've got—"

I heard him move away from the phone and a door close. "Then why did you call me, Charlotte?"

"Aubrey, it's not what you think," I pleaded, my stomach sinking. "I've got something else to do that's very important, something that I promise is going to make my life—maybe our lives—a lot easier."

Gena's phone rang. I watched her speak to someone for a moment, then mouth to me, It's *Terjanian.*

"Look, honey, I can't say anything more right now, but can we get together late tonight?"

He finally picked up the receiver. "I don't think so, Charlotte. I've got a lot of things to do myself this evening."

My heart felt as if it was about to explode, but Gena was motioning me to pick up the phone. "Okay. Will I see you at my parents' tree-trimming party on Sunday?"

"Your mother called me about it, but I didn't know if you—"

"Of course I do! And Aubrey . . ?"

"I'm listening."

"I . . . I'm sorry for that stuff I said the other morning."

There was a pause on the line before he said, "Yeah, okay," and hung up.

Nick Terjanian, one of the RHD detectives brought in on the Duncan case, was fairly bursting with news. "I'm on four in Questioned Documents with the copy of the vic's will and the proxy he allegedly signed," he said excitedly. "The technician up here said the proxy signature was definitely forged. And it's consistent with those indentations you found on the note pad on Duncan's desk. And Wozniak in Latent Prints said the fingerprints we took from Sheffield match that unidentified set on the desk near the pad."

"So Duncan was probably already dead, or close to it, when Sheffield arrived that afternoon and forged his signature."

"It's all a moot point, since Sheffield and Duncan are both dead," Terjanian was saying. "Just another loose end for the murder book."

Except for the fact that without Duncan's proxy, it would have been a five-five tie vote on the Still We Rise development project at Santa Barbara Plaza. "When will they have their report ready?"

"They're putting it together now."

"Would you leave a copy on my desk?"

While I finished reviewing the murder book, Gena went over to Robbery to talk to Detective Rudolph. She returned an hour later, a smile on her face. "Fluornoy and his crew are definitely going down," she said, then related how Rudolph had been cross-matching the items found in Fluornoy's house with items reported as stolen during the various home invasion robberies and comparing them with statements from the victims, who had been coming in all day to positively ID their belongings.

We were in a meeting with Stobaugh, the whole task force, and a senior deputy from the DA's office who was drawing up the indictments when we were interrupted by a Brooks-Brothered duo named Kramer and Lofton from Internal Affairs, there to interview Cortez and me. Stobaugh made his office available for us to be interviewed individually, although the mere presence of the wool-worsted IAD detectives in our department made everyone a little nervous. Everyone except Steve, who fairly gloated over our anticipated punishment for insubordination and neglect of duty in the investigation of the Duncan case.

Gena went first. It was more than an hour and a half before she came back to the conference room. As planned, I met her in the lavatory a few minutes later. "How'd it go?" I whispered.

She gave me a weary smile. "I don't know if I'll have a job after this, but I did what I had to do. Kramer's left to start the paperwork now."

"Good," I said, then took my turn in the box with Detective Lofton.

Gena and Lieutenant Stobaugh had already left, but other members of the task force were still there by the time Lofton cut me loose over an hour later. Firestone looked up from a conversation he was having to ask, "So what's the verdict?" a smirk on his face.

As much as I wanted to kick this asshole to kingdom come and back, I forced myself to remain calm. "Can we talk for a minute, Steve?"

I led him into Stobaugh's office. Firestone immediately went and sat at our lieutenant's desk, just as I'd predicted he would, put his feet up, and rared back in the chair. "I'm studying for the lieutenant's exam," he informed me smugly. "Think I'd make a better lieutenant than the Golden Boy?"

I sat in the chair opposite him. "If Cortez has her way, none of us will ever get promoted."

His feet came off the desk. "What do you mean?"

I dropped my head, purposely refusing to look him in the eye. "I'm really not supposed to talk about it, but I feel like . . . given the heads-up you gave me about her . . . I ought to warn you."

"Warn me about what?"

I got up, went to the edge of Stobaugh's desk, turned on his desk lamp, picked up one of his paperweights, exchanged it for another. "That Lofton from IAD was asking me some strange questions," I whispered. "Made me wonder . . ."

"What did he ask you?"

I shrugged, rotating the paperweight in my hand. "Funny stuff. First he started grilling me about the Duncan case, why we were pursuing it while on restricted duty, you know the routine. By the way, did you forget to tell Stobaugh you asked me to pick up Duncan's wills from his attorney?"

"I might have," he said vaguely. When I didn't continue, he said, "Yeah, I probably did."

I stared at him for a moment. "You need to correct that, Steve. It makes it look worse for me than it really is, you know what I'm saying?"

"I'll take care of it."

"You sure, 'cause I don't see the point in sticking my neck out for you if—"

"Dammit, I *said* I'd take care of it," he said irritably, waving his hand. "Now what did Lofton ask you about Cortez?"

I put down the paperweight and turned away. I had never mentioned Cortez as the subject of Detective Lofton's questioning. The fact that Firestone had jumped to that conclusion made me smile inwardly. I'd found his soft spot. And now that I'd found it, I could manipulate it. But could I get him to take the bait?

I returned to my seat. "It wasn't so much about Cortez, but Cortez and Ninety-fifth Street."

"Why Ninety-fifth Street?"

"You remember—the captain requested that IAD do the interview on Gena's shooting instead of our guys. Avoid a conflict of interest." I leaned forward and whispered: "I really wished it was one of our guys doing the investigation, you know, because we could have contained it. I mean, everyone knows Gena's not a team player, that she tries to deflect any shit coming her way."

"What did she tell them about Ninety-fifth Street?" he demanded.

I sat back as if I was trying to sort it out. "I'm not sure, but it seemed like they already knew a lot. For instance, they'd already talked to somebody about Tolliver and Fluornoy, because Lofton knew all about them. He even had copies of their files from South Bureau CRASH. Guess they got that stuff from Mike Cooper, huh?"

Firestone's face went a little pale, and he raked his fingers through his curly hair. A veil fell over his hazel eyes, but behind it I see his wheels turning: Had Cooper told IAD about the call he'd made to South Bureau to check out the tip on the Toyota prior to sending us out to Ninety-fifth Street? The call that had alerted him to the fact that Tolliver and Fluornoy were too dangerous to send detectives out without prior surveillance and sufficient backup?

"What else?" he asked uneasily.

This next part was going to be tricky, but I was stepping out on the hunch that I'd correctly interpreted Manny Rudolph's cryptic conversation with me this morning. "And then Lofton wanted to know specifically who told me about the tip Tolliver's mother called in, you or Rudolph. I think Rudolph must've told Cortez something this afternoon about his taking the call originally that was different from what you told me."

Firestone shot out of his seat and started pacing the room. We both started talking at once.

"That little bitch! She's trying to set me up."

"I didn't know what to tell them, so I just told the truth. Set you up how, Steve?"

He turned on his heel and retraced his steps, a caged animal. "Trying to make them think I sent her out there to get ambushed!"

"But why?"

"She kept making passes at me, and when I turned her down, she went *Fatal Attraction* on me, said she was going tell the lieutenant I'd forced her or something."

Knowing what Gena had told me and Internal Affairs about the rape and knowing too that DNA evidence could be obtained from the fetus, I was delighted at the size of the hole Firestone was digging for himself.

He shot me a sidelong glance. "Everyone's gonna know that's bullshit, right? I'm a kidder, but I never really hurt anybody. You could tell them that, couldn't you, Justice? And I could make things right for you on the Duncan investigation."

I thought back to the moves Firestone had tried to make on me last spring, the snide remarks he'd made about me as recently as last week. And here he was, asking me to forget all that to help him save his sorry ass.

He was right where I wanted him. Now was the time to set the hook.

"I'll do whatever I can, but don't think this is just about you, Steve. I think Cortez is trying to set us both up, make it look like we *both* tried to throw her to the wolves out there yesterday."

Maybe I laid it on too thick, because he stopped in midstride to stare at me. "Why you?"

"You know she's never liked me. She's always thought I was trying to be the queen bee of the department hive or something. Stupid female stuff. Even you tried to warn me, remember?"

I could see his mind working as he looked out the window. "Yeah, I did."

"But what bothers me most is that Lofton kept getting in my face, asking how the Tolliver kid came to our attention, and what assumption I was under when Gena and I went out to his house."

I noticed Firestone's eyelids flutter for an instant, then he turned veiled eyes toward me. "And what did you tell him?"

"No more than you told me. The call you got from Bernita Tolliver about her son and his girlfriend seeing the Toyota and all, how it turned out not to be true, the mother in the wind, you know."

"And what did he say?"

"Not much. You know how tight-lipped those IAD suits can be. But I got the sense that they were going to track down Bernita Tolliver and confirm the statements she made to you and Rudolph. Then Lofton started asking me about Cortez, how long she'd been working here, who she worked with, how we all got along."

Firestone came behind my chair and said softly. "You didn't tell them what I said about her, did you?"

I felt a momentary ripple of fear, but I kept my mouth shut and rode out the feeling, letting him sweat a bit, letting him think for a moment that he was truly lost. I finally twisted around in the chair to face him. "No, I wouldn't do that, Steve. You told me that stuff in confidence, right?"

He moved a little closer. "That's right, and we should keep it that way."

I rose to face him, saw the veiled threat, and the fear, in his eyes. "What now?"

His mind was still working behind those hazel eyes. "Nothing. Go home. I'll take care of it."

I went for the door, paused, and turned back. "I did the right thing by telling you, didn't I, Steve? I know we've had our differences, but I couldn't let those IAD pricks and Cortez ruin your career. Or mine."

He followed me to the door, a hand on my shoulder. I tried hard not to flinch. "You did the right thing."

"I just wish we could lay our hands on Bernita Tolliver. She could straighten this whole thing out."

"She sure could," he said slowly.

Everyone had gone when we emerged from Stobaugh's office. "You walking out?" I asked, going to my desk and shoving the report Terjanian had dropped off into my purse.

"No, I've got some work to do before tomorrow."

I walked out, thinking, *I'm sure you do.*

I went to the lobby to sign out in the log and then, as previously arranged, doubled back inside and walked up to the sixth floor. I knocked on an unmarked room near Internal Affairs and was admitted by Detective Kramer, who had changed into a flannel shirt, corduroys, and a leather jacket. "Did you get all that?" I asked.

"Yup," Lofton said from the recording equipment positioned against one wall of the room, his dark face intent. He'd changed, too, from his suit to a knit cap, baggy jeans, and a Raiders football jacket. "But you kept moving around so much you had me worried for a minute."

"I was trying to keep within range of the bug you put in the lamp. But you got everything Firestone said, right? And this is all admissible?"

"Judge signed the warrant two hours ago," Kramer said, holding up the paperwork. "But it's not enough without some hard evidence of him conspiring to harm the both of you."

"What about Cooper and Rudolph?" Gena asked from the conference table. "They both gave you statements, right?"

"They'll help, but I'd like to be able to get the Tolliver woman to verify what she actually said to Firestone and Rudolph."

Lieutenant Stobaugh rose from his spot at the conference table, but there was no joy on his face. "So where do we go from here, Jerry?"

"We've got a couple of unmarkeds downstairs from Central Bureau who'll pick up his trail soon as he leaves the office," Kramer replied.

"You really think Firetsone's hiding her?" I asked.

My lieutenant handed each of us a flyer featuring an old mug shot of a thin-faced woman. "South Bureau's had a be-on-the-lookout alert for Bernita Tolliver since last night. We've checked her family, friends, all of her regular haunts, plus every hotel and safe house we use, and we've gotten nothing yet. So I'm willing to give this a shot."

"And as worried as Detective Firestone sounds on this tape," Lofton added, "it's a sure bet he's going to do something to try to ·make things right for himself."

The phone rang. Kramer answered, spoke briefly into the receiver, and hung up. "Firestone just signed out of the building. Let's roll."

As the three men gathered up their equipment, I said: "I want in on this."

"Me, too," Gena added.

"Not on your lives." Lofton slid a couple of hotel keys across the table. "We've got rooms for you tonight at the New Otani Hotel down the street. Don't even go home to get your things, in case he shows up there. We'll call you as soon as we know something."

"And how long is this supposed to last?" Gena said, a worried look on her face.

"Not long, Detective," Kramer replied.

Gena started to protest, but I was already picking up and pocketing my key. "Thanks. I could use the rest."

U N D E R S T A N D I N G

We waited all of two seconds before heading downstairs ourselves and over to my Rabbit. "Why not take the department car, so we can pick up their radio transmissions?" Gena asked.

"Too many department cars might catch Firestone's eye. We'll just have to stick close to the unmarked carrying the IAD guys and our lieutenant."

"What if they spot us?"

"They'll be so busy looking ahead they won't even think to look behind them."

We followed them as they trailed behind the unit dogging Firestone. He led us first to an ATM machine at a minimart west of downtown, where we watched everyone scramble while he got some cash. But the transaction didn't last long, nor did Firestone seem to be aware of the many pairs of department eyes on him.

The caravan reassembled as he pulled away and stayed with him until he pulled into the parking lot of the Kismet Gardens, one of those L-shaped no-tell motels on Western Avenue near the Coliseum. "You familiar with this place?" Gena asked as we drove by.

"It doesn't look like any of the spots we've ever used for stashing witnesses."

I circled the block and parked in a crowded lot across the street in time to catch a glimpse of Firestone entering a room in the middle of the second floor. A couple of undercover cops crept to a location in the shadows beneath the stairs while Stobaugh and Lofton went to the manager's office. Through the window I could see them showing a photo to an elderly man and checking the register.

"Well, he's either here meeting the Tolliver woman or some trick," I observed as I settled in to wait.

"Why should he pay for sex when he can take it by force from naive females like me?"

"There's no need to beat up on yourself, Gena. It was an error in judgment, nothing more, nothing less."

"Yeah, but this one may end my career," she said bitterly.

The old man in the office picked up the phone and dialed a number, Stobaugh and Lofton watching on intently. The next few minutes stretched like hours, exacerbated by a particularly exuberant revival meeting going on in a nearby church. "God, do you think he's up there killing the poor woman?" Gena asked fretfully.

I shook my head. "That's why Stobaugh had the manager call up there. Besides, our guys stationed outside would hear it if he tried."

"But what if—"

Gena broke off as the door of the room opened. Firestone emerged with a large suitcase. He was accompanied by a gaunt woman of indeterminate age, dressed in a too-short dress, spike heels, and a bad wig. They started down the stairs and towards the manager's office when they were intercepted by the undercover cops, who quickly separated them and walked a few feet away with the woman.

While Firestone was loud-talking Detective Kramer, I could tell the uniforms were asking the woman for her ID. They peered at the wallet she offered, then looked toward the manager's office, giving Stobaugh and Lofton the thumbs-up signal.

"They've got her!" I cried, beating my fist on the steering wheel in triumph, blowing the horn in the process.

Firestone peered across the street, but I hoped he couldn't see my car in the crowded lot.

Or did he?

Gena sat trembling in the seat next to me. "I can't believe it," she said, tears welling up in her eyes. She made a move to open the car door. "I'm going to look that asshole in the eye, make him understand—"

I held her back, hoping no one across the street saw our movements. "You'll get your opportunity, Gena. They've got a long way to go before they can close the book on Firestone, so I'm sure you'll be seeing him again. Don't let your need to blow off some steam screw up their chances of building their case, of bringing that asshole to justice."

She gave me a lopsided smile. "No pun intended."

I tried to smile back, but, feeling the exhaustion of the last twenty-four hours weighing on me, it was all I could do to turn over the ignition on the Rabbit and shift it into reverse. "Let's head down to the New Otani so we can be there when they call."

Bernita Tolliver turned out to be as good as gold. First of all, she confirmed she'd had identical conversations with Manny Rudolph and Steve Firestone regarding her son's association with Bobby Fluornoy and the home invasion gang. But, more important, she had in her possession Steve Firestone's handwritten directions to the Kismet Gardens, which he'd given her when they'd met the day after the shooting and he'd offered her money to go into hiding until he could get her out of town.

By Friday morning, Firestone had already gotten himself not only a union rep for his sit-down with Kramer and Lofton, but a real attorney, which was a sure sign of a cop who knew he was in trouble.

As for Gena and me, our sit-down with the chief of police went a lot better than we expected, much better than we deserved. By the time Lieutenant Stobaugh and Captain MIA had briefed him on the details of our involvement in both the Duncan/Sheffield and home invasion cases, the good we'd done had pretty much balanced the bad.

Almost.

Although we still took our bows at the press conference that afternoon with the brass and the Home Invasion Task Force, minus Firestone, it was our last appearance in RHD for a while. For our insubordination and neglect of duty, we got heavy days off. We were suspended for two deployment periods—roughly sixty days—without pay, followed by another sixty days with pay, the punishment signed personally by the chief and duly noted in our personnel jackets.

Although the reprimand and punishment stung, "it's a lot less than Firestone wanted them to hang on us," I reminded Gena as we were getting our personal things together that afternoon.

"But that's on top of my sick leave!" Gena complained. "I don't know, Charlotte, I'm thinking of appealing this to the Board of Rights."

"That's certainly your prerogative, but you might want to consider whether you want to open up the door to IAD nosing around into what happened between you and Firestone."

"They're going to hear his side of it anyway. If I let this go down, I probably won't be able to come back to work until sometime in the spring! And they're saying I probably won't be able to return to RHD even then."

"They told me the same thing. But think about it, Gena—would you even want to?"

My question stopped Gena in her tracks. She gazed around the bull pen that housed the dozen or so detectives in our unit as if emerging from a bad dream. "Guess I've got a lot of time to think that over. What are you going to do?"

My mind went to my conversation with Aubrey the day before, the promise I'd made to do something that would make my life, our lives, better. At the time I thought I was talking about tying up Steve Firestone, but I suddenly realized there was something else I needed to do if Aubrey and I were going to move ahead.

I looked at my partner and smiled. "A little housecleaning, I think."

The next couple of days were busy ones. I took Beast for long walks in the neighborhood and had a new alarm system and exterior floodlights installed at my house, in case Steve Firestone made an unscheduled appearance. But I doubted he'd have the nerve, given his more pressing concerns.

I bought boxes and rolls of tape and wrapping paper, not for Christmas presents I'd yet to buy, but to finish packing up the rest of my husband Keith's and daughter Erica's things. In the process, I drank a few Scotches and shed more than a few tears over the brief time I'd had them in my life. Sometimes I felt as if I'd never stop crying—for them, for myself, for what had become of our long-ago dreams. But as I boxed up fourteen-year-old books and papers, toys and clothes, I finally realized what was past was past. I had to live for today, if I was going to live at all.

And for the first time, I began to think about my life, who I *really* was, not just as a crusading detective, long-suffering widow, or disappointing daughter, but as a grown woman on my own. I was thirty-nine, and it was high time I stood up for what I believed in, even if it didn't fit other people's notions of how I should live my life. And the sooner I came to that understanding, the sooner I'd be free. God forbid it should come as late for me as it did for Maynard Duncan.

Which brought me on Sunday morning to Peaceful Shepherd Missionary Baptist Church, not so much for the spiritual enlightenment as to resolve a few things for Maynard Duncan's sake and my own piece of mind.

As I slipped into Pastor Henley's office between the eight and ten o'clock services, I noticed something new had been added since my last visit—an architect's rendering of renovations to Green Pastures Nursing Home.

The good pastor walked me through the plans himself. "We'd

been planning an AIDS hospice unit for a long time, but we hadn't been able to attract an angel. Brother Duncan's bequest will allow us to equip and staff a four-bed unit, bearing his name, of course," Pastor Henley explained. "It was his fondest wish that those less fortunate than he wouldn't have to suffer their last days without adequate health care or separated from God's healing touch."

The comment made me wonder if Duncan knew all along about Philippe Baptiste's suffering, if this was his way of making amends. "So you were aware of Mr. Duncan's condition?"

Henley wagged his head solemnly. "I *was* his spiritual adviser, Detective. Of course, I never let on to Sister Ivy. There was no point in embarrassing the poor woman any more than she already was."

"But surely this—or other things that'll eventually come to light—will embarrass her even more," I said, thinking of the forth-coming revelations in Duncan's documentary.

"Although he was by no means perfect, Brother Duncan was a creative, courageous man, Detective Justice. With prayer and reflection, I'm sure Sister Ivy will come to understand that."

Henley folded his hands on top of the plans, glancing at his watch as he did so. "But you came to see me, Detective, and here I am going on about our good fortune. Is there something I can do for you before the next service?"

Taking the envelope out of my purse and sliding it across his desk, I said, "I thought you should see this."

Henley opened the envelope, read the report from Questioned Documents that Terjanian had provided me. "The proxy was forged!" he exclaimed. "So when Brother Sheffield was supposed to be meeting with Brother Duncan to get it signed, he was already dead?"

"More than likely."

"Does that mean Brother Sheffield murdered Brother Duncan?"

"Or set up Mrs. Amargosa to do it. With all of them dead, only God knows the answer to that question."

Henley fell back in his chair and clenched a knuckle between his teeth. "This could destroy the church's reputation! How can we possibly proceed with the project at Santa Barbara Plaza under these circumstances?"

I picked up my purse and headed for the door. "That's up to you to decide, Pastor. I just thought you ought to have a thorough understanding of what you're dealing with."

Climbing the hill to the Nut House that afternoon I checked out the cars on my parents' block, and the one leading up to it. Since I was pretty sure Firestone didn't know my parents' address, I was on the lookout not for him, but for Aubrey. I hadn't called him Thursday night, or the nights that followed, thinking both he and I could use the break. But when I didn't see his black Infiniti parked out front, I understood with a certainty I had not dared to admit before how much I missed him, how much I was hoping he'd be here.

My mother's Cadillac Eldorado was in the driveway, though, the Christmas lights my father had strung around the front of the house reflecting red and yellow, blue and green on the car's expertly waxed hood. Everything in Joymarie's world was just so, from her immaculate car to her showplace house to her high-achieving children.

Except for me. I'd struck out on my own when I became a cop, breaking away from my mother's expectations for her oldest daughter and her insulated, protected world. But I was still connected, still craving her approval, still vulnerable to her criticism, her undermining me in word and deed, and I knew more than ever that it had to stop. It was up to me to stand up for who I was and what I believed in.

If I believed in anything at all.

I almost turned away, retraced my steps back down the driveway, got into my car, and drove home. But I didn't, realizing if I was going to face down my demons and claim a life that was truly of my own making, it had to start at the Nut House. *Face the music right now and get this over with,* I thought as I mounted the steps and used my key to let myself in.

The music part wasn't so bad—Nat King Cole's "The Christmas Song" was playing on the stereo—and things looked pretty normal. In the living room by the fireplace, Uncle Syl, Perris, and Louise were untangling the Christmas lights while the twins ran into my legs as they chased each other with Christmas stockings intended for the mantel. "Hi, Auntie Char! Look what Unca Syl made us!" they chimed in unison.

My uncle looked up from what he was doing, came over to greet me with a kiss. "Baby Girl! You're early. Did you see the *Times* today?"

"I tried to avoid it, actually."

"Well, other than the story about you and the Home Invasion Task Force, there was an article in the Calendar section about Maynard Duncan's documentary being screened at the Directors Guild next February. And Tristan Cavender, no less, is taking time out from one of his projects to supervise the postproduction work on it."

"How interesting."

He eyed me suspiciously, then swatted my arm. "Fine, don't say anything! Go in the kitchen and sample our new eggnog recipe. Your mother and I tried to duplicate the one I had at Maynard Duncan's repast."

I hope not exactly, I wanted to say as I headed for the kitchen.

And walked up on Joymarie and Aubrey, two of the people I most wanted to see and dreaded seeing this night. Their backs were to me, and Aubrey was putting down a glass cup from which he'd been sipping. "That's pretty tasty, Mrs. Justice. It's got a tropical kick to it."

Wiping her hands on a dish towel, Joymarie said: "I just hope Charlotte can get here in time to have some before it's all gone. God knows she's got no excuse, since she doesn't have that crazy job to keep her occupied." She turned to walk to the refrigerator and almost ran into me. "Oh, Charlotte, you gave me a fright! I didn't see you standing there."

"Evidently not."

Aubrey remained facing the sink, his stiffened back telling me he was very much aware of my presence.

"Can we talk?" I said.

"I'll just leave you two alone," Joymarie said, edging away.

"No, it's you I want to talk to. Can you excuse us for a minute, Aubrey?"

"Sure," he mumbled, hefting the punch bowl. "Want me to put this on the bar, Mrs. Justice?"

"That would be fine, darling." The room empty now, Joymarie and I stood sizing each other up until she broke eye contact and moved around me toward the refrigerator. "How's it feel to have a few days off?" she asked.

"It's more than a few. I guess I have you to thank for that."

Joymarie wheeled around to confront me, both hands on her hips. "Now, don't go jumping to conclusions, young lady! I've heard your wild accusation about me having something to do with trouble you were having on your job—"

"Did you or did you not tell Uncle Henry about Detective Firestone harassing me on the job?"

Her lips compressed, Joymarie turned to check on the roast in the oven. "I might have slipped and mentioned something about it when I saw him at church."

"Do you know what your little slip did to me? Uncle Henry said something to my boss, who said something to me *and* Firestone."

She grabbed an oven mitt and a spoon and started basting the meat. "Well, that's a good thing, isn't it?"

"But, Mother, you had no right—"

"Putting him on notice to leave you alone?"

"No, putting him on notice to try and get rid of me!"

She turned toward me, face slack with disbelief. "What do you mean—'get rid of'?"

"It's a long story, which I won't get into because I don't know if I can trust you these days."

She pulled off the oven mitt, started rotating it in her hands. "Try to see it from my perspective, Charlotte," she said at last. "After almost losing one child to those animals in that police department, I don't want to risk another."

"Get off it! You know Perris was shot by a gang member."

"There's more to it than you could possibly understand," she snapped.

"Like what?"

A cloud passed over her face. "By my lights, if he hadn't been working for the LAPD, it wouldn't have happened!"

"Regardless of what happened to Perris, you've got to realize this is what I do. I *am* a cop. I chose it, it is my calling. And all the sniping you do about the LAPD—why I stay there instead of getting a good job like my brother, blah blah blah—has got to stop or I won't be coming around here anymore. Is that what you want?"

She made a tentative gesture in my direction, dropped her hand when she saw the anger in my eyes. "I'm just so afraid for you, Charlotte," she murmured. "You can't blame a mother for that, can you?"

Her face held all the love and anguish I'd seen in Dolores Amargosa's when she raged about what the world had done to her son. I sighed at her in exasperation. "I don't blame you for having those feelings, but I *do* blame you when you try and interfere in my job, when you put down what I do in front of the man I love!"

I saw the look of shock on her face, but I plunged ahead anyway.

"Whether you want to acknowledge it or not, I'm grown, Mother, and I've been making my own decisions for a long time. And whatever I decide to do, on my job or in my relationship with Aubrey, it's *my* decision to make, not yours!"

I was so involved with my own feelings that I almost missed seeing the slight tremble in my mother's regal frame or the tear slip down her face. Stunned, I moved hesitantly toward her.

"You're going to mess up your make-up," I said, reaching up to touch her cheek, brushing the tear away in the process. "Is that a new blusher?"

"Your father's using me as a guinea pig for a new line he's developing," she nodded, sniffling quickly. "It's called Bronzed Joy. You like it?"

"It suits you."

"Thanks, baby." The tears welled up again in my mother's gray eyes, eyes that were very much like mine. "I . . . I'm . . . I *do* love you, Charlotte. I just have difficulty showing it sometimes."

She moved to give me one of her clumsy hugs, but this one lasted a little longer than most. "I know, Mother," I said, brushing away my own tears. "It runs in the family."

People were starting to arrive, and I was soon caught up in the onslaught of congratulatory hugs and kisses being bestowed by relatives and friends for my success with the Home Invasion Task Force. Little did they know the other side of the coin.

My brother was under the mistletoe, stealing a kiss from his wife, Louise. I asked them if they'd seen Aubrey. "He was talking eggnog with Uncle Syl," Louise said, "but I don't see him now."

"Hey, we need to talk about your suspension," Perris said.

"Later."

I went to the bar and got a cup of cheer myself, hoping it would lighten my mood. I downed one, then two, and then got a third as I headed outside to sit by the pool.

The chill in the air had kept everyone away, except for Aubrey, who was standing at the far end of the yard, staring into the customized zodiac inlaid in the bottom of the pool. I walked toward him, stopped a few feet away, and took a seat on the diving board, between the mosaic-tiled portraits of Martin Luther King and Langston Hughes. "We had many a party out here when we were kids, remember?"

"I remember swimming over Langston's and Martin's heads, and the hot dogs your father used to grill."

"I remember watching you and Perris race in this pool, and you diving off this board." I gazed out over the pool, savoring the memory. "You were the most gorgeous boy I'd ever seen."

Aubrey drained his cup and came to stand before me. "I don't want to talk about me and Perris when we were fifteen, Charlotte. I want to talk about you and me, today."

I cleared my throat, and, "There is something I wanted to say about today, or the other day."

"I'm listening."

I got to my feet, felt the world tilt away as my stomach grazed against the firmness of Aubrey's body. I put my arms around his waist to steady myself, felt his go around me. I tried to smile, felt my eyes fill with tears instead. "I—it's been so long—I'm not sure I know how to say this, Aubrey."

"Try one word at a time."

"I . . . I guess I—"

"Slow down."

"I . . ." I felt as if I was going to lose it.

He started rubbing his hands along the length of my back, soothing me as if I were a baby. "Go on."

". . . love you, okay?" I finally got out. "Is that what you want to hear?"

He pulled away from me. "It's not about what *I* want to hear, it's about whether you mean it."

"What?"

"*Mean* it, Char. Because I love you, too, but I'm long past the days of wasting my time on a woman who doesn't appreciate me, or return the love I have to give."

Frightened, I took his hands in mine. "Aubrey, I appreciate everything you've done for me, the way I feel like I'm growing when we're together. And I *do* love you and I want to be with you." I dropped my head. "It's just that . . . losing Keith the way I did, and Erica, I'd convinced myself I'd never allow myself to feel that much love, that much pain, again."

Aubrey's brow creased with an unspoken emotion. I reached up to smooth away the tension I could see there. "I always thought throwing myself into policing was a way of dealing with the pain, making it go away by helping others. But in the last few days, I've seen too many women lose themselves in fantasies that only camouflage the truths that they thought were too painful to face. And all their efforts seem to bring them was more pain! I don't want that to happen to me."

I was crying in earnest now. Aubrey tried to wipe the tears from my eyes.

"Don't," I said. "I've got to let this out. I've lived my life for so long cut off from my feelings that I just have difficulty showing them sometimes."

"I know." He gave me a crooked smile. "It runs in your family."

"Were you eavesdropping on me and Joymarie?" I asked, pulling away.

"Not intentionally. I was coming back to get the dipper for the punch bowl when I overheard what she said to you."

I punched him in the arm. "You're despicable!"

He held me close, whispered in my ear: "But you still love me, don't you?"

"Don't press your luck!"

After holding me a few more minutes, he whispered, "I've got something for you."

"What?" I asked suspiciously.

"Come on, I'll show you."

I dried my eyes and we sneaked like children, hand in hand, through the house and out the front door. He took me to a brand-new Mercedes parked in front of the house and opened the door. "Oh, my God, Aubrey," I gasped. "You didn't buy this for me, did you?"

"Uh, not quite," he said, opening the passenger door before getting in the driver's seat. "This is my new company car. But there's something in the glove compartment for you."

I got in, opened the glove compartment, and saw something even more shocking than the car—a small, glossy box in that unmistakable Tiffany blue, wrapped in a red ribbon.

"You should never leave something so valuable in your car, Aubrey!"

"Quit playing cop and open it," he commanded.

I held it against my chest to calm my racing heart. "Wait a minute. I don't know if I'm ready for something like this."

I held the box in my hand, shook it, heard a slight rattle, and felt the lightness of it in my hand, the weight of it on my mind. "Can I open it Christmas Day?" I asked, thinking I'd have plenty of time over the next few months to figure out how it, and my relationship with Aubrey, fit into this new life I wanted to build for myself.

His smile widened. "If you promise to open it Christmas morning at my house, in your bathrobe."

I leaned over and kissed him. "I promise."

A C K N O W L E D G M E N T S

Thanks go to: Candace D. Cooper, Associate Justice, California
Court of Appeal, and Andrea Van Leesten, Esq., for assistance in
legal matters; Detective Roseanne Perino for assistance in understanding the LAPD's procedure for investigating officer-involved
shootings; Detective Pat Barron of the department's Detective
Services Group for insight into administrative issues; Amal
Johnson, R.N., for her help on continuous infusion pumps; Doug
P. Lyle, M.D., for invaluable help in understanding drug interac-
tions; Gerald Friedland, M.D., Director of the AIDS Program at
Yale University School of Medicine, for assistance in recreating the
symptomoly and treatment of HIV and AIDS in 1992.

To Katherine Forrest for continued writerly advice and sisterly support; Jill Moore Raab, for assistance in locating the right
Yeats poem; and Jan Burke for a listening ear.

Appreciation and gratitude to Michael Connelly—both east
and west—for your support and enthusiasm for my work. Ditto to
Carl Coan—and thanks for the use of the name.

And to my friends in the LAPD—Chief J. I. Davis,
Lieutenant Evangeline Nathan, Captain Ann Young, and Detective

Rosibel Smith—thank you for your support of my writing and the city we all love.

To booksellers, book groups, and readers all over the country for embracing Charlotte and her world. And to the Black Caucus of the American Library Association and Mystery Readers International—thanks for the recognition and honor.

To the team at W. W. Norton—Drake McFeely, Jill Bialosky, Bill Rusin, Oliver Gilliland, Rick Raeber, and the entire sales and publicity team—thanks for your enthusiasm and drive to make Charlotte's adventures a success.

To Bill Green and Chris Spry—thanks for the use of the Lodge.

To Michael Flot for helping me to keep my head straight during the writing process—in more ways than one.

Last, but not least, to Faith Childs, Felix Liddell, and Ann Wang for keeping me honest.